THE FLOTSAM TRILOGY

By Peter M. Ball

The Flotsam Trilogy

Exile

Frost

Crusade

Peter M. Ball

Apocalypse Ink Productions
Kenmore, Washington

Credits

Edited by Jennifer Brozek
Interior design by Jeff Brozek

PUBLISHED BY

Apocalypse Ink Productions
6830 NE Bothell Way, STE C #404
Kenmore, WA 98028
http://www.apocalypse-ink.com/

First Published November 2015

Limited Edition ISBN: 978-1-940444-16-1
Trade Paperback ISBN: 978-1-940444-17-8
Electronic Edition ISBN: 978-1-940444-15-4

Table of Contents

ACKNOWLEDGEMENTS

The nice thing about having all this collected is that it creates a much bigger book. When you're writing novellas, whose page-counts are comparatively slim, it feels ostentatious to sit down and write a long series of acknowledgements. Once you collect a bunch of them together, throwing in all the extras, it already feels ostentatious, so there's really nothing to lose.

First, I'd like to extend my thanks to Jennifer Brozek, Jeff Brozek, and Sarah Hendrix, the Shadow-Minion of the Apocalypse, who have made up the team at Apocalypse Ink Productions as I worked on these stories. The first version of *Flotsam* got its start in 2010, when I pitched it as a serial to Jennifer's *Edge of Propinquity* zine, and her prompting has kept me adding and evolving Keith Murphy's story in the five years since then.

I encountered Mark Ferrari by accident, in the art room of the Brighton World Fantasy convention, when I was seeing the cover art for *Exile* for the first time and slightly surprised to discover *anything* at a World Fantasy convention with my name on it. I burbled my thanks then, as shocked and slightly jet-lagged people are wont to do, but his cover stuck in my head as I wrote the second draft of *Exile* and his work got progressively better as the series continued.

Adam Windsor let me hole up in his spare room for a number of years significantly longer than we originally agreed when I moved, giving me the opportunity to do any number of writer-type things I wouldn't otherwise have a chance to do. *Flotsam* was definitely one of them. Thank you for the place to stay, and for the tradition of the Trashy Tuesday Movie, which had a far greater impact on this series than I would have thought.

Thanks, also, to the troll under the stairs, Sarah Blue, who would occasionally insist on nicking off the pub at improbably hours and coaxing me along. It helped.

I was always told that writing would be a solitary profession, but it turns out people lie about that. Special thanks go out to Chris Lynch, Chris Green, Dan Braum, and Jess Irwin, who agreed to my crazy plan to meet regularly and talk about our various plans and projects in order to keep ourselves on track. Thanks, also, to Kevin Powe, who remains the most peepy of the peeps and the person I'm most want to talk to when shit goes wrong.

The crew at the Queensland Writers Centre, who provided me with a day job I love in addition to an opportunity to meet and work with any number of writers. You folks are awesome, thank you. When I started this series, Meg Vann was my boss. When I ended the series, she was no longer my boss, but was definitely my friend. I thank her for both. There is something to be said for any employer who understands why "Dropped my laptop; lost 20,000 words of manuscript" is a worthy reason for taking sick leave.

My sister, Sally Ball, took a lot of photographs for the serialized version of *Flotsam* and a number of them became reference points when I set out to write this version of the story. Thanks, Sal. You're awesome. My parents, Terry and Margaret Ball, gave me a place to stay on the Coast when I needed to go down and re-acquaint myself with the city, in addition to moving us there in the first place. I have mostly forgiven them for the latter, now.

Despite my occasional grumbling and attempts to bring down the apocalypse on its doorstep, I do have the occasional good memory of the Gold Coast. My thanks go out to the various writers, artists, freaks, and weirdos who made my years on the Gold Coast bearable, despite my aversion to beaches, theme parks, and sunlight.

Finally, my thanks go to out to my write-club buddy, Angela Slatter, who has spent the past few years providing a regular place to write, tasty food, and a sounding board for weird ideas and plot problems. There are some friendships so invaluable that the words thank you really don't seem up to the task required, and this is definitely one of them.

EXILE

Book One of
The Flotsam Trilogy

PARADISE CITY

THEY FOUND ME in the Hard Rock. Thursday night, a little after ten. A good crowd for a Thursday, all things considered. Lots of girls with inscrutable, backpacker accents clustered around the bar. Plenty more heading up the stairs, attracted by the cover band's caterwaul. Blondes, natural and peroxide; a Gold Coast epidemic. Exposed skin, despite the cool nip in the air. Twenty-dollar cocktails named after natural disasters: Typhoons; Tsunamis; rum-soaked Hurricanes.

I'd racked up four hours sitting in the downstairs bar, drinking coffee and reading my book at a cosy table for four. Ignoring the crush of the late-night crowd, the heady mingling of sweat and perfume and the salt-water from the nearby beach. Ignoring the irritated, dark-eyed waitress who kept offering me coffee in the hopes I'd fuck off and free up the spot. I wasn't waiting for anyone else. Just me and my beat-up copy of *Persuasion* on yet another stake-out. Not waiting for the local talent to spot us. Not waiting for that at all.

I'd picked a table in the back of the room, wedged between one of Keith Moon's polyester shirts and Mark Occhilupo's surfboards. Earlier, when I'd been eating dinner, tourists would come past and read the brass plaques. Personally, I didn't give a shit. I'd picked the table 'cause it gave me sight lines on the downstairs bar, on the sliding doors leading out into the crowded street, and the brightly lit Hard Rock gift shop that emptied onto Cavil Mall.

They had a shitty cover band working the upstairs bar. I kept reading a line in my book, something about fine ladies and calm waters, and kept losing my place as they launched into another faintly off-key cover. When the big guy walked in, they'd worked themselves up to the Gunner's *Paradise City,* the bellicose crowd joining in on the chorus.

The big guy came in via the gift shop, all swagger and white teeth. He was six-nine, maybe. Athletic and well-built. Tight black jeans and red Converse high-tops, a tan just brown enough to be real instead of spray-on. I didn't recognise him, but I recognised the type. Even if you can't pierce the veil of the Gloom, there's always something off about the way the Other carry themselves.

He scanned the room like a predator, making note of every warm body crammed in around the memorabilia. I drained the last of my lukewarm coffee. Dog-eared the page in my book and slid it into my jacket pocket. The short, dark-eyed waitress stopped by my table and removed the empty coffee cup. Asked me if I'd like another, and actually broke into a grin when I told her I was almost done.

I pulled a twenty out of my wallet, folded it and slid it beneath the salt and pepper. Went back to watching the big guy as he started his rounds. Talking to girls. Flashing that smile. Flirting as easy as most people breathe, utterly unconcerned when the girl said no.

It took him a good five minutes before he found one that liked the look of him; at first, I thought she was part of the act. She laughed too loud when he made his approach, leaned in too readily as he started working his magic. She was exactly the kind of girl you dream of meeting when you show up at a place like the Hard Rock: bleached-blond; white t-shirt; tanned and smooth and very friendly, her cut-off jeans showing of the pink hibiscus tattooed on her right thigh.

The big guy glanced my way before making his move, just making sure I knew he was there. I recognised him, vaguely, from the old days. Robert? Ridley? One of Sabbath's boys, at any rate.

He stepped in close to his victim and whispered into her ear. One hand pressed against the small of her back, slipped beneath the t-shirt to make contact with the skin. The other touched her bare shoulder, and the veins closest to his fingertips turned dark as he siphoned a fragment of her life-force.

He did it fast and subtle, like a pick-pocket filching spare change. Made contact, sucked out a little of what he needed, broke away and moved on to the next girl who'd give him the time of day. Kept working the room like he hadn't even noticed me there.

That, on its own, meant he was faking it. I had that, just-got-off-the-Greyhound look that came from too long without a shower or decent sleep. I wore a long-sleeve flannel shirt to keep my tattoos covered and the SIG tucked into my belt hidden from plain sight. Demons are dumb, but they aren't that dumb, usually. Especially not if they work Sabbath's territory. Of all the Other on the Gold Coast, they were the most alert to intruders and potential threats.

If he hadn't made me, it meant he was faking. Playing decoy so they could approach me while I was distracted and my guard was down. Part of me—the part that's basically dumb as rocks—felt flattered I still warranted that kind of caution.

Then I felt the hard kiss of a .38 pressed against that hollow spot where my ribs gave way to my gut. Wesna settled into the chair beside me, her free arm slung over my shoulder like we were a pair of old friends getting together, catching up.

"Well, shit, Murphy," she said. "I guess this is welcome home, eh?"

The Wesna Holjack I'd known before leaving the Gold Coast had been tall, lean, and tough as boiled leather. She'd gone through high-school pretending to be one-of-the-boys, only she cared less about fitting in with the young, athletic surfer types and spent her lunch hours hanging with the freaks I ran with.

Looking at her, sixteen years later, you could argue that nothing had changed. She looked exactly like the woman I remember: same black hair hanging over her face; same long, bulldog jaw that she hated throughout high school; same look of irritation in her eyes, like she'd caught me fucking up yet again and knew she'd have to cover my ass.

Except I couldn't trust that look, not anymore. 'Cause the Wesna Holjack with a gun at my ribs still looked twenty-three, which meant, in my absence, she'd let them stuff a demon under her skin. Any memories I had of her were completely unreliable. Possession changes people, no matter what the demons say when they offer you the deal. Parts of who you are get lost to the thing from the wrong side of the Gloom that cohabitates in your body.

I figured I'd play it safe. Put both hands on the table. Made sure they were clear of anything that could qualify as a weapon. Wesna nuzzled my neck, feigning affection we'd never shared. She cracked her gum, nose against my cheek. From the outside it probably looked affectionate. Or what passes for affectionate in a bar at ten PM.

"So here's the deal," Wesna said. The barrel of the .38 never wavered, steady as a rock against my ribs. "You play along, and I don't shoot you. We have ourselves a conversation, all nice and private-like. Maybe you live through it. Maybe you don't. Tell me you understand."

"Jesus, Wes'. I know how this goes."

"You should know better than to blaspheme."

"I'll keep that in mind." I took a deep breath, risked moving my hands a little. "I'm armed. SIG, in my waistband. Back, right hand side."

Her free hand slid down, slow and professional. She found the gun, pulled it free. Consigned it to the small bag hanging over her shoulder.

"Anything else?"

I shook my head.

"Not like you." She leant back, flicked her hair. Checking out the rest of the bar. "Who's your back-up?"

"No back-up," I said. "I'm not looking for a fight."

She chewed on that for a moment. Weighed the options, how public we'd need to make things if she started a real fight.

"I'm putting the gun away now," she said. "I trust you'll behave?"

I said nothing, and she took it as a yes. The .38 disappeared, pointed somewhere other than my spleen. My spleen shivered with relief, along with the rest of me. Wesna shifted to the far side of the table, watched me like a snake waiting for a mouse to move. I took a deep breath, focused on her face.

Most days I'm as blind as anyone else. I spent years perfecting that, learning to ignore my natural talent. You're not supposed to see the things that go bump in the night. You're not supposed to know many of them walk the world beside you. I taught myself to keep the façade because it kept me sane.

But when I focused on Wesna Holjack, I saw things as they are.

Her eyes were gone, decayed to hollow sockets with a crimson fire in their depths. Skin burned dark and ashen. Little scraps of light that used to be a human spirit waging war against the thing she'd agreed to become.

The headache thundered in, right on schedule. The effort of looking into the Gloom taking its toll.

Wesna shook her head. "I should be calling Sabbath," she said.

"Yeah?"

"Give me a reason not to."

For a moment I caught a glimpse of the woman she'd been, fighting her way to the surface. I wanted to smile, to tell her it was good to see her. Neither was a good idea, not if I wanted to keep on living.

"Well, shit," I said. "I got nothing."

"Nothing?"

I folded my arms. "Guess you'd better call, eh? Be a good little soldier an' all?"

"Fuck," she said, and the phone was in her hand. She watched me, looking for tells, waiting for me to give her something. We both knew the threats Sabbath made when I left the coast. We both knew the price of coming home.

Wesna hissed , thinking things over. I waited, palms flat against the table. It's the only play I had. Wesna Holjack had been dangerous before she'd been possessed; if she decided we were going to fight, it was going to end fast and messy.

The band in the upstairs bar was still working their way through the best of Guns and Roses, segueing from *Sweet Child of Mine* into *November Rain*. Their guitarist could play. Their singer just liked to make noise. Good enough for a Thursday night, though. All the crowd demanded was noise and something to sing along to.

Wesna snorted and tapped her phone against the table. "Lot of noise in this bar," she said. "Hard to hear, you know what I'm saying? I gotta go out to make this call. Should be, what, five minutes? Ten? Depends how easy the boss is to get hold of on a Thursday night."

Her eyes were dark and hard as fuck. She'd just scraped out all the mercy she had left, fighting to remember we'd once been friends. Giving me one last chance to run and avoid the rain of shit she'd be forced to rain down on me.

I folded my arms, threw it all back in her face. "I appreciate that, but you should call him now. I'm not running, Wes'. I need to talk to the old fucker."

Wesna swore beneath her breath, her jaw pulling tight. "He ain't interested in talking, Murphy."

"Then you may as well pull the trigger," I said.

She let out a long, frustrated breath. Dialled a number from memory and waited for someone to answer.

"Yeah," she said, "it's me."

Her eyes stayed on me, hoping like hell I'd change my mind and run.

"It's him," she said. Then: "Yeah, I can do that."

She killed the call with her thumb, returned the phone to her jacket. Turned and signalled big guy, waving him over to our table. He broke off from the backpacker he'd been chatting up, cut through the crowd like a tall, good-looking shark.

The big guy looked me over, unimpressed by what he saw.

"This is Randall," Wesna said. "He'll be escorting you."

Randall glanced at her, raised an eyebrow.

"This is Murphy," she said. "Don't let the smell fool you."

The other eyebrow rose. Randall looked at me again, showing off teeth when he smiled. "Well, shit," he said. "I've heard of you, man."

I nodded, slowly. “Only good things, yeah?”

“No,” Randall said. “Not really.”

DOUBLE-TAP

THERE ARE FOURTEEN reliable ways of killing a body possessed by a demon, but the number starts dropping the longer the demon's been in residence. There are six effective methods of eliminating the fey once they're on our side of the Gloom, eight ways of taking out a lycanthrope if you're not picky about saving the human half, and any number of ways you can eliminate a sorcerer or witch once you've bypassed the protective magic they've used to keep themselves alive.

All of these things get harder when you aren't equipped with a talent for magic yourself. There's a lot more opportunities for things to go horribly wrong.

"Way I hear it," Randall said, "you're not one of the bosses' favourite people."

We were standing out front of the Hard Rock, underneath the goddamn neon guitar that shed whisky-coloured light over the crowd. Wesna stood at the curb, phone pressed against her ear, calling for a ride. Randall stood behind me, his tan even darker under the neon light. He hadn't said a damn thing since they'd escorted me from the table, one in front and one behind, shutting down the easy routes if I decided to break and run.

Part of me kept screaming that running was a good choice, but I put that down to paranoia. I'd been on the road four straight days, looking over my shoulder, grabbing a few quick hours of sleep in the back seats of stolen cars.

"Never met someone the boss outright hates." Randall pitched his voice just below the hubbub of the crowd, leant forward to make sure I could hear every word. "Ordinarily, he's all, you know, all business. No time for grudges or nothing." He puffed out his cheeks, exhaled slowly. "Way he acted when your name came up, when we heard you were here, just eating a burger..."

Randall shook his head. "I never heard him talk like that," he said. "Man has a grudge."

I turned, met his stare.

"You know how long it's been since the boss gave me the all-clear to really *hurt* a man?" There was nothing pleasant behind Randall's pristine smile. "Tonight? It's going to be a good night, man. A real good night."

"Ah-huh," I said.

"Unless the boss wants to get his hands dirty." Randall squinted, thinking that over. "Even then, I'm guessing I get to watch. Almost as good, watching, you know?"

I shook my head, trying to tune him out. Partially 'cause I knew the shtick, had done it plenty of times myself when me and Wesna were partnered together. Partially 'cause I had a bad feeling, and I've been in my job long enough not to ignore my subconscious when it starts telling me shit is going wrong.

I turned, scanning the crowd, trying to keep things subtle.

"You really do smell like arse," Randall said. "Hope the boss hoses you down 'fore we go to work on you and all."

"Shut-up," I said. "Your four o'clock."

Randall squinted, confused.

Realised too late what I was talking about.

He'd been loitering outside the Hard Rock ever since we exited, doing his best to blend with the crowd and avoid getting noticed. Mid-thirties, maybe; the beard made his age harder to peg down. Tight black t-shirt worn over a broad, surfer's chest. He looked like one of the local old boys, still cruising the clubs and hitting on chicks, being a low-key asshole. The kind of guy that's too old to call people bro, but doesn't really give a shit 'cause he thinks he's still twenty-six.

He put effort into the image, but the tattoos gave him away. They ran down the soft parts of his inner forearm, the mystic runes partially disguised by the Chinese dragon that wound between them. They were tether marks, allowing him to tap into the Gloom, use it for things ordinary people would end up calling magic.

I figured he'd been there an hour or so, long enough to start tapping the shadows and drawing out what he needed to do some damage. He saw Randall jerk around, searching for trouble, and figured he'd make his move. Shadows swam over him, tenebrous strands of darkness reaching from beneath parked cars and the weird angles cast by the neon.

On a street full of people coming and going, he focused on staying still, drawing the Gloom around him. He stood on the corner, shoulder pressed against the building. Held a smoke with his left hand, never pulling it far from his face.

His right hand hung at his side, clenched tight, blood dripping through his fingers.

It took effort, drawing that much of the Gloom into our world, binding it into something you could use as a weapon. The air hummed with the potential of it, blended with the rhythms of the ocean just two blocks away.

The sorcerer on the corner flicked his cigarette into the gutter, raised the bloodied fist.

I grabbed Wesna by the arm, hauled her to the concrete. Her phone spilled out of her hands, clattering against the concrete. Randall reached for me, still not entirely sure what was going on; realised his mistake as black flames speared through the crowd. The attack caught Randall in the chest, knocked him onto his arse. The dark mockery of fire clung to his chest, burning through the fabric.

Randall writhed, desperately beating at the unnatural flames.

The crowd outside the Hard Rock started screaming, their subconscious alerting them to danger their conscious minds refused to process. I reached for my SIG on instinct, realised it was still in Wesna's bag. She kicked free of me, pulled the bag out of my reach. Produced her own gun, the snub-nosed .32 she'd pressed against my ribs.

Steady hands lined up the shot, picked the moment. Her finger tightened against the trigger, two shots in quick succession. The first ricocheted. The second caught the sorcerer in the right arm, digging deep into the muscle.

More blood on the concrete. More screams from the crowd.

The sorcerer just laughed.

Sorcerers are a bitch to kill. They're worse when you're stuck with wounding them, instead of finishing the job. Wesna emptied her clip, another seven bullets pumped into our attacker. Not trying to kill him, just slowing him down. Ensuring he had to think about things before he built up to another blast of fire.

"Up." Wesna knelt beside me, sliding a new clip home. The sorcerer sagged against the wall, blood staining his shirt. Randall's wet breathing cut through the air. I rolled over, got my feet under me.

There were cops coming down the street, from the patrol that worked the nearby mall, shouting warnings, telling everyone to get down. Randall crawled, chest still burning. Wesna grabbed him, hauled him over one shoulder. She took one look at me, her eyes hard as stone.

"I think we should run," she said.

I nodded, lurching into motion, pushing through the crowd. Wesna followed, her partner on one shoulder. We went south. Away from the crowds. Away from the cops. Away from the sorcerer no-one was going to find, now that he'd disappeared into the Gloom and made his escape.

My name's Keith Murphy. I specialise in killing things from the Gloom who deserve a few bullets in the head. I'm not a sorcerer, but I worked for one, a guy named Danny Roark who saw me on a bad path and gave me an alternative. For sixteen years, we'd worked together; a two-man unit, the best of the best. Roark did the magic and I handled the guns. Hell, I did whatever needed doing in order to get the job done.

Running didn't bother me. Running's a survival trait.

What bothered me was running without having Roark for back-up. What bothered me was the sorcerer's ambush and me slinking back to my old boss for protection.

What bothered me was the nine multimeter bullet I'd swallowed, the one with the soul of my last victim trapped inside it. I'd killed Michael Wotan four days earlier, double-tapped him in a restaurant, Brunelli's, while he was drinking his coffee.

His followers wanted that bullet back. They're half the reason me and Roark split up. I'd come home for the first time in sixteen years 'cause shit had gone horribly wrong, and 'cause Danny Roark gave me strict orders about where to run.

Left to my own devices, I would have disappeared into Melbourne or Sydney. Or gone bush and hidden out in some rinky-dink outback town, killing time in the local pub until Roark gave the all-clear and work resumed.

The Gold Coast wasn't friendly territory. There were good odds I'd end up dead by sunrise, at Wesna's hand or her bosses or by someone else I knew.

That would be okay by me. I'd gotten used to the idea of dying.

When you'd fucked up as badly as Roark and I, the threat of *only* getting killed rated pretty well on your list of options.

SABBATH

WE TOOK REFUGE in a dinky little Thai place three blocks down from the Hard Rock. One of those hole in the wall joints, perpetually empty and around forever. Every city has 'em. Maybe you wonder how they stay in business. Maybe you never give 'em much thought. Either way, you don't go in. The things that run them prefer it that way.

We sat by the front window and watched the sirens roll past on the highway. The red and blue lights cut through the gloomy evening, cops expanding their search perimeter in order to track us down. It was coming up on eleven o'clock. Close enough to closing time that we had the place to ourselves. The owner of the restaurant kept coming up to Wesna, asking her questions in his native tongue.

Wesna responded in kind, kept her answers short. He glanced at me, glanced at Randall; shook his head as he retreated to the kitchen, bellowing at his employees. Wesna perched on the edge of her seat, peering through the glass window. Randall slumped in the chair beside her, drawing wheezy breathes as he prodded the blistered skin on his chest. "Fucking hell, that hurt," he kept saying. "Fucking-A, that hurt."

Wesna told him to shut up, but it just dropped his complaints to a whisper. Demons heal quick, a lot of the time. They just like to bitch while it happens. My own ribs ached from the quick sprint. I steadied my breathing, trying to slow it down.

"He doesn't sound happy," I said, nodding towards the kitchen.

"Ben's an old friend," she said. "He just dislikes disruption."

"I know your old friends, Wes'. I used to be one of them."

Wesna's head jerked towards me, her finger raised in anger. She held it there, about to tee off, but the tirade didn't come. She glanced at Randall, then back at the kitchen. Clenched her fingers and lowered her hand to the tabletop.

A few blocks up the cops were cleaning up outside the Hard Rock, trying to figure out exactly what went wrong. The stories from the crowd wouldn't be much help. They'd be hazy about what started the fire, stories about Molotov's conflicting with those who figured Randall spontaneously combusted. The only thing they'd be sure about was the chick with the gun, and even then the details wouldn't quite match up.

Wesna wasn't working with details that clashed, though. Eventually she'd figure out that I was the target. I didn't want that. Negotiating with people who want you dead is harder when they think you've brought trouble onto their patch.

I went on the offensive. "You guys been having problems with locals again?"

That earned me an angry look. "How 'bout you shut up, Murphy."

"Just saying, he looked like a local," I said. "Nothing wavered when you plugged him, so it probably wasn't glamour."

"And you're running," she said. "Fuck knows what from, but it's the only reason you're home."

"You ever seen the beaches in Adelaide, Wes? Only thing between you and the Antarctic ice is the occasional humpback whale."

I went silent, let her think. She brooded, hissing like a kettle after it's done boiling. It wasn't long before her phone rang, drawing a frown as she checked the number.

"Yeah?" she said, answering, glaring at me the entire time. She listened to the voice on the other end, frown growing deeper as the seconds rolled past.

"Unavoidable," she said, after a while.

Another few seconds past. Her eyes stayed locked on me, cold and suspicious. Then: "Yeah, we picked him up."

Then: "No, I don't think that's the case."

I could see the fires burning in her pupils when she hung up. There wasn't much left of the woman I'd known in there, not when she got that pissed off. I grinned at her, stoking the anger. The longer fury kept her distracted, the longer I could play things like the attack wasn't my fault.

"Sabbath still wants to see you," she said.

"He's not worried about the fire fight that just went down?"

Wesna stood, hauling Randall to his feet with one hand. "No," she said, "he's really not."

We caught a cab to the front doors of Jupiter's Casino. Fifteen minute drive. Twenty-bucks on the meter. Wesna paid the cabbie, led me through the lobby. Randall stayed in the cab, his chest raw and blistered from the sorcerer's assault. The casino is a fairly open-minded place, the tuxedo crowd drinking alongside the country boys in flannel shirts and the hipsters from the local uni with their skinny jeans and first, half-hearted attempt at a beard. Egalitarian by virtue of greed and the unity that comes from desperation and the white heat of waiting for the next spin. You could stretch that a long way, but there were limits. Mostly they went like this: no shirt, no shoes, no service.

Security watched us walk through the lobby. Most of 'em were human, but one standing by the entry to the Prince Albert pub had the angular look of something stuffed into human-shaped skin. I figured it was close to midnight, maybe a little after, and the Albert was still in full swing, filled with the slurry of noise that comes from too many drunk people crowded into too little space. The pub crowd skewed younger than the bars down by the gaming floor. More interested in drinking, less interested in blowing money.

We settled in to wait for an elevator. Wesna with her back to the wall, her eyes locked on me. It wasn't needed. I didn't need the reminder that I wouldn't get away, not here in the heart of the Casino, waiting for a trip to the twentieth floor. Sabbath owned the place in every way that mattered, even if his name never appeared on the deeds. He'd bought in when they built the place, back in eighty-five. Hung around like a tick, feeding on the desperation that hung in the crisp, dry air they pumped through, growing bloated and powerful over time.

The elevator came. We rode up in silence. The elevator chimed after twenty floors, opened out onto a hallway extending in both directions. Twenty floors up. One below the penthouse suits. It's the way Sabbath played things, hovering just below the level that drew notice. Displaying just enough importance to let you know he meant something.

Gold Coast decor runs towards beige. They call it sand, explain all the ways it connects the inside to the beach, but beige is fucking beige. There's no way of avoiding that. Sabbath never went with that. His suite was done in white and black, like he considered colour an insult. White walls. White lights. White tiles. A black couch and a deep, black coffee table. A sidebar lined with crystal decanters. A big, fuck-off type television mounted on the wall, big enough to see like your own private movie screen. It ran a feed from the cameras downstairs, showed people all through the casino engaged in the task of losing money.

Wesna dumped my pack on the coffee table, patted me down in one last time. She took her time about it, removed the contents from every pocket. There wasn't much. Spare change. A paper-clip. Three spare rounds for the SIG. They joined my pack on the coffee table. Wesna pointed towards the black couch.

"Sit," she said.

I sat my arse down.

"Wait," she said.

I waited. Wesna dumped the contents of my pack on the coffee table, sifted through them carefully. When she was done, she crossed the lounge room. Knocked on one of the big black doors leading into Sabbath's study. It opened slightly, and she talked with the person on the far side. I couldn't hear the specifics. I didn't really need to. The door closed when they were done, and Wesna fell in beside the couch, close enough to hurt me if I did something stupid.

The study doors opened ten minutes later. A short, neat man stepped into the room, bodyguard trailing behind him. The bodyguard was sleek and wide-shouldered, built to play front-row in the Rugby Sevens. Sabbath wore glasses, kept his greying hair cropped close to the scalp. He sat on the black couch opposite mine. Folded his arms. He wore a white linen suit that shone a little under the bright lights. Three hundred dollar sandals, his manicured toe nails on display.

He looked at Wesna. Looked at me. Looked at my shit, spread out over the coffee table. He picked up the paperback, my copy of *Persuasion*. Paged through it in an idle way, eyes skimming over the pages. “I wouldn’t have picked you as a reader, Murphy.”

“I wasn’t, when you knew me.” I kept my voice even. The sight of him flicking through the book made me irrationally angry, but anger was just going to get me in trouble. I took a deep breath, steadied my nerves. “It’s just a habit I picked up along the way. Lots of long nights in my job, now.”

“Lots of long nights,” he repeated, thumbing through the dog-earned pages, checking out the points I’d marked. He shook his head. “So a few hours back, I hear this rumour. Someone says Keith Murphy is back in town, chowing down at the Hard Rock on a burger and fries.”

He looked up, the dark pits of his eyes focused in my direction. “Now, me? I told them they were crazy. I told ‘em Big Keith Murphy fucked off out of town fifteen years back, and he sure as hell knows better than to come home. I told ‘em what would happen if Big Keith showed his face again, ‘cause we had ourselves a deal and it laid all that out. I told ‘em in intimate, bloody detail. It made me a little warm, you know?

Sabbath took a deep breath, tossed my book into the pile of clothes scattered across the coffee table. “My mood is not substantially improved by discovering you’re catching up on the classics, instead of getting bloated on junk food.”

“I did eat the burger, if that helps.”

His eyes narrowed, fighting a smile. "That depends. How was it?"

"Alright," I said. "Too much cheese."

"Huh." He lost interest in my pile of stuff, turned toward Wesna. "You got his gun?"

She produced the SIG, handed it over. Sabbath freed the clip, held it to his nose to catch the familiar scent. His expression soured. "Holy water?

"Soaked the top halves for a good four hours," I said. "Found a Pastor downtown who really, earnestly believes in the almighty. Stopped in to say hi to him on the way through."

"Impressive." Sabbath slid the clip in place, held the pistol at arm's length. "Ultimately non-lethal."

He put the SIG on the coffee table, close enough for me to reach if I was stupid enough to make a lunge for it. I would have been, once upon a time. I wasn't anymore.

"Maybe I wasn't looking for lethal."

"That," Sabbath said, "would be a very poor choice on your part." He dropped his weight back into the couch, tapping his index fingers together. The hollow darkness where his eyes should have been stayed fixed in my direction. "You're something of a conundrum, Mister Murphy."

"Don't know why." I glanced down at the table, all my stuff strewn across it. "Not like I'm hiding much, right now. I can strip down to my skivvies if that's what you want."

Sabbath's frown grew deeper. "Don't pretend to be an idiot, Murphy. I know you're not."

"No?"

"I know about Adelaide," Sabbath said. "The unfortunate incident with the head of the Ravens down there. Messy bit of business, that. All sorts of consequences."

"Angry cultists," I said. "An irate soul. Some kind of death curse, the way I hear it."

I feigned confidence, forced myself to keep breathing. Watched Sabbath wrestle with two sets of instincts. The first set told him to rip me apart, just like he'd promised to when I first walked away. The second set warned him that I could be useful, even if I did come with all sorts of baggage. Desperation made people pliable, and Sabbath loved working with the desperate.

"That's a lot of trouble," he said. His lip curled a little.

"Not so much," I said. "We've got it under control and all."

"We?"

"Roark and I," I said. "You remember Danny, right?"

That earned a low, glottal snarl from Sabbath. Yeah, he remembered Danny Roark. For a moment I caught a hint of light in the shadowy depths of his eyes. He beat it down. Played it calm. A demon without a grudge. "Where is Mister Roark? I'd like the chance to reacquaint myself."

I looked at him, held steady. "Like you said, I'm not an idiot."

Sabbath nodded. He liked that. "I could have Wesna break fingers until you felt like talking."

"All that gets us is ten broken fingers."

"Maybe," Sabbath said. "But then we get creative." He looked up at Wesna, smile playing at his lips. "It's been a long time since we broke someone. Perhaps we should go there, just to keep our hand in?"

"Okay," I said. "We can go that direction. You want to make me scream, I'm pretty sure it'll happen. You want me to beg, I'm sure it'll happen. Roark? It won't get you any closer to him. We ain't stupid, Sabbath. We took precautions. I'm here. Roark's not. I won't even hear from him until after this meeting's done, and I don't know where he is til he tells me."

Another nod. "Smart," Sabbath said.

"It's not like I came back on a whim." I glanced back at Wesna. She had the .32 out, discretely tucked under her free hand. Not pointed at me, not yet, but waiting for the order. I turned back to Sabbath, watched his smile finally bloom into life.

"Tell me about Adelaide."

"Big city. Middle of the desert."

"Cut the shit," Sabbath said. "I only have so much patience. You've been allowed to live this long because I may have use for you, and that just weighs out against the pleasure I'd get from having you ripped apart." He leaned forward, fixed me with a horrible stare. "Convince me you're actually useful, Keith. You're only going to get one shot at it."

"Alright, then," I said. "Let's cut the shit. You already know about Adelaide, and you've already guessed why I'm here. I need to lay low. I pissed off a cult. Turns out, when it comes to the Ravens, it's not a case of cutting off the head and leaving the body to die. And 'cause you know about Adelaide, you know about the rest. All the jobs that went right. All the things we eliminated, me and Roark. That's what I'm offering."

Sabbath sat back, did the thing where he tapped his fingertips together once more. "I've got ways of taking care of problems."

"You've got blunt instruments."

He shrugged. "They get the job done."

"Then why am I sitting here? Wesna could have left me to bleed out in the Hard Rock bathrooms."

I watched Sabbath sort through the ways he could play this, examining each bluff and setting it aside. He enjoyed the game, always did. Bluff and counter. Looking for tells. He wouldn't go all-in on my presence, not without knowing more, but he'd pay to see the cards. That'd buy him time to figure things out. Buy me time to figure out the next step.

"Alright," he said. "I've got some local nuisances I'd like to see eliminated, and your status as someone outside my organisation makes you a somewhat useful tool. I'm willing to trade you a period of tolerance inside the city limits, in exchange for some of your specialised talents."

"How long are you offering?"

"I'm thinking six months."

I thought about Adelaide. The mess we'd made down there. "I may need longer. A year at least."

"Then we'll find ourselves back here, negotiating a second extension," Sabbath said. "You get six months, and in return I deploy you to take care of three problems. I give you the targets and I give you the time-frames. And all you get is a promise that none of mine are coming after you, not until your time is up. I've got no interest in defending you, Murphy."

"I'm not looking for a bodyguard." I stood up, glanced down at my gear spread across the coffee table. "You know there's a limit on who I'll hunt."

"Even with your life on the line?"

"Even then."

"Well, then. Best I commit to picking my target's carefully." Sabbath spread his fingers. "Relax, Murphy. I won't ask you to shoot any mortals that don't have it coming."

"By whose standards? Yours or mine?"

Sabbath grinned. "Yours, I suppose. If that's the way to get this done."

I nodded, pointed at my gear. "I assume one of yours will bring all that down to the bar, once you've contented yourself that none of it is interesting?"

Sabbath shrugged again, his attention on the TV screen. He got what he wanted. Now we were done. Wesna put a hand on my shoulder, guided me towards the door. The air was cold, inside the casino. Cool and dry, courtesy of the air conditioning. "Twenty minutes," she said. "Assuming we find nothing."

I caught the elevator down to the ground floor alone, the only thing I had worth finding burning like a hot coal in the pit of my stomach.

I sat in the bar, nursing a bourbon. Waiting for someone to bring down my bag. I knew what they were looking for. It's half the reason they'd let me live. If word was out that we'd killed Wotan, then everyone knew we had his soul. Sabbath and Wesna would go through my shit with a fine-toothed comb, making sure I wasn't sneaking the soul cage into their city. They wouldn't find it. Couldn't, unless they wanted to cut me open and get messy.

I finished my bourbon. Ordered another. Wesna showed up halfway through the drink, handed me the backpack. "Your six months starts now," she said. "I call you in a week or two and we discuss the first job. You and me, not you and him. Sabbath would prefer not to see you for a while."

"The feeling's more than mutual." I sipped my bourbon. Rolled it across my tongue. "Where we meeting?"

"Wherever you end up staying." Wesna produced a cell phone, tucked it into my pocket. "Burner phone. Untraceable. My number's the only one in there."

I put down my glass. Picked up my pack. "Pleasure doing business with you, then."

She gave me a hard look. "Screw up once, and he'll have you. He's not fucking around with that. Whatever shit you're running from, don't let it screw up your deal."

I slung my backpack over one shoulder. "You worry too much, Wes."

"Like hell I do." Wesna flagged the bartender, ordered a scotch of her own. "You planning on seeing Nora while you're in town?"

I'd spent sixteen years working with Danny Roark, learning how to keep my emotions in check when talking to demons. I'd gotten pretty good at it, 'til I heard the name. When I abandoned the Gold Coast, Nora Otto was the only thing I gave a damn about leaving behind. I hooked my pack over one shoulder. "Nah, I don't think so."

"You know she looked for you, right? Tracked me down and started asking questions about where you'd gone."

"And you told her?"

"Just what you'd want me to tell her: that you were an asshole and no one knew where you ran off too." Wesna tried to hide the grin behind her glass of bourbon. It didn't really work.

"Good call," I said. I looked into my empty glass, contemplated having another. Decided against it. The past is better left in the past, I think, and getting drunk in front of Wesna would give her a chance to fish.

Plus, the soul-cage in my gut sat there like a stone, an insistent reminder to keep on the move until I'd finally reached somewhere safe.

"Listen," I said, "I'm off. You get a job, you call me. Otherwise, shit, just leave me alone."

I stopped off at the payphones by the lift, dropped coins into the slot and dialled the number Roark had me memorize in case we ever found ourselves separated and in deep shit. It rang a half-dozen times before a brisk, female voice answered: "So, you're still alive, then?"

"For the moment," I told her. "We've come to an accord."

"And now you need a ride?

"I do indeed."

"I'm down in the car park," the voice said. "Third floor. Row J. I'll keep an eye out."

SAFETY IS A STATE OF MIND

I FOUND HER parked on the far end of the lot, near the exit that looked over the shopping centre across the road. Holly Langford perched on the bonnet of a less than pristine HR Holden. The car looked out of place in the lot, as if the boxy, sixties design was being mocked by the rows of sleek hatchbacks and four-wheel drives. Holly flicked her cigarette into the garden outside the lot, slid off the car and scuffed her docs against the concrete. "Well, shit," she said. "It went well, then?"

"It went okay."

"It thrills me when you say that, mate. It inspires all kinds of fucking confidence."

I didn't blame her for being pissed. She'd known me for exactly twenty-four hours, ever since I'd called her and invoked Roark's name. She owed Roark some favours, from his life before we met. Like most sorcerers, she believed in paying back her debts.

Trusting her went against all sorts of instincts, but I climbed into the HR when she unlocked the passenger side. She had a second cigarette lit by the time I climbed in, lips pressed tight to hold it in place as she put the car into reverse. The big car suited her. She was six-three. Skinny. Looked about forty-five. I didn't trust my guess there, 'cause the piercings through her nose, lip, and eyebrows made it easy to low-ball her age. So did the dreadlocks that hung past her shoulders.

Thick, knotted tattoos covered her forearms; Celtic work, mostly. Designed to obscure the tattoos with actual power. She put the car in gear, headed into the outside world. "So what great and terrible hi-jinks are hidden behind your 'okay,' then?"

I pressed my head against the window, watched the once-familiar landscape slip past. "Who says there's hi-jinks?"

"History," she said. "I know Danny Roark. I've seen the kind of shit that tends to nip at his heels."

The cigarette smoke burnt itself into my nostrils, thick and pungent. I coughed into my fist, but she didn't take the hint. Just stared at me, eyes bright and focused. "Well?"

"Three jobs. A six-month stay of execution."

"Jesus."

"It's not that bad," I said. "No worse than I expected going in."

"Spoken like a stupid git who's spent too long around Danny." We hit the highway and she pressed her foot against the accelerator. Six cylinders of analogue engine roared, making a lie of the car's beat-up exterior. Langford took care of the engine, lavished the same attention on it that'd gone into the powder-blue shell of the vehicle.

"When this is done," Langford said, "I'm making myself a voodoo doll and spending some quality time giving you a headache." Her thin, tattooed arms danced around the wheel as she passed the slow-moving traffic. "You sure you don't know where Roark is?"

"West, somewhere. That's all he said."

She held the cigarette between two fingers, skinny arms working the wheel. I closed my eyes and kept my mouth shut, listened to the rhythm of Surfers receding into the distance. We were heading south, away from the tourist heart of the Coast, away from the casino and the shopping mall and the rows of pristine towers designed for temporary occupation. I'd been running on fumes sine Adelaide. I wanted a place to shower, a hamburger, and a place to shit out the 9mm shell lurking in my intestines.

Langford fired the stereo, found an old punk song on the FM dial. "So tell me about Adelaide," she said. "I mean, I asked around, while you were meeting with your demon friends, but..."

I yawned and covered my mouth with a fist. "It's not much of a story."

"That's Roark for *I don't want to talk about it.*"

"Yeah, I guess it is."

"He wouldn't get away with it either," she said. "Now with what you're asking. If we're going to hunt the local denizens of the Gloom, I'd kinda like to know you aren't a complete incompetent."

The bitterness in my laugh surprised me. "Yeah. I guess that's fair enough."

"So?"

I watched the once-familiar landscape roll past, stitching new and unfamiliar landmarks over bits of memory. Every block or so, as we rolled past the cross-street, I'd catch a glimpse of the beach framed between the rows of buildings. "Roark picked us a target in Adelaide," I said. "Some necromancer type, head of his own cult. It's serial killer central down there, so he had plenty of juice to work with. Enough to build up a serious following."

"And?"

"And we underestimated that. We got the guy, no trouble. Siphoned his spirit into a soul trap, so they couldn't bring him back. It should have been a clean, easy job. In and out. Next thing I know, Roark is giving me your phone number and telling me to run. Says he'll be heading out west to draw them off."

"Shit." Langford frowned at the steering wheel. "You went after Wotan?"

"We did."

She swore again, eased the car around the long curve at Burleigh Heads. For a moment the rows of high-rises gave way to an open expanse of park, stretching towards the pristine water. Another turn and they were gone.

"You know of him?"

"Who?"

"The hit," I said. "This Wotan asshole."

"I know him." Langford took a drag on her cigarette, stubbed it into the ash tray. "Wotan's old enough to remember the Gloom before it became corrupted. Rumour said he followed the Old Gods, cut deals with the Giants that sleep in the bottom of the darkness. I mean, shit, there were people who said the Old Crow was immortal." She shook her head, dreadlocks brushing against her shoulders. "Why in fuck would you try to take him down?"

I shrugged. "Roark said it was necessary."

"It didn't occur to you he might be wrong?"

The punk song ended and she went back to the stereo, searched through until she found the classic rock station. Led Zeppelin blared through the car, loud enough to make my ears bleed. I went to say something, decided against it. I needed Langford. That wasn't a feeling I liked.

We hit the end of Immigrant Song and she dialled the volume down a few levels. "So who's got the soul cage, you or him?"

She said it quietly, like the possible answers frightened her. I kept my face still, gave away nothing. "You say that like Roark would let me out of his sight with something like that. He trusts me, more or less, but I'm just the trigger guy. I don't mess with anything beyond the very basics."

Langford nodded. Adjusted her grip, thin fingers fluttering against the wheel. "I'm going to make this clear right up front," she said, "I'll get you to the safe house. I'll help out with your deal, 'cause I owe Danny that much. The moment I pay that back, I'm out of all this. You understand me?"

"Yeah," I said. "I get it."

"This part, though, I want real damn clear," Langford said. "Anything associated with Michael Wotan is asking for all kinds of trouble. If you're lying about the cage, if his soul or his followers show up and cause trouble, I'll abandon your ass so fast you'll wonder if I ever truly existed."

She folded down the visor, lifted another cigarette out of the pack she stored there. "I never bought in to Danny's crusade. I don't owe him enough to get started now."

Langford set me up in a safe house on Currumbin Hill. She let me in, handed over the keys, then loitered in the kitchen while I checked the place out. Two stories. Long windows looking over Currumbin Beach. Narrow, like they'd built the place inside an oversized picket dug into the steep slope. A million dollar holiday house built to catch the sunlight and the breeze, hidden behind a beige wall like every other house on the ridge.

I dumped my gear in a bedroom with a king sized bed that doubled as modern art. Stood at the high windows and watched the sun coming up over the ocean. I felt like shit. I'd been awake too long. My stomach weighed me down like I'd swallowed a sandbag.

Under different circumstances it would have been a nice view. The eastern slope of the Hill had been given over to a nature preserve, the steep slope leading down to the beach covered in thick scrub. The melodic chortle of magpies launching into the morning chorus mingled with the steady pulse of the waves. The ocean stretched out, uninterrupted, to the horizon. If it wasn't for the high-rise at the base of the hill, I could have convinced myself it was someplace pleasant.

I stood at the window for a stretch. Migrated to the bathroom after that, where a couple of futile minutes were spent trying to combat the oxycodone and antacid. I curled up on the toilet, stomach cramped to hell. Tried not to think about what would happen if my stomach acid breached the condom tied 'round the bullet.

Langford was making coffee by the time I emerged. Plunger, not instant. The mugs were pristine and white. "So what do you think?" she said.

"I'm used to cheaper."

"You're used to squalor." Langford handed me a coffee mug, nursed the other one in her left hand. "I've worked with Danny. I know his routines. The man lives for dingy hotel rooms."

"He's not that bad," I said.

"Say that after you've slept in a bed that's never known the presence of bed-bugs." Langford settled into the leather couch, watched me pace the room. "It belongs to some friends of mine, currently overseas," she said. "The neighbours are seasonal - no one around this time of year - and even if they were people are used to visitors dropping in and out. I'm assuming you know enough to ward the place?"

"I'll get by." I tried perching on the windowsill. Decided against it.

"Try to keep it neat and discrete, then." Langford frowned, distracted herself with the coffee. "Try not to trash the place, if someone tracks you here."

"They won't," I said, trying to make it sound like I really believed that was true.

"Please," Langford said. "I've worked with Danny."

"I'm not Roark."

"That isn't exactly a comfort." She finished her coffee, dropped the mug in the sink. "Once I leave this place, I'm forgetting you're here," she said. "We meet out in the city somewhere. You find your own way there and your own way back. You cover your own damn arse."

I made positive noises, like I understood where she was coming from. Hell, who knows. Maybe I actually did, somewhere down below the fear and the anger I still pretended I wasn't feeling. I was back on the Gold Coast. I was working for Sabbath again. One fuck-up on a job down in Adelaide and I'd wiped away everything good about my life, reverted back to the same piece-of-shit I used to be when I was twenty-one and scared as hell about the things I saw in the shadows.

Langford wasn't Roark. Trusting her didn't come easy. I drained my coffee, put it down. Looked her in the eye.

"I'll take care of things," I said. "Sixteen years, I did my end of things. Adelaide's the only time we fucked things up."

Langford thought about. Nodded once. "Alright," she said. "Alright."

She gathered her keys and stood up. Looked me over one final time, then decided I could take care of myself. "When do we hear about the client?"

"Wesna calls me. I call you," I said. "My guess? About a week."

"I'll see you in a week then," Langford said. "You've got my number."

I sat by the front door, watched her leave. Waited a good hour before I hiked through the scrub to the bottom of the hill, then caught a bus to Palm Beach and the twenty-four hour chemist. The girl behind the counter offered me a friendly smile.

"How can I help ya?" she said.

I asked her about laxatives and her smile faded fast.

THE FIRST HIT

MY PREDICTION ABOUT the first hit was out by three days. Wesna rang me mid-way through my evening work-out, invited me to dinner at the twenty-four hour McDonalds up on Burleigh Beach. She laid out the client's details over cheeseburgers and vanilla shakes, slipping me an envelope with a trio of grainy photographs printed from a cell phone.

"His name's Eddie Darius," she said. "He's a small-time cultist operating out of the parks in Southport, recruiting kids from the homeless that camp-out on the foreshore. We don't know who he worships, but they're strictly small-time. You want to keep the photos?"

I shook my head. The photographs weren't great quality, but they gave me a pretty good idea what to look for: short and thin, unwashed hair hanging over a face like a shark's fin. Flannel shirts habitually tied around his waist. Army surplus backpack slung over one shoulder. A lot of the photographs showed him on the foreshore, hanging out with guys whose wide-eyed expressions said they'd seen too much. I kept flipping through the images, found the one I wanted: a close-up on his right arm, covered in dark ink.

"His tat's look Sumerian." I flipped the photograph around, pointed out a marking of a multi-headed snake. "Tiamat, maybe, if that's anything to go by. Where in hell do you find a ritual that'll let you contact something that old in this part of the world?"

Wesna rolled her eyes. "Who he worships doesn't bother us. It's how that's become a problem."

I placed the photographs back into their envelope. Pushed it across the table. "Sloppy?"

"Sloppy enough," she said. "His disposal techniques leave something to be desired. Sabbath's agreement with the mortal powers-that-be..."

She didn't bother finishing that. She didn't really need to. The Other thrived on the Gold Coast because they lived beneath the radar, taking advantage of the transient population where no one really stuck around for all that long. The cops looked the other way when people disappeared. They started paying attention when the bodies started showing up.

"Alright," I said. "Give me a time frame."

Wesna's lip curled. "Two weeks."

"For surveillance?"

"For the whole thing," she said. "He's built his rituals around the full moon. The cops haven't seen the pattern yet, but they will, over time. They're on the verge of saying serial killer. We'd prefer they don't get to the point where the occult is suspected of being involved."

"Two weeks isn't a lot of time."

"Then call it a rush job," Wesna said. "Assuming you're up to it."

"Come on, Wes'."

"Come on, nothing. I gave you the opportunity to run. You elected to make a deal instead." She folded her arms, stared me down. "There's a part of me that would still regret pulling you apart. It would take the fun out of things, if Sabbath ordered it."

I waited for the smile to come, letting me know it was a joke. She left me there, still waiting, and exited the store, disappearing into the rainy night to do whatever Sabbath had her doing.

It isn't easy, killing a sorcerer. Even a minor, bottom-of-the-totem-pole motherfucker as useless as Eddie Darius. You need to spend enough time watching them to be certain who their worshipping, what kind of defences they've set up to cover their arse, and how they'll respond to being killed. You don't want to be haunted by the sorcerer's soul. You don't want to be plagued by their death curse. You sure as hell don't want to be on the run, hiding a soul cage beneath the floorboards in your safe house, hoping like hell the wards will hold if the cultists ever track you down.

I called into Langford, laid out the job. She bitched about the timeframes, but she took up the lion's share of the passive's role, scouting the target as he went through life, looking for the routines and the little daily rituals. Occasionally I'd spell her, taking a shift in the van we used to follow Darius around, giving her time to go do some research or catch a few hours sleep.

It wasn't ideal. It never is.

Eddie Darius spent his morning haunting the big, antiquarian bookstore on Scarborough street. Langford figured that for the place where he found whatever ancient book had got him into magic, and I couldn't really disagree with her. Despite its name, the store primarily carried the same collection of cheap paperbacks every other store on the Gold Coast carried: years of accumulated holiday reads left behind by tourists. Its antiquarian section catered to select clientele, and the owner usually kept his day staff away from those who knew they carried more than first-edition copies of Moby Dick and Great Expectations.

He spent his afternoons down on the park by the Broadwater, just by the bridge leading across the river to Surfers. A lot of the local homeless gathered there, motley clans of runaway teens who gathered around the assorted junkies and mentally unhinged that made up the core residents of the park. Years ago, back in my time, Southport hospital had been home to a mental health unit and a rehab clinic. Both were gone now, cleaned out by changes in government policy, but the people they'd serviced stayed close despite Southport's best efforts to drive them out with acts of urban renewal and regular sweeps of the riverside parks.

Darius wasn't homeless. He went there to deal heroin to the junkies and spend hours listening to the ramblings of the craziest of the mental cases. It wasn't unusual. It's a phase most aspiring sorcerers go through, not long after they realise that there's more to the world than they've realised in the past. A lot of them theorise that the ramblings of madmen are connected to the Gloom. A lot of them quickly realise they're right, even if there are more lucid sources where the information isn't quite so distorted and broken up.

We spent the two weeks on surveillance, waiting for the full moon and the night of his rituals. I sat in the passenger seat of the van, doing the final watch.

Langford sat behind the wheel, working her way through a pack of Windfield Blues.

"I don't know about you," she said, "but I kinda hate this guy." She took a long drag on her cigarette, eyes never leaving the park. Darius was talking to a sixteen year old girl, a blonde with matted hair and a grubby blue Quicksilver jacket. "Third time he's talked to her in a week. Dollars to donuts, that's who he's hoping to take home for a sacrifice."

I peered at him through binoculars. "It's that big a break in his pattern?"

"Big enough," Langford said. "Ordinarily, by this point, he'd have stopped by and given her whatever smack he's going to give her, burned through his spiel about the glory of whatever pissant entity he's lucked into worshipping. Then he'd head further down the bank, where he can listen to Old Mate down by the swings rant a bit."

She pointed to an elderly bloke who camped out on a patch of grass by the swings. I nodded and mulled it over. "You figure you've got his defences scouted?"

"Sure," she said. "They're basic wards. You could break them, if you put your mind to it. You thinking of making his dreams come true?"

"It's neat," I said. "It takes care of the body, and Sabbath wants these looking accidental."

Langford sucked on her cigarette, free hand toying with the end of a dreadlock. "Ordinarily I'd tell ya we need more lead-in," she said, "but this guy's a lightweight. I'll give you ten bucks on him shitting himself the moment a portal actually opens."

"You reckon we can pull it off?"

"So long as you hold up your part," she said. "Keep watch on our friend here, and I'll go set things up."

Eddie Darius rented an apartment on the second floor of a converted Southport motel. The sign out the front still read Palm Cove, despite the absence of either on the property, but it didn't look like they'd lit it up in over a decade. There were two stairwells leading up to the landing along the second floor. The lights in the stairwell at the back of the building were blown. In the two weeks we watched the place, none of the residence had used it after dark. I figured that'd work. It gave me somewhere to wait, while Darius was out, doing his thing. Plenty of darkness to hide in. Close access to his front door, three spots down on the landing.

I settled in around nine o'clock, waited a few hours for Eddie Darius to return. It's the hardest part of the job, sometimes. Sitting there, doing nothing, making sure you're not spotted. I busied myself with a minor charm Roark taught me, one of the ones that encouraged people not to see you if they glanced your way. It gave me something to concentrate on, instead of pacing the narrow stairwell.

The target showed up a little after eleven, escorting the girl he'd spent the week working on. She was blonde and street-kid skinny, had the instincts to sense I was there despite the charm I'd woven around myself. She glanced my way as the target fumbled with the keys, backed away a few steps when I emerged from the shadows.

The target kept talking to her, not really paying attention. I got halfway along the landing, produced the SIG and held it in a low, steady grip. "Mister Darius?"

He looked up at me, surprised. Looked at the SIG. Put two-and-two together real quick, for a moron like him. "Oh man," he said.

I kept the gun low. Looked at the girl. "Miss, you may wish to leave now," I said.

Darius whipped his head around just in time to see her retreating. He turned back to me, eyes narrowed. He'd moved past the shock now, stumbled into the phase where he was trying to work out what my presence meant.

He glanced down at the SIG again. The part he couldn't work out. Most sorcerers expect their enemies to fight magic with magic.

"Let's go inside," I said. "We can talk in private."

For a moment I saw hope rise up within him, but it died when he realised his wards were disabled. He stepped into the kitchen. I followed him, closed the door behind me. There wasn't much to his apartment. Shitty kitchen. Shitty lounge room. Where most people had a couch and TV, he had a big square of granite, a ritual circle carved into the dark stone. Lots of effort went into that circle. Four feet wide, candles at even points, dried blood in the centre. The knife resting in the centre looked like a prop from a B-Grade movie. That didn't surprise me. Amateur shit, all of it. The training wheels set up by a newly-minted sorcerer, unable to shape the Gloom without all the horror-movie trappings to prop up his confidence.

Darius edged close to the granite. Tried to hide the way he glanced down at the knife.

"Don't," I said.

He stopped. Waited for my next move. I still had the SIG pointed at the floor, held in a steady, two-handed grip. Darius whet his lips, mind whirring. "Listen, man," he said. "I don't have nothing worth stealing, right?"

"Bull."

"Come on, man. Look at this place. What in hell do you think you're taking?"

"Everyone's got something worth taking." I lifted the SIG, held it on him, and whispered one of the first spells Roark ever taught me. The twelve candles spread around the circle caught alight in unison. "Don't try to shit me, Darius. I know what you do here."

Darius stepped away from the altar, an easy smile forming on his lips. "Well, then," he said, "I suppose that changes things, somewhat." He dipped his knee slightly, approximating a bow without ever lowering his hands. "Welcome, brother, to my san——"

"If you say sanctum, I will shoot you where you stand," I said. "It's a goddamn lounge room, kid. There's not enough candles and blood in the world to transform it into anything but."

He closed his mouth. Bit his lower lip. "If you knew what I did here—"

"I know," I said. "I can even guess exactly what good you've done with it. Week after week, trying to open a portal. Killing those kids, carting off the bodies. Lazy work. Unimpressive."

"Lazy?" He couldn't quite process that. I almost felt sorry for him. The kid had learned the basics from someone, figured out enough to put together a ritual circle and contact one of the entities that lay in the Deep Gloom. With tutelage, he probably could have been a solid sorcerer. As it is, he remained a goddamn menace to those around him.

"Lazy," I said. "All that blood. All these goddamn props. You've got no idea how any of this shit actually works, do you?"

"I know enough," Darius said.

"Yeah?" I slipped the SIG into my waistband, picked up the gaudy knife he used in his rituals. "Well, then, Darius, I guess it's your lucky day. I don't want to hurt you. It's not my job. I'm just here to stop you from making another mess. You show me how much you know, how much you can do without dumping girls in the river, and you'll get through this evening without a bullet in your skull."

Darius whet his lips again, glanced down at the circle. "But—"

He cut himself off the moment I looked up.

"Yeah? But?"

"I need blood," Darius said. "A sacrifice. Mother Tiamat demands it, before she'll grant me—"

I grabbed his wrist with one hand, sliced the gaudy knife across his palm. For all his faults, he kept the blade sharp. Blood pooled immediately, swelling out of the wound. Darius swore three or four times, but I kept a tight grip on his hand.

"Blood," I said, slapping his palm down on the circle. It left a long, crimson smear over the older, darker stains. "And now there's a sacrifice. Lesson one, Darius. A thimble's as good as a bucket, when you're dealing with the Other."

"FUCK!" Darius nursed his bleeding hand, pressing it against his t-shirt. It didn't stop the blood from flowing, but it left a pretty impressive stain.

I dropped the knife, pulled the SIG again. That got his attention, blood or no blood.

"Don't focus on the pain," I said. "The pain is only temporary."

"I don't..." Darius said. Fear robbed him of the ability to finish the sentence. "I don't..."

"Kneel," I said.

He knelt.

I stepped back from the granite, gave him plenty of room. "Go ahead," I said. "Introduce me to your goddess."

"I can't—"

"Yes, you can," I said. "Deep breaths, concentrate, focus on what you want to achieve."

He went to object, but I raised the SIG and trained it in his direction. The gun seemed to give him focus, clarify the world so he understood the two options available to him. He knelt by the altar, dripped blood from his palm over the circle. Slowly, quietly, he started to chant. I didn't recognise the words, but I recognised the rhythm.

Nervously, desperately, Eddie Darius reached out to the far side of the Gloom and tried to contact his goddess. I held my breath, waited, let the unsteady cadence of his chant fill the room. The temperature dropped as darkness spread through the circle, seeping out of the circle like a stream of dark tears.

Darius hesitated, started by the unexpected result. "Don't," I said. "Keep going."

He swallowed and resumed the chant, eyes wide. The darkness congealed, thickened. Became something more than darkness and shadow. Eddie Darius stopped chanting, his voice going still. He stared at the Gloom, unable to look away from its depths.

A long, tenebrous tentacle reached out of the depths and caressed the side of his face. More of them reached along the edges of the circle, testing for restraints, found none. Darius retreated, hit the wall. He kept trying to go back, like he hadn't noticed he'd run out of room.

"What the fuck?" he whispered, over and over. "What the fucking fuck? "

Part of me pitied him.

I put a bullet in right leg, just above the knee. Eddie Darius shrieked, what little self-control he still had shattering in that instant. The tentacles shivered, feeding on his shock and the sudden rush of agony. As one, they reached for Darius and wrapped around him, dragging him into the circle with cold, implacable purpose. Eddie Darius screamed for a few short seconds, then he disappeared into the depths of the circle, drawn into the place on the far side of the Gloom.

I kept my breathing steady, did my best to feel nothing at all. Waited a full minute before I risked moving. The older entities of the Gloom, little-worshipped and mostly forgotten, were generally easy to placate. A brush against the world, a terrified victim; whatever Goddess Darius worshiped probably didn't even wake out of her slumber after she took him.

But you never assume that, not once a portal to the Gloom's been opened. I let the darkness thin in the centre of the circle, made sure there was nothing but granite underneath it. Then I collected the shell from the single shot, slipped it into the pocket of my jeans, and let the front door lock behind me.

DOWNTIME

I SPENT A few weeks building a routine, making it easier to keep my head down.

The safe house didn't make it easy. The tall, thin rooms encouraged horizontal living. All the furniture was pressed against the western side of the house, leaving a clear path along the windows that faced out towards the horizon. They weren't even windows, really. More a single wall of glass, looking down on the world through the trees and branches. When daylight broke, it came into the bedroom and slapped me awake. Made it damn near impossible to get back to sleep.

In theory, I was okay with that. Sleep is the enemy when you're hiding out. Sleep is the time when you're at your most vulnerable, trusting that your defences will keep you secure. I got by on as little sleep as possible. Spent my mornings working out with the free-weights I found in the bedroom wardrobe. Spent my afternoons taking care of the place, keeping it tidy. Reinforcing the wards. Keeping an eye out for trouble. Cleaning the SIG on the glass-topped coffee table, making sure the pistol did everything I wanted it to do.

Once a week I'd pull out the small wooden box I stored beneath the bed. I'd lift the wards and open it up, check the bullet with Michael Wotan's soul. Afterwards, I closed the box, then reinforced the wards on it. Slipped it back under the bed along with the SIG and my go bag.

I ordered in groceries from the nearest supermarket, had them delivered once a fortnight on a randomly selected day. In the evenings I put the television on, pretended to watch it. That ended around ten o'clock, when anything worth watching was entirely over-and-done with. Most nights, I'd just sit there, listening to the waves. Re-reading *Persuasion* for the second or third time. Killing days while I waited for Roark to call and tell me our exile was done.

It didn't help. Not really. Sitting tight worked on my nerves, left me feeling unsettled and ready to hit something. Staying put wasn't in my nature, not anymore. Sixteen years I'd worked jobs with Roark, drifting from city to city. We'd put down demons, fey, and sorcerers. We'd done the work that needed doing. Routine was the thing that got them all killed. Routine and the ability to pick apart their defences. I knew how easy it was to do my kind of work.

All you needed was time, a good deal of patience, and the certainty that you were doing something that needed to be done.

I met Wesna in the McDonalds up at Burleigh Heads, discussed the details in a quiet table in the corner of the building. She slid the envelope across the table, gave me a one month timeframe before the target needed to die. She watched my face, smirking, hoping for a reaction. I kept my cool, nodded. Told her it wouldn't be a problem.

I put a few blocks between us before I started swearing. Called Langford from a payphone down by Burleigh Beach, organised to meet with her an hour later.

The park by the beach wasn't a bad place to wait. Unlike the majority of the Coast's beachside parks, it actually deserved the name: a wide, green expanse that ended at the dunes, lots of tall pines that gave shelter to flocks of lorikeets in the afternoon. Families ended up there, during the holidays. The local feral tribes used it for drum circles and fire twirling every Saturday night. Surfers gave the place a wide berth, preferring the break on the far side of the headlands.

It was early, when I put the call through, so I claimed a table and waited. Langford showed up with two cups of coffee, slid one across the table as she sat down. It smelt good. Better than the cheap instant I'd been ordering back at the safe house, and way better than the McCafe garbage I'd been drinking a few hours earlier.

"Thanks," I said.

Langford shrugged. "You sounded like you needed it."

Her smile dared me to try and deny that, but there wasn't much point. I sipped my coffee, stared at the dark horizon. "The next target is Nora Otto," I said.

"She runs a club in Broadbeach, right under the Demon's noses."

"The Hell Bar," Langford said.

"You know it?"

"I've done business there, time to time," she said. "It's that kind of place, you know?"

"You ever met Otto?"

Langford shook her head.

"I have," I said. "We used to be friends."

Langford thought that over. Sipped her coffee. "Alright," she said. "You had to figure that was coming. You make a deal like yours with a demon who's holding a grudge..."

"Yeah," I said. "I figured it was coming."

"And?"

"It's still a surprise," I said. "Nora wasn't the kind of friend I figured for getting involved with the Other."

"Ah," Langford said.

"Yeah, fucking 'ah'."

"And how does that change things?"

"That depends," I said. "How bad is the bar?"

"Bad." Langford flexed her long, thin fingers, adjusted her grip on the coffee mug. "Exactly the kind of club you and Roark go after, actually. Lots of mortals brought in to be preyed upon by Other, lots of people given a shit-load of money in order to keep things hush-hush. I'd be surprised your demon friends want it taken down, if it wasn't for the personal connection to the mistress."

"I doubt her death will close things," I said. "Not for long, anyway."

Langford closed her eyes a moment, thinking that over. "Otto would be a hard woman to replace," she said. "Lots of experience handling the fey, eager to deal with the minor players. Lots of people trust her to keep the club neutral; the moment that changes, they start looking for safer options. No one's going to trust Sabbath to do that, even if they suspect that Otto's in his pocket."

"Is she?"

"Is she what?"

"In his pocket?"

"Who knows?" Langford considered her coffee, raised the paper cup to her lips. "You operate in Broadbeach and you're doing some kind of deal with Sabbath and his crew. How deep the deal goes is anyone's guess, but the illusion they've created is pretty convincing."

She drank, stopped. Looked me in the eye. "If you're asking me if she deserves to die, that's something I can't tell you."

"Yeah." I drank coffee, not really tasting it; tried to swallow too much hot liquid. It hurt as it went down, muscles contorting to force things down.

Langford thumped my back as I coughed and spluttered. I waved her off, wiped my mouth with the back of my hand. "Shit," I said. "I remember why I hate it here."

Langford waited, letting me process. She finished her coffee, dumped the empty cups into a nearby bin. Sunlight bloodied the horizon.

"Well," she said, "it's your move, trigger. Is that something we use, or a reason to call this whole thing off?"

"Neither," I said. "It's business as usual. We start surveillance, put together a plan. We've got thirty-one days to get it done; we either know it's worth doing by the end of that, or I've got all the reason I need to accuse Sabbath of lying."

"You think that's likely?"

"No," I said. "He's smarter than that. If he's put her on the list, he's confident I'll kill her. He swore that all his targets would deserve what they had coming."

"Yeah?" Langford snorted and rubbed her hands together, trying to generate some warmth. "By whose standards?"

"Mine," I said. "He was real damn careful about that one."

SURVEILLANCE

THERE WERE RAVENS on the power-lines outside the Oasis complex. Two of them, sitting wing-to-wing, positioned so their dark eyes could scan the street. I crouched by the window, watched them through the tinted pane of glass. Langford lay on her belly beside me, binoculars pressed to her face. I pointed at the birds, said, "How long have they been there?"

Langford lowered the binoculars and followed the line of my finger. "The birds?"

"Yeah, the birds," I said.

"A couple of hours, maybe." The binoculars went up again, her attention focused on the front door of the Hell Bar.

"How many hours?" I said.

"Two? Three? I don't know." It'd been three weeks since we started surveillance, and my presence was getting on her nerves. She wanted to ignore me, do her damn job, and get the hell out. My presence increased the odds of something going wrong, especially since I pushed for signs that Otto deserved to get hit.

"Big difference between two and three," I said.

Langford abandoned the binoculars, flicked me an angry glare. "They're birds, trigger."

"Yeah," I said. "They're ravens. It's not a good sign."

"You big on omens, you and Danny?"

"Omens, no. But Roark believed in knowing your enemy. He spent a damn month making sure I knew the difference between a raven and a crow, before we went and did the job down in Adelaide."

The steady rhythm of Langford's breathing halted. She sat up, binoculars dangling from her neck. Gave me a hard, stern look. "Shit," she said. "And you're sure they're ravens?"

"Too big to be anything else. And the curve happens towards the end of the beak," I said. "On a crow, you'd see it starting halfway down."

She looked through the binoculars, then nodded, dreadlocks bobbing. “Alright,” she said. “I’ll give you that. Doesn’t mean they’re trouble.”

“Doesn’t mean they aren’t,” I said.

“If they were trouble, I’d pay attention to ‘em. That’s what you’re paying me for.” Langford made a show of looking at her watch. “Twelve-oh-nine,” she said. “Your girl arrives in a couple of minutes, and we still haven’t got her process for bypassing the wards on the bar. You want to keep arguing about the damn birds?”

“I’m inclined to think about it,” I said. “Given all the things that’ve happened.”

“Shit.” Langford snorted exasperated air into the still room. “And if they are familiars for whatever cult you’re running from, how does it change your deal with Sabbath?”

“Well,” I said, and Langford raised an eyebrow at me. When I didn’t have anything to add, she pressed her eyes against the binoculars again and went back to watching the bar.

I left her to it, went to the small kitchenette to make us some shitty instant coffee. Three weeks of watching Nora Otto hadn’t improved my feelings towards the job. The residents heading into the Hell Bar weren’t exactly the company I’d choose to keep, but I’d be willing to bet Langford knew a dozen Other with similar reps and called them friend. Roark knew even more, tolerating the existence of all kinds of creatures we’d have killed in other circumstances.

That’s how it goes, once you’ve seen behind the Gloom.

“She’s here,” Langford said. “Usual park, down by the Surf Club.”

I left the steaming mugs of coffee on the bench and walked back to the window. Watched as Nora Otto exited her beat-up Daihatsu and crossed the road. She moved with short, clipped steps, her gait limited by the leather skirt she wore to the bar every night. Langford clicked her tongue at the choice. “Your girl has terrible fashion sense.”

"Depends."

"Depends on what?"

"Whether she's doing it to make a statement," I said. "A fuck-you to the creatures of the night, who naturally expect every mortal to run."

"If that's the case, she'd pair it with heels," Langford said. "Not a pair of steel-toed docs."

The part of me that still thought with a sixteen-year-old's hormones wanted to make a counter-argument. People noticed Nora Otto when she walked, and it wasn't just the skirt that got their attention. She paired the leather skirt with a professional jacket, midway between corporate and punk. In the sixteen years I'd been away, she'd grown into a lithe, pale beauty with a shock of dark curls and a full-sleeve of tattoos covering her right arm.

Nora approached the front door of the Hell Bar, slid the keys into the lock. Langford shushed me, focused on trying to make out the things Nora said or did to bypass the wards. The security on the Hell Bar didn't look like much. Two front entrances; one to the main bar, one to the beer garden. More access via the loading dock on the bottom floor of the Oasis centre that the bar suckled up to like a lungfish on a shark. The bouncers, by and large, looked regulation issue; big guys, all shoulders, in dark shirts and slacks.

You could kid yourself into thinking it'd be an easy job until Nora showed up, pausing in front of the double-doors to whisper to herself and spill a pinch of salt across the threshold of her joint. Langford watched it all, made notes in the ragged moleskin where things got puzzled out.

The bar doors opened and Nora disappeared inside. Langford watched it all, making note of everything. The ravens did the same.

"Keep an eye on 'em, eh?" I said, nodding to the birds.

"Ah-huh." Langford didn't look up from her notes, just chewed on a pencil as she thought.

"I mean it," I said. "They could be—"

Langford looked up, her expression set. "You want to back out on the job, trigger, say the word and I'll leave all this glamour behind."

I shook my head. "It's not about backing out."

"Course not," Langford said. "You're just the kind of unprofessional fucker who gets up your partners arse for the fun of it, then?"

I opened my mouth to argue. Shut it again, right smart. "Fine," I said. "I'll go finish making coffee."

Langford nodded and went back to her notes, getting lost in the work. After leaving the black coffee at her elbow, I retreated to the couch and dug my copy of *Persuasion* out of my pack. Was still there an hour later when Langford looked up, blinking, and said, "Why are you still here?"

By Saturday night Langford had stopped giving me shit about the ravens. They were still there, perched on the wire, still watching the front of the Hell Bar like black feathered cops on a stake-out. I'd come to my senses and cleared out of the apartment, headed back to the safe house to sleep and prepare, but Langford called me a little after nine o'clock and asked me to come check something out.

The Hell Bar was a different beast on a Saturday night. It attracted a younger crowd; lots of jeans, lots of t-shirts, lots of hairstyles that bosses and parents were probably complaining about. They were less polished than your standard club crowd on the Coast, a little wilder around the edges. The DJ's music bled across the mall, a mixture of old-school metal and punk.

Langford let me into the apartment, pushed the binoculars into my chest. "On the street," she said. "Below your goddamn birds. You aren't going to miss him."

I looked. Found the sorcerer right where she said he'd be, loitering in the shadows just outside the street lights, eyes closed as he smoked a cigarette and communed with the birds on a wire above him. I recognised him right away. Mid-thirties. Bearded. Tight black t-shirt over a Gold Coast tan. The asshole from the Hard Rock, except this time he wasn't playing it subtle.

"Showed up with a team of five about an hour ago," Langford said. "He's been sending his boys into the club, one by one, slipping 'em past the bouncers. I recognise some of them, from the past few days of watching."

"Shit," I said.

"You know him?"

"He tried to take a piece out of me, back when I first arrived."

"Shit." Langford scrubbed both hands along her face, trying to rub away the exhaustion. I could see her mind working, sorting through all the reasons the sorcerer could be here. None of them were good news.

I stood, pulled the SIG from its holster. "Tell me about the boys that went in."

Langford just looked at the gun. "What the fuck?"

"He's scouted the place," I said. "He's sent his boys in. Letting him kill or capture Otto isn't going do shit for keeping me on Sabbath's good side. Tell me about the guys he sent in."

"Five. Younger blokes. They wear those t-shirts like it's a uniform, jackets a little too heavy for the weather" Langford said. "All of them did the salt thing, while they waited in line, so they know enough to try and bypass a ward."

"You figure they succeeded?"

"Bouncers let 'em in." Langford turned back to the window, surveyed the street. "He's waiting for something."

"Right." I checked the safety on the SIG and slipped it back into the holster. "Best you pull out," I said. "I think this one's off."

Langford hesitated, glancing at the window. "Yeah?"

"Yeah," I said. "I'm going to have a word with our friend with the beard."

"You sure that's smart?"

"Not at all. But I don't like the coincidence, eh?"

She nodded, and I returned the nod on my way out of the apartment. I found the fire-door and took the stairs down two at a time. My footsteps echoed against the concrete walls. It smelt heavily of pee and stale cigarette smoke. I hit the ground floor and stepped out into the lobby, kept my pace steady as I exited and crossed the street.

The sorcerer stood beside a grey SUV, cigarette hanging from his lips. He watched the club with a terrible focus, never really blinking, and I could feel the slight tug of something happening inside as I got close. His flunkies, probably. Taking position in dark corners, tethering themselves to the Gloom. Dangerous to do, but they were trying for subtle, getting themselves all set up before the boss-man followed them in.

I took the long way around, coming through the back of the parking lot. Got within three car lengths before one of the ravens cawed a warning, getting the sorcerer's attention. He turned slightly, cigarette in hand. Spotted me hovering beside a red hatchback with faded paintwork.

I stepped out of the cover, SIG in hand. No point trying to hide once you've been made.

"Last time I ran into you, my friend messed up your arm," I said. "Trust me when I tell you, I'm a better shot."

He snorted and flicked his cigarette away. Stepped away from SUV with both hands exposed. "So, you'd be Keith Murphy," he said. "Don't worry. I know your rep, sir."

"You, on the other hand, are just some dude."

"As it should be," the sorcerer said. "I prefer to work low-key."

"Humour me. Give me a name."

"Well." He smirked at me, hands open. "I guess you can call me Thirteen."

"I've called people dumber things."

"I'm sure you have." He glanced down at the gun. "That's a very pretty firearm. How long do you think you can wave it around before it gets noticed and cops show up?"

"I dunno. It's nice and dark 'round here." I edged a little closer, lowered the gun. "Put your hands down, Thirteen. I don't need to look like I'm mugging you."

"I'd prefer to keep them up. A better chance someone will notice and all that jazz." He grinned at me, all confident. "Unless you'd like to shoot me, just to get me to comply."

I kept the SIG trained on him, covered the space between us. "It's tempting," I said. "Real tempting."

Then I kicked him between the legs, let the pain do its job. Thirteen doubled over, hands dropping to clutch at his damaged privates. I grabbed a hank of his greasy hair, used it to haul him upright and jab the SIG into the hollow of his throat.

"You've got five men inside that club. I can already feel them tethering. Do you want to tell me what they're doing, or do we skip to the part where this gets messy."

Thirteen grimaced. "You aren't this stupid, Murphy."

"People keep telling me that. I'm not sure where they got the idea," I said. "I don't know shit about you. I don't know what wards and curses are going to chase me when you're dead. I don't know that I care, either."

"Idiot," Thirteen said, and I felt something cold and sharp stick into my neck. Pain burned through my muscles, jammed them tight. One of Thirteen's flunkies stepped into my field of vision, grin plastered over his face. He held up a silver needle, point beaded with thin tendrils of shadow that writhed around the metal. A simple paralytic spell, one of the rookie sorcerer's tricks.

I'd gotten overconfident and paid the price for it.

"To answer your question, Mister Murphy, we were sitting on the bar in the hopes you'd show up. Local whispers say you and Nora Otto have a history, and our other attempts to track you proved ineffective." Thirteen straightened, took a tentative step, favouring his groin. "A desperate step on our part, but we needed to find you."

My jaw ached from the effort of trying to talk back. Thirteen grinned at me, let his flunky gently the lever the sig from my frozen fingers. "We need the soul of Michael Wotan," he said. "You don't understand what his death has set in motion."

His flunky handed over my gun, started going through my pockets. Searching for the bullet with Wotan's soul inside, or clues that'd tell him where I'd hidden it. I wished him luck; there wasn't much to find. I had the key card for the apartment on the far side of the mall. Enough cash for a cab home, plus some extra to take care of any incidental problems. The flunkie handed everything over, and Thirteen's smile started to wilt.

"I'm not sure what he's done, but I'd advise you to step aside." A low voice, soft and feminine, speaking from a point somewhere behind my head. I recognised it straight away. Sixteen years hadn't changed it that much. "I'm not doubting he deserves it, whatever you've got planned, but I guarantee you, he's pissed me off worse."

Thirteen arranged his face into a pleasant grin. "Miss Otto," he said. "We're not looking to cause trouble."

"Five punk sorcerers come into my bar, disrupt the wards and start juicing up in the shadows like their aiming to cause trouble. Forgive me if I don't take you at your word." Nora stepped forward, just inside my field of vision. Still wearing her leather skirt, a vintage Pistol's t-shirt with a blazer over the top, a discrete .32 nestled in her hand. "I'd take it as a kindness if you gave Keith back his voice now."

The flunk stepped forward, putting his body between Thirteen and Nora Otto's gun. "You don't understand," he said. "The killer must—"

Nora whipped the thirty two across the flunky's face. The weapon blurred, split the skin open just above his nose. The flunky dropped hard, fingers going to his face, the silver needle dropping to the bitumen. My aching jaw started moving. Muscles unclenched, aching from the prolonged effort. It was all I could do to keep on my feet.

Thirteen had a phone in his hand, pulled from his pocket while Nora dealt with the flunky. He held it in a tight grip, thumb hovering over the keypad. “I don’t think you comprehend the depths of shit that await you,” he said. “I have need of Mister Murphy. I cannot allow you to interrupt us.”

“And yet, I’ve got the gun,” Nora said. “And I doubt you’ve got any hoodoo that’ll save you in this instance.”

I tried to warn her, but my throat wasn’t up to it. All the words came out as a deranged croak. Thirteen smiled. Nora saw the phone. She fired as he mashed his thumb against the keypad.

The bar exploded outwards, dark flames filling the night with a wash of hot air. It wasn’t entirely natural. It wasn’t entirely magic. Part of me respected that, even as the blast wave knocked us all to the ground.

THE SECOND HIT

PEOPLE WERE SCREAMING. Thirteen lay on the ground, bleeding from the stomach. Crawling to the safety of the Gloom. My SIG was gone, tucked into some place in the shadows of his jacket. Nora Otto lay on the ground, eyes closed, her .32 dropped amid the chaos. My arms and legs protested as I crawled after the sorcerer.

My ears rang, unable to focus on anything but the screaming and the echo of the explosion's roar. Thirteen reached into the shadows, pulled out something tangible and dark. It wrapped around him, tendrils lashing onto his arm and drawing him in.

I reached for Thirteen as the shadows pulled him away, came up with a handful of air. Someone called my name. It sounded dim and far away, partially lost among the cacophony of screams and oncoming sirens.

"Murphy, come on."

Langford had her van parked on the edge of the lot, the door opened and waiting. I grabbed Nora, hauled her onto my shoulders. Forced my aching body to cover the short distance between me and the vehicle. We collapsed into the back, a heap of tangled limbs, and Langford had the van moving before I had the door closed. There were sirens nearby, too close for comfort, and Langford floored the accelerator in order to put distance between us.

"Thought I told you to pull out," I said. Hell, I probably shouted it, still unsure of how far I could trust my hearing.

"I owed you," Langford said. "I don't like being wrong."

"Cheers," I said.

"You're welcome." She took a hard corner, put us on the highway. Eased back on the accelerator so we attracted less attention. "What in fuck happened back there?"

"Someone went looking for me," I said. "He got inventive when Nora interrupted our discussion."

"Nora, as in, the target?"

"That'd be the one," I said. "We're going to need a place to stay. Somewhere a little more secure than the safe house. They jabbed me with a Gloom pin, just to keep me paralysed. I'll need some time to purge that. Nora's unconscious, probably hurt—"

"It's okay," Langford said. "I've got a place in mind."

"I need a new weapon," I said. "Asshole took my gun. I've got a stash locally, but—"

"I'm on it," Langford said. "You just start putting together a plan that'll take care of the shit that'll follow."

Langford drove us out to the Valley, up close to the national park where they used to log cedar in the days before the Coast was actually a city. You could still find remnants of logging camps hidden in the park, but the rest of the Valley was given over to small farms and forest getaways. Langford's place sat right up the back, high on the slopes of the mountains. From her veranda you could see a good kilometre of the winding road that came through the Valley, plus a herd of disinterested cows that occupied the slopes on the far side of the road.

We got Nora into Langford's spare room, then I crashed out on her threadbare couch with one arm thrown across my face. I slept fitfully, woke a little after dawn. A gentle rain tapped the corrugated roof of Langford's home. An old, analogue clock said it was five-thirteen in the AM, and the old familiar instincts told me trouble was coming. Langford padded out from the bedroom as I put on my shoes. She carried a worn, well-cared for .303, handed me the rifle without a word. I checked the lever action, joined her at the sliding door that led out to the balcony. I could just make out the black sedan parked at the edge of her property, just outside the boundary line where her wards began.

We eyed the car for a couple of minutes. Finally, I asked: "Thirteen or Sabbath?"

"Sabbath," Langford said. She picked up one of dreadlocks, toyed with it absently as she studied the car. "It feels like demons, in any event."

"Right," I said. "I'll go take care of it." I put the rifle on one shoulder, headed for the back door.

"They can't get in," Langford said. "Not without making the kind of noise Sabbath usually tries to avoid."

I nodded. "How long they been there?"

"I felt them arrive before sunrise," Langford said. "Figured the wait wouldn't hurt them any, since you were still sleeping."

"What's in the rifle?"

"Bullets," Langford said. "Nothing fancy 'bout them, trigger. I don't go picking fights with the local demon tribes."

"Ah-huh."

Her eyes narrowed. "Hope you aren't thinking about messing that up for me."

"That depends."

"Depends on what?"

"On how well-informed they are."

I let myself out. Trudged down the muddy driveway, struggling to keep my feet. Langford's place had a long drive, a couple of hundred meters. It took time to get down there, especially in the wet. Rainwater dripped into my eyes, left my flannel shirt clinging to my chest. I focused on keeping a good grip on the rifle, carried it under one arm like a hunter out for a stroll. No point in levelling it right off the bat, giving them no choice but to go defensive.

Wesna and Randall stood beside the low-set Holden, giving themselves a good six feet before they'd hit the fence. Randall held an umbrella in place, every inch of him tall and prissy. Wesna just put faith in her jacket, let the rain slick her dark hair against her forehead.

"So a bar down in Broadbeach blew up last night," she said.

"Ah-huh."

"Sabbath asked us to track you down, see if you knew anything about that."

"Ah-huh," I said. I adjusted the grip on the .303,

made sure I could get it up in a hurry.

"Don't give us Ah-huh," Randall said. He took an angry step forward, but Wesna caught his arm and hauled him into line.

"This isn't a pleasant kind of morning," she said. "Any chance we can come in, discuss this like reasonable people over coffee and warm biscuits?" She smiled pleasantly, like it wasn't raining out. Like she wouldn't be putting a fist through my face if the wards on Langford's property kept her from approaching.

"I don't mind the rain," I said. "Reminds me I'm alive."

Randall produced a knife, surging forward on a wave of anger. "You fucking cu—"

I got the .303 up, levelled at his head. Wesna gripped his shoulder again, fingers cinching tight. "Don't," she said, voice low and even. "Mister Murphy here is a professional, you will treat him like one."

Randall glowered at me, lowered the knife to his side. I kept the rifle up.

"Apologize," Wesna said.

Randall mumbled something I couldn't hear through the rain. It could have been an apology. It could have been a promise to cut out my damn tongue. Either way, Wesna removed her hand. She offered me a pleasant smile. "So the first thing we should check: is Nora Otto dead?"

"That's what you hired me to do," I said.

"You really expect me to accept that answer?"

"Depends," I said. "You really want to start this conversation by telling me I'm unprofessional?"

Wesna stared. Randall fumed beneath his umbrella. The rain kept falling on all of us. "Alright," Wesna said. "We'll come back to that one. Let's move on to the explosion."

"Not my idea."

Randall barked out a short laugh. "No shit it wasn't your idea."

I tapped an irritated finger against the stock of the .303. "You wanted these done quiet, so the blame could be portioned off to others. I still had another week before Otto should have been dead, I was figuring a way to do it quiet."

"And?"

"And a third party got involved. I ended up improvising."

"I figured," Wesna said. "You'll have to forgive Randall. Friends of his frequented the bar. They were present when what happened, happened."

"So, what, you figured you'd threaten me a little? See if I could bring 'em back?"

"We're not here to make threats." Wesna pushed wet hair back from her face, smile showing teeth for the first time since the conversation started. "For one thing, there doesn't seem much point. You've retreated to a place of moderate safety, acquired an ally of considerable power in the form of Miss Langford. Not that breaking in there is beyond our capabilities, but we're being reasonable men, Murphy." She paused and glanced back at Randall. "Most of us, at least."

She left a pause there, a place for me to comment. I let the rain fill it in for me, adjusted my stance in the muddy soil. It takes effort to hold a gun on someone for a prolonged conversation. The Enfield .303 weights about four kilograms. No one wants to hold that weight at their shoulder for five minutes.

"Here is the question that's bothering me," Wesna said. "You're not responsible for the explosion. This collaborates many of the things we've heard, looking into things ourselves and getting copies of the police report. Miss Otto isn't listed among the dead, which means you're either lying about her death or very good at your job."

"I'm not lying," I said.

"I said we'd come back to that." Wesna brushed water out of her eyes, signed quietly into the rain. "You did good work on that first job, Murphy. We gave you the target. The target disappeared. No sign of their deaths to cause trouble with the mortal cops. No ghosts hanging 'round in the Gloom 'causing trouble for the rest of us. I can appreciate that kind of work. I know how hard it is. Sabbath appreciates that approach, but he isn't happy right now. He's got no confirmation that the target is dead. He's got a new player making trouble. Explosions aren't how we do business."

"Tell Sabbath it wasn't my fault," I said. "A third party stepped in. "

"You really want me to tell Sabbath you brought a new player into his city?" Wesna shook her head. "We know about Thirteen, Keith. We know he's a disciple of Michael Wotan, and we know what happened in Adelaide when you and your partner fucked up. I protected you when he first showed up, said nothing about my suspicions when he jumped us at the Hard Rock. Sabbath is unlikely to be happy to learn about that. It may yet tip him over into expending resources on Miss Langford's wards, getting a team of his less savoury employees in to make a mess of things. It may convince him to make noise, Keith, and neither of us wants that."

"I do," Randall said. He'd retreated to the car, leaned his weight against it. The finger I had resting against the rifle trigger itched to apply pressure, to nail the prick from under ten feet. A bullet wouldn't hurt him, but six of them would do some damage and I knew the next step for putting him down for good.

Instead, I lowered the .303. Stood there in the rain, looking from demon to demon.

"You can both get fucked," I told them. "Pass it on to Sabbath. Next time I see you, I'll put a bullet in your head. You can get your asses back to the Gloom and stay there."

Wesna cocked her head. "You're in a bad mood," she said.

"'Cause Sabbath promised me no one who'd offend my sensibilities."

"Maybe he stuck by that," Wesna said. "Maybe your old friend Nora wasn't so nice as you'd like to think."

"You're very fond of twisting words."

"Words are the foundation of an agreement." Wesna showed off rows of neat, white teeth. "Words are what kept you alive, Mister Murphy, the first time you left this city. They're what's keeping you alive right now, 'cause we've got no evidence you've reneged on our agreement."

Wesna's smile didn't waver, but the humour drained out of her features. "When we find that evidence, this conversation will go a very different way."

"You're not going to find shit," I said. "Nora Otto's—"

Wesna's long, handsome face became something garish and horrible. She took a step forward, raised her right hand. Slowly, deliberately, she pressed forward, up against the limits of Langford's wards. Darkness pooled around her palm, thin wisps of magic gathering at the point of contact, whirling around it like a hurricane. It had to be hurting her. Had to be agony. Wesna showed nothing but that hideous, empty smile. She stared at me through the film of magic forming between us.

"The next time you see me, Keith, I'll have your third target. We'll pretend this conversation never happened and behave like professionals."

She retracted the hand, worked feeling back into her fingers. The unrelenting rain fell around us, forcing me to blink away the water as she retreated.

"Or we'll know for sure you're lying. That won't end well."

She climbed into the car, waited patiently for Randall to close his umbrella and take the driver's side.

The storm swallowed the tail lights as they disappeared into the valley.

PLANS AND REMINISENCES

I SPENT THE rest of the day seated on Langford's veranda, watching the road. The rain came down in a torrent, relentless and constant. Round sunset Langford emerged with a pot of coffee. She put a mug on the table, the coffee beside it. "Drink," she said.

It smelled good. Better than any coffee she'd brought me in the field. Langford settled into the chair beside me, put one foot on the railing. She went barefoot in her house. Wore jeans and a long-sleeve shirt that covered her tattoos. Her dreadlocks were bound back, away from her face. She looked older. Worn. The bones in her face were sharp, stark reminders of the skull underneath. I poured a cup of coffee, nursed it for a while. The rain had brought the cold with it this time.

"You see anything out there?"

I shook my head. "You?"

"Nope, but they're there. I can feel them out there, watching the place. Sabbath wants his pound of flesh."

"More than a pound," I said. "Sabbath doesn't worry me."

Langford ran her fingers over her jeans. "He worries me."

"Sabbath, we know. Sabbath, we can predict."

"That's why he worries me."

"They'll let me roll out of here. They won't want a fight on your doorstep."

Langford nodded. Her eyes were fixed on the horizon. "You want me to dig into Thirteen," she said. "Find out where he came from, how he fits in with Wotan and your bullet."

"I want that," I said, "but I'm not going to ask for it. I think we've used up whatever favours you owed Roark."

"That you have," Langford said, "but I'm going to do it anyway."

"Can't ask you to do that," I said. "No way I can pay you for it, not the way this shit is going."

Langford stood up, stretched. Thin, tattooed writs

poked free of her sleeves. "You survive this, Murphy, you owe me a favour. Seems to me you're the kind of son-of-a-bitch who remembers what he owes people."

"I just lied to a demon who used to be my best friend." I finished my coffee, put the mug on the table. "The odds of me surviving are pretty damn low."

"I'm willing to take my chances," Langford said. "Tell me what you already know about Wotan's organisation."

I took a deep breath and told her, everything Roark had drilled into me, all the men we'd taken out on the way up the food chain. I told her about the soul, trapped and taken, although I stopped short of telling her about the bullet Wotan's was hidden in. Langford listened. Nodded. Took the occasional notes.

At the end, while she nodded, I asked her for one last favour. "I'm going to take Nora with me," I said. "She needs to disappear completely for this to work."

"She going to go for that?"

"Probably not."

"Awful big risk, then."

"I owe her, and right now, she's my responsibility. I've got a few days to talk her into going along with the plan. But that means there's something back at the safe house that probably shouldn't be stored there."

Langford raised an eyebrow. Nodded. "Alright," she said. "If you're sure."

"I'm sure," I said. "Get it, take it, keep it hidden 'til I ask you for it. Figure you can do that?"

Langford just smiled. She went inside and left me standing vigil on the veranda, only emerging a few hours later to tell me Nora Otto was awake.

The bedroom Nora slept in had sunflowers on the curtains. She sat up in bed, drinking Langford's tea, and I settled into a wicker chair in the corner of the room. My arms still ached a little, my legs burned. Bad as I felt, Nora looked worse. She'd caught the explosion, got pretty tossed around, but it wasn't the physical injuries that took the real toll. She'd lost her bar. Lost employees. Regulars. Customers. Having me in the corner of the room, watching her sip tea, wouldn't be doing her any favours given our goddamn history.

She spent a long time looking at the window, studying the seam of sunlight caught beneath the curtains. Then she turned to me, her face set and steady, determined to cope. "You should have some tea," she said.

"I'm not really thirsty."

"It's really good tea," Nora said. "Whatever else your friend is good at, she's got a knack for beverages."

"I've drunk plenty of Langford's tea. I know what I'm missing at this point."

"Ah," Nora looked towards the open door, the living room beyond. Langford had retreated to the kitchen, giving us plenty of space. "So, you're back, then?" She said. "When did that happen?"

"Weeks ago," I said.

"Weeks?"

"It wasn't really planned," I said. "Things got fucked up. I needed to lie low."

She nodded slowly, put the tea down on the bedside table. "I get that," she said. "I remember how it was, before you bailed on me and all."

"I didn't bail. I had to leave."

Nora glared at me, her jaw set. Blue eyes under dark curls, burning with anger. Her jaw pulled tight as fencing wire. "You bailed," she repeated. "It took me a long time to forgive you for that, Murphy. Don't fuck it up by pretending it wasn't running away."

I kept my mouth shut. Didn't bother with any more explanations. Maybe she was right. Maybe I did run, all those years back. I was younger then. Stupider. Less aware of options.

"So you came back," Nora said, "and you thought you'd bring a shitload of trouble down on my place of business."

"No," I said. "I came back and cut a deal with Sabbath. Agreed to do some work for him, in exchange for a hassle free stay. I didn't plan on coming near you. Figured I'd fucked up you and me enough for one goddamn lifetime."

“Don’t play the martyr,” Nora said. “It doesn’t really suit you.”

“You either,” I said.

“What’s that supposed to mean? I’m the one who got left behind.”

“And I’m the one who got sent to kill you,” I said. “Sent by a demon I could have sworn you didn’t know existed back when you and I were dating.”

Nora blinked, her blue eyes suddenly cold and hard. “Oh,” she said. “We dated now?”

“Didn’t we?”

“No,” she said. “Not really. You and I, Murphy, we just fell into each other’s orbit. Dating’s a terrible word for that. It implies you actually cared about me, instead of just using me as the temporary escape when your other life got too much for you.”

“Well, you were a good escape.”

Her eyes narrowed dangerously. “I saved your ass last night,” she said. “Why don’t you at least try to get through this without fucking insulting me.”

“Alright,” I said. “Why’d Sabbath want you dead?”

“I owed him,” Nora said. “I wasn’t paying up. Not the smartest play, I’ll grant you, but I’ve spent the entire time since you’ve been gone trying to stay ahead of my debts. You know what he’s like when you owe him for too long. You, better than anyone, yeah? Isn’t that why you left?”

“No,” I said. “I didn’t owe him shit by the time I left.”

“Your friend take care of that? The one Sabbath’s got a hard-on for?”

“Roark,” I said.

She nodded.

“Yeah. It’s one of the things he took care of when he got me out of the city.”

“He the one who told you to leave me behind?”

It was my turn to nod.

“Your friend Roark’s an asshole,” she said.

“Nora—”

“No,” she said. “You don’t get it. I was nineteen, Keith. My boyfriend, more or less, just up and disappeared. Maybe he wasn't a good boyfriend. Maybe he didn't talk much about what was troubling, and maybe he seemed a little sketchy when you looked at the people he hung around with, but he was my goddamn boyfriend and I thought I was in love."

Her voice cracked. She took a deep breath, fought to regain control. "It makes it hard, not knowing what happened, when that sort of shit goes down. Even at nineteen, I went looking for goddamn answers. I tracked down Wesna, got her help. Put all the pieces together until I found my way to Sabbath. She didn't want me going there, getting up close with him. Didn't know how to stop me, either, and your name opened up his doors 'cause he still wanted ways to hurt you and I seemed all kinds of useful in that regard."

"You shouldn't have done that."

"No fucking shit." Nora turned towards the window, watched the light growing dimmer beneath the curtain. "After a few years, I figured out you weren't coming back. By then, I was involved, doing little jobs for Sabbath. Lots of people knew me. Lots of people puzzled out my connection to this asshole I used to go out with. I threw in with Sabbath 'cause that was the safest option, given the number of enemies you left here when you bailed."

She took a deep breath, then sighed. "Sixteen years is a long fucking time, Murphy. Let's not pretend we know each other, or trade on what we had. I assume you're not planning on killing me, given that I'm still breathing here."

"I never planned on killing you," I said. "I was just looking for options."

"So you went with blowing up my bar?"

"Not me."

"Oh, not you, just people who wanted you dead. People who'd tracked you here and figured out I knew you once." Her voice cracked a second time, accompanied by a momentary anger that washed across her features. "I built that fucking bar, Murphy. I built it out of nothing. If you're going after the asshole who blew it up, I want to be involved."

I stood up, shook my head. "I'm not sure that's a good idea."

Nora rolled out of bed. Moved a little steadier than I was.

"I'm not sure I give a fuck," she said. "I think you'll find you owe me, Murphy, and I fully intend to collect."

"You're leaving town," I said. "Same way I did. Sabbath's got reason to believe you're dead. I'd like him to keep believing that."

"If you're going after Sabbath, I want in on that, too."

"Look—"

Nora raised a finger.

"I don't run," she said. "That's not what I do. You present me with a problem, I figure out how to solve it. If Sabbath thinks I'm dead, that gives me an advantage. I could use an advantage, Keith. I can kill that motherfucker dead."

"Jesus, Nora."

"Jesus, Nora, nothing."

"Do you even know how to—"

There are fourteen reliable ways of killing a body possessed by a demon. She covered eleven of them in quick succession, stumbled a little over the twelfth.

"I'm not the girl you left behind," Nora said. "I figured this shit out, and I don't need saving."

"Okay," I said.

"What I need," she said. "What I've needed for a long damn time, are allies who aren't afraid to work alongside me."

She backed away from me, sat down on the bed. Reached for the kettle on her bedside table. "So you going to work with me, Keith? Or you really think you can convince me I gotta slink off quietly after all the shit you've pulled?"

THE RIGHT CALL

WE LEFT LANGFORD'S place a few hours after sunset, followed the winding road out of the Valley until we saw the lights of the suburbs. We'd been on the road about five minutes when the headlights appeared in the rearview, keeping to a safe distance. A professional would have chased me, forced me to take a corner at speed. Deaths happened all the time in the valley, particularly when it's wet, but that's not how demons do things. They're creatures of another time, obsessed with killing you face to face.

Nora sat in the passenger seat, nursing Langford's .303. She'd abandoned the leather skirt for a pair of Langford's jeans, hidden the bandages on her arm and shoulder underneath a borrowed sweatshirt. Langford used a little magic to disguise Nora's features. For the moment, she looked older, dreadlocked and pierced. From a distance, you'd mistake her for Langford. Up close, if you knew what to look for, the glamour would be obvious.

Nora didn't care. Her eyes stayed on the road, fingers tight against the rifle. She said nothing until we hit the main roads and I turned onto the highway.

"North?"

"Yeah."

"That's heading towards Sabbath's territory," she said. "And we've already got a tail."

"Necessary evil," I said. "Unless you're confident we can do this with a borrowed rifle and a rented van."

She buttoned her lip and let me drive. It'd been over a decade since I'd set up the storage locker out the back of Nerang, long enough that the once-isolated concrete complex had been surrounded by newly built units. It took us twenty minutes to get there, another ten to navigate our way to the back of the complex. My storage unit was in the rear, secured by an old deadbolt. I'd set it up years ago, when things were just starting to go south with Sabbath. The first of many around Australia, after working with Roark allowed me to fund the existence of others.

We got out of the car and I picked the lock, letting us inside.

The interior of the storage unit didn't look out of place. Lots of boxes. Old furniture, two decades out of date. Dust and damp and a single, overworked light bulb that gave us a bare minimum of illumination. I pointed Nora towards a box by the door. "There's an old flashlight in there," I said. "It'll have about three grand rolled up inside it, where the batteries would go."

She knelt by the box and started searching, sneezing as the dust rose. "Wouldn't a, you know, actual flashlight be a little more useful at this point?"

"Probably," I said, "but we've got what we've got."

I went to work on the rest of the place, unearthing all the tools of the trade I'd hidden there. Vials of holy water. A couple of sharp knives, one blessed by a priest and another by a local wiccan. A twelve gauge and three boxes of shells. Two P220s, earlier models of the SIG that I'd used to kill Wotan, along with ammunition for each. I loaded the first, slid it into my empty holster. Offered the second to Nora.

"Shit," she said, "weren't you the boy scout way back when."

I looked around the cluttered shed, thought about the gear I'd stashed in a dozen other cities. "This," I said, "this is nothing. Pick any other city where I keep a stash, and I could probably go to war with the gear I've got there."

We climbed back into the van, drove down to the McDonalds at the end of the block, and went inside to order. Wesna and Randall parked their car outside, doing their best to look inconspicuous. Nora peeled a twenty off the roll of bills from the storage shed and ordered us some food. Quarter pounders. French fries. Cardboard cups full of coke. I kept my eyes on the demons. She kept her eyes on her food. She chewed slowly, took regular sips of her coke.

"So, the asshole who took out my bar," she said. "Thirteen?"

"If you say so. I'm going to stick with asshole."

"Sure."

"What's he after?"

"Me," I said.

"That's the short version. I want something longer."

"Not sure what else there is. He's part of a cult. I killed their leader. They've been chasing me ever since."

"That's why you came back?"

"Ah-huh." I took a long pull from my coke. I could taste the soda water they used in the post-mix. Nora took a bite out of her burger. She sat there, chewing quietly. When she swallowed, she put the burger down. Watched me for a moment, then said: "Who else did you kill?"

I shrugged.

"Does that mean you don't know, or you don't want to tell me."

"It means it's what I do. What I've been doing for years now," I said. "I take out people who mess with things they shouldn't. Things from the Gloom that don't want to play by mortal rules. I don't feel the need to apologise for it."

"Was that your job while you lived here?"

"No," I said. "It came afterward."

"Is it why you left?"

"One of the reasons."

"What are the others?"

I took a long breath. "Youth. Stupidity. My own little fuck-up while handling Sabbath's business, which meant the other option was sticking around and getting dead. Roark came along and offered an alternative. I went along with it because it was easy."

"Are you sorry?"

"Do we have to do this?"

"Are you sorry you left?"

The rain was easing up outside. I could see signs of moonlight peeking through the clouds. "No," I said. "I'm not sorry I left. It was the right call, Nora. I know I'm not meant to say that, but it's the honest-to-god truth."

I pulled my eyes away from the window, met her

angry stare. Nora clenched her fists on the table. She reached for her coke, pulled it closer. Her eyes went to the counter, looking at the kids and the strangers ordering. Then she looked at me, her eyes big and very blue. She'd given up crying a long time ago. I could see that in her face. That didn't mean she'd stopped wanting too. It didn't mean she wouldn't be crying now, if she could find it within her.

I didn't blame her. I had plenty of regrets.

"Come on," I said. "We gotta find some place to crash tonight."

Traffic on the Gold Coast is a pain in the arse. It's a long, narrow city with two arterial roads and the kind of public transport system that hugs that coast. If you want to go most places, you're driving the two arterial streets. In a city of six hundred thousand people, that shouldn't be a big deal. Factor in the ten million who pass through every year, it quickly adds up to a nightmare.

We lost sight of Wesna's sedan about an hour after we left McDonalds, stayed on the road for another hour just to be sure we lost them. Eventually we dumped the van down in the Tweed, 'caught one of the local busses north, and checked into a hotel. We looked like hell, but the bloke behind the counter didn't bat an eye. He gave us the plastic cards that served as the room keys and told us about the complimentary breakfast buffet.

Nora sulked as we rode the elevator to the fourteenth floor. Our room looked over the beachfront. From the window, you could see the sand and the dark mass of ocean. The windows were layered glass, designed to help combat the heat. An air conditioner did the rest, made sure things were comfortable. Nora eyed the bed in the centre of the room. It was big and wide and entirely comfortable, but there wasn't any other place to sleep. She sat on it and hit the remote for the TV. A cheerful, smiling woman worked out on some revolutionary exercise machine you could set up over a door. Nora watched it for a few minutes while I stowed my gear.

"So, where you going to sleep?" she said.

"I was planning to use the bed."

"And I'm going to sleep?"

"Wherever the hell you want," I said. "The bed will be fine, believe me. I don't sleep much anymore, especially not with someone hunting me. If you want, we can take turns. I'll trust you not to run."

"Jesus, Murphy." She curled her legs up on the bed, hugged them close to her body. I left her to it, went to work securing the room. Basic wards on the doors and windows, powered by a few stray drops of blood. Then I fished a book out of my pack, settled in to the room's single armchair. I kept the SIG P220 close, resting on my lap, and opened to an unread page of *Persuasion*. I proceeded to read the same page about Anne Elliot's time at Uppercross a half-dozen times, not really able to concentrate on it. My brain kept looping round, running through everything that'd happened. Wesna. Nora. Sabbath. Michael Wotan down in Adelaide and his friend Thirteen. I didn't like not having a plan. I didn't like not having Roark around to do the planning for me.

"Murphy?" The way Nora said my name, all soft and gentle, did more to get my attention than the word itself. She'd crawled into bed wearing a t-shirt Langford had loaned her, left her jeans in a small puddle beside the bed with her belt and her shoes beside them. Her head was resting against the pillow, stray hairs falling across her face. The glamour faded. She looked like Nora again.

"This thing you did," she said. "This thing with Roark. I want to know about it."

"There's nothing to know," I said. "Not really."

"It's the thing—" she hesitated, bit her lower lip. "It's the thing you chose instead of me," she said. "I'd like to know something, yeah?"

I thought about that. Figured it couldn't hurt. Started telling her about the last sixteen years. Nora lay in the bed, watching me. I stared out the window, mouth working on its own, running through the training and the hits and the little things that wore away at me. The things we'd taken down and made the world a better place. An incubus running brothels down in Kings Cross. A handful of werewolves up north, hunting the local backpackers who wandered into the bush. The hotels. The hours of setting things up. The painstaking rituals required to keep something dead that knew plenty of ways to come back from the grave.

I told Nora about Michael Wotan in Adelaide. The way Roark told me we were hitting the necromancer, the little chill that went through me despite my pretence that I didn't know what was coming. I told her about the cult he ran, the girls that went missing every full moon. About the pall that hung over Adelaide, Australia's own capital of murder and serial killers, all because he lived there and clung on like a tic. I told her about Roark's instructions, about the clear moon overhead that night before I went in and pulled the trigger. About the little things I couldn't quite remember that may have been mistakes, about having to run with the soul in the shell despite the fact I didn't really know what to do with it.

I told her all of it, 'cause she'd asked me to, and 'cause some part of me thought I owed her, and she listened to it all with her serious expression and the blankets pulled up around her shoulders. And when I was done, I just sat there, watching her in the dim light. Wondering what things would have been like if I hadn't run away from my problems. If I hadn't taken Roark up on his offer and run around killing bastards that needed killing.

"Murphy?" Nora said.

I shook of my reverie. "Yeah?"

"We're adults," Nora said. "You can use the damn bed."

"I'm okay," I said. "I won't sleep for a while."

"Murphy," she said, like I was missing something, and then I caught her eye and caught up with things, and I put my book down and shucked off my pants while she watched me. When I peeled off my shirt her eyes followed the scars and the tattoos, trying to read the missing years between the lines they'd left on my body. I didn't give her long to do that, not before I was under the covers alongside her, throwing an arm around her and pulling her close. Nora wriggled back, put her arse against my groin. I didn't complain about that. She didn't complain when parts of me started remembering the times we were more than friends.

She rolled over and pressed her lips against mine. Her fingers went lower, searching for a way into my underwear.

"Listen," I said, "are you sure about this?"

Nora nodded, and her fingers found what they were looking for, and after that I wasn't really focused on asking anything. After that we just peeled off whatever we were still wearing and remembered what it was like when things weren't so complicated and she didn't really hate me, and I remembered what it was like to care about something other than the job.

The next morning I rented a sky blue hatchback and drove us both down to the safe house. The rain had cleared overnight, replaced by the clear light of morning, and the view from the house stretched out across the water. Nora spent a few minutes exploring the place, whistled beneath her breath. "Doing what you do pays better than I expected," she said. "Maybe you were right to bail."

I shook my head, promised her my usual spots for lying low involved more fleas and less impressive views. "This is Langford's doing," I said. "She knows people with money who owe her favours."

"Good for her." Nora strolled over to the window, rested her forehead against it. She was still wearing the borrowed jeans, coupled them with a sweater we'd picked up at the gift-shop below the hotel. "You think her friends have got something a little less conspicuous hanging around in their wardrobe?"

"Good odds," I said. "Bedroom's through and to the left."

Nora nodded and disappeared into the bedroom, leaving me alone in the kitchen. I took a few moments to check the wards, then made coffee with the plunger. We hadn't mentioned the events of the previous evening. I wasn't sure if I should have started that. I was almost done with the coffee when Nora emerged, a slightly too-large t-shirt hanging over the jeans.

"Langford has big friends," she said.

"Sorry," I said.

"You sure this Thirteen asshole will have my apartment covered?"

"If they don't," I said. "Sabbath will. Either of them is liable to take a shot at you, given the circumstances."

"I'm going to need clothes, Murphy."

"We'll get to that," I said. "This'll do you for a day or two, 'til we get something sorted. First priority is making sure they buy your death, while we keep us from getting dead. That matters more than the size of your shirt."

I handed her a coffee. Black. Two sugars. The way she'd drunk it as a teenager. Nora sipped it, winced at the flavour, but she didn't say anything. I watched her pace around the lounge room, then settle into the couch.

"So here's the deal," I said. "You wait here for a day. Lie low. Watch some TV. Raid the refrigerator when you get hungry and all. The most important thing is staying here, out of sight, behind the wards. They've kept me safe this long, with Thirteen looking for me, and Sabbath hasn't seen fit to come down here and blow the place up, which is a pretty good sign they don't know I've been staying here."

"And you?"

"I'm going to talk to an old friend," I said. "See if I can start undoing some of the mess I've made of your goddamn life in the last twenty-four hours, then see if I can get a lead on Thirteen so I can dissuade him from further acts of terrorism against people I used to know."

"You think you can do that?"

I grabbed one of the knives we recovered from the storage shed, tapped my fingers against the older SIG P220 in my holster. "I plan on being convincing," I said. "It usually brings people around."

I left her sitting at the kitchen table, nursing a cup of coffee. Nora smiled as I left, like she was already thinking of me coming home. For a moment, I let myself believe it.

TRUST

I CALLED WESNA'S number and asked her to meet me. Just her, no Sabbath, no Randall riding shotgun. She called me an idiot, then told me it wasn't possible, then told me to take a walk through the mangroves along the creek. I took the rental car, drove until I hit the creek. From there I followed the water inland, parked alongside an old RSL. There were paths that followed the creek from there, wooden decks that jutted over the water on the parts where the shore wasn't worthwhile. Eventually they disappeared into mangroves, thin clumps of trees and wooden decking that cut between them. I followed the path, found a seat in this covered alcove about halfway through the walk.

The mangroves smelt of gasoline, inheriting the smell from the river. Kids used the alcove to get drunk and stoned, the small trash can overflowing with empty bottles and beer cans. I could see the wide expanse of Currumbin Bridge through a space in the trees. Behind it, the side of Currumbin Hill that looked out over the suburbs instead of the goddamn beach.

The waiting got to me pretty quick. I stuck my hands in my pockets and wondered what Nora was doing right now. Wondered how much truth there was in the story she'd spun about owing Sabbath money. I'd started theorizing about other possibilities when Wesna showed up, coming around the bend in the path at a light jog. She'd dressed down for the occasion. Sneakers. Sweat pants. A plastic visor protecting her face. Just another Gold Coast fitness freak running the mangrove path.

She came to a stop, hands on her hips. Her expression wasn't friendly. "For real," she said. "Is Nora Otto dead?"

I stared at her, saying nothing.

"I should wring your neck," she said. "Twist your skull free off that annoying carcass and take it back to Sabbath as a trophy."

"You really should," I said. I grinned at her, wry and careful. Hoping she'd take it as a joke, instead of tacit permission. "I mean, this? This isn't smart, Wes'. Not smart at all, goddamnit."

"Don't blaspheme." Her expression didn't budge. "An' you don't want to run that play right now. This is against-my-better-judgement shit, Murphy. Don't push it, okay?"

"Okay," I said.

We stood, facing each other, listening to the mosquitoes and the river and the distant sound of traffic. I backed off first, retreating to the wooden seat. Wesna watched, arms folded, waiting.

"I wouldn't have picked you for a jogger," I said.

Her expression grew severe.

"Alright," I said. "Business." I took a long breath, let it out. It didn't help any, except for buying time, but at that moment, time was enough.

"First up, I need to figure out, you know, given what's gone down here—"

"No," Wesna said.

"No?"

"Not at any price you're willing to give him," she said. "You fucked a job. That's it. He's going to set the hounds on you, revel in your damn pain. That was always the plan, though. You knew that."

"I did."

Wesna took off the visor, studied me as I watched the river. "Why ask, then?"

"I like knowing where I stand. It makes it easier to figure out which moves are really there," I said. "Shit's going to get bad, sooner than you think, and having Sabbath on my team doesn't seem like a bad idea."

"You like to dream big," Wesna said.

"That I do." I crouched, picked up a discarded bottle cap from the debris on the platform. I lined it up on my index finger, sent it spinning into the creek with my thumb. "So what's he offering Nora, that she's so willing to forgive me?"

Wesna raised an eyebrow, half-amused at the prospect. "You really think anything Sabbath says can make her forgive and forget?"

"I'm willing to bet he can," I said, "'specially given the situation. She came to him after I was gone, offered to work for him in exchange for knowledge. He kept her in the back pocket in case I ever came home, playing a long game in case he ever had a chance for revenge. You're not going to tell me it's beyond his capabilities?"

"It's not," Wesna said.

"So?"

"It's not his play," she said. "He set her as a target to hurt you, sure, but that wasn't the only reason. The Nora you knew, she's gone, mate. She's spent too much time running the place where black market deals got done. Sabbath wanted her gone because she'd become a threat. Nora Otto knows secrets, these days. Used them to pay off her debt years ago."

"Not the story she's telling," I said.

"No reason she should." Wesna crossed the platform, settled her arse on the bench beside me. "The Boss isn't too pissed her bar went up in flames, even with the time he's putting in keeping the cops from losing their shit. Nora's bar going boom is good fucking news for him; one more up-and-comer losing their power base before they can come and challenge him. Even with that gone, she's dangerous. Knows too many people. I know you got history and all, but..."

She didn't finish that thought. She didn't need too. Sabbath had sworn he wouldn't send me after anyone who didn't have it coming, and odds were good he'd lived up to that. Demons lied. They lied through their teeth, sweated lies out of their borrowed pores. But there weren't many that swore an oath they didn't mean.

I stood and dusted off my jeans. "If this is where you plan on turning on me, now's the time," I said.

Wesna shook her head. "Not this time. This is just two old friends catching up on things."

"Appreciate it," I said.

"You shouldn't," Wesna said. "It makes the part where I do have to hurt you sting a little worse, and you know you're going to pay for that once I get into the swing of things."

"Maybe we'll get lucky and never see each other again," I said.

"No one's that lucky," Wesna said. She put her visor back on her head, preparing to jog into the shadows. "I swear to god, Murphy. Not even you."

My father used to rent an apartment on Burleigh Beach. We lived there three years, longer than I spent anywhere else in my childhood years. It never felt like home, exactly, but it felt closer to it than anyplace else I'd lived. Roark always said that's what made me good at the job. Not the sight I'd learned to ignore, or the skills I'd picked up breaking legs for Sabbath. Just my habitual refusal to belong somewhere, putting down roots that get mirrored in the Gloom, getting twisted into weapons that could get used against me.

I drove out to Burleigh and parked on the beach. Found a payphone, one of the few that still existed, and dialled the number I wasn't supposed to dial. It rang out twice, spitting out my change, but I fed it back in and dialled.

I got an answer on the third attempt. Danny Roark said, "Keith?"

"Yeah."

"You weren't supposed to call," he said.

"Yeah."

"Then I'm assuming it's bad, and we need to make this fast," Danny said. "What do you need, Keith?"

I studied the phone booth, the graffiti and tags scratched into the glass walls. The line snapped and popped, the distortion of old copper landlines trying to connect with cell. I became aware of my own breathing, in out and, marking off the empty seconds.

"Roark?"

He took a long breath. "Yeah?"

"Things are going to get bad here," I said. "The cult tracked me here. They've got people in the city. Sabbath..."

I heard the click of a cigarette lighter, louder and clearer than the line distortion. The pause as Roark inhaled, thinking things over.

"We knew Sabbath would be difficult," he said. "The cult following you was always a possibility. You know how to play this, Keith. You know what's at stake."

"No," I said. "Not really. The way Langford talks about Wotan? The way his followers are coming after me? They're blowing shit up, Danny. Attacking me in the midst of a crowd, screw the collateral damage. They don't care if they get noticed, and that ain't normal."

I left that out there, waiting for Roark to pick it up.

He didn't. Just smoked his cigarette. "Did you keep the soul cage secure?"

"Yeah, but—"

"But nothing," Roark said. "It's all that matters, Keith."

"No," I said, "it's not."

I leaned against the car, stared at the old apartment building. Listened to the waves rolling into the beach behind me. "What the fuck did we start, Danny? Why the fuck did we take down someone we weren't ready to take down? Just once, give me details. Treat me like a partner."

The silence on the other end of the phone seemed like it would last forever.

"Roark?"

"Still here."

"Come on, man. I need to know."

"Yeah."

Roark sighed, low and quiet.

"Ragnarok," he said. "He wanted to start an apocalypse."

I chewed on that. Absorbed it. "That's a new one," I said. "How close did he come?"

"Close enough."

Roark hung up the phone, left me alone with the beach and the dial tone.

ESCHATOLOGY

SPEND ENOUGH TIME peering into the Gloom, and you become a student of eschatology. Ragnarok. The End of Days. The long count on the Mayan Calendar and the last days of the Kali Yuga. Myths and religions are replete with scenarios that mark the end of the world, and once you realise that demons and magic are real, it's not long before you start to do the math.

The end of the world is inevitable. Every species of Other that emerges from the Gloom, every faction that finds its way here, believes that the end is coming. They just disagree on how it will happen, when it arrives, and who will finally kick it off.

Very few of the options end well for humanity. Which makes it easy to sway people to your side, once they've brushed against the Gloom and realised that something's coming.

The promise of self-preservation against inevitable catastrophe appeals to pretty much everyone.

I went back to the safe house. Nora Otto was already gone. I knew it from the moment I opened the door, felt the cold, sterile emptiness of the place. I fumbled for the lights, turned on the row that led down the short flight of stairs from the front door to the lounge room. I didn't bother calling Nora's name. Instinct said she'd already bailed, and all that really remained to find out was how badly she'd fucked me on the way out.

I made my way in, saw all the signs of someone tossing the place, just like I was meant too. All the drawers in the kitchen opened, their contents strewn over the floor. Couch cushions torn and spread across the hardwood, ensuring there was nothing hidden within. Solid work, methodical. I checked the duffle bag we'd taken from the storage shed, discovered the knives, spare SIG P220, and cash was gone.

I drew my gun, edged my way into the bedroom. Of all the shit in the safe house, only one thing really mattered, and I knelt to retrieve the warded box from beneath the bed.

I heard something behind me, straightened just in time to see a big man emerge from the shadows. Not Thirteen, but he looked like the sorcerer's Neanderthal older brother. Big. Bearded. Tattoos exposed for all to see, skin tanned to the consistency of leather. He grinned widely when I pointed the SIG at him.

"Stay," I said.

He hesitated a moment. All I really needed. I put a bullet into his shoulder, in the fleshy part well away from the bone. The kind of injury that'd hurt like hell without doing too much damage, making him think twice about doing something stupid while I had the gun in my hand.

Pity for me he wasn't inclined to go along. There's an optimal range for firearms, and we were well inside it. The Neanderthal stepped forward, closed a meaty fist around my gun and wrenched it out of my grip.

"Hear you killed the Master," the Neanderthal said. "You trapped his soul in steel and lead."

A fist the size of a brick connected with the side of my face, got me seeing stars.

"You shouldn't have done that," the Neanderthal said. "The Master kept us safe."

He swung again, but now my adrenaline had kicked in, giving me enough to roll free. I came to my feet with the bed sheets in hand, flung them at the bigger man on instinct. He brought his arm up, guarding his side on instinct. I punched him below the ribs, put all my weight behind it. Felt like I was punching a side of beef, not really doing shit, but I heard the Neanderthal wheeze for a moment, his breath knocked out of him.

I pulled the knife I'd taken with me. Four inches of steel, a red rubber grip. Not the kind of weapon you go out using if you're looking for a fight, but it fit in my pocket and didn't attract too many questions. The blade bit into the Neanderthal's shoulder. The second stab got him in the arm.

The Neanderthal screamed a bit, came charging in to do more damage. The knife hurt him, but he didn't see it doing any damage. Just bled him a little, and he had plenty to bleed. I changed tack, stabbed low and up. Got him in the stomach and kept the knife there, working it along instead of pulling it free.

That seemed to get his attention. His fist caught me on the ear, knocked me sideways, and I let go of the knife. Crawled across the floor to the P220 lying on the bare boards.

The Neanderthal pulled the knife free. Scowled at it like he couldn't understand why anyone would bother with such a thing.

By then I had the SIG in hand and a clear shot at his big frame. Two in the chest. Two in the head. Just like Roark taught me.

The Neanderthal took a long time going down, but he hit the floor eventually. I lay there, breathing heavily, reached for the box beneath the bed. I already knew what I'd find there, but I let myself hope I wouldn't.

The bullet containing Wotan's soul was gone. I reached for me phone, dialled Langford's number.

"The safe house is blown," I said. "I think we need to talk."

I hung up. Took one last look at the carnage they'd wrecked upon the place, with or without Nora's help. Then I grabbed my gear and got the hell out of dodge, before someone came looking to figure out if the Neanderthal needed some back-up.

Langford met me in the food court of the Southport Mall, at one of the raised tables that looked across the river to the theme parks on the spit. She took one look at my face and put together what happened. "Gone?"

"Gone."

"Shit," she said. "I'm sorry."

"My choice to trust her, see how she'd play it," I said. "My mess to clean up, now that we know which side she's on. You bring the gun?"

Langford nodded. She pushed a small bag across the lunch table, looked away as I stowed it in my backpack. "Glad you sent me in, then," she said. "It'd suck if you owed me for having this thing for no good reason."

I nodded quietly, felt the familiar weight of the bullet and the soul within settle around me. I'd put a lot of trust in Langford, in her ability to create a convincing fake Nora could mistake for the real soul cage and smuggle the real one out.

Hell, I'd put a lot of trust in her ability to hand the damn thing over, once she knew what was inside.

"Tell me about Thirteen," I said. "What'd you find out?"

"A lot, and none of it happy news. I found plenty of contacts who knew about it, thought he was just some random sorcerer who showed up on the strip a few years back. Way I figured it, that makes him one of Wotan's first apprentices. Someone outside the chain of command of whatever cult you disrupted down there with Roark."

"What's he been doing?"

"Nothing major." Langford speared a French fry with her fork, chewed it slowly while she thought through her notes. "Little things. Favours. The guy knows how to be discreet. Plenty of people have worked with him, or done some kind of business. No one really knew where he came from, or who he served to get his powers. Mostly, he's just been consolidating, firming up his place on the totem pole without raising the wrong kind of attention. The only surprise..."

"He didn't work with Sabbath?"

"Got it in one," she said. "Any dealing's he's had with Sabbath's crew have been through intermediaries. It's like he's been avoiding a confrontation with the big dog."

"He worked through Nora?"

"A few times."

I nodded. Swore. "He's the bolt hole," I said. "Wotan sent him here so there was someone outside his cult, someone capable of lying low in case someone like Roark and me came along."

"Which means he didn't follow you here 'cause he's been here all along," Langford said. "Playing the same game you've been playing, only he's been doing it for a fuck-load longer."

"Any of your friends know where Thirteen lives?"

Langford speared another French fry, offered me a smile. "He's got a place up on Tamborine Mountain, overlooking the city," she said.

"Expensive place to nest."

"He's got expensive tastes," she said. "Unlike you, he seems to prefer blending in with the pricey end of town, rather than staying in squalor."

"If he's been here this long, he'll be dug in," I said. "It'll take us too long to unravel his defences, especially if he's got Nora onsite."

Langford nodded. "You'd need an army to take him. The whole fucking place is teeming with cultists. I think the whole lot of 'em relocated once word got out you were here.

"Well then," I said, "I guess we go get an army."

"There's only one army worth getting around these parts."

"Yeah, I know. That's going to be the bitch of it." I dabbed my mouth with the serviette, left it crumpled on the brown plastic tray. "I don't think Sabbath plays by the enemy of my enemy rule."

"Sabbath's got nothing but enemies," Langford said. "It tends to make life easy for him."

THE NEW DEAL

GETTING PICKED UP by Sabbath's crew wasn't exactly hard. I went back to the Casino. I made myself visible. By and by, someone spotted me and reported me up the line, which meant Wesna and Randall came down to find me. Wesna's face gave away nothing. Randall grinned at me like it was Christmas. He took lead, asked why I was there, and I told him I was giving myself up. I told him I had a plan for repaying Sabbath after my failure when it came to killing Nora Otto.

Randall gave me a disappointed look. "I thought you were professional, Murphy. This here? This is bush league." He signalled Wesna and they both stood up. Waited for me to join them. "Come on," Randall said. "Let's go talk to the big man."

I followed them out of the bar, into the elevator that led to Sabbath's floor. Soon as the doors slid closed, Wesna planted a fist in my stomach. Worked my ribs a few more times, kept going 'til I had some trouble standing upright. When the bell chimed to tell us we'd hit the sixteenth floor, they carried me out of the elevator supported between them. My chest was a bruise. It hurt to breath.

They carried me into Sabbath's apartment. He was out in the lounge room, waiting to see me. He had his glass of scotch already.

"You're a stubborn son-of-a-bitch," Sabbath said, showing off his teeth, and the smile set off something primal inside me, the same way my instincts knew to be afraid of grinning sharks and serpents with exposed fangs. "I made you a deal in the spirit of generosity, Keith, and you come back to me after spitting in my face a second time. You really think I've got it in me to let you burn me a third time? I promised you a world of pain. I promised you'd see what your own innards look like."

"Learned my lesson about Otto," I said. "Won't make—"

"No," Sabbath said. "I'm not interested in what you've got to tell me."

Then he sat in one of the big, leather lounge chairs and held his drink in place. Sat there with the sun sinking into the mountains behind him, sipping from his bourbon while Randall and Wesna did the work. They took turns. Randall started things off with a fist to the face, tight and hard against the side of my face where the jaw and my skull come together. Wesna went to work on the soft part of my belly, kept working it 'til I found myself spitting blood on Sabbath's tiled floor. I tried to make a show of it. Tried to stay on my feet and look Sabbath in the eye, to show him he couldn't break me.

That wasn't going to fly. Not this time around. They had me on the floor within seconds, and once I was down there, hurting and bleeding, they kicked ten kinds of shit out of me while Sabbath sat there grinning. I lost track of time pretty damn fast. Maybe I blacked out a little. Maybe I didn't. All know, by the time they got it out of their systems, there wasn't any sign of daylight behind Sabbath's head. I know because Randall was down on one knee, jerking my head up by the ears, forcing me to look at his boss.

Every part of me hurt, but I hadn't been shown my internal organs yet. Sabbath's cold eyes studied me, calculating his next move.

My next move was easy. I passed the fuck out.

Someone was trying to give me water, and the mess that used to be my lips objected to this course of action. Strong hands. A deep voice. They had me upright.

"Come on," they said. "Come on, drink."

I opened my mouth to object, but all I managed was a moan. And moaning hurt. It hurt even more than having the water forced upon me, now that I'd given whoever held the glass an opening. I swallowed. Gagged. Wished like I hell I could go back to the dark, sleepy place where I'd been for god knows how fucking long.

I processed my situation, on instinct. It didn't take long. There was pain, and there was more pain, and then there was the queasy blur that appeared before me when I tried to open up my eyes. Opening my eyes hurt like hell, like they'd found a way to bruise my fucking eyelids. Closing them hurt too, but at least I didn't feel like hurling.

The water glass found its way to my lips again. This time, through the pain, I registered being thirsty. I forced my cracked, bloodied mouth open and took a cautious sip. Somewhere, far behind the pain, I could taste something sour and metallic in the water. Once I swallowed, and it was still there, I figured it for blood. I could still feel dry, sticky blood plastered across my face. They'd kept me somewhere warm and humid. The blood on my face had dried, but my skin felt slick and sticky on its own, the legacy of several hours spent perspiring.

"—need to rehydrate," the voice was saying, glass back at my lips. "He ain't decided to kill you yet, and that's a tiny fucking miracle. Don't give him the pleasure of dying on him now. Drink the damn water, Murphy."

I risked opening my eyes for a minute. The world stayed still long enough to make out Wesna's face. She'd taken off her jacket, rolled up the sleeves of her shirt.

"Try to stay awake," she said. "You may have picked up a concussion."

I tried to nod, but pain shot through my jaw. I mumbled a soft, "Hurts," into the air.

"'Course it hurts," Wesna said. "We had orders to hurt you. Randall, he took it personally. Man really doesn't like you. Think he might have broken your nose."

Soon as he said it, I wanted to try sniffing the air, just to see how big a mess they'd done to my nasal passages. I forced myself to ignore that instinct, to take steady breathes through the wreckage of my mouth. Your instincts mean shit when you've been beaten to all hell. After a certain point, your body just forgets how to avoid pain. It assumes the pain is everywhere, so it falls back on the familiar instead of the smart.

"Sabbath," I mumbled.

"Sabbath ain't done with you."

"Deal—"

"Told you before, the deal is off the table," Wesna

said. "You're simply out of things that Sabbath really wants, Murphy. Not sure you got anything he's interested in."

I smiled a little, even though it hurt. Whispered, "Soul," before I lowered myself back to the warm tile floor. I closed my eyes again, focused on my breathing. Wesna put her glass down. Leaned over me 'til she got so close I could feel her warm breath on my cheek. "You offering us a soul? You really dumb enough to do that?"

"Soul." I kept my eyes shut, so I didn't need to watch her reaction. Wesna stood and brushed her hands. I heard her boot heels clip the tiled floor as she exited the room.

I hurt worse than anything I'd felt before this time.

Somewhere along the line, I passed out and let the darkness wash over me.

The next time I woke up, I was back in Sabbath's lounge room. My back was against the leather couch and they'd washed the sweaty, sticky blood away from the worst of my injuries. I could see daylight out the window and the pain had receded a little. I figured it for two days out, recovering from the beating. My ribs hurt and my face hurt and I felt like I was built from cardboard, stiff and unbending and terribly, terribly fragile. A demon stood by the couch, watching me like a hawk. The moment he felt sure I was awake, he disappeared through the doorway. A few moments later, Sabbath appeared. He wore a white suit with a bright carnation in the pocket. Wesna stood behind Sabbath's shoulder, sunglasses back in place, watching me.

I tried to lift myself off the couch. "How long was I out?"

"About three days." Sabbath lowered himself into the couch, angled forward with an eager look. "I'm impressed with your resilience, Murphy. Taking a beating from Wesna and Randall isn't something most people come back from."

I nodded slowly. It fit. I had that empty, hollowed-out feeling that came from too long without food.

"Hungry," I said.

"I'm sure you are." Sabbath folded his hands on top of his ample belly. "Question is, Murphy, do I waste food on you? No point feeding the dog if you're planning to take it to slaughter in the morning."

I nodded a little to acknowledge his point. "Most people feed the dog 'cause it's humane."

"Like I've ever given a shit about humanity." Sabbath's thick tongue wormed its way across his lips. "So Wesna says you're willing to sell your soul. Tell me, Keith, is that really true?"

"It may be," I said, "if the deal were good enough."

"If the deal..." Sabbath grinned, suddenly delighted. "And where are you going to get a better deal for your pitiful, blackened soul than you'd get through me?"

"Sarcasm doesn't suit you."

"Then don't toy with me, Murphy. I kept you alive because Wesna thinks you're sincere, and I'm a businessman before I'm anything else. That sack of meat you walk around in...all those instincts, all that physical memory. It's an appealing package, Murphy, even before we take into account the little pleasures that come from having your soul to torture on a rainy day. What do you want?"

"Not here," I said.

"Here," Sabbath said. "You're not in a position to argue. Make your pitch."

I hung my head, tried to look vulnerable. It wasn't hard. They'd beaten me bad enough that I couldn't do much to fight back, and I'd never been the kind of guy who waded into a fist-fight.

"Nora Otto's been working with a guy named Thirteen," I said. "A sorcerer, a new player in town, trained by the guy I shot down in Adelaide. They're trying to bring Michael Wotan back from the dead. I'd like your help ensuring Wotan is truly dead. That whatever curse he's set upon the world is done and no apocalypse is forthcoming."

"And in exchange?"

"You get what you wanted," I told him. "Otto's

dead. A potential threat is neutralised. When I die, however that happens, you get my soul to play with and my body as a vessel."

He rose, standing over me. "I like you desperate, Murphy. It makes you...amusing."

"Do we have a deal?"

"Not yet." Sabbath's long stride ate the distance between the couch and the door. "On the plus side, Murphy, you may have earned yourself food."

The worst part of negotiating from a position of weakness is the waiting. When your opponent has all the leverage, they're not in any hurry to give you an answer. They'll stretch the hours out and give you time to think through your position. They'll try to make you realise exactly how little power you have in the situation, in the hopes that you'll rationalise down your expectations. In any negotiation, whether it's for a used car or the state of your soul, it's the person who's willing to walk away who has the real advantage.

Sabbath's crew left me in a bare, stifling room near the back of his apartment. It should have been a nice place; the walls were painted a light shade of sand, the floorboards were dark and polished to a sheen. Instead, they gave the room a terrible symmetry that didn't quite belong, and the only things that broke it were the red leather couch and my shuffling, aching body.

I took my time doing laps of the room, getting a feel for the lay of the land. The door was locked, solid enough that I didn't want to try and kick it down. Especially not with the beating they'd put on me. The window in the corner of the room looked over the Broadbeach mall. They had a brass band playing in the gazebo while people shopped. There were restaurants on the mall; Chinese, Italian, Indian, Thai. The scent from their kitchens made its way to the twentieth floor. My stomach protested, loudly, the fact that I still hadn't eaten.

I finished walking the perimeter of the room, went back to the red couch to wait.

I didn't hear from Sabbath for a long time, but after a few hours Wesna unlocked the door and slid a plastic bag full of take-out through the gap. My mouth watered when I caught the rich scent of butter chicken, but I didn't crawl for it immediately. The first rule of dealing with the Other is never accept any gifts. Don't take a drink, don't eat their food, don't do shit that could leave you beholden to them.

Me, I was long past that stage. Whatever hooks I'd let Sabbath get beneath my skin, they weren't going to get in deeper by eating the take-out. I resisted because there were real good odds of Wesna or Sabbath watching the room, paying attention to how I acted. I forced myself to stay on the couch, ignoring the food for a couple of minutes.

Then, when the rumble in my gut became an ache, I let myself give in.

I ate fast, eager to fill the emptiness in my stomach. Afterward, I dragged my ass back to the sofa and settled in there, stretching my arms and legs so I could figure out where they really hurt. Near as I could tell, Wesna was right. They'd been real careful not to break things. My jaw hurt like hell after the beating Randall put on it, and my ribs were a black mess of bruising and pain, but neither had been broken. They'd heal, sooner or later, assuming I didn't get into more trouble.

Sabbath reappeared after sunset. Wesna came in behind him, can of Coke in hand. He popped it open and held it to me, waited for me to take it. I stared at the drink, stared at him. "It ain't poisoned," he said. "That wouldn't be smart."

I took the can and swallowed. After a long day in the pressure cooker Sabbath called an apartment, the chilly bite of the cola against my back teeth was pretty close to heaven.

"I don't buy it," Sabbath said. "Sixteen years, Murphy. That's how long I've wanted to get my hands on you, how long I dreamed of paying you back for all your little betrayals. In all that time, the one thing that galled me was the knowledge your soul was safe. Even at sixteen, you were smart enough to guard that and refused to let me have it."

"And now I'm here, all grown up, offering it to you on a platter?"

"Precisely," Sabbath said. "Precisely that. It's not the kind of move you make, Murphy. As Wesna is fond of saying, it seems...unprofessional."

"Me and professional parted ways a couple of weeks back," I said. "The moment we fucked the Wotan hit."

"If that were true, you would have come after me with both guns blazing. You're playing a long game, Murphy. I can taste it."

I nodded, then winced. My jaw still ached. "Ragnarok," I said.

"The twilight of the gods?"

"My guess is that's an imperfect translation, given it came from your side of the Gloom," I said. "Something out there, something deep in the Gloom, had this vision for how the world would end and that's what a bunch of Vikings transcribed."

"And this is important because?"

"That same thing, in the deep Gloom, was responsible for Michael Wotan," I said. "He was trying to kick off Ragnarok when me and Roark put him down, 'cept we fucked the job and his cult seems to think everything's on schedule. One of the possible ends of the world is coming, and I kinda doubt it's the one your kind wants to win out."

Sabbath thought that over. Broke into a grin. "And that's what brought you back?"

"That, among other things."

"Alright." Sabbath's smile belong on some kind of predator. A big cat. A shark. Something fast and efficient and utterly sure of itself. I'm not sure he believes me. I'm not sure he cares. His fire-bright eyes search mine. "You don't expect to survive what's coming?"

"Not really."

"And your soul?"

"Is pretty much doomed either way," I said. "Better the devil you know, you know?"

Sabbath shook his head. "I don't want your soul, Murphy."

He stood, and walked over to the window, arms folded as he glared at the people below. "When you first came back, I intended to use you like a tool. Eliminate those who opposed me, from the irritating to the dangerous. You failed me in that, but I've done some digging. I've confirmed what you've told me about Thirteen, about his connections and his…alliances." The last word slipped out in a wary, sibilant hiss. "I don't want your soul, Murphy, I want your service. I'll help you stop Thirteen, because that's good for business. In return, when it's done, you'll come back and work for me. You'll work off the debt you owe me, the one for your failure and the one for your betrayal. You'll kill who I tell you to kill, mortal or Other; you'll work with whoever I want you to work with, and I'll hear no complaints. If I tell you to start training one of mine, then you'll damn well train them. You're going to do it all with your soul intact, 'cause I want to enjoy each moment of pain it causes you to be one of my agents."

I forced myself upright, one hand pressed against the couch to keep myself stead. "I liked you better when you were vindictive, Sabbath."

"I liked you better when you were a punk," Sabbath said. "You didn't try to play me, Murphy, back when you were a kid."

"I didn't have anything worth playing for," I said. "Otherwise I would have tried."

He held out his hand. I shook it, hating myself the whole time, and I felt something dark settle over my soul. There's more than one way to hurt a guy, and Sabbath knew almost all of them.

THE THIRD HIT

I WENT UP Tamborine Mountain in an SUV packed to the gills with demons. Randall in the driver's seat, Wesna riding shotgun. Me in the back with three guys I didn't recognise, but all of them had the familiar, empty stare of demons who'd been there a long, long time. Sabbath's crew for dealing with trouble was somewhat stronger than it used to be. A second SUV followed along behind us, more guys loaded up and ready for trouble.

We sat in silence while the car took the mountain curves, stayed silent as the road straightened at the peak. From the top of the mountain you could look out over the whole damn coast. It was night, and the lights glittered and shone like your own private fairyland. Beautiful, almost, from a distance. We rolled through the empty streets, passed mountain-top farms with orchards full of avocados and limes. Pulled up a half-click short of the property identified as Thirteen's personal fortress.

It didn't look like the kind of place a cult would flourish. A small half-acre with a two-story house up near the cliffs, looking out over the Coast. Its own orchard covering the grounds. House in good nick. The kind of place that cost more than anyone ever associated with the cowls-and-chants crews, even if they had shit wrong.

We hoofed it over the last half-K, went over the wire fence one at a time. I had my SIG back, loaded and ready. The demons were all armed, all peering through the darkness with their superior vision. We crept through the orchard, all quiet. All professional. Occasionally Wesna would hold up a fist, bring us to a halt. One of the demons would peel off from the pack, disappear into the shadows, and when they reappeared there was blood on their hands. Sentry positions. Wandering guards. Sabbath's blunt instrument knew their job. Knew how to work quiet, even if they did it bloody.

We made it through the trees. Split up as we approached the house. Thirteen wasn't stupid. There were floodlights set up around the exterior. Motions sensors attached to them, so they'd go up if someone tried to approach. Not the kind of thing your average suburbanite goes for. Not even the kind of thing your average Tamborine commuter would write off as normal. It didn't matter. This was the Gold Coast. Eccentricities were written off, embraced as little streaks of character.

Wesna and Randall crouched down beside me, studied the house and the set-up. Wesna put a finger to her lips, pointed to three spots around the house. I squinted, saw the moving shadows. More guards. More cultists, standing vigil beside the house. One by one they went away, taken out by demons who understood how to avoid the floodlights. Wesna nodded, satisfied. Reached out and grabbed my arm. We both knew what was coming next, but I wasn't looking forward to it. It was one of those tricks I hated, even if I knew it had a purpose.

Randall reached into the darkness, gathered it together until it thickened. A portal to the Gloom, a place beyond the real world.

Then Wesna stepped through, pulling me in behind her.

The transition between real world and the currents of the Gloom felt like the first stage of drowning. First the cold hit, then the sensation of spiralling out of control, getting sucked beneath the surface by a strong rip and whipped by the wild eddies and tides of the place. The realisation, in this place, that you no longer possessed any real mass. Mortals weren't built to be there. All we saw, based on what I knew, were vague impressions of our surroundings. Shadow, indistinct reflections of the places we knew in the real world.

Wesna dragged me behind her, the grip around my arm cinched tight. I closed my eyes, tried not to scream. Let the cold darkness wash over me.

Then it was over, Wesna dragging me through a second portal, wrestling me free of the Gloom that didn't want to let go. Warm hands held mine, getting feeling back into my fingers. My ragged, panicked breathing grew steady.

I opened my eyes, pushed myself upright. We were up against the walls of the house, under the motion sensors. Close as we could get via Gloom, given the wards Thirteen erected around his damn house. Getting us this close was Wesna's job. Getting us inside was mine.

We were closest to a side door, probably exits from the laundry. I inched my way over, went to work with the lockpicks. Worked slow, cautious, to keep the noise down. The lock clicked, too loud for my taste. I eased the door open, felt the push of Thirteen's wards. Those eased when I dug the bullet out of my pocket, pressed the reliquary with Wotan's soul up against the intangible barrier.

The bullet bucked in my fingers, the soul awakened by the contact. I gripped it tight, forced it back into my pocket. Held it there until the spirit eased, going dormant again inside its prison.

Randall slipped past me, into the house. Wesna followed, crouched low, wincing a little as though she expected the wards to catch her. We were in the laundry, heading into the kitchen. There were two cultists there, loitering. Both were dead by the time I entered, their necks twisted into modern art by the demon's furious strength.

Wesna looked at me, eyebrow raised. I gestured. Up. With the Raven Cult, it was always up. They liked their rituals close to the sky, and their leaders slept on the upper floors.

We heard the chanting before we saw them. They were on the upper deck, this long expanse of woodwork that jutted over the cliff. Odds are, Thirteen had bought the place just for that deck, the open space exposed to the sky, a place where he could do the things that needed doing.

They'd carted a big chunk of granite into the centre of the deck, surrounded it with twelve men in dark robes and deep hoods. Thirteen stood in the centre of it all, the false bullet sitting in the centre of his stone. Nora stood at the edge of the circle, gnawing on a fingernail. Still wearing the oversized shirt from the safe house, the borrowed pair of Langford's jeans. They'd armed her, left her to serve as a guard dog. A short, dressed-down punk with a big Winchester pump action.

Thirteen had his hands raised, palms open to the sky. I didn't recognise his chant, but that didn't mean much. Michael Wotan had prayed to entities older than anything I knew about, things that slept in the deep parts of the Gloom ever since their worshippers died off. Usually, those worshippers took their languages with them.

They'd tethered themselves, all thirteen men. Tapped into the Gloom and started drawing on its power, preparing to invest it in the nine millimetre shell they'd placed at the centre of their ritual. You could feel the energy hanging in the air. The hair on my arms stood to attention. They were going for big magic, the kind of shit most sorcerers tried to stay away from.

Easiest way to kill a cultist is to disrupt his rituals, let the magic feed on him instead of his preferred victim. Only problem, on this scale, was figuring out what to disrupt. With so much energy floating about, it'd feed on anyone standing by, regardless of whether they were involved. I glanced back at Wesna, caught her short nod. The kind of rift they were looking to open tended to be bad news, regardless of whether you were mortal or Other.

The ritual hit a fever pitch, dark flames appearing around the bullet. Thirteen's chanting hit a crescendo, his eyes rolled back in his head. They were waiting for that energy to crack the wards on the reliquary, free their leader's soul from the tiny, insignificant purgatory. Instead, it blew the bullet to dust, reducing the lead and steel and powder down to component atoms.

Thirteen opened his eyes. Stared at the results of his magic. Realised what'd happened and howled in anger, turning on Nora and stalking forward. She reacted like you'd expect, switched over to self-preservation mode. Levelled the shotgun in his direction.

I nodded to Wesna and Randall, stepped out of cover and onto the balcony. The SIG kicked in my hands, targeting the closest member of Thirteen's little circle. He went down, blood spilling from a hole in his chest. The magic they were channelling bucked, forcing the circle to focus on getting it under control. Thirteen felt the kick, glanced in my direction.

Nora Otto seized upon the distraction and fired the big Remington into Thirteen's chest.

Thirteen staggered. Blood oozed out the front of his robe, through the holes the buckshot tore through the fabric. Magic kept him upright. All the energy he channelled, unsure where to go. It just stayed in him, kept him moving, advancing on Nora until he could smash a fist into her cheek.

Wesna and Randall were moving now, working their way around the circle. Necks were snapped. Throats cut. Knives buried deep in the stomachs of those who truly resisted dying. Any semblance of control evaporated. Things caught fire. The wooden landing. One cultist's hair. Parts of Thirteen's body. I levelled the SIG. Fired twice. Thirteen charged me, knocked me to the floor. The SIG skittered out of my grasp. Thirteen's foot caught me in the ribs.

He had no control of the magic anymore. Fire ripped along his arms, burnt away his black t-shirt and most of his hair. His eyes were dark chasms, deeper than any demon's gaze. Too much energy running through him. Eventually it'd burn out, but 'til then he had all kinds of options. He swung at me, more magic than muscle. Took out a chunk of balustrade when I ducked away from the punch. I heard the wood shatter, splintering around his fist. Didn't even bother trying to fight back. Nothing I hit him with would do much more than annoy him.

His arms lit up, flames leaping higher. I figured Thirteen was running on anger, letting his thwarted rage propel him through the pain. He jumped at me, fingers extended. Tried to fix his fingers around my throat as the flames singed my face and chest. I fought back, scrambling. If he locked in the choke, I knew I was dead.

However fast this was burning out, it wasn't fast enough. I kicked at him, trying to push free. Got lucky when his head jerked back, Wesna coming up behind him and hooking fingers into his nose. She punched him in the face, put all her strength behind it. Demon strength. More than I had. It bloodied him, bust his mouth open. Thirteen rounded on her, roaring with laughter.

I dove for the SIG, rolled with the momentum. Came to a halt against the balcony railings, jarring my shoulder hard. Didn't matter. I had the pistol up, a clear shot. I emptied everything in the clip into Thirteen's back. Five rounds. Dead centre. Started fumbling for a spare clip as he stood there, still on fire, teetering between life and death.

He turned slowly, legs unsteady. I slammed the new clip home.

Wesna hit him from behind, both hands clenched together, a hammering blow to the neck. Thirteen stumbled.

I fired one last time. Caught him in the head. There wasn't enough magic in the world to keep him upright after the mess that made.

Wesna crossed the balcony, pulled me to my feet. The bulk of the cultists were running, trying to get the hell out of the killzone the balcony had become. All of them learned, the hard way, about Wesna's back-up team, still sitting outside the house. Wesna looked at the carnage around us, nodded with satisfaction.

She pointed to a huddled, bloodied figure slumped by the ritual granite block. "What about her, then?"

I nodded. Raised the SIG. Nora looked up at me, through her curls. Her lips bloody, smiling, defiant. Still just a little bit punk. "You going to kill me, Murphy?"

I thought about that. Finger on the trigger. Screams came out of the darkness. Still plenty of Thirteen's cultists around, running into demons in the dark. Still plenty of assholes that needed killing, if only so we could ensure the world was a better place.

EXILED

I WENT DOWN the mountain in the back of the SUV; Randall drove, unhappy as hell. Wesna rode shotgun, mouth pulled into a grim line. It was six in the morning. Sunlight coming over the horizon. The rest of the demons were up at the house, eliminating any signs of our involvement. Not all of them, I figured. They'd keep some traces of my presence there. Insurance, in case I did something stupid. In case I tried to back out of Sabbath's deal, go my own away once more.

Nora sat in the seat beside me. Bound and gagged. Zip ties on the wrists and ankles. Old rags stuffed into her mouth. Randall offered to kill her for me, couldn't understand why I told him to back off. Wesna did. She didn't like it, but she understood. No matter how much demon they stuffed in her, there were parts that remained stubbornly human.

We rolled through the national park, through the back of Nerang where the estates and the prize-homes sat side-by-side with industrial parks. Sunday morning. Quiet and sleepy, in this part of town. It's the surfers who rose early, padded down to the beach with boards under their arm. I needed to remember that. Get the hell away from the beach.

We pulled into the parking lot at Nerang Station, empty as hell at that time of the morning. I got out, went round to the door on Nora's side of the SUV. Wesna was already there. She looked me in the eye, wanting to be sure I knew what I was doing.

I nodded. Produced a knife. Cut the zip-ties around Nora's arms and legs before I let her out of the car. She climbed out, eyes full of fire, but Wesna's presence kept her from taking a swing at me. Nora, on her own, might have had sufficient fury to beat the crap out of me, but she'd expended a lot of it recent days. Tried to change the world, or at least her part of it, and realised there wasn't anything she could do to affect the way things were.

"You can't stay here," I said. "You're sure as hell not going to win, if you take on Sabbath at his own game."

I offered her a roll of bills. Salvage from the cult's lair. Nora looked at the money. "You seriously think I'll run, Murphy?"

"I'm seriously hoping you'll try."

She thought about that. Took the cash off my hands. About six hundred, give or take. Enough to put some distance between us.

"Spend some time in Melbourne first," I said. "You'll like it there. Good coffee. Lots of bars. It shouldn't take long to set yourself up."

Nora's eyes narrowed. "I don't need your advice."

"Take it anyway." I met her eyes, holding her stare. "This isn't letting you go, this is giving you a head start. If Sabbath still wants you dead, he's going to send people. Make sure you've got some place you can defend, or you've hooked up with someone that'll make him think twice."

"I can't believe you're doing this."

"You'd rather end up dead?"

"Maybe." She looked me in the eye, and I could see she wasn't joking. A part of her hated leaving. Hated giving in. "I'm not like you, Murphy. The idea of running does nothing for me. I'd rather stay and fight."

I nodded, slowly. "You can try that."

Nora looked towards the car. Randall glaring at her. Wesna standing there, arms folded, expression stern.

"No, I really can't." She leant in, kissed me on the cheek. "Welcome home," she said. "Don't think I ever said that."

I stood there, saying nothing. Wesna cleared her throat, the noise close to a snarl.

"Right then." Nora grinned. "Fuck you all, then."

She walked up the station, bought a ticket that'd take her north. Brisbane, first. God knows where after that. Somewhere far, far away if she was smart, and I hoped to hell she was. I climbed back into the car. Sat there in the back seat, waiting for the train to come and take her away.

Then, when the train was gone and we were sure the station was empty, Randall gunned the engine and reversed us out of the lot.

FROST

Book Two of
The Flotsam Trilogy

DECLARATIONS OF WAR

THE HIT ON Eli Penny went sour before it ever got started. They'd sent me and Finn out to do the job, one more man than the hit really needed, but for once I couldn't place the blame on Finn and his amateur tendencies. His only role was to lure Penny out, get him to the Sailboat Bar down on Currumbin River. None of the Rebels were supposed to know that Finn had turned on them. Hell, the Rebels weren't even supposed to know what they were really up against.

That's the problem with working for demons, I guess. They get so goddamn cocky when they're picking fights with mortals.

I was hidden round the back of the Sailboat, crouched down in the kitchen with a loaded Mossberg and a bad feeling. Finn was out in the main bar, hammering down vodka like his life depended on it. It was a Monday night, three hours after closing. The back door of the place was locked at the dead bolt. The front door was open, waiting for Penny to show up. The kitchen was narrow, a galley space designed to handle bar food and the occasional toasted sandwich. One of the kitchen taps dripped, the water hitting stainless steel just above my head, followed by three seconds of silence before the next drop fell.

It was late November, coming into summer, but winter wasn't done with us yet. My breath steamed in the cool night air. The tiles were cold against my arse. I heard Penny's bike pull up out front. He took his time getting off, letting the engine idle. That bothered me. It bothered me a lot. The growl of the idling Harley covered all other sound. I counted off three seconds, had trouble hearing the dripping tap that was less than a foot away from me. Counted another three and the engine was still running.

Another three seconds.

Another.

Suspicion got me moving when the engine didn't cut off. I got traction on the cold tile floor, slid my back up the wall. Caught sight of an unfamiliar shadow looming at the back door, heard the scuffed step of someone big and sneaky trying to keep a low profile. I eased down the galley, closer to the door. Heard the soft click of something metal getting slid into the doorjamb. I figured it for a crowbar. Crude, but effective. Out front, the door to the main bar opened. I heard Finn call Penny a cunt, inviting him in for a drink. Luring him well inside the bar where, if all was going to plan, my shotgun would end his life.

Penny stood at the door, responded with a single question: "You really think we wouldn't know, Finn?"

That's when I knew we were fucked.

Gunshots from the bar meant Penny had a gun. Light, small calibre. Just enough to piss Finn off, given his recent transformation. That meant Finn would start fighting back. That meant things were getting messy.

Me? I had my own problems. The crowbar did its work, levered the back door open. No mistaking the guys who did the job for anything other than Rebels. Two of them, full moon at their back. Big men. Leather jackets. Beards thick enough you could lose a boy scout troop in their depths. The first came at me, brandished the crowbar. Guess he missed the Mossberg in the dark. I swung it round, jerked the trigger. Felt the shotgun kick. Nothing accurate about it, but that's the Mossberg's charm. They packed a lot of shot into a twelve gauge shell. Accuracy isn't a factor; it's your basic point and shoot kind of tool. Crowbar ate his fair share of the blast, reeled back against the bench.

I pumped the action, ejected the empty shell. Ducked the desperate, half-arsed swing that sent the crowbar at my head. The biker pushed off the counter, lurched forward. It wasn't really fair. The crowbar wasn't built for a room the size of the kitchen. He couldn't get the momentum he wanted on the swing. The Mossberg handled the lack of space just fine. It kicked in my hands, spat lead shot into the biker's stomach. He was a big guy. Flab over muscle. The second shot put him down, left him lying there with a messy hole in his guts.

The other guy jumped me. Came flying in over his gut-shot friend, crash-tackled me to the floor. He wrapped a big arm around me, grabbed the Mossberg in a meaty fist and jerked it to the side. I fought back. He held on. Made it hard to use the shotgun without blowing holes in me as well. His other hand pounded away, hard jabs to my ribs. They hurt like hell. Metal chain wrapped around his fist. He was softening me up, beating me til I struggled less. Until I let the Mossberg go and became a little less of a threat. Then the chain-wrapped fist would hammer into my face a few times. That wouldn't be pretty.

I struggled. Kept coming up short. I'm not the guy you send into a fist fight. Against the kinds of targets I'm normally after, going hand-to-hand is a sure sign that shit has made contact with the fan. The biker had the height. He sure as hell had the strength. He ripped the Mossberg out of my grip. Let it slide across the tiles. Wrapped his arm around my throat. Tightened. Squeezed. Cut off my air. His breath hot against my ear. The word *motherfucker* repeated over and over. I grabbed at his arm, trying to wrench it free. Tried to get it to budge an inch, just enough to get some air in my lungs.

He'd stopped punching once the choke went on. The chain-wrapped fist went away. Left behind bruised ribs, a dull ache that wouldn't bother me much if I didn't get air soon. I kept struggling. Kept fighting. I caught sight of his free hand in the corner of my vision. No chain this time. Something small. Something glass. He smashed it against my chest, big hand smearing the glass across my shirt. Shards bit into skin. Water soaked into the cuts. Grunted like he'd done something good, ended the fight on his terms.

He let me go. Let me breathe. Stood up and produced a knife. The whole thing made a horrible, terrible sense. I would have laughed if I had the breath.

The biker loomed over me. Called me a cocksucker again, but this time he put some force behind it. Buried his steel caps into my ribs. In his mind the fight was over. He'd slapped me with holy water. Burned a hole in my chest. Weakened the demon inside me just enough for the knife to do some damage. In his mind, I'd be writhing in agony. Someone had given him the details, told him how to hunt the possessed.

Pity for him the possessed guy was out in the bar, trading gunshots with Eli Penny. I was just the stupid human fucker who got by on his wits and charm. I had my SIG holstered at my waist, a back-up in case the Mossberg wasn't up to the job. Be prepared, you know? It's how I lived my goddamn life.

I drew the pistol, pointed it. The first shot surprised the hell out of him. He teetered, unsure whether to fight or fall.

The second shot took that choice away from him.

I lay on the cold tile, chest heaving. My ribs hurt. Every breath I took hurt like a motherfucker. I didn't much care. I kept trying to breathe deep, wincing against the pain. Did it until the adrenaline faded, letting me think a little clearer.

I listened to the soft plink of the dripping tap. Realised I couldn't hear shit coming from the bar. That wasn't good. Didn't matter who killed who out there, it rated as not good. I forced myself into motion. Stood up. Recovered the Mossberg. Ejected the spent shell and limped towards the swinging doors that led out into the main bar. Paused and edged the door open a crack with the barrel of the shotgun.

"Finn?"

He didn't answer. Neither did anyone else. I eased the door open a little further, and caught the shape of someone tall and broad slumped against one of the tables. It lifted a bottle in my direction. "That went fuckin' well, eh?"

I limped through the door, let them swing shut behind me. The open windows gave the bar a little more light than the kitchen. Made it easier to see the mess. Finn sat at the table, finishing his vodka. Eli Penny lay on the floorboards, head twisted in the wrong direction. Exactly the kind of thing that'd draw the wrong kind of attention once the coroner got his hands on the corpse.

"Stupid fucker came at me with a gun," Finn said. "Didn't think anything of it until he threw fuckin' holy water into my face."

He leaned forward, into the light. Let me see the patches of burned skin where the water eroded his human features. Demons are good at hiding. They're damn near indestructible compared to your average human. I knew about fourteen ways of taking a demon down once it's gotten its hooks in a human. Holy water was the least efficient, but it hurt more than the other options.

"Fuckers in the kitchen tried the same thing," I said. "Whoever fed them information didn't do a good job of it."

"Doesn't matter. They know, and that's all Sabbath needs to get pissed at us." Finn took one last swig from the vodka bottle, dropped it to the floor when he was done. It rolled across the floorboards, came to rest against Eli Penny's corpse. "He's going to blame you for this. Ya know that, right?"

"Must be one of those days that ends in a fuckin' Y, then." I limped toward the front door, surveyed the parking lot. Eli Penny's bike sat out there, along with the vintage Holden Commodore Finn boosted to drive to the bar. No other bikes, which meant my playmates in the kitchen had come up on the place by foot. Easy enough to do, but it took time. I didn't like things that took time, not after the fight we just had. Time meant planning. It raised the probability of a Rebel with some kind of Plan B in mind showing up and making a bigger mess than we were already in.

I pulled out my phone. Dialled Wesna Holjack's number. She answered on the first ring, didn't say a word. Just waited for my report, so she could pass it on.

"They came at us with holy water," I said. "Penny, two others, all of 'em eliminated. I think it's a safe bet they know what they're up against, and they aren't really afraid of going to war."

"And the site?"

“Compromised.” I turned, looked down at Penny’s body, the head turned to face me while his body pointed in the other direction. “Really, really compromised.”

Wesna swore. Repeated what I said to someone else.

When she came back on the line, she gave me exactly the order I’d expected. I hung up, turned back to Finn. He waited, half-smile in place.

“She wants us to burn the place, right?”

I gave him the good news. Let him set about the preparing the place for arson. There’s something about fire that puts demons in a good mood, but it’s never been my favourite way of dealing with a hit gone wrong.

Fire’s the tool of amateurs and by-the-hour thugs. I’d been a professional, once upon a time. I’d killed things that truly deserved to die. I thought about the two men I’d gunned down in the kitchen. Not innocent, not really, but definitely mortal.

It was hard to shake the feeling I was on the wrong side.

DEBRIEF

I'D BEEN WORKING out of an apartment in the southern edge of Broadbeach that week; this quiet, furnished holiday flat with palm trees on the shower curtain and plumbing from the fifties. Technically, I was still on the run. Trying to avoid the mess I'd made down in Adelaide. The same one that'd drawn Wotan's Raven cult to the Gold Coast and gotten me embroiled with Sabbath in the first place. I kept to basic protocol, despite being stuck inside the city limits: pre-paid phones; temporary rooms; avoiding a routine, as much as I could manage. Sabbath liked to bitch about it, but he didn't stop me doing it.

I took a long shower the morning after the hit. Let the hot water wake me up before I started checking my bruises. I hurt like a motherfucker, my ribs covered in varying shades of purple. Nothing broken. That was the good news. I put antiseptic on the cuts. Pulled a shirt and a jumper over the bruises. Slipped the SIG into my waistband before I left the house.

It was seven AM. I'd had exactly five hours sleep. I needed coffee, better than the instant shit I kept in my apartment. I went down the street, found a cafe on the water. Ordered. Waited. Watched the surfers limping up the path, their hair hanging around their faces, damp wetsuits partially open despite the winter chill.

Breakfast came. Bacon. Poached eggs. Inch-thick doorstop toast. Weedy strands of rocket laid over the whole damn thing, pretending lettuce had a place on the breakfast table. I ate slow. Drank my coffee. The cafe was built for alfresco dining, a chance to get tourists up close to the saltwater, but the brisk air encouraged the other diners to stick to inside tables. It was cold out and the waitresses were dressed in black jumpers. The other patrons huddled inside, behind the windows. They stirred their tea. Ate their meals. Said shit about the unseasonable cold, then moved on to other topics.

I fretted about the cold, too. I fretted about a lot of things. The death of Eli Penny gave me plenty more for the list. It escalated things between Sabbath's crew and the Rebels. It added the complication of the bikers knowing about the demons, coming into the fight with some idea of what they were facing. What'd been an annoyance on Sabbath's radar now became a threat.

Sabbath didn't handle threats well. It tended to get bloody.

I was halfway through my meal when my cell phone rang. I checked it. Wesna. Thumbed the phone to life. "I'm eating. The cafe on Victoria Ave, closest to the surf."

Wesna hung up without saying a thing. That meant I was due a visit. Broadbeach was Sabbath's turf, and the suburb isn't that big. An SUV pulled up in under two minutes, parked in between a couple of sedans. Wesna made a beeline for my table. She was tall and pale, carried herself like a woman who intended to knock some motherfucker's head off. She hid that behind a business jacket and expensive jeans; perfect Gold Coast business-casual. She sat at my table, her dark eyes focused on my breakfast and the coffee beside the plate.

"We aren't particularly happy with the way things went last night," she said.

I shrugged and focused on my food. Shovelled toast and egg into my mouth, chewed it mechanically. That didn't bother Wesna. Few things did. She flagged down a waitress. Ordered a coffee. Waited me out, quietly, until the mouthful was done.

"Last night," she said, sternly.

"It wasn't my cock-up." I sat back in my chair, reached for my coffee. "I spent weeks watching over those assholes. I found you the weak link to tempt into joining your side. I planned the hit on Penny myself, gave you all the reasons to take down the two-I-C instead of going straight after Kodiak."

"I have the paperwork."

I picked up a slice of toast, already going cold. "Then why come give me shit about crap that wasn't my fault?"

Wesna grinned. She liked that question. "'Cause some of us do what we're told," she said. "And we try not to cock things up."

"It wasn't my cock-up," I repeated.

"A-huh." Wesna drank her coffee. Pushed her fringe out of her face. We'd gone to school together. No way you'd pick it now. She'd been preserved at twenty-three, the age she'd been when the demon slipped in beneath her skin: tall, statuesque, coal-dark hair that dangled in her face. I wore the additional thirteen years like an old, shabby coat. I guess that's what happens when one of you is possessed, and the other signs up with a mad fucker who teaches you to kill things from the Gloom for a living.

"Tell me what happened," she said. "All of it. From the start."

I sighed. Put my coffee down. Went through the previous evening from memory. She'd be checking it against Finn's story, making sure all the details were more-or-less alike. Demons don't trust people, least of all their own kind.

"How's Finn?" I said.

"Healing."

I nodded. Demons would heal gunshots in a matter of hours, put him back on the streets. The holy water would slow that down, leave him with plenty of scar tissue, but he'd still be up and about far sooner than I would. Still, I felt sorry for him. It was my fault he was hurting. I'd picked Mick Finn, out of all the Rebels, as the weak link in the gang. Demons don't possess people when they aren't wanted. When Sabbath wanted a man on the inside, it had to be someone who'd agree to have a demon inserted. There's plenty of ways to do that. Plenty of techniques that don't qualify as coercion.

But in the end he'd heal. And his injuries meant we'd end up going to war with the Rebels. "Sabbath got a plan?"

"Find the sorcerer. Shut them down." Wesna took a deep breath, blew her fringe out of her face. "Take care of the Rebels ahead of schedule, in case they start getting ideas."

I nodded. I knew what most of that meant. “I’m pretty banged up. Got a bruise where my ribs should be.”

Wesna smirked. Pushed a small, white scrap of paper across the table. I picked it up. Read the contents. *Hell Bar. Thursday. Six AM.*

“You’ve got three days,” she said. “Heal up as best you can.”

Three days was longer than I’d expected, but it meant bad things. It meant we were taking a scorched earth approach, wiping the enemy out before the Rebels could encroach on Sabbath’s business any further. I was going to end up shooting people. Real people, not sorcerers or creatures from the Gloom.

That was the reality of working for Sabbath. And that was the deal I’d cut in order to save my life.

INEFFECTIVE COPING MECHANISMS

I NEEDED A drink. Hell, I needed several. Part of me considered going out and drinking alone, but when you run a list of enemies as long as mine, it's always safer to have someone there to help you watch your back.

Holly Langford wasn't really a friend. More an old ally of my former boss, a talented sorcerer in her own right. In a city full of former friends, she remained the only woman I trusted. It's half the reason I kept calling her, asking to hang out.

I wasn't sure why she kept showing up. I didn't dare question it.

We met down in Palm Beach, in the beer garden at the pub. She was a long, skinny woman. Older than the average patrons, but the dreadlocks and piercings made it hard to pinpoint her age. She wore a woollen cardigan, ragged jeans, and Docs. I found her in the midst of lighting a cigarette, ignoring the no-smoking signs posted on the walls. Other patrons didn't seem to notice.

"You look like shit." She tucked the lighter back in her pocket, waved the cigarette in my direction. "His Nastiness got you doing something that's got your conscience riled?"

I sat at her table, pushed a beer in front of her. "You know I can't talk about work. That's part of the deal with us hanging out."

"If you call it hanging out, I'm heading back to the Valley and you drink on your own. This is me checking in on you, mate, seeing how much damage your stupidity's done now." Langford sucked on her cigarette, exhaled smoke in my direction. "Heard there was a fire last night. Bar down by the creek."

I shrugged. Drank my beer.

Langford snorted and ground her cigarette into the table. "Three bodies dragged out of the ashes, so you did a shit job of hiding 'em. Human, based on what I've heard, although that doesn't mean much these days. His Nastiness has been expanding territory lately, pushing up against people who don't like being pushed.

That's not a healthy environment for a man like you, Murphy. If Roark were here—"

"He isn't, though, is he?"

"No. And ain't that a fucking pity." Langford shook her head. She was already reaching for a second cigarette, tapping it free of the pack, searching her pockets for the lighter she'd only just put away. "He got you training anyone yet? Paired you up with another bright young flunky who can be honed into a deadly instrument?"

I glared at her over the top of my beer. "We done with the lecture yet, or you want to keep going?"

Langford shrugged and reached for her glass. "I'd keep going, if I thought you'd listen," she said. "Never would have helped you, when you first showed up in town, if I thought it'd end with you and Sabbath on the same team."

"I never would have asked, if I knew that's how it'd end," I said. "On the plus side, it ain't the end of the world. That was the alternative, remember?"

Langford snorted. Said nothing for a little while. I'd come back to the Gold Coast with the apocalypse on my heels, the cult of the Raven following me and the promise of Ragnarok in the air. It wasn't all that surprising; spend enough time around sorcerers, peering into the Gloom where bad things come from, and you become a student of eschaton scenarios. The problem with my return is that the Raven cult were too damn close to succeeding.

"Well," she said, "That one we blame on Roark, useless bastard that he is." Langford raised her glass in salute, waited for me to do the same. "To absent bloody warriors and the mess they leave behind 'em."

I tapped my glass against hers. "To Danny-fucking-Roark."

She sipped from her glass. I drained mine empty. The beer hit my stomach, cold and hard, and I pointed towards the bar. "Seems I need another," I said. "Let me know if you're up for another round."

"You really think beer is going to help?"

I shrugged. "It's all I got right now. Roark always said to use the tools available."

"Somehow I don't think this is what he had in mind."

I caught the bus up to Broadbeach, staggered the two blocks home from my stop. My ribs still ached like a motherfucker, but the beer took the edge off the pain. Let me walk upright without listing to the side. Let me reach out with my right arm without wincing in pain. There were clouds coming in off the Pacific, the night sky filled with brooding darkness alleviated by the occasional patch of stars.

I turned onto my street, noticed the darkness. Pulled up short and reached for the SIG, hidden beneath my jacket. When you spend your life around magic, darkness is always relative. There is darkness that's just the absence of light, and darkness that comes from the Gloom. Darkness so deep it touches another place, creates doorways that demons and fey and worse can use to slip into our slice of reality.

The darkness around my front door wasn't Gloom, not yet. It came close enough to make me nervous, even half-drunk and needing to piss. I slid the SIG out of its holster, edged towards the stairs leading up to my flat.

I'd been in the place about three weeks. Warded it against intruders on the first night there, etching protective circles into the door frames, powering them up with little dabs of blood. They were solid work. The first thing Roark taught me, when he took me under his wing. I'd never make a full-fledged sorcerer—never felt the need or the inclination to learn more than the basics——but I could manage enough magic to keep out unwanted intruders.

I made it to the top of the stairs, edged along the narrow balcony I shared with the other three flats on the top floor of the Palm Tree Lodge. Darkness clustered around my front door, thickening into tenebrous knots. Something scratched at the wood on my door from the depths of the knot, rattled the knob a couple of times in case I'd left it unlocked. If it noticed me creeping along the balcony, SIG pointed in its direction, it certainly wasn't bothered by my presence or the gun.

If I'd been sober, that would have bothered me plenty. Even half-drunk and willing to do something stupid, creeping up on whatever hid inside the shadows was enough to make my back teeth ache.

I raised the SIG, aimed for the centre of the mass. Squeezed off a single shot that echoed, loud and sharp, against the natural canyon formed by the row of high rises on either side of the streets. The bullet disappeared into the knot of darkness. Did fuck-knows-what to the thing hiding inside.

For a moment the shadows knotted into a tight, compact ball of darkness.

Then expanded again as the shadow charged, barrelling down the length of the balcony. The sight of it connected with something in the back-brain, the little knot of instincts that still tells you to run when faced with a predator you can't outfight.

I ignored those instincts. I'd spent years training myself to do it, focusing on what needed to happen in order to put down things from the Gloom and keep humanity safe. I stood my ground and fired a second time, got a third shot off before the darkness enveloped me and robbed me of what little light I had to guide my aim.

It didn't really matter. Whatever sat in the middle of that knot of shadows hit me a half-second later, connecting like a wrecking ball fuelled by rage and a particular dislike for me and my goddamn gun.

For a moment I was flying, the SIG ripped loose from my hand.

By the time I landed, the darkness was gone. I lay against the newly-bent railing that ran around the landing, ribs burning like they'd replaced the bones with detcord and set it all alight. I wasn't really drunk anymore. I wasn't really sober either.

Mostly, I was just in pain, fighting against the urge to pass the fuck out.

PROTOCOLS

IT HURT TO breathe. That wasn't a good sign. It meant I'd broken a rib hitting the railing, compounding the damage done by the biker a few hours earlier. Possibly more than one rib, judging by the pain. I focused on short, shallow breathes. Kept myself moving.

I'd learned to travel light when I first left the Gold Coast, giving up any notion of having a home in favour of staying on the move. Even after coming back, setting up as one of Sabbath's flunkies, I'd kept the habit of being ready to go. I limped through the flat, collecting my bag and the small box underneath the bed. Made myself go back outside, searched the balcony for my SIG. It wasn't there.

I went down the stairs, scanned the front garden. Found the handgun near the base of the palm tree planted dangerously close to the driveway. Kneeling to pick it up almost caused me to pass out, but I got it and slid back into the holster. Pulled my jacket over the gun as I shuffled towards the street.

I knew the pain would get worse. I'd gotten this far on adrenaline and training, fuelled by the knowledge that gunfire would catch the neighbour's attention and start attracting cops. Paranoia that the things that attacked me would come flying out of the darkness to finish the job. That wasn't going to last. I made it a block before my breathing became a wheeze. My jacket no longer kept me warm, and my hands were shaking.

I made it less than half a block before I coughed up blood.

The SUV slid to a stop beside me. It wasn't one of Sabbath's cars. Too old. Too beat to shit. I was on the sidewalk, curled over my burning ribs. Trying to focus just enough to hear the sirens coming. To get my SIG to the storm drain in the gutter, sitting just out of reach. A door opened on the far side and heavy boots scuffed the bitumen. Big guys. Shaved heads. Rebel colours on their jacket.

They clustered round me. Someone planted a boot on my wrist, pinned the hand with the SIG to the dirt. A thin, reedy voice said, “Shit, he the one?”

“He’s the one,” someone answered.

A boot made contact with my ribs. I squeaked. Tried to curl up. It hurt to curl. It hurt to lie straight. Being in between didn’t do shit to help.

“Not much of threat, then. Thought these boys were big and bad.”

Another kick. More pain.

“This boy’s human, according to sources.”

I couldn’t make out faces, not from the ground. They were silhouettes. Voices. Too many threats for my drunk, broke ass to handle. One of them knelt down and his face caught the streetlight. He was a big, broad-shouldered motherfucker. Beard thick enough you could mistake him for a bear. Scar tissue round his left eye, where someone had been dumb enough to go at him with a knife. Big, bad Cody Patton. AKA The Kodiak.

Thick fingers ripped a hank of hair out of my skull. The Kodiak looked at his crew, grinned a little. “Yeah, it’s him,” he said. “Bring him. We want to get out of here ‘fore that thing comes back.”

“We don’t need the whole guy,” the reedy voice said. “All we need is—”

“Bring him.” The Kodiak growled the words out. No one bothered arguing. Lots of hands reached for me. Hoisted me into the air. Pain kept me from fighting back. Kept me from doing much but screaming. I let myself scream.

I’m not one for magic. It required too much focus, too much sacrifice to make it work. I learned enough basic sorcery to do what needed doing, left the rest to a partner like Danny Roark on the jobs that needed more than that. With my gun gone, a whole lot of pain, and too many opponents to fight en-masse, I wracked my memory for something that’d help. There wasn’t much. I could ward a room, protect myself, siphon a soul into a prepared receptacle. Nothing that would stop four big-ass men loading my injured arse into the back of an SUV.

Sure as hell nothing that would give me an edge against a man like the Kodiak if he decided to take me apart.

Turns out I didn't need it, 'cause some days my arse is lucky. The part of me still processing things, deep behind the pain, registered the headlights at the far end of the road. Caught the roar of the engine, the slammed doors. Wesna's voice giving orders as the possessed opened fire. The Rebels still worried about cops and bodies. Wesna was beyond that. The guys trying to carry me were quickly down a guy. They dropped me. Ran for it. Disappeared in a squeal of rubber. I lay on bitumen, banged up and bleeding, laughing like a crazy man.

More orders. No more gunfire. This time, when they lifted me up, I felt safe enough to finally give up and let protocols be damned. Someone hammed their fingers into my neck. Feeling for a pulse.

"Trust you, Murphy," Wesna said. "Trying to find ways to get your dumb arse killed before things start to get interesting."

I wanted to smile. To burble something in response. Neither option worked for me, so I passed out instead, let the dark and the pain take over until there wasn't much else to think about.

The sunlight filtered in through a crack in the curtains, woke me up a little after six AM. I was in the casino hotel, racking up recovery time in a five-hundred-a-night suite. Sabbath's territory. Safe, for certain definitions of safe that focused exclusively on the short-term. I limped to the bathroom. Relieved my bladder. Limped back and forced myself to stretch, working the ache out of muscles that'd been pushed to their limits.

I wasn't too sore, for a guy who'd just been curb-stomped. That means they'd wasted resources on getting me healed, some two-bit sorcerer in Sabbath's employ coming in and whispering spells over me while I lay there, unable to stop them. It wasn't that I objected. I'd used magic to heal before. It's just never as reliable as letting things happen the old-fashioned way, and someone always pays the price for thwarting nature's will.

Wesna showed up around quarter to seven. Came bearing coffee and a spare SIG for my empty holster. I searched the wardrobe. Found my clothes hanging. They'd ransacked my old apartment, moved my meagre possessions into the suite. "Consider this the end of your independent living," Wesna said. "You're staying here for the duration. Sabbath's orders, so take your shit up with him."

I grunted something that could be agreement. Went and stood by the window. It'd started raining while I was asleep, the world outside turned grey and cold and wet. From my vantage point, in the casino tower, I could see through to the beach. It wasn't far. The highway. Three blocks of buildings. A thin line of sand between us and the water. The rain made everything a little blurry. Fat drops of water rolled down the tinted window glass.

"There was something at my flat," I said. "Something before the Kodiak's boys jumped me. It wasn't human."

"We found the aftermath," she said. "I sent Randall in to collect your shit and clean things up. Turned out it was a bigger job than expected."

"I don't own that much, Wes'."

"But you did leave a dent in the balcony rail," she said. "Warped the thing a good foot out of shape, so you're lucky you're still alive. Most people don't live through things that hit that hard, mate."

I thought about that. Nodded.

"Jesus," I said.

Annoyance flickered across Wesna's features. "Don't blaspheme."

I apologised. Drained my coffee. Left the paper cup on the windowsill. I felt better, with the caffeine in me. Capable of walking. Capable of thinking. "I take it Sabbath wants to see me?"

Wesna rose, already heading for the door. "Orders said to bring you as soon as you were upright." she said. "Better to get it over with than piss him off by having him wait."

HELL, MID-RENOVATION

HELL BAR SAT at the beach end of the Broadbeach Mall, attached to the second floor of the Oasis Plaza like a slightly malignant mole. Once upon a time it'd been the local neutral ground, a meeting place for the things that go bump in the night; where they could drink and negotiate, free from prying eyes. That'd ended when some cultists blew the place up, trying to lure me out of hiding.

Now Hell Bar was a construction site, barricaded off from the rest of the world with plywood barricades and signs that warned you about the necessities of a hard-hat on site. Work on the site started early; it was just after seven, by the time we walked over, and the crew was already at it. Saws; nail guns; the sound of men sweating and swearing in equal measure.

We hammered on the wall. Waited, quiet-like. Heard people yelling Cuddy's name. Heard footsteps on the stair well. Mick Cuddy appeared at the edge of the barricade. A squat guy, broad-shouldered, stomach like a pasta bowl. He wore a hard-hat, a safety vest, and a harried expression. He wasn't pleased to see us.

"Jesus," he said. "He know you two were coming?"

"Michael, please," Wesna said. "We've talked about blaspheming."

"We talked about having random strays on my site, too, but it hasn't stopped shit from happening." Cuddy edged back a little, shaking his head. "You gotta talk to him about conducting business somewhere else, yeah? We aren't meant to have folks wandering in and out."

Wesna shrugged and edged her way past the foreman. "What makes you think he listens to me?"

"Hope, mostly." Cuddy grinned. "And the fact that I'd listen, darlin', if you started talkin' to me."

"Everyone should have a dream, mate." I slipped past Cuddy, waited for him to slide the barricade into place again. "What's his mood like?"

Cuddy laughed, out loud. "He's doing his impression of a pissed-off motherfucker trying to pretend he's not pissed off."

"Same as usual, then."

"Yup." Cuddy gave me a hard-hat and a safety vest of my own. He'd long ago gave up trying to foist them onto Wesna. I'm not sure he ever tried it on Sabbath.

We called the job a renovation, but the truth ran closer to rebuilding. Work crews swarming the place like ants, hard hats and safety vests everywhere. The initial stages of construction had been dominated by the repair of load-bearing pillars and much of the external wall, trying to shore up the worst of the damage.

That'd given way to detail work about a month back, specialists coming in to work on design and décor, crafting the interior to reflect Sabbath's vision. The bar was a wide, circular room covered in a fine layer of concrete dust. Cuddy had two guys sweeping the floor, preparing for the team that'd come through to polish the concrete. Heavy pillars had been re-envisioned, a series of up lights situated at the base to cast hellish reds and yellows against the high ceiling. It'd probably be a nice effect, once the bar was dark. This hour of the morning, with the work crews around, it just looked like a bunch of guys spending quality time on the electrical system.

The real genius of the design was the decision to go split level, breaking up the flat lines of the bar to create quiet nooks where patrons could hide, with central depressions creating a natural amphitheatre where those in the mood to show off could stay in the public eye. Sabbath's plans called for glass-topped tables and curved railings for people to lean against. The former were in storage, waiting for renovations to hit their final stage. The latter were being installed, solid curves of glass stretching around the raised platform with the central bar. Sabbath figured the balustrade for his masterpiece; LED-lights ran through the solid chunk of glass and plastic, designed to light up the railings with the same hellish glow as the pillars.

Cuddy's men were good at their jobs. They worked fast, worked early, and they kept their safety gear in place. Sabbath stood in the centre of it all, the odd man out. He was a compact older guy, neat and tidy; one of the tanned, white-linen suite brigade that filtered their way to the Coast on retirement. A lean, jogger's frame; grey hair cut close to the scalp. He studied one of the balustrades through wire-framed glasses, all business, expression neutral. When we arrived, he glanced in our direction for the barest hint of a second.

"They look rather gaudy, don't they?" His voice was bland, disinterested. The same tone you use when people ask for the time at a bus stop. "I've been assured they'll look spectacular once the room is dark and they're lit, but for now..."

Sabbath walked the length of the plastic rail, jumped down the two foot drop from his level to ours. He crouched, viewed the balustrade from the underside. "I hear we have a problem with the Kodiak?"

"Something like that." Wesna straightened, her eyes following Sabbath as he continued his slow inspection. "Some of Cody's boys came after Keith last night. Tested the wards on his apartment; kicked the crap out of him when they found him in the street."

Sabbath's eyes narrows. "When you say they tested the wards?"

Wesna glanced back at me, took a deep breath. "They sent something from the Gloom after him. Whoever's been giving them information has gone a little further than holy water and combat tactics."

Sabbath came to a halt. Crouched down to put the banister on eye level. He ran his fingers over the smooth, plastic surface. The faintest hint of a smile ghosted around the edge of his mouth. "And yet you're up and around, Mister Murphy?"

I stepped up, cleared my throat. "I got lucky," I said. "Fought off whatever they sent after me. Wes found me before they could finish the job, saved me from having the crap kicked out of me."

“Fortunate.” Sabbath straightened, gestured to one of the workmen. A teenage kid, maybe nineteen; a dark-haired surfer kid who wore the tan of someone who snuck in an early morning at the beach before he hit the job site.

“You,” Sabbath said. “Come here.”

The kid looked up, eyes wide.

Sabbath pointed at the banister. “There’s a crack.”

The kid blinked, not sure how to process the information he’d been given. “Sir?”

“There is a crack,” Sabbath repeated. “A flaw in the construction of the banister, or something you and your Neanderthal friends have instilled in the set-up of this section. I want you to take care of it.”

“I’ll have to get me—”

Sabbath grabbed the kid by the neck, forced his head down to banister level. “Do you see the crack?”

The kid squirmed, trying to get free. No chance of that. His eyes rolled, looking for back-up, but no-one seemed to care.

The contractor, Cuddy, came over. “Is there a problem, Mister Sabbath?”

Sabbath met the bigger man’s gaze, held the kid in an iron grip. “I found a flaw in your work,” he said. “I was pointing it out to your employee here, making sure he was aware of it.”

The kid continued squirming, gaining confidence now that Cuddy was up close. He grit his teeth, swore a few times. Tried his hand at making threats. “Let me go, you—”

“Nick.” Cuddy’s tone cut the kid off. The contractor shook his head, warning the kid to be silent. “We’ll take of it, Mister Sabbath. My apologies for the problem.”

Sabbath nodded, once. Released the kid. Cuddy edged a little closer, hauled the kid out of Sabbath’s path. Probably a smart move; the kid was ready to pick a fight. That wouldn’t end well. Not for him. Cuddy pulled the kid out of the line of fire, throwing quick glances over his shoulder.

Sabbath produced a handkerchief, wiped his fingers. "People," he said. "You have to watch them."

There wasn't shit wrong with the balustrade, not that I could see. That didn't really matter any. Wesna nodded. I nodded. We waited.

Sabbath screwed the handkerchief along the length of his pinky finger. "So this business with our Rebel friends? I take it we've moved beyond handling things delicately?"

I glanced around the half-built bar, all the people in close proximity who didn't know what walked among them. "They're loading up to fight demons," I said. "From what I've seen of the club, back when you had me look into them, they'll make a fight of it."

Sabbath made a thoughtful noise in the back of his throat. He turned to Wesna. "You agree with Keith's assessment?"

"Almost certainly."

"Almost?" Sabbath finished with his handkerchief, folded it into quarters. "This is not a matter where I appreciate evasiveness."

"Apologies." Wesna grimaced slightly, scowling as she thought through her words. "I don't like having an unknown quantity out there, destabilizing things. I don't like the possibility that we could lose men. I sure as hell don't like them having the ability to send things after us; there's no threat at the casino, but here, where the wards aren't done yet?"

She paused, took a deep breath. Sabbath nodded, hands on his balustrade. "The wards here will hold," he said. "I've made sure of that."

"You're sure?"

He didn't bother answering that, just made a thoughtful noise in the back of his throat. "Best we go do something about the problem, then."

Wesna nodded. "What kind of something?"

"Something permanent." Sabbath sucked breath through his teeth, finger tapping a staccato pattern against the railing. "Something quiet; take off the head, and we'll see if the body has it in it to survive. Our friends in the police service will appreciate quiet and permanent. It's so much easier to overlook our activities when we keep them from making noise."

I exchanged a look with Wesna, thought about the thing that attacked me. Quiet wasn't really its modus operandi.

"And if the body survives the attack?"

"Then things get bloody." Sabbath turned to me, smiling. His teeth where very white and even in his plain, tanned face. "We hit a point, Keith, where the cops can go fuck themselves. I don't feel the need to play this subtle, and I'll appreciate every minute we get to stain your precious hands with blood."

THE OUTSIDER

WE HIT THE Rebel clubhouse on a Wednesday. A cold, wet four AM assault, two through the front, two through the rear. I'd been assigned to the back door, crouched low in the scrub with Finn. He went to work on the chain link fence, the soft clip of the wire-cutters making a hole to crawl through. He wasn't happy about being partnered with me, kept glancing over his shoulder to make sure I had his back. It was basic, amateur shit; the professionals had the front door assault. More ground to cover as they crossed the yard.

The clubhouse wasn't much to look at. It was old, the paint peeling in long strips, nothing keeping the weeds down in the yard but the constant passage of bikes rolling in and rolling out. Yellow light spilled through open windows. Corrugated iron roof, weatherboard walls. A long, broad veranda surrounding three-quarters of the house. The whole thing up on short, thick hardwood stumps to keep the white ants out of it.

We'd been in position a half-hour, no signs of movement. The snip of the wire cutters seemed too damn loud. I picked my way through the muddy ground, looking for a better vantage point. Three times I'd done surveillance on the place, preparing for the raid. It was never still. There was always someone guarding the fort.

"You gotta—"

Finn held up a finger, still focused on the wire. I fell silent, observed, adjusted the grip on the SIG. Finn finished cutting his hole, hauled the Mossberg off his shoulder. Cradled the shotgun, eyes burning. The smile saying everything he wanted to say: Finn didn't gotta do anything. Except maybe kill some motherfuckers, and Finn didn't need me for that.

Finn was a fucking idiot. I'd been working that theory for a couple of weeks, hadn't found anything to contradict it. He'd been a thug with a hair trigger before they stuffed a demon inside him; possession hadn't done a thing to curb those qualities.

I grabbed his arm, pulled him back as he lurched for the hole in the fence. Finn fell back, landed on his ass. He wasn't smiling anymore.

I nodded toward the well-lit clubhouse. "You smell anything?"

"From here?" Finn shook his head. "Too much rain and mud."

"Fine. So what do you hear?"

Finn squinted. "Mostly, just some bitch."

His grin came back. I ignored it. "Inside the club house, asshole."

Finn crinkled his nose and stared at the house. "I ain't hearing shit."

"Then we ain't going in," I said. "Call Wes. Wave her off."

Finn shorted. Adjusted his grip on the Mossberg. "Like that's your call."

He pulled back the chain links, slipped through the hole he'd cut in the fence line. I swore under my breath, went through the fence after him. We hustled across the open yard, skidded to halt by the stairs to the back door. Finn took them two at a time, applied his shoulder to the door. He'd been a big man before he was possessed. The demon only made him stronger. The door burst open, hit the limits of its hinges.

Finn swept into the room, shotgun ready. I came behind him, SIG in a two-handed grip. The theory was simple: the Mossberg would make a mess of any resistance we encountered; I'd pick off the stragglers with the SIG and let Finn move on. We could hear Wes and Randall working from the front door, their heavy boots on the floorboards, doors getting kicked open as the pair surged into a new room.

The clubhouse wasn't large. We were done in less than two minutes, met up in the central room filled with half-empty beer bottles and torn leather couches. There wasn't anything worth seeing: no resistance; no signs of life; no evidence of where the rest of the Rebels had gone.

"Well, then," Finn said. "This is a fucking pile of shit." He kicked a small pyramid of beer cans, watched them bounce off the wall. Turned back to find Wesna and Randall glaring at him.

"No one's arguing with you," Randall said. He was a tall, athletic guy. A tri-athlete, before he'd been possessed. Now he just looked young and pretty. Lean, heavily tanned, perfectly white teeth; Sabbath's long-term muscle. He snarled at Finn, took a position by the window. Peered out into the darkness, a second Mossberg held at the ready. The shotgun didn't suite him. "They left bikes out there."

Wesna clicked her fingers, pointed Finn towards the door. "Go check it."

Finn scowled. "Why me?"

"'Cause I said so." She took a few steps closer to Finn. Stared down at him. "We got a problem, Finn?"

He thought that over. Glanced at me. "Nah," he said. "No problem."

"Then go check out the bikes," she said. "I want to know why they're sitting there, and how they got left behind. Keith?"

I looked up.

"Do your thing," she said. "Find me something we can report to the big man."

I took my time tossing the room, content to let the demons stand guard. Randall hovered by the door. Finn worked the yard. Wesna followed along behind me, waiting for me to give her some good news. It got on my nerves, but I kept my mouth shut. Wesna Holjack had been dangerous before she got possessed, I sure as hell didn't want to tangle with her now that a demon was augmenting her speed and strength.

I found what we were looking for in a bedroom up the back of the house, half-hidden under a double bed covered in blankets and stained sheets. It wasn't a large circle—maybe a foot wide, the runes scratched into the floorboards, wax melted into the grooves after multiple uses. I called Wesna's name, waved her over.

"Someone needs to check the scrub," I said.

"You think they botched a summoning?"

"They carved it into wood," I said, "that doesn't exactly scream competence. Even if they did get their shit together long enough to make this work, it'd be easy to sabotage."

"Easy for someone like you, or actually easy?"

I pointed to the first rune, at the top of the circle. "The woods already warping. They're lucky their sorcerer didn't blow himself up trying to hold things steady."

Wesna considered that, eyes narrowed to slits. "Randall?"

The tall demon peeled away from the window, alert.

"Take Finn. Search the scrub," Wesna said. "Blow out a knee if he objects."

Randall nodded, disappearing into the darkness. Wesna knelt down beside me. "You sure this is active?"

I scraped at the wax with my thumbnail. The lingering charge in the circle ran up my arm, as uncomfortable as licking a battery. "Yeah, I'm sure."

She swore under her breath, took Randall's spot by the window. I left her there, continued my search in the kitchen. Picked my way through the empty beer cans and pizza boxes, found the utensils hidden in the bottom drawer by the sink. A dozen candles, plain wax, picked up at the local supermarket. Two knives, gaudy and utterly unsuited for stabbing people, the kind of shit you'd pick up at your tobacconist alongside the replica blades from Conan and Lord of the Rings. Gold leaf on the handles, fake stones in the hilts. Blades that wove back and forth like a serpent.

I brought them into the lounge room, dropped them onto the coffee table. "These guys were either desperate, stupid, or they got themselves set up," I said. "This is one step up from birthday candles and a butter knife."

Wesna had her phone pressed against her ear. She nodded, absently, at the shit I'd dropped on the table. Hung up the phone and nodded towards the door.

"Come on," she said. "They found your bodies."

LOOKING INTO A VERY DARK PLACE

WE SLOGGED THROUGH the undergrowth, following the spot of a torchlight Wesna used for my benefit. She could see just as easily in the dark, could probably follow the scent of the dead to their resting place. The possessed can smell blood as well as any cadaver dog, even if you've got the bodies buried.

We were up in theme park country, out past Dreamworld and into the stretch of no man's land that neither the Gold Coast nor Brisbane had bothered to claim. The damp, earthy smell of the scrub was everywhere, but there wasn't any noise except the sound of our boots and my occasional curse as I tripped over the undergrowth. We'd been going a half-hour when Wesna came to a halt.

"Up there." She pointed, identifying a soft glimmer of light further up the incline. Finn's phone, we discovered, left in the crook of a tree as a signal. From there, even I could smell the coppery scent of blood on the far side of the ridge. Finn stood guard, his expression grim. Randall went from body to body, photographing their faces with his cell.

"We've found seven," he reported. "Partially buried, probably before the rain. They've been attacked by something big."

Wesna made a noncommittal noise. Australia's natural predators were small and poisonous. Big meant something from the Gloom, lending credence to my theory that someone had fucked up a summoning.

Finn adjusted his grip on the gun, nodded to the south. "Local theme park has a tiger exhibit?"

"We'd have heard something if one of those went missing." I holstered my SIG for the first time since the raid began, half-slid down the slope til I came across a body. No mistaking it for anything but one of the Rebels. Leather jacket. Dirty jeans. Tattoos and the long, out-of-control beard a lot of the Rebel's wore. A red and black bandanna was twisted around his right knee; Rebel colours, worn with pride.

He'd been savaged pretty good. Wounds to the shoulders, chest, and head. Big, bloody rents that tore through leather and flesh. Slick, wet internal organs were exposed to the air, the blood around them ugly and dark.

"Scratch off accident," I said.

Wesna's torch joined mine on the wound. "You're sure?"

"Whatever did this is big," I said. "If you fuck up a summoning, you can get big, but you don't get longevity. Whatever came out of the Gloom ripped these boys up good, half-buried them to try and hide the body, then cleaned up the clubhouse to try and hide its existence."

"Could be another person," Finn said. "Let the monster do the hard work, come in and clean up afterwards."

"I don't find that any more comforting than Keith's theory," Wesna said. "We know they had a sorcerer on board; we don't know who. The Kodiak never showed any aptitude for magic, but maybe—"

She froze. Sniffed the air. "Anyone smell the Kodiak among the dead?"

Randall and Finn exchanged a look, took a long sniff of the air themselves. I went about things the old-fashioned way, checking the corpses one by one, sliding my way down the slope until I found the last body pressed against the tree. The dead biker was a big, ginger-haired motherfucker. Barbed wire tattooed around his throat, half-hidden by the tangled thatch of beard. I recognised the guy. His name was Dan Rickman. He'd been the Rebel's toe-cutter for the better part of a decade. One of the Kodiak's closest friends.

"No Kodiak," I said, "but he would have been here. No way they summoned something like this without the boss around."

"You think he ran?"

"That, or he got transformed into the monster." I said. "Not to insult you all, but it wouldn't the first time someone made a mistake and let something from the Gloom send them crazy."

The demons didn't have a response to that. Wesna came down the hill a little. "Murphy."

I jerked my head up, met Wesna's stare.

"Do your thing." she said.

I looked at the carnage. "They're already dead, Wes."

"Not that," she said. "Your other thing. We need to know for sure that they're dead and staying dead."

Used to be I had a gift. As a kid, from around age six, I could see past the disguises of the things that go bump in the night. I could see auras, learned real fast what all the splashes of colour meant. I learned the existence of demons, and fey, all the species of Other that make their way out of the Gloom. I learned about the ghosts the hard way, on a trip to see my grandfather in the caravan he called home. I peered into very dark places and realised other worlds existed on the far side of the darkness.

These days I'm blind as anyone else, content to see the same façade that gets everyone else through their life. I taught myself to see the illusions all the Other prefer to hide behind, to lock down my natural gifts for the sake of my own sanity. I didn't need to see a demon's real face to know that it was dangerous. I sure as hell didn't need to see ghosts, not in my line of work.

I knelt down beside Dan Rickman's body. Took a good look at the bloody mess that used to be his stomach. "I ain't exactly a forensic specialist, but that looks kinda dead to me."

Wesna grinned. "And how exactly did you end up back in Sabbath's employ, Keith?"

"These guys ain't a cult."

"Weren't," Wesna said. "Who knows what the fuck they are, now that they're summoning shit with their crappy sacrificial knives?"

She had a point. I hated that. I hated everything she was asking me to do.

I knelt in the mud, closed my eyes. Focused on my breathing. In. Out. In. Out. Focused on the science of it, the mechanics: the contraction of the diaphragm; the drop of pressure in the thorax; the expansion of the lungs. The broccoli-like tangle of bronchial tendrils extracting oxygen from the inhaled air, transferring it to the bloodstream. Cold mud seeped through my pants, ensuring they'd never be worn again.

I could still slip the shackles I'd put on my vision. It took time, and it took focus, and a few seconds of seeing past the veil could give a migraine that lasted a month. I took a final breath, set my teeth against each other so I wouldn't bite my tongue.

"Ready?" Wesna said.

I nodded. Opened my eyes. The demon who wore Wesna Holjack's body loomed over me, feet firmly dug into the damp earth. She'd always been tall and imposing, but with the veil ripped away from my sight, I was forced to watch her skin blister and boil together, then decay into the char grilled mockery of her human features. Her eyes rotted, leaving behind hollow sockets where the demon's presence burned like a crimson fire. Her aura was a riot, flicks of silver light waging war with the dark fire, the last remnant of the human spirit who'd been Wesna Holjack before the demon came along.

She grinned at me, blackened skin flaking as her lips pulled into a rictus. "The bodies, Keith."

I wrenched my eyes away from her, forced myself to count off the breath. My mouth flooded with aluminium-tinged saliva, forcing me to spit. I kept my breathing steady, in, out, in, out. Focused on the corpses spread across the slope. They weren't any prettier; they were still dead, their wet innards exposed to the air, their stillness an affront to the cool night breeze that caressed the hill with its fingertips.

I could see the faint, pale light of magic surrounding Rickman's tattoos; sufficient evidence they'd been part of a ritual, perhaps enough to confirm he'd been capable of summoning something with the circle.

My blood hammered in my temples, growing tighter and colder. I kept breathing, kept focused, studied Rickman's corpse for signs of a ghost. Scrambled up the slope and did the same for his nearest comrade. They were freshly dead, no more than twelve hours since they'd been ripped apart and partially buried. Auras lingered. Ghosts hung around. It took time for both to dissipate, depending on who the deceased had been.

By the time I slid to a halt beside the third corpse, barely able to keep myself upright, I'd given up hope of seeing signs of either.

"Whatever killed them took their spirits," I said. "Or someone came past, right after the attack, and siphoned their souls into a ghost-cage."

Wesna appeared behind me, holding me upright. "You're sure?"

"I'm sure." I stood up, let my focus waver. The rhythmic pounding in my head could have been used to construct a housing estate. "They're clean, Wes. An' if this was something from the far side of the Gloom—"

I hawked and spat, trying to clear my mouth. My stomach roiled in response, ready to puke its contents over Wesna's combat boots. I blinked a few times, found myself sitting in the mud, the world preparing to lurch sideways as my equilibrium when to shit.

Then I saw it. The feather.

It was mostly hidden under the biker's bulk; the tip of the shaft poking free, just beside his hip; the downy afterfeathers at the base of the stem slicked together by the damp. A black feather on wet soil, easy enough for a demon's sight to miss on a quick perusal, but what I saw seemed to feed on the shadows around it. Thin strands of the Gloom clung to the thing, almost made it seem alive, and when I shifted the body to pull the feather free, it proved to be too large for any of the local fauna. Over a foot long, the Gloom-touched vane seething beneath my fingers.

It hadn't come from a bird. Whatever lost the feather was native to the Gloom, from the deepest parts of that world that rarely interacted with ours. It was the only way to explain its presence and its size. It felt cold to touch. Dangerous. My vision swam. I took a deep breath and held it. Counted backwards from ten. Focused on my own feet, the flecks of mud smeared against the sides of my boots.

Wesna crouched beside me, shone a torch into my eyes.

"You okay?"

I blinked at her, raising one hand against the light. She looked like the woman I'd known again; pale, dark, strong. Only the faintest glimmer of demon-fire visible in her eyes, where no disguise the Other have come up with has ever proven to be one hundred percent effective.

She repeated her question, and I nodded slowly. "Don't usually hold it that long."

"That's 'cause you're a lazy prick." She stood, offered me a hand. I ignored the offer. Placed the feather in her outstretched fingers. She lifted it. Studied it. Whistled, softly. "That's...big," she said.

I clambered to my feet. Held onto a tree until I steadied. "No shit, it's big," I said.

"No, it's really big," Wesna said. "It's almost like—" She crouched beside the corpse, peeled back the eyelid. "They were soul free?"

"Yep."

She swore a few times. Ran a finger along the feather's vane.

"Finn, get ready to torch the clubhouse. Randall, you're on corpse disposal. You've ten minutes. Don't fucking disappoint me." She grabbed me by one arm, hauled me up the slope. "You've got ten minutes to double check the clubhouse, make sure there's nothing we missed," she said. "If I find out you've blown this, Murphy, you won't need to worry about Sabbath coming after you."

I tried to shake her off. Failed to free my arm. "What the fuck, Wes? It's just a feather."

"Yeah," she said. "Giant-fucking-feathers and bodies empty of souls. Tell me what that sounds like to you, given the trouble we've had in the last year?"

I shut my mouth. Said nothing. I knew exactly where she was leading me and I knew it wasn't really possible. Valkyries don't come to our world. They're too far back in the Gloom, too removed from the places that would give them access. They were too old school, creatures of the Gloom when it was known by another name, before it was poisoned by industrialism and capitalism and a worldwide epidemic of people who didn't believe in magic.

Valkyries didn't come to Earth, not without a damn good reason.

BAD CHOICES

FINN TORCHED THE clubhouse before we left. Randall took care of the bodies, made sure the cops would never find them. The basic precautions of the underworld, criminal and metaphysical; both believed you couldn't be too careful, especially when there were corpses involved. Arson seemed to calm Finn down. He sat in the back seat, on the passenger side. Hummed quietly as Randall found his way back to the highway, turned the black SUV south and rolled past the knot of theme parks.

It's a twenty-minute ride from theme park country to Broadbeach. Forty, if there's roadwork and traffic, but we ran into neither at that hour of the morning. It was quiet out. A Wednesday. There are parts of the Coast that never sleep, but they tended to stay closer to the beach. The theme parks were inland, making something valuable from the bits of the Coast no one wanted. I sat on the back seat. Let the painkillers attack the edge of my migraine. I wanted to make a phone call. To Langford. To Roark. To someone who knew the rules of the Gloom better than I did; someone who could tell me that a valkyrie running loose wasn't going to be my fault.

Mostly, it was Roark I wanted. My partner. My friend. The guy I'd done jobs with for sixteen years, including the last one where we killed the one guy we shouldn't have killed. The one guy where we weren't good enough to get the job done, or the one where we just got sloppy. I kept Michael Wotan's spirit trapped in a bullet in a warded box. A basic precaution when you kill off a sorcerer. It limited their options for vengeance via death curse or haunting, kept their essence handy in case you needed it for another job down the line. It wasn't pretty. It wasn't ethical. But neither were the fuckers Roark and I used to kill.

Randall drove us down to the beachfront, parked in the lot opposite the Oasis and led us all up into the half-finished bar. It was early, yet. Still early enough that

Cuddy and his work crew hadn't shown up. That meant there were sorcerers working, a cadre of pock-marked little fuckers painting runes onto the walls, warding the place with blood and magic to keep it well defended. They were Sabbath's people, human but touched by something in the Gloom. Capable of just enough magic to get themselves in trouble and keep some bad things out.

Sabbath saw us marching in. Saw the look on Wesna's face and nodded towards the back rooms, the place where his office would be set up and give him a quiet place away from the bar crowd. We walked through the cold, half-painted bar. Lined up in the small, cramped room where Sabbath had a plastic table set up to handle his paperwork. He pulled out a plastic seat. Settled his arse into it.

"Well?"

Wesna told him. Went through everything, step by step. Mentioned my suspicion. Mentioned the goddamn fire. Sabbath sat there, hands clasped, index fingers tapping together as she reported in. The finger tapping stopped when Wesna finished talking. Sabbath sat there, very still. He glared at me.

"One fire in a month is sloppy." His eyes narrowed, just a little. "Two in the space of a week is like shitting in your own bed. It's a mess you don't want to clean up, but you do it, 'cause the alternatives are much, much worse."

"The fire wasn't Murphy's call. I—"

Sabbath shifted his stare to her. He held out his hand, waited for Wesna to hand over the evidence. For a long time he studied the length of the thing, running his fingers along the vane. "So you think we've got a valkyrie?"

Wesna shrugged. "I'd put money on it."

"We haven't seen a valkyrie loose in the mortal world for several centuries." Sabbath lowered the feather, turned his stare back to me. "Would have thought it'd be hunting your arse, Murphy, if one of the winged bitches got it together to manifest in this realm."

I set my jaw. Said nothing and tried to hold my ground. It didn't work. Sabbath could see it my eyes, the fact I'd already considered it. Put two and two together, given the cult who'd come chasing me six months back, screaming threats of Ragnarok unless I gave them back the soul I'd stolen when I killed the leader. "We can't be sure it's a valkyrie," I said. "Wes is just speculating, based on a feather and a lack of souls at the scene. I could rip off the souls, if I needed too. Someone could've planted the feather, trying to place us and get us to do something stupid."

"You were attacked," Sabbath said.

"If I were attacked by a valkyrie, I should be dead.'

Sabbath grunted softly, looked at the feather again. I could see him processing it all, sorting through the possibilities. He was judging the possibilities the feathers represented, weighing them against the potential trouble if *that's unlikely* turned into *well, shit, I guess I was wrong.* He didn't give much away. Sabbath never did. He'd made his fortune in the casino, adopted the kind of poker face most humans would never manage.

"I can look into it," I said.

Sabbath raised an eyebrow. Tried to hide his grin. "And why would I want you looking into things, Keith Murphy? I want you spilling blood, not running around playing hero."

"Do it 'cause you need to know," I said, "and because I do this kind of thing better than your people. It'll be faster and easier if you let me ask around, figure out what's happening before whatever left that feather behind comes back to cause more trouble."

Sabbath nodded slowly. Put the feather on the plastic table. "That's one possibility."

"But you want to take the long way around?"

"No." Sabbath smoothed his jacket, adopted a bland, unpleasant grin. "I want the more immediate answer. The one I think you can provide us with. According to Wesna, you were travelling with a warded box. I think we both know what's likely contained within."

I glanced at Wesna. She looked away. Finn and Randall looked confused, like they weren't sure of the game. But they knew trouble was coming, and they knew I was getting screwed. They were eager to see that part up close.

"You're going to take care of this, Murphy," Sabbath said. "You're going to collect your little box and contact one of your sorcerer friends, and then you're going to call forth a ghost who can answer some of our questions. If this is a valkyrie, I want to be prepared. If your apocalypse is still on the cards, I want to get that resolved."

Sabbath's lips were smiling, but it never reached his eyes. He watched me, easy and friendly, kept eye contact as he spoke. "You and I had a deal," he said. "I wouldn't want you to feel short-changed by the experience."

I looked around. Smiles on Finn and Randall's faces, a smile on Sabbath's thin lips. Wesna didn't look at me. She didn't really need to. I shoved my hands in my pockets. Glared at the black feather on the white plastic table-top.

"I'm not a fucking necromancer," I said. "I don't even know one in close proximity."

"Doesn't matter," Sabbath said. "We both know you'll do the job, in a pinch."

THE UNDERPASS

EVEN AS A kid, I knew the Underpass was bad news. There were rumours about it in school, stories told and retold about the dangers of going down there at night. Bad things happened in the concrete tunnel, accumulated there like layers of graffiti. When I was really young, I heard about the gang fights. Then the murders, and the rapes, and the urban myths about things that seemed weirder and more dangerous than both. Bodies found skinned, their internal organs missing. People who walked into the tunnel on one side of the highway, but never emerged from the far end.

It wasn't until I learned about magic that I understood; the Underpass was a thin point, an inlet on the shoreline between our world and the Gloom. That made it dangerous, and useful, all at once.

None of that meant I liked it there, breathing in the lingering scent of raw fear and human piss. I stared down the tunnel, the length of it visible thanks to the series of dim fluorescent lights the council installed a few years back. Three in the morning, and there were still cars on the highway above, the steady hiss of tyres on bitumen filling in the empty space.

Langford knelt by the mouth of the tunnel, working on the circle. Crouched so low her dreadlocks brushed against the concrete, forcing her to double-check her work multiple times. "You realise you should be doing this, right? It's stronger if it's your own work."

"It's stronger if it's done by someone competent," I said.

"I've seen you put together a ward."

"And yet we're having this conversation?" I shook my head. "Wotan knew magic. Understood it far better than I ever will. If the choice is your wards, or mine, who do you think is more likely to make an error he'll exploit?"

Langford made a soft noise, scuttled sideways around the ward, double checking her work as she went. She inspected the white lines: chalk, salt, a few drops of my blood to give it power the moment I invoked the darkness in the tunnel. Placed candles at the four points, lit them one by one. "Be sure you've got the call down. If you give him an opening, any opening—"

"I know. I've got it down."

She stood, lit up a cigarette. Studied her work as she smoked. "You got the bullet?"

I nodded. Tapped my pocket. "Makes me nervous, having it this close to the tunnel."

"Makes me nervous, just keeping a ghost in that thing." Langford finished her cigarette, flicked it into the shadows of the tunnel. We watched the burning cherry dim, the shadows reaching out to smother the light. "You realise this is ten kinds of stupid, right? You aren't a necromancer. You barely qualify as a sorcerer."

"That's why I owe you another favour."

"I'm starting to rethink my policy 'bout doing favour for idiots determined to end up dead." Langford grinned and cast one last look down the tunnel. Took a few steps away from the circle before tossing me the lighter. "Keep the flames lit, keep your chanting steady. Anything goes wrong..."

I waited for the advice. It didn't come.

"Hell," Langford said. "Anything goes wrong, you're basically fucked."

I sat in the middle of Langford's circle, watching the flickering candle flames. It'd been close to midnight, when we started. Well after that now, and getting later. A cold wind swept off the Broadwater, raised goose-bumps under my sweater. My watch counted off the seconds, ticking quietly as I waited.

There's a litany of things I dislike about magic. It starts with the people who use it, more or less. Sorcerers. Necromancers. Cultists and other crazy fuckers, all of them, willing to do a deal with something from the depths of the Gloom, trading off bits of their humanity in exchange for the ability to break the rules of science. Guys like Michael Wotan, who kept Adelaide in his grip. Forged it into a place of cathedrals and serial killers, serving his own ends.

I didn't like the practice of doing magic any better than the people. It involved too much risk, too much ritual, too much chanting. And it involved a whole damn lot of waiting, just to get what you needed done.

I put the bullet on the edge of the circle, watched the lead tip come alight. We'd trapped Michael Wotan's soul in the lead, held it there after I'd put two bullets in his chest, another two in his skull. The only way to kill a necromancer and have them stay dead, once they've spent enough time leaching off a city known for death. Siphon out the soul. Keep it somewhere safe.

I started chanting, let the words weave into the darkness. One by one, the lights running down the tunnel flickered and died away. Strands of shadow spread along the walls, a web of darkness growing thicker, growing stronger and more tangible. Tenebrous strands clawed their way free of the tunnel mouth, reaching out to cover the scant few feet between me and the entryway. Tendrils of darkness coiled around the bullet, testing the limits of the ward.

The candles flickered. Threatened to go out. I kept chanting, my voice steady. Watched the shadows spill out of the tunnel, growing thicker and deeper as they bulged and folded over one another. The hiss of car tires stopped; time ground to a halt. The edge between light and darkness became a physical thing, a border where the eddies and currents of the Gloom were visible.

I spoke Michael Wotan's name three times.

Settled in, amid the eerie silence, to wait for his ghost to appear.

A lean, haggard face appeared in the depths of the shadow. Hollow cheeks covered in three-day growth, the right eye-socket empty and cavernous. It floated just beyond the limits of the ward, hovering low enough to focus on the bullet and the blue-white spark of the soul within. I took my time studying it, trying to be sure. Feeding the wrong ghost was rarely a good idea, and the features seemed to shift beneath my gaze. It was like trying to identify a corpse that floated beneath the surface of the water.

I unfolded the blade on a pocket knife, nicked my thumb with the point. Placed pressure on the cut until a small bead of blood formed. The single eye moved from the bullet for the first time since the ghost appeared, alert to the blood's presence. I pushed my hand through the ward, bare flesh going numb as it hit the chill of the Gloom. The ghost's dark lips suckled against my cold skin, sucking at the small bead of life-force. Features grew solid, distinct. They looked much like the man I'd killed in Adelaide.

I pulled my hand back. Rubbed warmth into it, best I could.

Michael Wotan's single, ghostly eye fixed itself on me. "It didn't need to be your blood."

"Yeah, well, I didn't have any corpses handy, and I don't kill stray cats just to talk to former targets," I said. "My blood is what's on offer, mate. Take it or leave it."

The ghost considered me, the red point of its good eye burning through the darkness. It wasn't all of Wotan. Couldn't be, so long as I kept his soul trapped tight in the bullet. This was just a figment of the man, a memory given form by the shadows of the Gloom.

That didn't make him any less devious.

"Another drop, then. You can spare another drop, yes?" The ghost ran a tongue along the dark mass of its lips. "Call it a sign of good faith. Placate the part of me that remembers you and a gun."

I wrapped my fingers around my thumb. "I don't give a damn what you remember."

"If that were true, you wouldn't have called me forth." His face rose up, brushing close to the ward. Favoured me with a cold smile. "Tell me what you want, little wizard."

"There's something dangerous loose in my city. I believe it's a valkyrie." I tapped a finger against the tip of the bullet, let the soul light flare in response to my touch. "I believe your death set that in motion. I want to know how to stop it."

"Of course you do," Wotan said. "The alternatives would prove unpleasant."

"I assume you had a contingency," I said. "Long as you lived, there would have been all kinds of outs."

A cold smile formed on the ghost's lips. "You'll notice I'm not holding a grudge," Wotan said. "That's important, Keith Murphy. You killed me, more or less, and that's inconvenient, but you get used to these things in my line of work. You outran the initial death curse, which suggests you're moderately adroit and aware of how dangerous the path you're on can be. You've consulted seers and tapped sources of power, so you've prepared yourself for a fight. Your circle is weaker than it should be, and I choose not to probe or attempt to break it down. I choose not to fight you, Keith Murphy, brief as our struggle would be. I want you to understand that."

I nodded. Waited.

"Give me blood," Wotan said. "And we'll talk."

I squeezed another drop from my thumb, pressed it against the ward. The ghost's tongue brushed against my skin, cold and feathery and distinctly unpleasant.

"Enough," I said.

Wotan's ghost continued to suckle, trying to draw free another bead. I jerked my hand and ghost went to follow, came up against the ward. All four candles flickered, the barrier holding firm.

The lean, wolfish smile reappeared on the ghost's face. "You really think this will stop me, little wizard?"

"I think it'll do the job." I bunched my numb fingers into a fist, worked some life back into them. "You're not the real Michael Wotan. You're just a fraction of him, a memory of him that floats through the Gloom. Everything that made you dangerous is down there, caged and bound in that bullet."

The dark, cold eyes dropped down to stare at the bullet at my feet. I clicked my fingers, drawing its attention up once more.

"Here's what you can get, shade. You can tell me what the valkyrie is doing here, and I'll feed you a third drop of blood that will sustain you for a little while longer. You can tell me why it's killing bikers instead of me, and maybe you'll earn a fourth."

The ghosts eye widened a little, betraying his surprise. He didn't know about the Rebels.

"Or you can shit me, tell me nothing," I said, "and I'll let you dissolve back into the shadows. You exist because I allow you to exist. "

The ghost smirked.

"And if I tell you nothing?" Wotan said. "Do you know what happens then, Keith Murphy? You die. Your friend who drew that circle dies. Your friend Roark dies. Your family dies. Every woman you ever loved, every friend you ever cared for, all those people you pass in the street every day. Everyone, everywhere, ends up dead and their souls are whisked away by the servants of Ragnarok. I made pacts with ancient things, elder gods and giants, the kind of Other that lie dormant in the heart of the Gloom because humankind no longer believes in anything that terrible. When I died, they stirred in their slumber. If I stay dead too long, they wake."

The ghost grew closer to the ward.

"You want to stop Ragnarok, Keith Murphy? You missed that chance. My followers came here. They sought a means of raising me from the dead. You eliminated them, one by one, and now the Fimblewinter approaches and the angels of the Apocalypse hunt for my killer. Once they find him, once they take vengeance upon the man who caused my death, the end of the world will begin in earnest."

The ghost flung itself at the ward, spectral hands clawing at the barrier. Dark streaks formed in the barrier, candle light flickering and threatening death.

"Do you really think I care about nothingness, Keith Murphy?" The ghost shrieked. "Against the weight of all that's coming, do you really think your petty threats are going to sway me to your side?"

"No," I said, "I really didn't."

I closed my eyes, ignored the ghost's wail. Recited the chant to dismiss the Gloom and make the ward unnecessary. Wotan's shade threw itself against the barrier, trying to break free, but Langford's work held.

My chanting reached its crescendo, and all four candles were snuffed in unison.

I stood there, in the darkness. Ordinary, untouched by magic, and dangerous in its own way. One by one, the lights in the underpass came on. Eventually the traffic on the highway started up, the wet hiss of car tyres on bitumen letting me know the danger was passed.

LIFE LESSONS

LANGFORD DROVE ME back to the Casino, dropped me out front without saying a word. I thanked her, and she nodded once. Bailed on the scene before the demons came out to ask questions. I didn't really blame her. She didn't trust Sabbath. Barely trusted me. The only reason she still agreed to help out is because the end of the world gets people's attention, and no one wants to be on the wrong side of the process.

I caught the lift to the fourteenth floor. Listened to a woman in a gold lamé dress tell her partner about the problems with playing blackjack. It seems she didn't trust the dealers much, assumed they were rigging the games. Her partner just stood there, nodding. Flashed me that apologetic look quiet people give when they're trapped in an elevator with a talker.

We hit my floor. The elevator chimed and I stepped out. The woman and her partner still had another three floors to go. I bet she talked through all of them.

I found Wesna loitering outside my room. Leaning against the wall, arms crossed, her suit jacket folded and draped over one shoulder. She didn't look up as I came down the hall, waited for me to slide the key in the lock before asking, "How'd it go?"

I stood there, in front of my door. Thought about the answer. "Well," I said, "You were right."

Wesna nodded. Unfolded her arms and pushed off the wall. When I opened the door and stepped inside, she came into the room after me. "The ghost tell you why it's going after the Rebels?"

"No, but I don't think that's him." I threw my jacket on the bed. Dug round underneath for the box I used to store Wotan's bullet. "According to him, the valkyrie's after my blood before the world ends—it's payback for killing him, near as I can tell—but he's out of agents to work this side of things. With the Raven cult gone—"

"You're putting together theories."

I found the box, returned the bullet. Slid it under my bed once more. “You forget what it’s like to be mortal,” I said. “We don’t like uncertainty. Theories are all that’s keeping me sane, in the face of all this.”

Wesna went very quiet. Watched me, from her place by the window, her eyes cold and hard. She wasn’t happy with me. I’d said something stupid, crossed a line I didn’t know about. I stood and adjusted the fit of my holster. We stared at each other.

“Do you know what I remember about being mortal, Murphy?” Wesna crossed the room, stood just inside my reach. “I remember being jealous that you saw things, and I didn’t. That you got a way out, and I didn’t. I remember being pissed that a little piss-ant like you, too scared to really be a fighter, got all the attention. It’s easy to remember that. Possession brings out the worst in a mortal.”

She reached for my SIG. Pulled it free and slid the clip out of the gun. Tossed both onto the bed, one at a time.

“It’s harder to remember why we were friends,” she said. “Those moments when you weren’t being a prick. When the two of us hung out, or worked together, or had fun. Those times when it was you and me against the world, and the world was a far more dangerous place than anyone else knew.”

She stepped closer to me. Leaned towards me until I could feel her warm breath against my face.

“She clings to that, Murphy. The part of me that was mortal once, she clings to those memories of you, you little shit. Not her family, not her friends, just you. That’s how she thinks she’ll stay in the fight, even though that fight’s already over. And she hates the fact that I’m telling you this, and hates what might come next, but she can’t stop me Murphy. ‘Cause you’re a fucking miserable prick, and you keep trying to beat those good memories out of her.”

She pushed the holster rig off my shoulders; let the whole thing fall to the carpet. Slid a hand down my ribs, let it rest against my hip. “Do you know what’s going to happen, Murphy? On the day I finally extinguish the last of those happy recollections and leave me in here, dominant and guided by her baser impulses?"

I pushed back, made some space between us. "Yeah, I think I can guess."

"Good." Wesna gave a throaty laugh, backed off a few steps. "Then perhaps you want to stop making cracks about what it's like to be mortal. One of us has a much better idea about the difference between human and not; let's assume it's the person who has something to contrast the experience against."

She retreated to the chair, picked up her jacket. Slid it on and straightened her cuffs, professional and calm. "I'm going to go inform Sabbath that your suspicions were correct. You're going to take Finn, start looking into whoever helped the Rebels summon this thing. That's your first priority."

I let out a short breath. Reached for the SIG to reload and slide it into the drawer beside my bed. "I can do that," I said. "The valkyrie's going to find me, sooner or later."

"I'm pretty sure she already has," Wesna said. "We want answers to the other mystery. Tomorrow, you're going to talk to what's left of the Rebels with Finn, see if you can figure out where the Kodiak's gone hiding."

I nodded. "You sure we should wait til tomorrow?"

"You're tired," Wesna said. "You've just done the kind of magic that gets described as big and stupidly risky. Get some sleep, Murphy. You're safe enough, here, if the valkyrie attacks."

SHAZZA

THE TRIP UP into theme park country took about a half hour. We just followed the highway, turned right after Movieworld. Followed the road over a scrub-covered hill until we found ourselves a housing estate nestled in a hollow. They were everywhere, this far north. Selling the ideal of Gold Coast living on a budget, without ever putting you close to the beach. Finn drove us into the estate. They'd built all the houses off the same plan and looked the same. They were still new, still pristine. Their only distinguishing marks were the number on the letter box, the colour of the front door, and the car of the driveway.

"Kodiak's old lady lives out here," Finn said. His fingers tapped a pattern on the wheel, drumming to some riff I couldn't hear. "They bought in the early days, before the estate built up around them. Charming fucking place to live."

He took a left, eased down the narrow street. There were kids out on the front lawns, tussling over a football. Pushbikes were dumped in a pile on the nearest driveway. They stopped playing, watched us drive past. "Charming."

We took another turn. Another left, two rights. Deep enough into the tangle of the estate to make finding our way out difficult. Finn kept his mouth shut, parked us out front of a small, grey house in the heart of the estate. I checked the number, twenty-three, and the green door. Nothing in the driveway but a few oil stains on the concrete.

"Might want to let me knock," Finn said. "Shazza has a reputation."

"Maybe she dislikes the nickname?"

Finn rolled his eyes. "You want to do this?"

I held up both hands, let him make the approach. Took position just behind his right shoulder while he rapped his knuckles against the screen door.

"Shaz," he shouted. "Shaz, mate, it's Finn. We've gotta talk to you 'bout Cody."

The walls muffled sound from inside the house, made it hard to tell what was happening. We waited. Traded glances. When the front door jerked open, the first thing we noticed was the gun barrel. A twenty-two rifle, pointed at Finn's chest. The woman doing the pointing was slight, five-three and bottle blond, hair pulled back into a pony tail. Torn jeans and a faded Zepplin t-shirt promising a stairway to heaven. She looked about twenty-four. Handled the rifle like she knew how to use it.

"Cody says you ain't welcome 'round here no more, Irish," she said. "So how 'bout you and your friend fuck off, 'fore I start making some phone calls an' all."

Finn shook his head. "How 'bout you put the gun down and we have a chat, eh?"

"You really think I won't shoot you, Irish?" The rifle hitched a little, braced against her shoulder. More bluff than common sense. The screen door limited options, but the rifle was a long-range weapon. It was easy to grab for, easy to redirect if you get into hand-to-hand. Hard for the shooter to adjust, if the target ducked and weaved.

Still, I admired her guts. "It's not that he doesn't think you'll shoot," I said. "It's just that he doesn't care if you hit him or not."

The woman glanced at me, paid attention for the first time. Finn offered her a shit-eating grin, latched his fingers on the latticework covering the screen door.

"Listen, Sharon—it is Sharon, isn't it?"

She nodded, mute. Attention still focused on Finn.

"Sharon," I repeated. "I'm not sure how much your boyfriend told you, but the twenty-two isn't a threat to Finn anymore. If you hit him—and at this range, no matter how shit-hot your aim, odds are good you're going to miss—but if you hit him, it'll slow him down for maybe two seconds before he recovers and rips your throat out."

She looked me over. "I know you?"

"Not at all."

"Then you should probably shut your yap, seeing as you're friends with this arsehole."

I shrugged, stepped away from Finn. "Friends isn't the word I'd use."

"You're on my property together."

"Necessity," I said. "Calling Finn a friend suggests that I actually like him. I don't. He's too much of an arsehole, as you've noted, and there's something distinctly unsavoury about him. He approaches every problem like a hammer and spends half his time breaking thumbs."

Her eyes narrowed. She adjusted her grip on the rifle. "You're a man who likes words, aren't you?"

"I find them useful, from time to time."

"Yeah, for covering up bullshit."

"I only wish that were the case." I closed my eyes, exhaled sharply. "Finn, get the gun."

I felt him move, surging forward. The loud crack of the rifle echoed in the entryway, deafening me and the woman. Probably didn't do Finn any favours, although he moved like it didn't matter. He hit the screen door, punched through it. Ignoring the blood streaming from his shoulder, the flesh already knitting together and covering the bullet wound. He wrapped a fist around the rifle barrel, jerked it sideways. Sharon's next shot went into the ceiling. Punched a hole in the white plaster.

When I opened my eyes, Sharon was on the floor and Finn held the rifle. He held the weapon pointed at his victim, barrel pressed against her skull. I let myself through the screen door, pulled him away, and relieved him of the weapon. Finn stayed crouched over the woman, dangerous even without a weapon.

Sharon didn't stare. Didn't stutter or go into shock. She just glared at Finn. "Shit," she said, "you went to their side, didn't you? That's what Cody was on about, when he started giving warnings."

"If it helps, Finn didn't have much choice." I opened the rifle, emptied the ammunition. Discarded the weapon as I crouched beside the fallen woman. "Possession needs to be consensual, before a demon slips in beneath the skin, but they can make it seem awful tempting. My boss tortured Finn, played upon his own ambitions, made siding with Sabbath's organisation seem like the superior option."

"And you're, what, his handler? You lead him around like a fucking attack dog?"

"Depends on the day," I said. "And what we're trying to handle. Right now, we're looking for Cody Patton. Finn seems to think you know where he might be."

She set her jaw. Said nothing. Her eyes stayed on Finn.

"Finn?"

His head jerked upright, eager for the order to tear her apart.

"I'd like you to step outside, Finn."

He pouted a little. "Come on, Murphy."

"Fuck off," I said. "Go wait in the car. Make sure we're not attracting cops."

He sneered, showing off an incisor, but he did what I asked. When the screen door slammed shut behind him, I stepped back to give her some breathing room. "I don't want to hurt you, and I don't want to hurt Kodiak. Finn'll do it, if he gets to your fella first, 'cause that's the way he deals with problems. I prefer a precise approach—identify the problem, figure out the best way to eliminate it, do so with minimal casualties."

"And doesn't that sound spiffy." She risked pushing herself upright, lurching into a seated position. "You're the guy who does the job with a bullet, instead of ripping people apart with your fingernails, huh? Good for you."

"No," I said, retrieving my weapon. "I'm the guy who isn't possessed. If you shoot me, I end up in a pool of blood on your floor. If I find your husband, he's got a fighting chance. More importantly, I'm the guy who actually gives a shit about the consequences of this war. Kodiak brought something into this world. Something that shouldn't be here. It killed the rest of the Rebels before we could get there. It's the reason he's in hiding right now."

I held up the rifle in both hands, let her see it wasn't aimed in her direction. Put it down against the bench behind me, covered with photographs. "I can't guarantee you Kodiak is getting out of this alive. Against me, he's got a chance. Against Finn and his kind, he's got less. Against the thing that's chasing him..."

Sharon didn't answer. She wanted to trust me. I could see that in her face. Weird shit had started infiltrating her life, eroding her sense of control. I knew that feeling, know how tempting it could be when someone came along and talked like they understood the things you didn't. She was a woman who liked control.

"Here's the deal I'm offering: tell me where Kodiak is and I'll go in alone," I said. "No Finn. None of the other possessed in Sabbath's entourage. Just me and a gun and Kodiak with whatever he's shacked up with. If I get to him, I'll make him an offer that'll keep him alive. Everything that happens after that is up to him."

She jerked her chin towards the front door. "He's never going to go for that."

"He doesn't need to," I said. "Demons have rules, same as everyone else. Not many, I'll grant you, but if I make this promise, they'll respect it. They've got no choice."

She stared at me, weighing the options. Her eyes dropped to my SIG in its holster, hovered there for a few moments. She expected me to start threatening her again. Expected me to put a bullet into her, eventually. I kept my hands well away from the gun and sat down on one of the leather couches.

Her eyes drifted to the rifle. Did the math on reaching it, re-loading it, and firing. Figured out I'd cut her off before she could complete the first part of the plan. That was the end of it. The moment she gave in.

"Few weeks ago, he came home talking about this guy he met," she said. "Went by the name of Black. He offered Kodiak all kinds of help, explained why the Rebels weren't able to go toe-to-toe with your lot. It got Kodiak all excited, you know?"

She paused and shook her head.

"Sometimes, Cody, he isn't that smart. Lets himself get run by his ego, you know? Always wanting to be a little bigger. I told him it was stupid, tried to get him to back out of things. I knew a few things, yeah? I mean, I worked this club down in the Cross a few years back, learned the hard way our boss wasn't really *on the level.* He made me an offer. I went the other way."

She closed her eyes. Shuddered at the memory. "I saw what happened when things got ugly, didn't want to get between something like that again. Told Kodiak he needed to prepare for things to get bad, if he went with Black's plan. Told him he'd need somewhere safe to hole up if shit got real."

"Hopefully he listened to you."

She nodded, quietly. "A friend of his has a farm, out on the Downs," she said. "Three hour drive, if you don't get car sick."

"This friend got a name?"

"Pillman," she said. "Mick Pillman. Odds are, if things went south, Kodiak is hiding out there."

I nodded. Filed the name away. "What about this guy, Black? The one who helped Kodiak out?"

"All I ever had was a name," she said. "Kodiak talking shit about how Black was going to teach the Rebels everything they needed to know. Talked on the phone a lot. Never came around to the house."

I stood up. Nodded. "If he'd done that," I said, "you'd have warded your house against intruders like Finn."

I headed for the door. Sharon Patton stood, moved to follow me. Finn's growl gave her away, forced her to pause at the doorway.

"Stay inside," I said. "Your house is no protection against what's after Kodiak. Neither is your gun. I suggest you find some way of fixing that, once I'm out of here. I can hold Finn back for a while, but he'll come looking for revenge before too long. He's an eye for an eye kind of guy, these days."

Sharon met my gaze. Didn't budge. "Nah," she said. "I'm coming with you."

"I kinda doubt that," I said.

"Then I'll see you six or seven hours, when you try to find Kodiak and fail," she said. "Pillman doesn't know you, but he knows trouble's coming. Without a familiar face, he's just going to fuck with you. If I come along, I'm a familiar face."

She folded her arms. Waited. Eyes planted on Finn as he leered through the screen door.

"Besides," she said. "If you leave me here, with him, I'm more-or-less dead, right?"

I looked at her. Looked at Finn.

"Yeah," I said. "I suppose you're right."

ROAD TRIP

THE TRIP OUT to Inglewood took the better part of four hours. I left Finn behind, grumbling. Told him to cab his way back to the Casino, let Sabbath know what'd happened. Figured they'd know to fill in the gaps, if I didn't return within twenty-four hours. I put Sharon in the driver's seat, kept watch for anything stupid. She kept her cool. Drove normal. The shit with Finn had her rattled worse than anything I could do.

Inglewood wasn't a big place. Farms lined the roadway into town. No doubt they'd line the roadway all the way out. In the middle there were a cluster of buildings: service stations, a handful of stores selling local crafts and furniture, catering to the tourists who thought driving the hinterland was fun; a public school, a catholic school, some pubs, and a handful of churches. GPS put the Pillman farm a few kilometres outside of town. We followed the roads, drove through fields that should have been filled with sunflowers. Halfway through spring and there were no signs of crops growing. Frost got to them, killed them off. Left field after field of neatly-ploughed rows, patched with the handful of greenery where something struggled to stay alive.

Pillman's farm wasn't doing any better than the others. We took a right at the front gate, followed the kilometre long driveway up to the house. The fields were neat, wet rows of earth. A pair of cows, piebald and rugged up in canvas jackets, watched the car roll past their pen. Pillman was out front, working on his Ute. He emerged as we pulled up, wiped his hands on a pair of grubby jeans.

He was a big man; taller than me by a couple of inches, bearded and pot-bellied, with muscle sheathed in fat. He still carried a wrench as he stepped away from the Ute, closing the distance between us. Nothing threatening about it, but I knew it was there.

Sharon climbed out of the car first. Called Pillman's name. He ignored her, focused his attention on me. Spat into the grass, scratching his beard with the edge of the wrench. "I don't know you," Pillman said. "Don't much like having strangers on my land 'n' all."

"He's a friend, Pillman," Sharon said.

"Friend's don't walk onto a man's land trying to hide a gun," Pillman said. "Friend's usually give a man warning that they're coming."

"We didn't have much time for a warning." I eased back my jacket, gave him a look at the SIG holstered on my hip. "If this makes you nervous, I can leave it in the car. I don't want to cause any trouble here. I just want to talk to your friend, maybe get him out of the jam he's in. Get him out of your house, even, before unpleasant people come around."

Pillman's eyes narrowed. He dropped his gaze to the gun, focused on it for a couple of moments. He nodded. "Given what Kodiak's been saying, trusting strangers who show up armed doesn't exactly seem like it'll help him out."

"Trusting strangers who show up promising things is how all this got started," I said. "He's playing in a whole new league now, and he doesn't know the rules. I'm offering to help, keep him alive a little while longer. Whatever he did, back at his clubhouse, it brought something bad into the neighbourhood."

Pillman chewed that over, wrench tapping a pattern against his thigh.

"I can help him stop it," I said, "if he's willing to let me. Assuming we got here before the thing that came flying out here to find him."

The wrench stopped moving.

"And who the fuck are you," Pillman said. "That you can ride in like the man who fixes everything."

"He's a friend of Black's," Sharon said, lying through her teeth. "Cody tell you 'bout Black, Pill?"

"Yeah," Pillman said, his voice dark and angry. "Seems to me Cody was a damned sight happier before he ever heard that name."

"Him and me both," I said, "but he can still back out. This hasn't sunk its teeth into him. No need for it to pull him apart."

Pillman thought it through. Nodded. Jerked his chin towards a dirt road leading west from his farmhouse. "There's a shack about five paddocks out that way," he said. "Old place my grandpa used when he had some local drovers through. He's hiding there. Laying low. Doing fuck knows what to the place, trying to keep the devil out."

Pillman paused and spat into the grass again, narrowly missing the dog. "I think he's going crazy, sitting out there alone, but he ain't exactly open to me visiting. Threatened me with a shotgun, last time I tried." He shook his head. "Wish you better luck than I had, yeah?"

I knew we were too late before we even went inside.

There was no door on the drover's shack. It'd been torn free, left sitting on the overgrown grass beside the front deck. The hands that did the tearing had gouged the door frame, torn the hinges free. I had one hand out, stopping Sharon from getting closer. She didn't like that. She wanted to be in there, checking on Kodiak, making sure he was okay. The only reason she didn't fight me was the assumption that her presence wouldn't help, and Kodiak was already gone.

I freed the SIG from its holster, eased my way towards the door. Sharon followed, right on my heels, until I stopped and waved her back to the car. She hesitated, eyes still on black space where the door should be. I waved again, dropping into a crouch, and this time she complied. I edged closer, put my back to the wall. Stood beside the open doorway and listened. Heard nothing. Smelled nothing but dirt and trees and unwashed dishes left to soak in the sink. I looked back, caught Sharon's stare. Nodded once, to reassure her, before I edged my head 'round the door and peered in.

He'd put up a fight, before he went down. There wasn't much in the shack——a small kitchen table, two chairs, a fridge—but everything bore holes where it'd caught a spray of buckshot. Bloodstains, too. Dark smears on the floor and the wall, where the valkyrie had entertained herself, played with Kodiak the same way a cat plays with a cockroach. The shotgun lay by the door into the second room, discarded there when Kodiak realised he needed more than a gun.

I picked my way through the carnage, checked the bedroom. Kodiak's corpse on the floor, lying in a dark pool of his own blood. Eyes open. Face contorted. His t-shirt, jacket, and stomach all hanging in shreds where the valkyrie's claws did their work. He'd attempted to protect himself, here, at least. There were wards painted on the walls, crude and half-formed, barely up to the task of keeping out the weakest entities of the Gloom, let alone the thing that'd come to chase him down. I swore softly, knelt beside the corpse. Checked the tattoos that covered his arms and chest, recognised some familiar signs.

I sighed. Steadied myself. Regulated my breathing. Let my vision slip, just for a moment, and check things with my other sight.

The ink in the centre of Kodiak's chest writhed like it was a living thing, the Gloom-tainted ink struggling to break free of the skin. I lowered my hand towards that tattoo, watched the flesh bulge towards my skin. Whatever magic the Kodiak had inked into his skin, it reacted to my presence like—

I took a breath. Swore. Let my vision return to normal. Felt the headache thundering in, right on fucking schedule. The truth settled around me like bags of wet cement, building up a fortification between me and panic. The Rebels attacked me, took hair out of my scalp. No doubt they could scrape my blood off their shoes, once they had the idea in their heads and shit. It was enough to ink themselves with a little of my essence, make themselves living decoys when the valkyrie hit town. Sacrifices to keep me safe, for a little while, at least.

No one was dumb enough to do that voluntarily, but there were plenty of ways you could trick 'em into it, if you were willing to be that kind of asshole. I leant over the Kodiak's body, pulled free his wallet and phone.

I heard footsteps on the front veranda. Sharon letting her curiosity get the better of her nerves. "That's a lot of blood," she yelled, her voice wavering. "Christ, Murphy, that's a lot of blood, yeah?"

"Yeah, it is." I pulled free Kodiak's wallet, tucked it into my jacket. His cell phone followed, along with the keys to his bike. I listened to Sharon's uncertain footsteps as she crossed the small room, pausing at the bedroom door.

"Shit, that's—" her voice cracked, gave in to grief. "Christ, Murphy, we had a deal."

"This wasn't Sabbath."

"Bull."

"No bull." I pointed at the walls. "Those wards aren't great work, but they would have kept this place safe from your average demon. A guy like Finn, he wouldn't be able to push in here."

Sharon nodded, not really processing the words. Just letting the emotions hit, knocking her through the stages of grief. She pushed past me, knelt down beside her husband. "You stupid prick," she said. "You stupid, useless prick."

I gave her a moment. Put my hand on her shoulder. "Come on. We've gotta move."

"Like hell."

"Sharon—"

"He's my husband," she said. "Give me a minute, yeah?"

"No," I said, hauling her to her feet. "That's not how this works. Kodiak is dead, which means something killed him. Something that may well still be in the area, looking for more fleshy bags of blood to have some goddamn fun with."

"He's dead, Murphy."

"Then there's nothing I can do to help him," I said, "and I've got everything I need. You want to stay, you can stay, but I'm out of here before the valkyrie comes looking."

"What about Kodiak?"

"He's dead," I said. "I've seen all I need to. Now let's—"

"No," Sharon said. "What about his ghost."

"His soul is gone," I said. "The valkyrie took it."

"I don't believe you."

"You don't have to believe me." I turned and picked my way through the carnage, heading for the car. It was already getting dark outside, shadows growing long as the sun set behind the hills. Night wasn't our friend, not out in the open. Too few places to hide, too many shadows the valkyrie could use for transport.

I paused at the front door, looked back towards the bedroom. "You coming?"

Sharon appeared, eyes wet, scrubbing her nose with the back of her hand. She joined me out on the grass, didn't bother looking back. She settled into the passenger seat, eyes front the entire way.

"You going to call him?" she said.

"Who?"

"This Black guy who fucked with Kodiak," she said. "You took his phone, right? You figure the contact's there?"

I slid the key into the ignition, fired up the engine. "Yeah, I'll call him."

"I want to be there," she said. "I want to know why this happened."

"The answers don't help."

"Cody's dead," she said. "Nothing much is going to help, yeah?"

"Yeah."

"Then I'll take what I can get," she said. "Make the damn call."

I nodded. Fished the phone out of my pocket with my free hand, kept the other on the wheel. I scrolled through the short-list of names on Kodiak's call list, found the one repeated number that didn't have an ID attached. Then I thought through the tattoo, the one shared by Kodiak and the dead Rebels out at the club house.

"Sharon?"

"Yeah?"

"The new ink Cody had? On his chest?"

"He said it'd keep him safe." She snorted. "Idiot, I guess."

"He the only one who did it?"

Sharon Patton went very quiet.

"Nah," she said. "He made a couple of the boys do it. The ones he wanted kept safe. Said the design was a gift from Black."

I nodded. Things were settling into place, making an unpleasant kind of sense. "And you?"

"Yeah," she said. "I had my doubts, but he wanted me safe too."

I swore. Let her climb behind the wheel. "Drive fast, then," I said. "We really don't want to be out here."

SIXTEEN YEARS, NINE MONTHS

I DIALLED BLACK'S number. Felt confident I knew who'd be on the far end. It was exactly his kind of play, using one set of scum to upset the other. Sacrificing some to keep others safe. The phone rang out, then again when I redialled. On the third call, someone answered, the voice deep and familiar.

"Mister Kodiak?"

"Afraid not."

He recognised my voice. We'd talked on the phone a hundred times. Worked together long enough that it'd take more than a fake name to distract us.

"Keith," he said.

"Roark."

"Took your fucking time," he said. "Working for Sabbath made you soft, kid."

"Slow, maybe. Not soft."

"Where's Kodiak?"

"Dead," I said. "Looks like something from the deep parts of the Gloom mistook him for me, a few days back."

Roark paused. Sucked on his teeth. "Alright," he said. "You'd better come see me. This is going to move up my timeline a little."

The address Roark gave me was down in Burleigh Heads, one of the cheaper blocks of flats on the waterfront, just down from the park where the local ferals gathered to beat drums and spin fire every Sunday evening. I parked in the street, climbed out of the car. Sharon followed me, gave the flats a wary look. Two stories, ugly brown brickwork, tinted windows over grey louvers. Beach towels hung over the balcony rails on the top floor, surfboards and wetsuits taking up the available space.

I pointed at the flat on the bottom right. "That's the one."

She didn't look convinced, but the first brush of Roark's protective wards convinced her. She hesitated at the front gate, pushed herself over the threshold. Spent the short walk from the gate to the front door trying to brush something free of her skin. "Jesus," she said. "That feels horrible."

"That's what proper defences do," I said. "If you'd been Finn or one of Sabbath's demons, you'd be stuck out there, at the gate, writhing in agony."

"'Cept I ain't a demon."

"No, but you've touched their world. Brush up against magic and it leaves a taint." I knocked on the door, shouted: "Hey, it's me."

Roark opened the door, squinted over my shoulder. "You brought along a stray."

"Her name's Sharon. You just got her husband killed."

Roark studied her, eyes glassy. "You shouldn't have brought her, Keith."

"Then you tell her to fuck off and give her the cab fare to get home," I said. "Home, where she lived with Kodiak, unwarded, despite there being a valkyrie on the loose and snacking on bikers. Home where Sabbath's demons know how to find her and make her an object lesson about the perils of crossing the big dog, since they can't hurt her husband anymore."

Roark scowled. Exhaled through his nose. He was an old, cranky fucker; had been since we first met.

"She's got one of the tattoos," I said. "The one you gave Kodiak to 'protect' his men."

We stood there, staring at one another. Waiting for someone to give in. Roark gave first.

"Alright," he said. "Come in, the pair of ya. I'll make ya some fuckin' tea."

Roark's flat smelt of stale cigarettes and leftover pizza, same as every other safe-house the two of us had set up in. It covered the scent of blood that tended to linger in the air, legacy of the wards he set up upon moving in, and often provided some relief from the mold growing on the walls and ceiling. Roark aimed low, when it came to finding a place to stay; said we'd grown so used to overlooking the poor that it didn't take much magic to encourage others to look the other way.

Sharon sat in the lounge chair, watching Roark in the kitchen. She wasn't impressed by the flat and she wasn't impressed by the sorcerer. I didn't really blame her. Roark cultivated a look that made it easy to dismiss him as just another aging crank: a thatch of white hair that didn't get cut often enough; a white beard that jutted from his chin and extended the length of his face; thin, angular features that came from eating too little and smoking too much. He nursed a rollie as he made our tea, exposing the tattoos that covered his right arm to the wrist.

"I made it far as Perth before the cult lost interest in me," Roark said. "Figure that's when they came out here, starting poking their nose into your business. You have my apologies for that, Keith. It wasn't how it was meant to go."

I shrugged. "Turned out okay."

"No, it didn't," Roark said. "You were meant to stay away from that prick."

"Yeah, well, I made some hard choices. And you weren't around."

The kettle whistled, and Roark busied himself pouring water over teabags. He spooned in sugar, mixed it with the spoon. Delivered the first cup to Sharon; mine came next, sugar free. Roark's mug contained a solid shot of whiskey, surreptitiously added before he settled into the free lounge chair.

"Miss Patton, I'm sorry about your husband," he said.

Sharon froze, teacup on its way to her mouth. "You're what?"

"I'm sorry," Roark said. "I gather, from the fact you're here, that you're at least partially aware of what's out there. The Kodiak had placed himself into conflict with Sabbath, and through Sabbath, Keith. That ensured the valkyrie would find them, sooner or later, and I took steps to make that sooner in the name of preserving a valuable asset. Ordinarily, I'm loathe to involve others in a fight like this, but the stakes are considerably higher than I'd like."

"Yeah? How high is that?"

"Apocalyptic," Roark said. "In this case, Ragnarok."

Sharon raised an eyebrow and sipped her cup of tea. When she was done, she looked back at me. "Is he honestly talking about the end of the world?"

"Pretty much," I said.

"Jesus."

Roark snorted into his teacup. "If the apocalypse of Jesus Christ was starting, perhaps I'd worry less."

Sharon looked at me and Roark in turn. She wasn't sure how to take that, wasn't sure of much at all by this point. I just shrugged. Spend enough time with sorcerers and you get used to thinking about multiple eschatonic scenarios. Some were better for humanity than others, but none of them were good.

"So, you armed the Rebels with just enough magic to get the valkyrie's attention, and it focused on offing all of them instead on me and the demons." I put my teacup down. "That just means it's fed recently. It'll get stronger, smarter—"

"We want it smarter," Roark said. "Smarter means we can trick it."

"Sixteen years we worked together. How did I miss the fact that you were crazy as a cut snake?"

Roark produced his pouch of tobacco, started rolling himself a fresh cigarette. "Fucked if I know, kid. Maybe you just didn't pay attention."

"How you planning on taking out a valkyrie?"

"I got a plan," Roark said. "Beginnings of one, anyway. We'll need a couple of demons on board, but I figure you're positioned to figure out one or two children of darkness who'd be willing to help us out."

"Sure," I said. "All it'll cost me is a handful of souls."

"Don't be melodramatic, kid. They don't need souls." Roark licked the edge of his cigarette, pressed the paper together. "Whoever helps us is going to be the new top kick 'round these parts, slipping into Sabbath's position before his corpse is cold."

"Sabbath runs a tight crew," I said. "No one's dumb enough to cross him, even if the stakes are good."

"Sure there are," Roark said. "You've just gotta learn how to ask."

"Roark—"

"Kid, please." He held up one hand, focused on getting his cigarette lit. He took a long, deep breath and exhaled with something approaching contentment. "You've worked with them for nine months. I dare say you could identify those who are too far gone and those who are willing to take the risk. Ambition comes naturally to the entities of the Gloom, and there's always some who took the possession eagerly 'cause they wanted control over things."

"Fine," I said. "Then what?"

"Then we're going to use the valkyrie to eliminate Sabbath and free you from your promise," he said. "That's the first step."

"Yeah? What's the second?"

"That I'm still figuring out," Roark said. "Let's focus on freeing your soul, for now."

"My soul ain't traded away," I said. "I'm just pledged to work for the man, do whatever he asks of me."

"Your soul would have been a better deal," Roark said. "I'll be in touch, Murphy. Leave the girl here. It'll be safer for her."

PROTECTIVE COLOURATION

ROARK GAVE THE orders and I delivered. That's the way our partnership worked for the better part of sixteen years. He was the brains. I was the trigger. It felt good to have him back. To leave Sharon Patton sitting on his couch and drive away unfettered by the responsibility of keeping her safe. All I had to do was follow orders and play things cool, gather the intel Roark needed to instigate the next phase of his plan.

The rain had started while we were in Roark's flat, the clouds pelting the road with fat, stinging raindrops that left me soaked through by the time I reached the car. I sat in the driver's seat, cold and wet. Slid the key into the ignition and left it there, unturned. The wind whistled through the park between me and the beach, bending the palm fronds to its will. I cupped my palms together and breathed on them, trying to instil some warmth in my skin. It didn't work. Didn't help at all.

I caught a glimpse of myself in the rear view mirror. Wet. Cold. Thirty-six years old, with wet hair plastered over my face and the pale features of someone who didn't see enough sun. I scrubbed a hand through the wet thatch of hair, pulled it free of my eyes.

"This," I said. "This isn't good."

The face in the mirror gave me a lunatic grin. "Isn't this what you wanted, kid?"

Then the face in the mirror laughed. I was laughing too. Rain splattered the windshield. Tapped against the roof of the car. Lightning flashed in the distance, over the water, and the thunder rolled through a few seconds after.

I took a deep breath. Adjusted the rear view mirror, focused it so all I could see were the trees and the dark line of parked cars that lined the road. Exhaled slowly and checked the time. 2:44 AM. All the demons would be awake when I made it back to the casino.

"Just be cool," I told myself.

I turned the key in the ignition and put the car in gear.

There is no way to be cool when you're walking into a casino foyer in damp jeans and wet sneakers that squelch against the tiles. Even with the storm raging outside, staff and patrons alike looked up and shook their head at me, caught between amusement and sympathy for the stupid fucker who got caught in the rain without an umbrella. I stormed through, not bothering to hide the fact I was pissed. Most people kept their distance, but Finn broke free of the security guards working the front door and trailed me to the lifts. He caught up as I jammed my thumb against the button, stood beside me as I waited and glared at the doors.

"So," he said, grinning. "You want a towel or something?"

"I want a fucking shower," I said. "Followed by a few hours sleep in a warm fucking bed."

"Well, if you're lucky, you'll be getting one of those."

"I plan on taking both."

"Then revise you plans. The boss is still pissed with you, and you don't look like you've returned with good news."

"I return with news."

"The Kodiak's dead?"

I nodded.

"That's something, at least. What about his old lady?"

The lift chimed and the doors slid open. A Japanese couple stepped out, flashed me a bewildered look. I glared at them, pushed past to get into the lift. Finn apologised and directed them towards the gaming floor, one hand holding the lift open until he finished his conversation. When he was done, he let the doors close, turned towards me once more.

"Well?"

"Sharon Patton got away from me after the valkyrie attacked us."

"She got away alive?"

"Far as I know."

"Huh." Finn screwed up his face in a crude mockery of thinking. "Weren't you supposed to be some king shit assassin, Murphy? You seem to leave an awful lot of people walking away, still breathing."

We hit the twelfth floor and the doors slid open. I stood there, dripping on the carpet, watching Finn's shit-eating grin.

"This would be the part where you exit the elevator," he said.

I gave him the finger. Stepped into the twelfth floor hallway before the doors slid closed.

I spent close to twenty minutes soaking in the shower, running shampoo through my ragged hair and applying soap to the three-day growth on my chin. The hotel air-conditioning kept the room pleasantly warm, a stark contrast to the howling winds pelting a downpour against my window. I slid the disposable razor along each cheek, tested the shave with two fingers on my free hand and figured it would do. Rinsed and towelled off, unplugged the sink. Exited into my main bedroom with a towel around my waist.

Wesna sat on the double-bed, her dark hair clipped back behind her right ear. She glanced at my naked chest, smirked as her gaze rose to meet mine. I reached for a shirt, hauled it over my head. Kept the towel hitched against my hip bones as I searched for a pair of jeans.

"I liked it better when you knocked," I said.

"And I liked it better when you worked for us, instead of going freelance." Wesna crossed the room, pulled my spare pair of jeans out of the wardrobe. "Sabbath ordered these for you. They should be your size."

I glanced at the jeans, ran my thumb over the unfamiliar fabric. They were a dark, charcoal grey; softer than I was used too. "Sabbath ordered these?"

"Mostly he had orders given to the concierge, but the spirit is there."

"I didn't need new pants."

"There are plenty of people who'd disagree with you. We wanted to stop you coming into the casino looking like a hobo." Wesna shook her head, kicked at the damp clothes into a pile. "Put the pants on, Murphy. Sabbath wants to talk to you."

"I've been up close to twenty-four hours straight."

"So I'll order you a coffee to drink while we walk over to the club."

"Wes, come on, I've been—"

"I know Danny Roark is back in town."

She said it simply, like it was no big deal. I hesitated, one leg pushed through the dark jeans, mentally running through the list of weapons secreted in the room. Figured my best bet was the knife I'd slipped into place between the mattress and the bed, covered by the bedcovers and a minor glamour to keep the maids from noticing. That done, I went back to getting dressed, hoping she hadn't noticed my pause.

Wesna just stood at the bathroom door, arms folded. She slouched against the doorjamb, waiting, a smile teasing her lips. "I tracked him entering the city about two weeks back," she said. "He's been holed up down in Burleigh Heads, pretending no-one's noticed him. My suspicion is that he's connected to our current problems, if not the cause of them altogether."

She tilted her head back, smile growing a little broader. "How am I doing so far?"

I shimmied the jeans over my arse, slid the fly closed. "I don't know what you're talking about."

"A-huh." Wesna abandoned the bathroom doorway, settled into one of the suite's small seats instead. She produced a small phone, underhanded it my way. I caught it, brought the screen to life. It showed Roark standing at the doorway to his flat, cigarette smoke rising into the air as he painted a ward beneath the doormat. "That's dated over a week ago, just before we did the raid on the Rebel club house. He was providing them with information; my guess, he's the one who told them about the demons in Sabbath's employ."

I killed the image, tossed the phone back to Wesna. "He hasn't tried to contact me."

"You try to contact him?"

"Didn't even realise he was here until you showed me."

Wesna glanced down at her phone, slid it into her jacket pocket. She let her attention drift to the window, focusing on the storm. "You trying to bullshit me, Murphy?"

I buttoned up my shirt, ran my fingers through my hair. "Mostly I'm trying to figure out why Danny Roark ain't dead. Would have thought that's the first thing you tell Sabbath when shit starts going down."

"You're a professional, Murphy" Wesna said. "Don't pretend you're stupid."

"Right," I said. "You plan on using me for leverage."

"Not just you. I figure he's connected to the hippy with the dreads?"

"Langford?"

"If that's her name."

I nodded. No point in trying to hide it.

"The moment I tell Sabbath, he's going to order the old man shot," Wesna said. "That's going to take resources we don't have, given Roark's talents. Meanwhile we've got a city to hold and a winged bitch floating 'round out there, killing off our contacts. That makes Mister Roark a little secret between you and I, Keith."

She stood up, smoothed out the lines of her jacket. Offered me a cold, dead smile.

"I know what the old man's thinking: he's looking to eliminate Sabbath and free you from your promise, and that means working with someone who'll betray the boss and take over once Sabbath's gone. If that's the case, Murphy, you're going to send me. Until then, he's an ace in the hole. A little something I can give to Sabbath if I do something to earn his ire."

She stood and opened the door to my room. Waited there, arms folded, her expression stern. "Time to play things cool and pay attention for the signals," she said. "We'll get one shot at getting out, and I want you to be ready for it."

I stood and looked in the mirror, studied the effect of the outfit. Dark pants. Dark jacket. Dark shirt. I looked like Randall. Or Finn. Or Wesna. Another one of Sabath's boys, wearing the unofficial uniform. I couldn't tell if it was a victory for him or protective colouration for me.

"You look good," Wesna said.

"'Cause that's always been my goal," I said.

She raised an eyebrow. Hid a smile. Turned to check the hallways. "You'd better put on shoes," she said. "Sabbath wants to hear your report and he'll bitch like a motherfucker if you make him wait."

HOW TO PLAY THINGS COOL

CUDDY AND HIS crew were working overtime getting Hell Bar ready to open, which meant Sabbath hadn't left the place in over three days. I felt the soft tingle of wards against my skin when we crossed the threshold, a sign that Sabbath's sorcerers had been hard at work the night before. Going into the club with bad intentions would hurt like a motherfucker now, even if it wasn't opened yet.

We found Sabbath at the bar, studying blueprints, making notes. He was doing something to the Hell Bar that wasn't on-plan, but everyone assumed that. Like the wards, there were things you did because of the special clientele. Creatures with tastes for more than booze that needed looking after.

Wesna and I stood at his elbow, waited quietly. Sabbath ignored us for a minute, then led us to the back room to discuss things. Wesna stood by the door, watching the work crew do their thing, while I relayed all that had happened between hitting Sharon's place and the death of the Kodiak in the farmhouse. I omitted any mention of Danny Roark, left things with me returning to the casino after finding the body.

Sabbath sat there, fingertips pressed together, mouth pulled into a tight line. He listened to me talk, nodded at all the right places. When I stopped talking, he looked at me. I looked at him too, trying to stay nonchalant. Trying to look like just another one of his boys who'd toed the line and wore the uniform, black on black on black.

"You've had a busy night, then," Sabbath said.

I checked that line for booby traps, figured it was safe to respond. "Yeah, you could say that."

"Pity you survived it all."

"That's the part I was feeling good about."

"I've been thinking about that first attack, at your safehouse, a few days back." For a moment, Sabbath's lip curled and he thought about smiling. "It's a rare man who can survive an attack by an entity of the deep Gloom, let alone walk away unscathed."

"I'm good at what I do."

"Not that good." This time he did smile, but there wasn't any humour in it. "Roark may have trained you to be an excellent killer, but we're talking about an enemy far beyond his comprehension, let alone yours. That makes me suspicious, Keith. It makes me wonder what you're not telling me."

My chair tipped backwards and I found myself staring up at Wesna. She produced a knife, slid the point of the blade against my Adam's apple. Her expression gave away nothing.

Sabbath rested both elbows against his desk. "Is there something you're not telling me, Keith?"

"You really thought I was holding out, that knife would be in me already," I said.

Sabbath's nostril's flared. He nodded and Wesna let go. The chair went down hard, crashing into the concrete floor. I went with it, no way to roll with the impact. My shoulder hit the ground first. My head followed, teeth rattling as my skull bounced off the concrete. I lay there a moment, catching my breath. Wesna stood over me, expression calm. She folded her knife, returned it to her right pocket.

She looked up at Sabbath. "This isn't smart."

"Fun, though."

"Screw fun," she said. "There's something out there, hoovering up Rebels. Smart money says it's coming for us, sooner or later. I can beat on Keith all day if that gives you a hard on, but it's not the smart play."

"Noted," Sabbath said. "Pick him up."

Wesna knelt on the concrete. Grabbed my hair with her left hand, the chair with the right. Hauled both of us upright, set me down hard. Tore out a chunk of hair when she was done. I winced and rubbed my scalp. Glared at Sabbath.

"This isn't fucking necessary."

Sabbath rubbed his forefinger along the edge of his mouth. "Tell me what you learned about Black."

"Sorcerer," I said. "Ambitious. A little dangerous. Sounds like he's one of the Raven cult; some motherfucker we missed when we were wrapping things up with those boys, looking for some payback 'cause we fucked their shit up."

Sabbath's eyes narrowed. "I wouldn't have thought they had people capable of such magic, not after you eliminated their leadership."

I shrugged. "People slip through in any operation, no matter how thoroughly you take out the top. Someone knows a little more than you thought, or someone finds books and figures out all the shit their leaders weren't going to tell 'em."

Sabbath stared at me, perfecting his poker face.

"Cultists are like fucking roaches, you know?" I stretched my neck to one side, winced when it hurt. "You could nuke their fucking compounds and one of the little fuckers would survive and bring the thing back from the dead."

That brought a smile to his face. That smile said he didn't believe me, and he wanted me to know it. It said we were going to play things my way for a while, because Sabbath was in charge. He could have Wesna gut me any time. He could send Finn around to break my legs. He could send Randall out to do far, far worse.

"Alright," he said. "Let's say there's a cockroach out there. Why don't you get to work exterminating the little fucker?"

I nodded. Stood up. Sabbath watched me go, smile still locked in place.

"Keith?"

I stopped at the doorway. Turned around.

"Make sure you keep Finn close, this time. Don't run off alone. Don't make promises to housewives. There are dangerous things out there, yeah? We don't want you getting hurt."

ROACHES

I HUSTLED BACK over the highway, planted my arse in the casino bar. Waited for the bartender to bring me a double scotch—neat, no ice—to kill the dull ache in my skull. It didn't take long. Neither did the second glass. Say what you will about working for Sabbath, it got you good service at the bars where they knew him.

I was trying to figure out how to handle things. Stay cool. Keep my head down. Avoid letting Sabbath know there were people in town he'd rather not be here. Avoid letting Sabbath know that Wesna might be willing to betray him, if there was something in the deal that'd keep her from getting caught out.

I let the third glass of scotch touch the sides, slowed down a little once the bartender poured me another drink. The pleasant, heady buzz settled over me as I surveyed the bar, made a quick count of the demons and associated Other working the casino security. I stopped when I hit double digits, figured it was safer to start counting the mortals instead. Sabbath ran the casino like his own private kingdom, made sure he had talons in every pie available. He'd bought in early enough to make it possible, held his territory with the same jealousy big cats used to claim their hunting grounds.

It was quarter-to-five in the morning when Finn showed up, settling into the bar stool beside me. Slot machines sang their song from the gaming floor. The storm punctuated the chimes and squeals with the occasional burst of thunder. It was wet outside. Finn's hair was damp, curling against his skull. I was halfway through my fourth drink.

"Thought you were supposed to be sleeping," he said.

I raised my glass to him. "This is like sleeping."

"No, that's just being a motherfucker taking the easy way out." Finn flagged down the bartender, ordered himself a coffee. "I think I got you figured, new kid. You're willing to work for the boss, but you aren't sending your best self in to get things done. That's why we don't see king shit Danny Murphy when we're out in the fucking field. It's why Wes shits her pants over ya, despite the fact you're basically just a fuck-up."

I drained my scotch. Tipped the glass over and planted it on the bar. "When I sleep, I feel bad about things. It gives me bad dreams."

"Yeah, well, I've got some good news for you, new kid. Sometimes it doesn't take a high-and-mighty sorcerer to get surveillance done." He dug into his jacket, produced a phone. Slid it across the bar. "Bossman wanted you and me out there looking for cockroaches. Figured I'd save you some time."

I picked up the phone. Studied the screen. It showed Sharon Patton on a Burleigh Street, buying bread from the hippie bakery on the curve where the main road peels away from the beach. Holly Langford stood beside her, arms folded, dreads left to hang loose over her leather jacket.

"Shazza I recognise," Finn said. "The other one, well, I hear she's a witch who operates out of the Valley. Dangerous sort. Friend of yours, in an off-again, on-again kind of way."

I blinked and stared at the screen with a stupid expression on my face. "Off-again, mostly."

"Someone's got you sleeping on the couch, eh?"

"It's not like that," I said. "She didn't agree with..." I gesture at Finn, then the foyer. "All this, I guess."

"Every fucking conversation with you, it ends with the fucking violins." Finn snorted. Sipped his coffee. "Time to sack up, Murphy. Sabbath's decided there's a good chance they're our roaches, and he wants you and me to go pick 'em up."

I giggled. I couldn't help myself. "Just you and me, you mean?"

"Hell, no," Finn said. "The two of us, we ain't going toe-to-toe with a sorcerer that strong. We got a mission tonight. Twenty-three hundred.

"Sabbath told you to do this?"

Finn grinned at me, showing off his teeth. It didn't have the menace of Sabbath's smile. He hadn't had a demon inside him long enough for the teeth to start changing. "Yeah, new kid. Sabbath told me to do this. You and me and Wes and Randall, we're going hunting."

Langford owned a property out in Currumbin Valley, this breezy old Queenslander on the side of the hill, held up by hardwood pylons and a tangle of weeds too thick to let the place slide down. I'd stayed there before, when I first came to the Coast. Knew how well she'd warded things.

There was a weird mood in the SUV. Four of us packed in: me; Finn; Randall; Wes. Another car ahead of us, another four possessed thugs in Sabbath's employ. Maybe the mood in their car made more sense. Ours was just a mess. Finn all eager to spill blood. Randall a little more cautious. He'd been out to Langford's property before, knew how hard the wards would be to breach. His expression said he didn't know why we were crossing the line now, but he was going to do the job.

Wesna's expression remained impossible to read. She sat in the passenger seat, eyes forward, shotgun on her lap. Ready for anything. Giving away nothing. Ready to bark orders if anyone looked like they were straying.

It was quarter past ten when we came to a stop. The rain hammered the top of the car. Soaked us all through as we gathered on the side of the road. There wasn't much to see, that deep into the valley. Langford's side of the road was all gum trees and brush, a long driveway snaking up the slope of the hill. The far side of the road was a farm; empty paddocks, a handful of cows, barbed wire fences to keep people out and the animals in.

Wesna took charge. Did it all with hand signals. Two man teams. Two round the rear of the building. She'd go up the driveway with Randall and a crowbar. Finn and I would cover her. Lightning flashed. The thunder rolled over us, louder and closer than usual. The demons nodded. Broke off and disappeared into the brush. The rest of us lined up in front of Langford's gate, felt the goose bumps run down our arms as the ward picked up our presence. Wesna tapped my shoulder. Pointed me at the gate. I raised an eyebrow. Spat a mouth full of rainwater into the mud.

Her expression gave away nothing. I nodded and knelt by the gate, felt the rainwater soaking through the knees of my pants. Took a few deep breathes to steady myself and really looked, let my vision slip its shackles and pay attention to the things I never wanted to see.

Langford's ward should have been a complex thing, a knot of shadowed strands pulled from the Gloom to serve as a barrier few creatures could see. She'd spent decades protecting her place, layering the ward year after year, building up her own personal Great Wall that'd take a goddamn howitzer to break through.

The ward I looked at was a simple knot, the kind built by an apprentice sorcerer still afraid of their own power. I blinked the rainwater out of my eyes, stared at it a few moments, trying to pick the trick.

Then I nodded and flashed three fingers to Wesna, let her relay the information to the other teams over radio. Three minutes later the wards were down and we crept up the driveway, using the trees for cover as we closed on Langford's house.

There were thirty steps from the driveway to Langford's front door. We went up them one at a time. Randall. Wesna. Me. Finn. Spread out along the big veranda, crouched low to avoid being spotted through the windows. There was a light on in Langford's kitchen. Another in the bathroom towards the rear of the house. No immediate signs of life, but that didn't mean much. Wesna pointed. Finn and I broke off, went left while she and Randall went right. Queenslanders build verandas that stretch around three quarters of the house. Spend their summers outside, on the deck, rather than sweat through the humidity within. I followed Finn to the far end, to the doors leading into an unlit bedroom. He knelt in front of the lock, worked at it with a set of picks. I pressed myself against the wall. Listened to the torrential rain hammering the corrugated iron roof. We didn't need to be stealthy. The rain covered almost everything. I could have yelled orders at Finn, and he would have turned round and yelled back *what?*

That made it easy. Well, easier. There are fourteen reliable ways of killing someone possessed by a demon. Fewer, if you don't have a competent sorcerer to back you up. I let Finn finish the lock, followed him into the bedroom. I looped my right arm around his head. Ripped at his eyes with my fingers. Demon or not, the eyes are always vulnerable.

Finn screamed. Barely audible over the rain. He thrashed around. Bigger than me. Stronger than me, with the demon inside him. I held in, dug my fingers in. Levered my other hand around his throat and cinched as tight as I could. Demon or not, he needed to breath. The absence of air disagreed with him. He let me know by ramming himself, back first, into the wall. The bruises on my ribs burned like a brand new injury. My head buzzed, not quite aching. Finn bunched his shoulders. Tried to disrupt my leverage.

I got my thumb deep in his eye socket. Dug in. Hauled his head back enough to lock the choke in and put pressure on the carotid arteries. Waited for the blood to stop reaching his brain. It took longer than you'd expect, if you'd seen it done to a human. Finn sagged. Dropped to his knees. To the floor. Lay there, very still. Blood coming from his right eye where I'd done some damage.

I caught my breath. Stood. Readied the SIG as I stepped into the lounge room, heading towards the kitchen. Wesna stood there. Randall on the floor. Her teeth were bared, sharp fangs exposed. There was hostility in her eyes as she looked up at me, a hunger to keep fighting and killing.

I stood my ground. Kept the SIG trained on her.

She took a few deep breaths. Reigned the demon in. Stood and held her hands in the air.

"Oh no," she said, deadpan. "I fear this was all an elaborate ruse to capture me."

I shook my head. Slid the SIG into its holster. "Randall still alive."

"Mostly. Finn?"

“I didn’t come equipped to kill demons,” I said. “If I’d known...”

Wesna shrugged. “There’s still four men out there, coming down the hill, expecting to kill someone tonight. You really want to bitch at me, or do you want to get out of here.”

ALONE, IN THE GLOOM

ROARK'S APARTMENT GOT crowded with all of us in there. Langford sat on the single couch, Sharon on the floor beside her. Roark on the small chair by the table, the ashtray filled with the debris of his chain smoking. Me and Wesna on the double-seater couch. Roark watched us all, his dark eyes gleaming. He was in his element: planning; thinking of doing something crazy; convincing people to go along.

"We're going to be moving fast," he said. "Fast as is reasonable, given the situation. Langford's already given up her house for this. The weather ain't getting any better. Sabbath ain't stupid; he'll figure the play we've made before too long. He'll come after Wesna and he'll come after Keith. Then he'll come for the rest of us, and no one thinks that'll be pretty, yeah?"

He looked at as all, one by one. Waited for the nod. "So we're moving fast," he said. "And fast means doing it risky. We got a valkyrie out there, and we've got Miss Patton here to draw the bitch in. What we don't have is a means of fighting the bitch, but we've got the means of getting one. The deepest parts of the Gloom spat out our problem; they're going to spit out our solution."

Wesna raised an eyebrow. "We're going to call something else out to fight the valkyrie?"

"We thought of it," Langford said. "Too risky in the long run. We don't want to shut down one apocalypse, only to have another one roll in over the top."

"That depends on the apocalypse." Wesna folded her arms and smiled.

"You want to bring about your own eschaton scenario, you go out and work for it like everyone else," Roark said. "We're stopping this one cold. That means we're going for a weapon that'll let us hold our own."

Roark settled back into his chair, a satisfied grin on his face. He reached for a cigarette and lit it, meeting the collective stares of the room. Langford put down her cup of tea, rubbed at her right eye. "We're going into the Gloom for a weapon?"

"A sword, most likely," Roark said. "I suspect that's up to Keith, once he gets there. It's his subconscious we'll be working with, unless we've got someone better suited."

"I'm better suited," Wesna said.

"'Cept you'll be part of the doorway." Roark stared at her, eyes small and hard. "Mortal sorcery doesn't often touch the deep Gloom. It's too hard to get there. Too hard to get back." He paused, lit his cigarette. "We'll be relying on the part of you that's native to the other side to get Keith where he's going while Langford and I keep the gate open."

"And where am I taking him?"

"Wherever you can find," Roark said. "The resting place of Excalibur. The hiding place of Durandal, after it passed from Hector of Troy to Roland. Go find fucking Balmung in the forge of Wayland Smith for all I care. It doesn't really matter. They're all reflections of the same fucking sword, hidden somewhere deep in the Gloom. They all mean the same thing in the long run."

Wesna snorted. "Yeah, that you've lost your mind, old man?"

"Wes," I said. "Come on."

"No. No 'come on,'" she said. "I was willing to entertain some level of foolishness in the name of the reward Roark tendered, but this is..."

She shook her head, unable to find the word. I didn't really blame her.

Roark kept his smile half-hidden behind the cigarette. "You saying you can't do it, little demon?"

"I'm saying you're all fucking mad," she said.

"Desperate is different to mad."

We all turned to look at Sharon Patton, seated quietly on the floor. She stared at Wesna, her jaw set.

"Yeah?" Wesna said. "Easily said, given you're the woman who doesn't play a role in the plan."

"I play a role," Sharon said. "Once you do this? Once you get your sword? I'm the woman you're going to send out there, trying to lure the valkyrie into place. I'm the lamb you're using to trap the monster."

She took a deep breath. Eased it out. "On the whole, I'd rather be going into whatever nightmare the four of you are talking about. At least, then, you're doing something instead of waiting for the end."

"They'll be on you the moment you hit the Gloom. You've got to be prepared for that." Langford crouched low, cigarette in hand, glaring at the row of lights that ran down the centre of the underpass. Roark was down the other end, assessing the situation; he squatted and scratched something into the dirt, nodded in satisfaction.

Langford sighed and sketched a line of runes in the dirt. Finishing them gave her far less pleasure than it gave Roark. "You cannot fight a valkyrie over there, so don't even think about trying," she said. "Your only advantage on the Gloom side will be light and the ability to move fast, until you get yourself a weapon that'll let you fight on her terms."

I kicked at the gravel, snorted into the cold night air. "In which case, the valkyrie's just bigger and stronger than I am, with centuries of experience when it comes to ripping folk's apart?"

"Spoken like a man who knows exactly how fucked he is." Langford stood, tapped the ash free of her cigarette. "You should take the demon-girl through with you."

I glanced towards the car park, where Wesna stood beside her black SUV. Stark and tall and pale, arms folded as she observed. "I'm not inclined to trust Wes. Not with something like this."

"But you'll trust her to watch over me and Roark, while we get your ass to the deepest reaches of the Gloom to do a little B&E?"

"She'll want the sword," I said. "That means I've got to get back to this side of existence."

"That makes me feel so much better." Langford dropped her cigarette, ground it beneath the toe of her boot. "My life was pleasantly boring until you came into town, Keith. I don't think I'll miss you much, once we stop this shit and you leave."

She grinned at me from behind the dreadlocks, nodded to Roark. "I think he's ready to get started. Best you give us some space."

I retreated to the parking lot, took a position next to Wesna. Langford and Roark both opened their packs, started producing candles and twine and knives forged from bone and silver. The building blocks of serious magic, rather than the hasty spells we forged on the fly, paying a tithe of blood in order to keep things safe. They were going to open a tunnel in the Gloom, transport to a place disconnected from reality. Nothing about that was safe, least of all for me.

Wesna turned toward me. "You realise this is crazy?"

"Most things Roark puts together are," I said. "He treats magic like it's an extreme sport, and he wants to be king shit."

"And you go along with it?"

"Worked pretty well for us, most of the time."

She nodded. Satisfied. Folded her arms. "If we get separated in there—if I come back without you—I will kill them both while they're weak and take their corpses to Sabbath."

"If we get separated in there, I've got no way back," I said. "What happens to Roark and Langford rates pretty low on my list of priorities after that."

"Vicious little prick, aren't you?" A slow, easy smile spread across Wesna's face. "Some days, Murphy, I remember why my mortal half liked you."

The two sorcerers went to work, their whispered chants filling the cold night air. I started preparing myself to go into the Gloom, physically and mentally. Opened the boot of the car, started loading gear. Mag-lights, both heavy enough to be used as a club; Langford had prepared them both, carved magic into the rubber so the light would still burn on the Gloom side. A knife, blessed and bound up with magic, slipped into my pocket. My

SIG in its usual place, ready to be drawn. A heavier jacket, just in case.

I held up the second pack, offered it to her. "You want?"

Wesna shook her head.

"This is going to be bad enough," she said. "We don't go this deep, Murphy. Not when we're sharing a body with a mortal. Probably best for both of us if I'm not in there, armed."

I nodded. Went back to prepping. By the time I was done, they'd established the tunnel, replaced the dim light of the Underpass with a long expanse of Gloom that struggled against wards both Langford and Roark had erected. I used to think I knew what darkness meant. I didn't. It was like saying you understood the colour of the ocean because you've stood on the shore and watched the waves roll in. The Gloom I looked at wasn't from the shallows. It was from deep in the trenches, the parts of the Gloom where no human ever went. Langford's face was white with the effort of keeping it contained. I couldn't see Roark from our vantage point, but I was betting the old man was struggling.

Wesna clapped me on the shoulder. "Come on," she said. "They aren't going to hold this for long."

I nodded. Adjusted my grip on the mag-light. Waited for Wesna to lift me and charge us towards the darkness. She moved fast. Zero to holy shit in under a second. We charged towards the darkness. Hit the Gloom at full speed, and it felt like smashing into a wall. The force of it shucked the breath from my lungs, pain spreading down my limbs. For a moment I thought we were stuck there, left to break upon the darkness.

Then the Gloom wrapped itself around me, pulled me in.

For a moment, I fell, twisting and turning, utterly convinced that I'd never actually land.

ARMED AND DANGEROUS

I LANDED ON a hard, jagged ridge of black stone. Lay there, gasping for breath, while my senses adjusted to the realities of the Gloom. It was cold. My eyes watered with it. My hands and feet were numb already, my ears stinging where they were exposed to the darkness. I could hear wings overhead, the heavy flap of creatures twice my size holding their bulk aloft. I needed to move, but my body objected. It was too cold. Too terrifying. My adrenal system should have gone into overdrive trying to cope with all the stimuli, but it never kicked in. Biology never meant much, out in the Gloom.

Wesna lay beside me, curled into a fetal ball. She whimpered softly, hissed words I couldn't understand. There wasn't any hiding her demon half out here. It responded to the Gloom, asserted its dominance. "Wes," I whispered. "Wes, come on."

I reached out, grabbed her shoulder.

"Keith," she hissed. "Keith, just..."

I let go. Numb fingers wrapped around the mag-light, used it to help get me upright. My eyes burned in the cold air. My feet objected to movement. I kept low, under ridges of rock, all too aware of the creatures watching from overhead. The rocks provided some cover. She'd be safe enough, maybe. I made out the bulk of a building, further along the cliff. Single story, but big, sized for creatures that made humanity seem insignificant. Walls of grey, smoke-coloured stone. I edged towards it, inching my way through the darkness. The shadows seemed to breathe, swelling and subsiding on their own personal tides.

The building looked Scandinavian, an old Viking longhouse. That wasn't surprising, all things considered. The Gloom manifested things based on human expectations, tapping deep into the subconscious in order to gather form. I crept towards it, used a crowbar to lever open the front doors. The interior wasn't inviting. A long hall. A dormant fire. Empty tables and chairs, all covered in black ice. The soles of my shoes slid on the cold stone floor, searching for traction. My breathing echoed, impossibly loud, and I feared the winged creatures above would come searching at any moment.

“And so the lonely hero comes, searching for a way to save the world.”

Wotan’s cold, dead voice echoed across the chamber as he emerged from the shadows of the room. The lean, haggard features seemed clearer here; more like an obsidian copy of the man he’d been in life. His voice seemed to whisper from the walls of the building, rather than the cruel lips of his spectre.

“You shouldn’t be here, little killer. This is no place for the living.”

“No place for you, either,” I said. “You’re dead, Wotan.”

“Not here.” His shade floated forward, gathering mass from the floor. “Not in many of the ways that matter, little killer.”

I thumbed the Mag-light, let its illumination spill out. What should have been a bright, yellow glow came out muted and wavering, but it was still enough to force back Wotan’s shade.

I started walking, letting the light force him away from me. “I don’t have time for you.”

The ghost expanded, looming over me, still staying clear of the light. “You will make time, little killer. Little thief of lives. You don’t understand this place, but I do. I always have. I could call down the hosts of the valkyrie, all of them at once. I could wake the slumbering titans and draw them forth to punish you. I could—”

“You could shut your hole,” I said. “You’re just a ghost.”

Wotan deflated. Glared at me with his one good eye.

“You play a dangerous game, little killer.”

“Maybe, but not with you.” I shook the Mag-light at him, watched him glide back to avoid it’s glow. It was warmer, in the middle of the light; feeling seeped into my fingers. I extended my middle finger, pushed the ghost back. “Fuck off. I’ve got a job to do.”

The Mag-light flickered. First sign that the batteries were dying. I was working the back wall of the building, searching for nooks and crannies where a sword could be hidden. Wotan's ghost floated behind me, reedy voice echoing off the empty chamber. I tried to ignore him. Focus on the job.

"Do you know what happens when you die in the Gloom?" Wotan's face hung at the edge of my light, fixing me with his single eye. "You ever wondered what happens to heroes, little killer, when they're trapped in this side of the world?"

I had my fingers on the wall, pressed them hard against the stone. The contact sent sparks of pain down my arm. I'd pissed on an electric fence once, back when I was a kid. Low voltage. Enough to give you a kick. Making contact with the wall felt just the same. My numb fingers burned. It turned up nothing.

I stood by the wall. Watched my light flicker again. Wondered if we'd fucked up. Wondered where it'd happened. Was it Wesna, unable to get me here? Langford and Roark, unable to do their part? Someone just fucking with me, propelling me into the Gloom for no real use.

"Your light's going to fail," Wotan said. "When that happens, you're going to be mine, little killer."

I stood by the dormant fireplace. Looked at it. Wondered how long it'd been since someone lit a fire in there. Turned around and looked at the room. The long table. The rows of chairs. Black ice. Grey stone. The dark shadow of a chieftain's hall; whatever facsimile of it the Gloom could cobble together from my subconscious.

I went to the head of the table. Felt the stones shift in the floor. Not a lot. Not a lot at all, with the ice frozen over the stone. I got out the second Mag-light. Set it down next to me. Used the first one to chip away the ice. Free the stone underneath. Wotan's ghost stopped mocking me. Held its breath, a little afraid.

The flagstone weighted a ton. I needed the crowbar to lift it. The bundle lay there, in a crevice in the floor. Black leather straps. Grey cloth. About the right size. I pulled the bundle free and laid it on the floor. Unwrapped the leather straps, freed the blade from the cloth. It didn't look like much. A long, heavy steel blade. The grey steel just a little brighter than the Gloom around it. I wrapped numb fingers around the hilt; held it, blade first, towards the ghost.

Wotan backed away. Gave me space.

"Impressive, isn't it," he rasped. "This little spark of hope you're carrying."

I reached for the cloth. Wrapped it around the blade.

"It'll do," I said. "It'll do for now."

I found Wesna where I'd left her, half-hidden by a rocky outcropping, her face turned away from the open air. I didn't need to unshackle my vision to see the changes the Gloom was making to her. This far in, her skin looked ashen and burnt, like she'd walked through a furnace. The blackened hand that fended me had sharp talons at the end of each finger, little slices of obsidian that could slice me open without a thought.

I crouched beside her, called her name. Held the bundle with the sword inside it in an awkward grip, trying to reach around her and get her attention. "Wes, we need to get going," I whispered. "Come on, you and me, we need to get back. I've got the sword, Wes. I've got it. We can get the hell out of here, but it's going to be up to you."

A snarl formed deep in Wesna's throat and it never became words, just a low, threatening sound that demanded I get away from her, that I run and keep running. Sixteen years of hunting things that came from the Gloom, and it's one of the few things that ever made me shit myself. I held her tight. Kept talking. Braced myself for bloodshed.

The things that flew above us kept circling. Growing more and more curious about the happenings on the ground.

Wotan's ghost appeared at the edge of the light. Laughed, softly, at the sight of the hunched-over demon.

"You may have the sword, little killer, but your pet demon can't get you home."

"Fuck off." I reached for the straps on the bundle. Freed them and lifted the sword free. Held it at the ready, squaring off against the ghost. Held it and pointed the blade at him, ready to strike. "Fuck the hell off, Wotan. Or—"

Strong fingers wrapped around my leg. Latched onto me, holding me in place. Keeping me from advancing to strike. I looked down. Caught the burnt wreckage of Wesna's face. The dark, obsidian blocks that were once her eyes. She held on, pulled at me, struggled for control.

Then she tipped backwards, hauling us off balance, and the two of us were falling. Weightless. Lightless. Rushing through the Gloom. We slid hard and fast and dangerous and landed on the cold concrete path outside the underpass. My fingers were still wrapped around the sword, holding onto it like a lifeline. Wesna let go of my thigh. Fell back and howled at the night sky. Keening like a wolf in pain. I lay on the ground. Strained to see. Too long in the Gloom made it hard to process light. Everything seemed wrong.

"Well, fuck me, the two of 'em did it."

I blinked. Focused. Made out Finn standing over me. One eye was hidden behind a white bandage. His other eye glittered with malice. It took a few moments longer to see the small automatic concealed in his big, gloved hand.

Finn just smiled at me. Reached for the sword. "I don't doubt what you just did was all kinds of difficult," he said, "but I'm afraid you're going to be giving me that sword, Murph. Otherwise—"

He stepped back, avoiding the arc of the blade as I swung at him. He grinned, shook his head, and steadied his pistol.

Then someone stomped a steel-capped boot into the side of my skull, and I lost interest in hitting anyone with a chunk of magical steel.

Hell, I lost interest in almost everything, except for passing out.

PRISONERS

I CAME TO in Hell Bar, my wrists zip tied to one of the steel bars that bisected the room, my back to the steel wire that hung below them. They'd trussed up Roark to my left, Langford to my right. Both of them looked like hell, pale and wasted from the effort of opening the gate. Roark was bleeding from the temple. I figure whoever hit him did the same number on me, coming in off Finn's distraction to knock me out.

Randall leant against the bar; arms folded, smile in place. There was a big .38 holstered under his right arm, but he wasn't all that interested in pulling it out and shooting us. Finn stood behind the bar, glaring at me with his one good eye. He'd opened a bottle of vodka, started drinking without hesitation. The automatic sat beside his half-full glass, waiting for an excuse.

Sabbath sat on one of the bar stools, nursing the sword in his lap. He looked at it. Looked at me. Smiled to himself.

No sign of Wesna. That was good news, or bad news. I wasn't sure which.

Sabbath stood up, pulled the sword free of the bundled cloth.

"There were times when I had my doubts," he said. "But I have to admit, Keith, you proved to be a solid investment. You found me a weapon. You brought me bait. You flushed out the weak and disloyal among my crew. It almost made the risk of letting you keep your soul worthwhile."

He swung the sword in an experimental arc. Smiled at me when he was done.

"Nothing like the classics," he said.

I glared at him. My head hurt. The plastic pull-ties were cutting into my wrists. I went through the process Roark drilled into me. Evaluated the situation; figured out the options. It seemed like we were pretty fucked. It seemed like our options were limited. I was okay with that. Dying didn't seem so bad, so long as it happened out in the light.

"Where's Wes?" I said.

"A very good question." Sabbath smirked. He glanced at Randall. "Don't you think it's a good question?"

"It'll do," Randall said.

"Indeed." Sabbath gestured with the length of the sword. Pointed behind me, made me contort to get a glimpse of the dance floor behind my shoulder. Wesna was splayed out on the glass tiles. Bleeding. Broken. Her demon half struggling to heal her wounds.

"Miss Holjack was a very disloyal woman," Sabbath said. "That sort of thing has consequences. We're going to teach her that. It's going to take a very long time."

He lowered the sword. Dug its point into the floor.

"You'll probably like this, Keithy-boy. When we're done, she's going to be mortal again. We're going to rip the demon out of her, leave her human half in whatever remains of her body. It'll hurt. It'll hurt every day of her life. And it still won't mean a damn thing compared to the pain we'll put her other half through."

He took a deep breath. Exhaled slowly.

"That's tomorrow's business. Today..." he gestured at the walls of the club. "Today we put all this to the test."

He smiled at me. Waited for me to ask. I didn't give him the satisfaction. Just stared at him, picturing a place behind his skull and the ways I could find my way there with a round from the SIG. Pretending it was still possible to get out of this and hurt him.

Sabbath knelt down. Looked me in the eyes. "You know what's disappointing, Keith? Getting you here. Getting Roark here. Baiting a goddamn trap I spent months putting together. And yet we've got no guest of honour. The huntress...she's still out there. Still looking for someone, I take it, who isn't the two of you or your little friend Miss Langford."

His free hand darted out, wrapped around my jaw. Squeezed tight enough that I could feel teeth trying to worm free of my jaw, just to escape the pressure.

"I take it that Miss Patton is still alive out there," he said. "That's what Wesna implied, when I let Randall take a knife to her softest parts. She resisted for a long time, Keith. Her demon half let her do that."

He let go of my jaw. Dragged the tip of the sword along the tile, letting its rasp fill the room.

"I want Miss Patton, Keith. It's a simple deal. You and Finn are going to collect her. You're going to bring her here. We're going use the lure to bring in the valkyrie, and then we're going to take care of the winged bitch."

I twisted a little. Met his stare. "You seem very confident about that."

"Keith, you're a smart man." Sabbath stood. Put the sword on his shoulder. "Just smart enough to be dangerous, under most circumstances, but you're also predictable. Your mentor is here. Your friend is here. Wesna is here, and she'll feel pain every instant you're out there, wasting time. More importantly, I've got your sword, and you're pretty much fucked if the valkyrie comes for you without the blade in hand."

I leaned forward. Felt my shoulder give, testing the limits of my bound wrists. "Why send me, Sabbath. Surely your demons can find one girl?"

The small, grey-haired demon offered me a wan smile. Tried not to let the irritation show.

"You know where she is," I said. "You can't get in."

"Your mentor's wards are...effective."

Sabbath stared at me. Cool and calm. He was wearing the face of the businessman. The demon willing to subjugate in order to get what he wanted. What he really wanted was his claws in my throat. Ripping me apart. Decorating his new club with my blood and gizzards.

"You can refuse," Sabbath said. "But if you do, or if you cross me. If anything happens out there but you and Finn collecting the girl and bringing her here to me. If any of that happens, Keith, it won't end well for your friends."

He raised the sword. Slid it between the railing and the zip-ties binding my wrists.

"Do we have an understanding, Keith?"

I nodded. Sagged. Ignored the wide smile on Finn's face behind the bar.

The sword cut the zip-ties and I got my feet beneath me.

"Get out of here," Sabbath said. "Both of you. You've got exactly one hour."

PROTECTIONS

I FOLLOWED FINN down to the car park below the club. He hissed at me, threw me the keys. Covered me with a .38 until I climbed into the car. Produced a zip-tie and used it to bind my hand to the steering wheel before he went around to the passenger side and climbed in. I didn't bother making a move. There weren't any moves to make. I was tired. Hurting. My main advantage lay in Finn only having one eye, and that wasn't much against a demon at close quarters. I needed to bide my time.

The storm still raged, filling the night sky with wind and lightning. Fat raindrops splattered against the windshield. Slowed down the late-night traffic that filled the Gold Coast highway. Even in a storm, at three in the morning, the Gold Coast didn't really sleep. People drove places. People worked the late shift. There were still bars and clubs selling drinks and people willing to buy them. Places to buy more than that, if that's what you were after.

I kept our pace steady the entire way down to Burleigh. Ignored Finn's evil grin and the stink of vodka on his breath. He watched me. Waited for me to do something stupid. I didn't have any stupid left in me. Not in that car. Not with that storm.

I took the final turn. Parked on the slope of Burleigh Hill.

"That one," I said, pointing. Finn leaned forward. Stared with his good eye. Nodded before he exited the car, then came 'round to open the driver's side door and cut the zip-tie free.

"Out," he said, quietly. The gun trained on my ribs.

"Lead the way," he said, gesturing with the barrel. I did as I was told. Went to the front gate. Opened it. Felt the push of the ward against my skin. Pushed back, just hard enough, to create myself an opening. Finn came to halt at the fence line. Raised the .38 and held it in a two-handed grip. Lightning flashed. Lit him up like a pale, grinning ghost.

"You can take exactly two steps towards the door," Finn said. "Call her name, get her to come out. Do anything else, and I'll put a bullet in the back of your head."

I loitered by the gate. Put my hands into my pockets.

"You're down an eye," I said. "You sure you're able to make that shot?"

Finn laughed. He liked that.

"You sure I ain't?" he said.

I took two steps. Yelled Sharon's name. The storm tried to drown me out, but lights went on in Roark's safe house. Someone inside heard me. The silhouette appeared at the front door. I heard the latch click. The door swinging open, just a little. I blinked away the rainwater. Remembered the first time I'd met Sharon Patton. Hit the deck, hard, as the light spilled out of the open doorway.

I dropped, and Finn fired at me. The bullet whistling past my shoulder. I was face down in the mud when the shotgun went off. Rolled over just in time to see Sharon step though the door, pump the action and fire a second shot. Ejecting the shell for a third. Finn's swearing cut through the rain. She was using Roark's shotgun this time, not her husband's hunting rifle. Every round of shot was blessed by a priest, made holy in a way that few demons could tolerate.

I rolled over as Sharon fired a third time. Watched Finn's skin burn away, retreating from the shotgun wounds. He staggered. Swore. Tried to raise the .38 and fire at Sharon Patton.

She unleashed the final rounds in the shotgun. Left him lying in the gutter, melting in the rain. There are fourteen reliable ways of killing someone possessed by a demon. Round after round of blessed shotgun did the job well enough, even if it wasn't elegant.

Sharon walked to the edge of the garden. Spat on Finn's decaying corpse.

"I take it, since you're here," she said, "things are mildly fucked?"

"Yeah," I said. "Mildly fucked. But I think I've got a plan."

I went through Roark's place, gathered everything that could be useful. Shotguns. Handguns. Knives you could use in a fight. Knives you could break out for a ritual. There wasn't much there. Roark travelled light. I took the shotgun off Sharon Patton. Loaded a fresh SIG with rounds soaked in holy water. Sharon stood beside me. Picked through the remains. A handgun. A knife. A spare for both weapons, in case something went wrong. We were working fast, waiting for the cops to show. No chance the neighbours missed the shotgun, even with the storm.

Sharon had questions. She was locking them down, saying nothing, but they were boiling away inside her, ready to spill over the moment you took off the lid. I didn't take the lid off. I hustled her. Through the weapons. Through the yard. Into the SUV with a zip-tie still hanging from the steering wheel. The clock on the dash said we were coming up on five o'clock. Close enough to dawn that we should have seen the first streaks of light breaking over the horizon. The storm took care of that. Kept the world dark and wet.

I turned to Sharon. "You're on the clock," I said.

She turned away from the window. Looked at me. "What?"

"Outside the safe house. You're on the clock," I said. "The valkyrie's going to be looking for you. It's going to be hunting."

She processed that. Nodded. "Assuming you've got a plan?"

"Not a good one," I said. "Roark does the planning, usually."

"Well, now it's on you," she said. "How 'bout you dazzle me."

I started the car. Eased it onto the road. Took a right at the lights at the bottom of the hill and floored it down the straight road from Burleigh to Broadbeach. I told Sharon my plan on the way, laid it out step by step.

There wasn't much to it, really. It sounded kinda stupid, when I said it aloud. It involved a lot of chaos. A lot of chaos, and a lot of luck.

But it played to my strengths and the resources we had. And it wasn't like Sharon had any other choice.

I parked in the lot beside the beach, across the road from the Hell Bar. Cut the lights and the engine, took a deep breath. Watched the lightning flash across the sky. Sharon climbed out of the car. She had a knife in one hand. One of Roark's revolvers in the other. Her part in things was easy. Stay behind me. Let the chaos begin. Try and cut Roark or Langford free. Stay safe until the valkyrie arrived, then trust in Sabbath or me to get the fucker.

I climbed out of the car. Walked through the rain. When we got to cover, on the far side of the road, I paused a moment and listened. Tried to pick up the sound of wings in the air. Sharon stood beside me. Head cocked. Hands shaking. We couldn't hear shit over the rain, but you could feel it. The sensation in the pit of your stomach that told you bad things were on your tail.

I took a deep breath. Exhaled slow. "Ready?"

Sharon adjusted her grip on the knife. Nodded.

I took the stairs to the second floor two at a time, shotgun locked against my shoulder while I waited for targets. Sabbath had two demons guarding the front door. Security from the casino, thick necks in black suits. I didn't recognise them. Odds are, they didn't recognise me. That gave me the edge.

They heard me coming. Tensed up and reached for their guns, trusted they'd still be standing after I emptied shotgun's contents in their direction. Demons get confident like that. They're used to being invulnerable. I pulled the trigger. Let the shotgun kick against my shoulder. Caught them both in the blast radius. Shattered the brand new glass door separating the interior of Hell Bar from the outside world. The demons hissed and screamed. Sharon came up behind me. Finished them with her SIG. One to the head. One to the chest. Neither of us slowing down.

I followed the curve of the wall. Moved into the main bar with the shotgun still in place. Swept it in a wide arc, made everyone in the room. Wesna, still bleeding and prone on the dance floor. Sabbath, sword in hand, drinking a martini from the bar. Langford and Roark, all trussed up on the railing.

Randall, gun in hand, waiting for me to walk in. He fired at me once I cleared the partition, buried a bullet in the wall just beside my head. Kept firing as he advanced on me, picking up speed. Randall wasn't stupid. He knew better than to keep things at a firefight. Up close, he was bigger. Stronger. Better. Moved faster than I could follow.

At range, we were playing things my way. I jerked the trigger as he charged. Fired wild. Watched Randall's leg spin and slip out from under him, dumping him on the red tile. His .38 skittered out of his hands. Disappeared among the tangle of empty chairs and tables.

Randall made a pained nose. Screamed once.

I raised the shotgun again. Pointed it at Sabbath. He'd positioned himself by the railing. Made the shotgun an impractical tool. Too close to Roark. Too close to Langford. Too much risk of injuring either, and not enough time to trade the shotgun out and get the SIG out for close-up work.

Sabbath raised the sword. Rested it against Roark's ear. "I'm going to assume that Finn failed me," he said. "That's very disappointing."

I steadied the shotgun. "Put the sword down, Sabbath."

"Keith, please." A smile spread over the demon's face. He adjusted his stance, moving a half-step closer to Roark. The blade slid along the old sorcerer's skin, leaving a red mark below his ear. "The shotgun really isn't your weapon. It's too...imprecise. There's the risk of doing injury to your old friend Roark or this fine young lady with the dreadlocks."

Sharon crouched beside the interior wall, SIG in hand. She had her eyes closed. Refused to look at what was happening. I went right. Took my time making each cautious step as I circled round, one ear cocked towards the ceiling. Waiting for the valkyrie to come.

"You brought the girl, though," Sabbath said. "I can smell her, Keith. What'd you tell her she was going to do? Help you? Try and free the prisoners while you played hero?"

Sharon Patton's head jerked upright.

"You know why you're here, Sharon?" Sabbath licked his lips. Raised the sword a half-inch away from Roark's throat. "You're here because Keith wants all the monsters to fight each other. He can't kill me, but he can watch someone else do the job. Do you think that's going to be you, witch? Do you really think you can stop me?"

Sharon turned. Stared at me; eyes asking the question. I kept my eyes forward. Focused on Sabbath. Kept circling the room, searching for a shot.

Sabbath moved the sword away from Roark's throat. Spread his arms wide.

"Go on," he said. "Shoot me. Prove that I'm wrong."

I hesitated. Did the math. He was a demon. He was fast. I'd need to drop the shotgun. Draw a bead with the SIG. Hard to do with a mortal opponent. Harder with a demon.

I tried it anyway. Dropped. Drew. Finger to the trigger. My body froze, unwilling to follow through.

"Geased," Sabbath said. "Magically bound not to hurt me. Been working it over you ever since you signed on, Keith. A little extra insurance, in case you weren't up to fulfilling your promise."

He took a few steps closer to me, swinging the sword in an idle arc. I focused. Put everything I had into pulling the trigger. Sabbath kept walking and my finger stayed still.

Sharon broke cover. Pointed her gun at Sabbath. Her finger squeezed the trigger three times, shots echoing across the room. Sabbath ducked. Weaved. Avoided all three. Came charging at her, sword ready, prepared to split her in half.

She stepped into the charge. Let the sword sink into her, blade through her stomach, just below the solar plexus. Sharon sank into the steel. Grabbed at Sabbath's wrist. Dragged herself along the blade so she could spit into his face.

For a moment she hovered there, a dead weight on the blade.

Then Sabbath lowered the steel and she slid, pitching backwards, eyes staring into the sky. A lonely, empty shell where the woman used to be.

Sabbath rounded on me, smiling, eager for another kill.

Then he noticed the howl of the wind, the way it ripped through the doorway blown open when I arrived.

He noticed the sound of wings as the valkyrie arrived.

THE VALKYRIE

SHADOWS CRAWLED ACROSS the walls. Our breath steamed, got ripped away by the wind. I hunkered down behind Sabbath's bar, grabbed Wesna and pulled her behind cover. Sabbath lost his grip on the sword, crawled toward Randall down among the tangle of table-legs. Langford held her ground, one bloody hand held before her like she was preparing to start a ward. She shouted something I couldn't hear. The wind tore the words away and discarded them someplace several miles away, beyond the broken glass and the coagulating darkness.

Sabbath bellowed an order I could barely hear, attempted to throw the sword across the room. It fell short, slid to halt on the greying carpet. Randall started crawling for it. I did the same. He was moving faster, but he was closer to the dark bulge that'd once been Sabbath's windows. It all came down to simple mechanics. He was faster. He was tougher. He was closer to the point where things went wrong for everybody.

The spear burst free of the darkness, spiked down between Randall's shoulder blades and pinned him to the floor. The valkyrie followed her weapon, pulling free of the hungry Gloom with slow inevitability. It wore a woman's face, cold and cruel as winter frost, its faint luminescence visible in the dim room. Long, articulated fingers adjusted her grip on the spear, wrenched it free of Randall's spine.

The meat that'd been Randall's body fell away, a lifeless hump on the floor. His spirits—demon and mortal alike—remained pinned to the end of the valkyrie's spear. She studied them, expressionless, her gaunt body stooped to fit into the room, her wings brushing the ceiling as they beat an agitated pattern. She plucked the spirits free of her weapon, brought them to her cruel mouth and sucked at them.

I wanted to scream, but I couldn't. It was beautiful, watching her feed. The sight of it a seductive touch against the deep places in my subconscious; the places that courted death, adored its inevitability. The places that dreamed of a blissful endlessness where fighting, hell, surviving, was no longer necessary.

The valkyrie turned, eyes moving from face to face. She settled on Sabbath, pointed her spear. Advanced as quickly as the room would let her, sweeping chairs and tables aside. Sabbath crawled backwards, pleaded for someone to hold her off. I stared at her, open mouthed, eager to be her next meal. I screamed against the wind, trying to get her attention. The spear slid through Sabbath.

Then Langford touched my arm, and the terrible lure of the valkyrie's presence dissolved into bowel-clenching terror. "Sword," she yelled, pointing at the blade. "Time to fight, Keith."

Terror I could handle. Terror was an old friend, there since childhood. The reason I'd signed up with Sabbath and the reason I'd left him to work for Roark. I let the fear wash over me and set it aside. Processed things, step by step. Get upright. Stagger to the sword. Pick it up and hold it ready, prepared for the valkyrie to turn.

She moved impossibly fast. Wings spread, spear gleaming, whipping herself around in an attempt to break free. Sabbath's club did its job. Held her there, trapped, unable to fly away. The valkyrie's face contorted. Confused. Angry. Hungry for blood. She stabbed at me as I approached her. The spear went wide, but the shaft caught me in the ribs as she swept it across the floor. My lungs burned. I could hear Roark screaming something. Heard Langford's shrill cry on the floor.

Sabbath lay on the tiled floor. The valkyrie loomed over him, unwilling to leave him behind. She reared up with the spear, ready to stab down at me. I threw myself forward. Got inside her guard. Swept the sword up towards her ribs with everything I had. The blade bit into her. Blood colder than anything I'd felt in the past gushed out of the wound. A bunched fist caught me in the side of the head. Knocked me into the tables. Knocked the tables to the floor.

The valkyrie reached down. Wrapped sharp talons around my throat. She lifted me. Shook me, jittery and weak as a rag doll. Somewhere, down on the floor, Langford had gotten free. She had one of the guns. Fired it, repeatedly, into the valkyrie's side. Five shots. Six shots. Enough to get its attention. The thin, black face turned towards her.

The sword burned in my hand. Heavy. Dangerous. Unwieldy as hell. I swept it towards her. Caught her in the head. Blood fountained out of her wounds. She screamed a final time, high-pitched and weird. Her legs crumpled. I hit the floor.

Langford grabbed me. Roark was already on the move, limping for the dance floor where Wesna struggled to rise.

Hell Bar was burning again. I didn't think it was my fault this time.

Hell Bar was burning again and the valkyrie burned with her.

AFTERMATH

WE BURIED SHARON Patton in a lawn grave up in Southport. No headstones, just a small plaque, a quiet place located between a local church and the university. She didn't have family. Didn't have many friends, now the Rebels were dead. The mourning party was me, Roark, and Langford. Wesna sent her apologies, as she did to pretty much everything.

I went to breakfast at this café down in Palm Beach. Coffee. Bacon. Pancakes with syrup. Everything a growing boy could need, or a slacker like me really wanted. Roark had a new safe house down there. A base of operations he could use to fight the coming war. I was living in his spare room, listening to him ramble about the things that needed to be done.

I was halfway through breakfast when Wesna sat down. She looked older. Not my age, not yet, but older than twenty-three. Her black hair was slicked down, held in place by a clip. She wore a dark suit. A darker expression. Professional as shit.

"Got something for you," she said. She produced a briefcase. Flicked it open. Pulled out a set of paperwork and slid it across the table. "I've been going through Sabbath's business, figuring out what stays and what goes. That's on the list of things to get rid of, but I can't think of anyone I'd trust to keep it running."

I look down at the paperwork. The deeds to the Hell Bar.

"Figure you may find it useful, what with its ability to trap things in there."

I nodded. Put the paperwork into my pocket. Went back to eating my breakfast.

"Where's the sword?" she said.

I put down my fork. Stared at her. "Somewhere safe," I said.

Wesna nodded. Flagged down a waiter. Ordered herself a black coffee.

"I don't like having something like that in my city," she said. "I'd rather you stored it elsewhere."

"I'd rather we didn't have it all," I said. "Except, you know. Apocalypse."

Wesna smiled. Kind-of. "Yeah," she said. "Apocalypse."

The waiter came and delivered her coffee. She stared at her drink. I stared at my food. We were friends once, a long, long time ago. It's easy to remember and hard to remember, all at the same time.

Wesna sipped her drink. Put it down and lick her lips.

"I'm not going to be Sabbath," she said.

"Wes, that's not what worries me." I sliced a chunk of pancake free. Shoved it into my mouth. Chewed mechanically. Swallowed mechanically. Looked up into her big, green eyes. "Sabbath didn't start out as Sabbath. He grew into being a fucker, you know?"

Wesna nodded. Looks at her coffee.

"Yeah, suppose that's true," she said.

I exhaled slowly. Looked out the window. There were kids in winter coats out there. Parents rugged up against the breeze. It wasn't getting any warmer. The locals were starting to notice. Climate change, they called it. One of those weird things. The last three winters had been unseasonably warm. They were willing to take it on faith that the world was going the other way.

"Me and Roark, we got this thing to focus on," I said. "Once we're done, you know, it'll be like it always was. We shoot the assholes that need killing. You try to keep yourself from becoming someone we hunt. That's as close to détente as we're coming, Wes. I wish I could offer you more than that."

She sipped her coffee. Nodded a little.

"Guess that's all I can really ask for." She looked up and raised her cup to me, offering me a salute.

"To the end of the fucking world," she said. "And stopping it for another day."

It seemed a fair thing to salute to. I raised my cup to hers.

CRUSADE

Book Three of
The Flotsam Series

THIS IS HOW THINGS GO WRONG

DANNY ROARK DIED on the top of Kirra Hill, trying to stop the Fenris Wolf from breaking into our reality. It was a Friday night, cold and damp, a chill wind blowing across the ocean and leaving us all shivering. There were three of us there that night: me and Danny and Holly Langford, the only people Roark trusted to try and stop the apocalypse from happening.

The top of the hill was small and open to the elements. One side ended in a steep drop, straight down to the highway that ran beside the beach and the cliffs of Kirra Point. The only cover from the wind was a cast-iron statue of an eagle and a couple of barbeques set up beside the picnic tables. Roark sat by the barbecues, lighting his third cigarette. Holly Langford crouched beside him, ripping the wrapper off a Snickers. She bit into it. Grimaced.

"Two hours," she said.

Roark breathed against his cigarette. "We're all aware."

Langford took another bite, pushed the rest of the Snickers back into the wrapper. "It's like trying to chew a stone," she said, words muffled by the lump of half-chewed chocolate. "That's how fucking cold it is."

"That's why I'm over here," I said.

"Yeah, an' you look toasty warm." Langford grinned at me. She was a tall, bird-like woman, a witch from the dreadlocks and piercings brigade. One of Roark's old friends, which meant she looked forty-five, maybe, underneath the tats and the hair.

Danny Roark looked a hell of a lot older, a small, white-haired bloke with a neat beard and a nose that'd been broken too many times to be normal. He scanned the night air, his breath steaming a little even after he'd ground out the cigarette. "Keith," he said, "get up."

I obeyed out of habit, the legacy of sixteen years working as Roark's partner. He was the brains of the operation, the one who understood the rules of magic. I was the trigger man, back when I got to use guns instead of some oversized sword from the Gloom, descended from all those magic swords you hear 'bout in myth and legend.

Roark pointed at the fence line of the closest beach shack. "Down there. You see it?"

I squinted. The fence was a roll of chicken-wire held up by the occasional metal stake, marking the yard of a pale-blue fibro shack with the single light out front left on. The bright point of light shimmered and dimmed a little, then returned to its usual glow. It dimmed a second time, almost going black.

"How long, do you reckon?"

Roark sniffed the air like a bloodhound. "Not long."

"Right." I moved the sword into a ready stance, the point of the blade angled towards the incursion. "Best get to it, then, yeah?"

Roark's eyes narrowed. "Keith?"

I hesitated.

"This isn't..." His voice cracked, forcing him to hawk and spit into the darkness. "We've done okay, you and I," he said. "Killed a lot of things people said we couldn't kill. We made some mistakes, but mostly we've done good."

"Yeah?"

"This isn't like that," Roark said. "This is desperation, yeah? If it we didn't have that sword, I wouldn't even chance it."

He stared at me, eyes cold and blue. There was fear there. That was new. Roark didn't fear much, not in the years we'd worked together. I scrambled down the slope, boots skidding on the damp grass. The darkness between me and the porch light thickened, the murky night air growing tangible.

This was the twenty-first incursion, the name he'd given to the weak points between our world and the Gloom, letting through things you'd rather not think about. Myths and nightmares made flesh.

The Gloom bulged and something that could have been a wolf emerged, if you made a wolf larger and filtered it through the nightmares of a dozen terrified children. The head emerged first; a black-furred maw with fangs like shards of black glass. It loped out of the Gloom the size of a car, silent as a cat. The wolf's presence registered on something deep in the back of my mind, one of those primal responses that told me to run. I could hear a hundred whispers in the air, wordless rhythms I couldn't identify. Breathing hurt; cold air burning through the weak flesh of my lungs, seeping into my veins and muscles.

Up the hill, by the barbecues, Roark and Langford were chanting, using magic to try and contain the wolf or slow it down. The red eyes lifted, focusing on the sorcerers. Ordinarily I would have shot it a few times, used bullets to slow it down and make it easier to catch with the sword, but the cold was bad enough I didn't trust my hands not to tremble. Holding the sword in a two-handed grip was as close to sturdy as I could manage.

"Hey." I edged a little closer, jabbed the sword-point in the wolf's long face. That focused its attention, got it moving in a slow circle as it tried to gauge the level of threat. It's one of the few advantages we had when it came to incursions; it's been so long since most entities made it to Earth that they aren't sure how to cope with things when they first arrive.

I kept turning. Kept the sword between us. "You know what this is," I said. "You know what it means. I'm going to give you until three to go back where you came from, otherwise me and the letter opener from hell will have to send you back the hard way."

The wolf eyed the sword, unsure of the threat.

"One," I said, softly. "Two."

Then I jammed the sword into the wolf's right eye.

It didn't bleed, but I'd long ago given up expecting creatures from the Gloom to bleed when injured. The wolf reared back, exposing its belly, and I swung the blade across the soft underbelly. Clumsy work, on my part. In the hands of someone who knew what they were doing, the sword wound would have been enough to put the wolf down. From me, it just pissed the creature off, set it snarling and lunging in my direction, moving incredibly fast.

I focused on basic principles: don't get bitten; don't fall over; don't let the wolf slip past the blade. Up the hill, Roark and Langford built their chanting to a crescendo, voices growing louder and faster. Shadowy tendrils reached out of the night, trying to take hold of the wolf and drag it back through the knot of Gloom. It fought. Snarled. Shouldered its way past me as it pulled free, darting up the hill with speed I couldn't match.

The wolf slammed into the wards Roark and Langford had set around themselves. I followed, forcing my tired legs over the slippery grass, struggling as the dropping temperature started to sap my strength. I could hear the steady drone of two voices, Langford's strong tenor and Roark's snarled baritone; caught the edge of panic creeping into Langford's rhythm. Their magic hadn't contained the wolf. It barely kept them safe as it slammed against the wards again, trying to break through.

I wasn't fast enough. I knew that the moment I started up the hill, knew it the moment my legs screamed in protest. Roark and I were a team, one of the best, but we dealt in smaller problems than the wolf. Our prey were minor demons, lesser fey, and newly minted ghosts. The occasional sorcerer who crossed the line. Each of them took time and planning to eliminate. Weeks of it, if not months.

I drew my SIG and fired at the Wolf. The gun kicked in my right hand as I dragged the heavy blade in my left. I heard something break, up by the barbeques, right before Roark's rough voice lost its momentum. The old man swore.

Blue flames burst against the Wolf as Roark retreated into lesser magics, trying to beat the wolf directly. Langford's voice faltered. I dropped the SIG, forced myself into a sprint. Watched the rows of glass-shard teeth lock tight on Roark's skinny arm, dragging him to the ground. That wasn't good. I knew that. Roark was screaming. Langford was giving ground, trying to find somewhere safe. I charged, sword held in a two handed grip. Raised it up and swung it down hard, letting the anger carry me.

The blade smashed into the wolf's dark face, all my weight behind it. Tenebrous fur and bone gave way, part of the long maw disintegrating in the wake of the blow. The wolf's form shimmered, struggling to maintain cohesion.

The wolf whipped its injured head from side to side. Slowed, then stopped as its form discorporated. I hit it again, hard as I could. Never be afraid of ensuring a target's taken care of.

Roark was on the ground. The wolf had torn through his jacket, savaged his right shoulder pretty bad. Dark blood pumped out, leaving a stain on the ground. In the distance, I could hear sirens. There was plenty of space on the top of Kirra Hill, but gunshots attracted too much attention, even on a Friday night.

Langford pulled herself together. Knelt down beside me, checking Roark's wounds.

"Shit." She slapped Roark's cheek. "Danny? Hey, Danny?"

The old man opened his eyes. Coughed up a mouth full of blood. His mouth moved, trying to say something. Bubbles formed in the dark blood around his lips. He exhaled hard. Didn't breathe in again, after.

I grabbed Roark's hand. Held it. Felt the shudder as his body stopped fighting the pain.

Langford put her hand on my shoulder. "Keith," she said. "Keith, we've gotta go."

I lifted my head. Sniffled. The siren's were getting closer, coming round the curve at the bottom of the hill

"Right," I said.

It seemed the better choice than pointing out we were fucked.

FUNERAL RITES

WE CREMATED DANNY Roark three days later, let the wind take his remains as Langford poured a handful from the urn at seven different locations around the Coast. Funeral rites get tricky when you're dealing with sorcerers, particularly those with Roark's experience. Strong spirits had a tendency to re-appear in the Gloom, manifesting as ghosts or other malevolent entities. Some liked to think they could come back from the dead, reanimate themselves like some B-movie villain. Roark never wanted that. "One day we'll fuck up," he said. "When I'm dead, I'm staying dead."

His instructions specified cremation. They told us when and where to discard his remains. It took the better part of seven hours, Langford and I sitting side-by-side in my rental car. We didn't talk much. We didn't have the time. Once the talking started, we'd start to grieve, and there simply wasn't time.

We sucked it up. We did what was necessary. And when we were done, I dropped Langford off at a bus stop and drove north, to a bar that didn't open on Mondays. I opened the front door and walked through to my office, sat down at the unfamiliar desk, and made the phone-call I didn't want to make.

"We should meet," I said. "Given the circumstances, I'm going to need more help."

It's a phrase every demon lives for. Wesna Holjack took the news better than most.

I went out front and let myself in behind the bar, opened a fresh bottle of scotch and poured myself a glass. It went down easy, barely touched the side. I took my time with the second glass. Nursed it while I waited for Wesna to arrive, studying the empty booths that lined the walls. For a long time Hell Bar had been neutral ground, the place where mutual enmity was set aside. There were wards built into the place, stronger than steel. They'd been tested pretty thoroughly, proved themselves strong enough to hold a valkyrie in place. When the end of the world finally happened, I figured the Hell Bar was going under last.

None of that stopped Wesna Holjack from letting herself in, stepping past the wards as though they weren't even there.

She studied the empty room with a faint air of irritation, like she was wondering why she'd relinquished ownership of the place. Her scowl deepened when she saw the open bottle of scotch. She was a tall, good-looking woman with black hair that hung over her face and a long, strong jaw line she'd hated when we were in high school. Not that you could tell we were the same age anymore. The demon they'd stuffed beneath her skin kept her looking twenty-three. I wore the extra years a lot harder, and I've lived every minute of them.

I kicked out a second chair with my heel, pointed to the empty glass. "Scotch?"

Wesna flicked an irritated look at the offered chair. "My contacts in the police service called about something recently," she said. "They were investigating multiple phone calls about shots fired up on Kirra Hill and they found evidence of...well, the local five-oh like to call it 'potential occult activity.' They found some blood stains and a pair of ritual circles."

"Yeah," I said. "That was us."

"I figured." She settled into the chair, pulled it right up against the table so she could lean forward and fix me with a steady glare. "That kind of shit is sloppy, Keith. It makes it harder to convince the law to look the other way, particularly given the current state of the weather systems. There's only so long people will buy into global warming, especially with the temperatures dropping as summer comes on. What in hell was your boss thinking?"

"Not much," I said. "Roark's dead, Wes."

For a moment, she didn't say anything. She eased back, sinking into the chair, but her glare didn't soften. "How?"

"We had an incursion, something from the deep gloom. It got past me and went after the sorcerers, punched through Roark's ward. Messed him up pretty good before I caught up and put the sword through its skull."

"You're usually better prepared than that," she said.

"We were expecting another valkyrie."

Wesna nodded, waiting for me to elaborate. I didn't.

"So all this was three days ago?" she said.

I nodded.

"And I'm hearing about it now because?"

"Because we were busy," I said. "Langford and I were taking care of things."

"Define 'taking care of things?'"

I busied myself with pouring another glass of scotch. "He left instructions, Wes. He was specific. End of the world be damned, he gave his entire damn life to preventing anything from the Gloom getting a foothold on this plane of reality. I wasn't prepared to let you stuff a demon into his corpse just 'cause it'd mean some part of him kept living."

"You make it sound unsavoury."

"It doesn't take much effort."

Wesna grunted. I watched her sort through her preferred responses. There was still enough human in her to acknowledge I was right. There was just enough demon in her to be irritated, pissed that an opportunity had slipped through her fingers. She'd allied with Roark to eliminate her predecessor, sliding into position as the head of a small empire that stretched across the city. She'd stayed civil because she wanted access to me and Langford. We were easier to manipulate, and either would be dangerous with a demon riding shotgun and following her orders.

The human side won out. She nudged her glass, let me fill it with a generous measure. Raised it in a momentary salute. "To Roark, then," she said. "A useful ally, as these things go."

I raised my glass. Drank.

"You know that's not why I asked you over here."

A faint smile touched Wesna's lips. "And here I thought we were friends."

"With Roark dead, we're pretty much flying

blind," I said. "I'm just a weapon, Wes. I need someone else to point out the targets. Langford rode shotgun on a couple of jobs, knows a little about what Roark had planned, but with the Wolf manifesting on this plane of reality, it's safe to say things aren't going well. We need allies."

"We are allies."

"Not what I meant."

"I know." Wesna toyed with her glass, twisting it to the left. "Ever hear of a guy named Bruce Mim?"

I shook my head.

"He runs a card game up in Southport, recruits pretty heavily from the taproom of the Dell. He's an old-school fucker, been here longer than Sabbath could remember. Claims to be capable of prophecy if the mood strikes him or the price is right."

Wesna stood up, brushing off her jeans. "He keeps a low profile for all that, which is how he he's lasted. I don't know if he was as long-lived as Wotan, down in Adelaide, but I'd put money on it being a close thing."

"Sounds like the kind of guy Roark would have recruited," I said.

"He tried," Wesna said. "Mim told him to get out. Warned him what'd happen if he ever came back and tried to initiate a conversation. He doesn't look it, but he's a scary guy when he needs to be. Scary enough to keep your friend Roark out of his hair."

"You figure I've got a better shot?"

"I figure you're desperate," Wesna said. "You've inherited a crusade to save the world, but you've got no fucking idea how. That's the curse of being a foot-soldier, Keith. It's the reason I wasn't willing to stay one, 'specially if you can't get your shit together and stop the end from happening." She stopped playing with the glass, pushed back on her chair. "We've had some dealings with Mim's organisation. I'll set something up, get Dale to escort you over there. He'll make sure you come back in one piece, more or less, but after that, you're on your own."

"Agreed," I said. Then: "Thank you, Wes."

She nodded. It was the kind of nod that suggested there weren't going to be many more favours coming my way.

THE NEW DEAL

IT WAS WEDNESDAY before I got the call telling me the meet was on. Thursday before Dale showed up at the bar to escort me into Mim's territory. It was a slow night, but he got attention. Couldn't help that. Dale had been a good-looking kid, before he got possessed. A tall, heavily tanned kid with a surfer's physique. Late twenties, maybe, with a slightly off-kilter grin that showed off perfect rows of white teeth. He moved like a guy with plenty of confidence, aware of the attention his features attracted, and utterly at ease with being on display. All that was veneer now, a disguise the demon wore for the sake of convenience. I caught him as he was making eyes at a couple of backpackers seated at the bar.

"Hey," I said, "with me. I've gotta collect my kit."

Dale turned towards me, letting the facade drop. Followed along like a petulant teenager and hovered at the door to my office, watching me collect the SIG from the drawer and strap the goddamn sword over my right shoulder.

"Boss wanted me to introduce you to Mim," he said. "Not send you over there to start a damn war."

"She also stressed how dangerous he is. It's not like I'm going in there unarmed."

"Fair enough." He watched me finished my prep. When I was done, he held up his right hand, flexed his fingers a few times. "Gloves are a good idea, if you've got them. Mim likes things cold."

I pulled a pair of leather gloves out of my kit, tucked them into my waist. Adjusted the way the sword hung in its sheath. It didn't sit right, but that wasn't a surprise. I was used to guns. The sword never sat right. The dull end of the sheath dug into my kidneys.

I joined Dale at the office door. He looked me over. Sniffed. "The steel will 'cause problems," he said. "No chance you'd be willing to leave it behind?"

"You telling me you're going in unarmed?"

Dale grinned at me, his expression wolfish. "I'm just saying, the sword will make them nervous. They're that kind of organisation."

"Let them be nervous, then."

We hit the Dell around ten o'clock. It was an old-school pub that'd been caught in the wave of urban renewal, but the renovations hadn't done much to change the clientele. You could gussy the Dell up with carpet and brass fittings, but it remained a bloke's pub, dedicated to those who did work with their hands. Rows of big men crowded around the bar; builders and chippies and electricians, the occasional plasterer and plumber in the mix. They showed up with jackets pulled over work shirts, still wearing their steel-capped work boots. Ordered beer, for the most part, although a few had upgraded to spirits. They crowded into the sports bar, stood there, shoulder to shoulder, while they drank.

That made it real fucking easy to pick Bruce Mim out of the crowd.

He looked to be about sixty, all neat and dapper with his carefully trimmed beard. Short, like most sorcerers tend to be when they're getting on in years. Old as he looked, I'd put money on his real age running into centuries, dating back before breeding and modern nutrition made blokes who cleared six feet a regular occurrence.

Mim held court in the back of the Dell, nursing a pint-glass of Coopers Pale. He dressed like a guy on his way to a cocktail party; black pants, black jacket, a powder-blue shirt with the collar spread open, exposing the leathery skin at the hollow of his throat. He stretched his legs out, spit-polished leather shoes gleaming in the dim light. He looked up as we entered, fixed his glassy eyes on me.

Dale pointed, unnecessarily. "That's him."

We were intercepted halfway across the room, a big wall of flesh rising up from one of the tables, stepping into our path with a dour look on his face. The bloke was tall enough to look Wesna in the eye, but he coupled it with a hard mass of belly and a piggish head with no visible sign of a neck.

Dale just smiled at him, turning on his demonic charm. The big man turned to me. Studied me carefully, lingering on the point just over my right shoulder, the point where he'd be seeing the sword if he had a talent for magic. "Met your boss once," the big man said. "Old bloke. Well dressed. Came here looking for help. Mister Mim was pretty clear about what would happen if he came back."

"I'm not him," I said.

The big man grunted. "No, guess you're not."

"And he's not my boss anymore," I said.

The big man laughed and stepped aside, pointing me toward Mim's table. There were three or four people gathered round the old sorcerer, but they all found better places to be as I made my approach. Mim took a long pull from his pint-glass, tried to hide a smile as I sat down and adjusted the sword for comfort.

"So, you're the pup Danny Roark recruited." Bruce Mim had a soft, reedy voice that invited you to lean forward to hear things clearly. Up close, I could see the faint redness of an old scar around his throat, a sign that he'd been strangled by someone with a vested interest in seeing him dead. He scratched at it, idly, then reached for his drink. "That would make you the man who pulled the trigger on Michael Wotan, down in Adelaide, yes?"

I nodded. "That would be me."

"You two made a bit of a mess down there."

"That wasn't our intention."

"You say 'our' like the blame can be apportioned equally," Mim said. "I knew your mentor, Mister Murphy. Knew him even better than you did, for all that you're going to deny that's possible. Take comfort in the fact that your mentor was fallible, which is why you've ended up here, preparing to beg an old man for help."

"You're well-informed."

"I'm a seer," Mim said. "I read the fucking future." He paused and belched into his fist. "Beyond that, mate, I'm not a stupid man, eh?"

"I'd hardly be here if—."

"Kid, please, don't try that shit on me." Mim clicked his tongue, shook his head. "You're here because you want to fight against the inevitable, and 'cause you don't read the portents I read in the morning. I know when to fight, mate, and I know when to give up."

"And now's a time for giving up?"

"Don't patronize me, you little bastard. I know what you set in motion."

"I'd hardly be here if you didn't." I settled back in my chair, fixed my eyes on the sorcerer. "I'm not denying responsibility; Roark and I killed Michael Wotan and we fucked up. Maybe you're right when you say the blame is his, but that doesn't matter much. The end of the world is coming and I'd like to stop that. Right now, according to people who know, you're the only practitioner on the continent as old as Michael Wotan. No doubt you've got your own precautions against unreasonable death, possibly even some way of avoiding the worst of what's going to happen. I'm here because you know things. I need someone who knows things, someone to point at targets I can take down and stop."

"And if those targets don't exist?"

"I don't believe that."

"Assume I do." Mim lifted his pint glass in mock salute. "Assume that's why I'm going to sit here, with my friends, such as they are, and I'm going to get fucking plastered 'til the end of the world arrives."

He drank. Part of me wanted to start swinging, to lash out and pick a fight. It's a natural response when you can't fight the real enemy. Bad things were coming and I didn't know how to stop them, but I did know how to plant my fist against someone's jaw.

"I assume that's the same answer you gave Roark when he came to visit you."

Mim's smile showed off a handful of missing teeth. "More or less."

"You're that certain that the world is going to end?"

"Not at all," Mim said. "I merely knew you and Roark didn't stand a chance of saving it. And witness, if you will, how that prophecy is turning out. One of you is still alive. One of you is not."

"If Roark is out of the equation, how does that change things?"

Mim raised his head, looked at me for the first time. He blinked a few times, like he couldn't get me into focus.

"Well," he said, "there's two problems. First, you're not going to succeed, not the way you're going."

I nodded. "Right. And two?"

"Two," Mim said, "I've peered into the future, mate. I've seen what happens if I get involved. I've seen the way the ripples change things. I could tell you, but you won't believe me. Right now you think I'm a bit of an old drunk."

He stopped and drained his glass of beer.

"Which is a pity," he said, "'cause you're going to be dead before this night is out, and that's going to make things a whole lot fucking harder than it should have been."

I should have met that news with more than a shrug. Should have, but I didn't; people had been telling me I was going to die for as long as I'd been working with Roark.

I raised an eyebrow at Mim and fought off a smile. "If we wanted to change that particular ripple, how would we go about it?"

Mim shook his head. Stood, and headed towards the bar. "You go back in time," he said, "and you let Michael Wotan live. Some things can't be altered, mate, once they're set in motion."

I nodded. "If that were true, you wouldn't meet with me."

"Sharp," Mim said. "Very sharp." He turned to the room. "Mister Carleton, this one is sharp, aye?"

The tall, piggish bloke nodded in response, turned back to his drink at the bar.

"Mister Carleton predicted you'd be sharp," Mim said. "It's one of the things I like that about you, Mister Murphy."

"Lucky me," I said.

"You're right, of course," Mim said, "I wouldn't

meet with you if your death were truly unavoidable, but you're misreading the situation. There's nothing you could have done to prevent that particular ripple, but there's every possibility you'll uncover something in the hours that come, now that you've been warned. That's why I'm meeting with you, Mister Murphy. I want to see how you handle things."

He finished his beer and beamed at me, one hand already raised to call over the waitress. "You're not convinced."

"Not entirely."

"That's perfectly fine by me," Mim said. "No skin off my nose, as they like to say. The events of the following twenty-four hours are more-or-less set in stone. So, here's the deal I'll offer you: if you're still alive tomorrow evening, return here with the soul of Michael Wotan and we'll begin our formal arrangement. If you're dead, or if the price doesn't agree with you, I'll ask you to fuck off and let me enjoy my drink in peace. There is no negotiation on this front. You want to save the world, that's my price. One soul, stored however you and Roark managed to store it. "

I blinked. "What do you want with a soul?"

"That would be my business, and none of yours," Bruce Mim said. He offered me his hand, and his grip was surprisingly strong. "I wish you luck, Mister Murphy."

I shook his hand, frowning. Stood, and slid my chair in. "If I can ask?"

Mim raised his glassy eyes, tried to focus on my face.

"What changed?" I said. "Why give me a different answer to the one you gave Roark?"

"Because you're different people," Mim said, "and you'll respond to my advice in very different ways. Mister Roark assumed he knew the game and how it should be played. He passed those assumptions down to you, but you learned them in a very particular way."

He raised his beer glass in mock salute. "You believe in the rules he taught you, but you don't really care if you understand them or not. That means you can be taught. Danny Roark would have broken my nose already, getting this far into the conversation. He never would have trusted me enough to stop things going wrong, but it's possible you might."

THE COST OF DOING BUSINESS

I GOT DALE to drive me back to the bar, watched the lights of the Gold Coast slip by as we followed the highway south. He dropped me by the external stairs at the back of the Oasis centre, right beside the chalkboard sign we put advertising the Hell Bar's presence up on the second floor. I walked over to the stairs, huddled there in the cold breeze. Watched Dale's car turn the corner at the end of the block, heading back to the casino on the other side of Broadbeach. Reporting back to Wesna, keeping her in the loop. Letting her know I was thinking of giving up Wotan's soul, simply 'cause one of her rivals said it was necessary. I figured she wouldn't be happy about that. Wesna wasn't happy about much anymore, least of all when it came to me.

I put in a few hours behind the counter, learning the art of mixing drinks from the kids I'd hired to work the place. They were generally younger and faster than me, more adept at working the loud environment and capturing people's orders. I stayed until we closed things down a little after three AM. Cashed out the registers and ushered the last of the staff out as I put the night's take into the safe.

When I was done, I went to the second safe, the one hidden beneath the floorboards at the back of the office. I pricked my thumb with a silver needle, put pressure on it until a bead of blood formed. I smeared it against the side of the safe before I started on the combination, felt the certainty of the code as it clicked into place.

Inside, protected by the wards, were the handful of things I cared about: a spare SIG and two clips of ammunition doused in holy water; a handful of false IDs that could get me out of the city in a pinch; about six grand in cash, go-money that would get me moving if I had to abandon the city; a silver knife Danny Roark had given, way back when we first started working together.

And behind all that, a wooden box. Old and varnished and covered in runes, the worn copper latch a little tarnished with age. Inside was a nine millimetre bullet that glowed softly in the dim light of the office, the soft lead and copper jacket both covered in etched symbols designed to keep a ghost caged and trapped inside.

We'd used it to trap Michael Wotan's soul, the night me and Roark did the Adelaide hit and set things into motion. I'd gone on the run to keep it out of the cult's hands. I'd killed people, made deals with the devil, and risked my life more times than I'd care to count.

I pressed a finger against the bullet, felt the angry presence of the soul trapped within. Thought long and hard about whether to give it up. Decided I'd do a better job after a few hours sleep.

I'd rented a unit in Palm Beach that month, a two-bedroom holiday place just off Eighteenth Avenue, one of thirty in a brand new block. I climbed the stairs to the fourth floor, followed the outside landing to the rear of the building. The first sign that they'd hit the apartment came when I saw the door. It hung open, the deadlock ripped out of the door frame, making it impossible to close the door properly. Crude work, probably some guy with a crowbar, but it got things open and it got them inside. I pulled my SIG out of its holster. Crouched low and pressed my back to the wall as I listened at the door. Heard nothing but silence. Saw nothing but darkness when I poked my head around. I used the SIG's barrel to edge the door open, slipped inside without hitting the lights.

They'd done a number on the place. I'd rented it fully-furnished and they'd taken a knife to everything, sliced open the couches and bed mattresses as they'd searched. There were holes in the drywall where they'd gone at it with the crowbar, gouging lines into the white surface so they could search the spaces behind.

There was nothing to take. Anything of value got stored in the bar. Had been ever since I'd inherited the place and built a warded safe in my office. It'd seemed a good solution, back when I first thought of it. It seemed a little less safe, looking at the wreckage of my former apartment. There was a go-bag in my wardrobe. I picked it up and dropped the apartment keys on the kitchen bench. Walked down to the highway intending to catch a bus and pretend I'd never lived there.

I found Bruce Mim's muscle waiting at the front gate. The tall, neckless kid with the jowls and piggish eyes. He was standing beside a brand new Ute, one of those sports models where they'd taken something built for work and turned it into a status symbol. It was black, spit-polished, and the tray was covered with a tarp the colour of dried blood. It made me wonder what the kid carted round in the rear.

We stared at each other a moment.

"Carleton, right?" I said.

He nodded.

"You have anything to do with what happened up there?"

He shook his head. "Boss just wanted me to check in," he said. "See if you were still alive, like."

There was something soft and girlish about his voice. It didn't match the layers of muscle and fat packed onto his tall body. It wasn't there when he shouted to be heard over the bar, but out here, in the quiet morning, he spoke soft and looked ready to wring my fucking neck.

I glanced at the car. "This one of those forking path things? Or you allowed to give me a lift?"

Watching Carleton shrug was like observing tectonic plates in motion. "Depends on where you're going," he said.

I thought about it. Ran through the list of places it was probably safe to be.

"Oasis," I said. "If they hit here, I want to go check in on my goddamn bar."

He nodded. "I can do that."

And he opened the passenger side door.

Hell Bar had dedicated staff parking in the underground lot beneath the Oasis building. When the cult tried to get inside the bar and found the wards too strong, they'd set up down below and waited, setting up an ambush site that played to their advantage. They'd come prepared: weapons, a solid plan, a safe place to keep their pet sorcerers and give them a vantage point on the action. They were prepared for sorcerers. Someone like Langford and Roark who took more than a bullet to eliminate for good. Sorcerers are hard to kill, especially when all you're dealing with are bullets. Someone needs to strip down the wards. Someone needs to seal the deal that keeps the sorcerer dead.

They hit us with a seven man team. Locals, probably. The sorcerers were Raven Cult, the leftover followers of Michael Wotan. A pair of fanatics doing their best to keep the apocalypse happening right on fucking schedule. The rest were professionals. Armed and ready for things to get bloody. They didn't care about magic. They were there to make sure the right person got filled with lead.

They'd done a good job of hiding themselves. Me and Carleton rolled down the short slope of the driveway, went the length of the lot to get to his park. I sat in the passenger seat, fretting about the state of the bar. Carleton sat in the driver's seat, silently following directions. They split their squad between two SUVs, parked on either side of the building. We didn't notice 'em, going in. SUVs are everywhere you look on the Gold Coast. Big cars with surf racks that never went off-road.

The team reversed both vehicles out, once Carleton killed the engine. Cut off our escape route and boxed us in. The professionals spilled out, took cover behind the parked cars: two shotguns; two handguns; an old-fashioned Uzi and a whole lot of cover. We abandoned the Ute, dove for cover. Carleton took refuge behind the nearest concrete pillar. I hit the floor, crawled until I found safe place behind the Ute's engine block. The sound of five guns in the closed quarters of the lot was deafening. I pulled my SIG from the shoulder holster, added my own weapon to the mix. Not really trying to hit anything, just reminding them to keep their heads down.

The adrenaline hit, right on schedule. I kept low. Kept breathing easy. Adrenaline isn't your friend in a fire-fight. It's built on a flight or fight reflex, the kind that makes you want to take things up close and personal. I could do that, if I was stupid. I had my fists. I had the SIG. If I could get to the stairs, make it to the bar, I could unleash all kinds of hell with the sword stored in the safe up there. Adrenaline is stupid in all kinds of ways. I took a deep breath, assessed the situation. Started figuring out an exit strategy.

Carleton looked over from his place behind the pillar. I could barely hear his yell over the cacophony of gunfire. "You got any defences this far down?"

I shook my head.

"Guess you're going to owe me a favour, then." A gleeful grin passed over Carleton's face as he crouched low behind the pillar and produced a small knife. He pricked his thumb, squeezed until a bead of blood appeared.

"Brace yourself," Carleton said. "This isn't going to be subtle."

He whispered beneath his breath, eyes rolling back as he focused. His thumb made contact with the dusty floor, grinding the blood into the concrete. The energy in the parking lot shifted. My skin shivered, covered in goose bumps. Carleton slumped against the pillar, nodding to himself. "Engine blocks," he said. "Two bullets in each."

They were easy shots to make. Pointless, under ordinary circumstances. Hollywood tells plenty of lies about the protective quality of an automobile, but your standard cast-iron block will stand up to a low calibre gunfire. Cars don't often explode when you shoot 'em, so you're better off aiming elsewhere.

Magic messes with your expectations, though. I put two in the engine block, just like Carleton told me to. It went up in flames, forcing me to take cover as a wave of heat rolled over us. I was upright and shooting again in a moment, hitting the second car before the cultists had a chance to run. The explosion rattled the car park, set off the sprinkler system. Carleton whooped with satisfaction, grinned as he walked through the deluge of water.

He grinned at me, jowls wet. "Well, then," he said.

“Lucky for you I was here tonight.”

I pointed at the stairwell. Motioned him along. “Come on,” I said. “We don’t want to be here when security arrives.

NEW BOSS

WE ARRIVED AT the Dell a little after nine AM. Early enough that the pub wasn't yet open to the public. Carleton produced a spare key and let us into the main bar, escorted me through the tables with chairs stacked on them. Took me through to a back room, up a set of stairs. Mim sat at a small card table, shuffling his deck. When we arrived, he stopped long enough to pick a piece of non-existent lint from the green felt. "My private room," Mim said, "for the nights when I'm feeling a little less social and mornings where I'm forced to conduct business."

I looked around. Bare walls. Bare floor. A couple of crates the pub used for storage. "It's nice," I said.

"It's serviceable," Mim said. "Never really felt the need to get anything more than that. The demons, they want to rise and conquer, but my lot has always been content to make do with a little."

I sat down at his table. Placed a small wooden box in front of me.

"You're offer still good?"

Mim's white eyebrows rose. "It's still good."

I nodded. "My apartment was ransacked by the cult last night. They were lying in wait below the bar when I showed up to check security there. I'd be dead if your boy Carleton hadn't been there to help me out."

I pushed the box towards him. Mim whet his lips as he reached for it, taking his time unlatching it and tipping the lid back. It wasn't large, but the contents sent a soft glow over the dim back room. "So, this is Wotan's soul?"

"However much of it we managed to cage."

Mim lifted the glowing 9mm bullet, studied the lights that danced around the tip. "Can I ask why you used a bullet?"

"We had one handy," I said. "The steel jacket is strong enough to hold the binding runes. The lead is soft enough to let a soul seep into it. Plus, it's one less thing to carry. So long as I've packed the soul-cage last in the clip, I know exactly where it is."

Mim nodded slowly. "And if you shoot someone with it, before it got used?"

I shrugged. "It never happened."

"Not once, in twelve years?"

"Me and Roark were a good team. We didn't make many mistakes."

Mim returned the bullet to the box, flipped the lid closed with a nod. "You were saving them all up, I suppose, til you could make a really big mistake and make sure everyone noticed."

I stared at him. "This going to be a thing?"

"Relax," Mim said. "I'm fucking with you. That's something you'll need to get used to, Mister Murphy." He reached into his pocket, pulled out a sheet of paper. Put it on the table next to my box.

"What's this?"

"Instructions," he said. "Times and places for the next handful of incursions, most of which will consist of entities you'd rather not have roaming the city. Valkyries, mostly, unless I'm reading the portents wrong. That is what you wanted, isn't it?"

I opened the paper. Scanned the details. "There's a half-dozen times on this, going ahead a couple of weeks."

"I tried to look further, but it simply wasn't there. Things are in flux right now, Mister Murphy. You can regard this as a positive sign, I think."

"What about a plan? What do you want us to do when they arrive?"

"Honestly?" Mim grinned at me. "Use your initiative. This is your crusade, Mister Murphy. I'm merely the man behind the throne, passing on information."

"I'd assumed—"

"Assumed what? That I'd take an active role? That I'd wade out into battle with you, trying to fight the monsters? That strikes me as futile, Mister Murphy. Not least because I am a monster, one of those things you and Roark used to travel the country eliminating. Had I been a little more aggressive in my dealings, had folks like Wotan been a little more circumspect, I have no doubt I would have been on Roark's list and it would be my Ragnarok you're trying to circumvent."

He'd moved one hand over the box as he talked, resting his fingertips against the runes that kept it warded. "Tell me if I'm wrong, please."

"No," I said. "You're not wrong."

"Then let's not pretend this is anything otherwise," Mim said. "I agreed to help you, in my own way. I have no desire to pick up where the departed Danny Roark left off. I'm not a man equipped for standing vigil on a cold winter's morning, Mister Murphy. I have no desire to tangle with the forces that are waking in the depths of the Gloom. Particularly not if the portents prove right and their victory remains the most likely outcome."

He reached out and snagged the box from the table, took it to the safe at the back of the room. "I'm a pragmatic man, Mister Murphy, and I don't pretend otherwise. It's how I've lasted this long, below the radar of men like Danny Roark. It's why women like Miss Holjack don't regard me as a threat."

He touched the safe, whispered a few words. Stepped back as the door swung open. It was a neat trick, showing off for my benefit. There were things Mim used magic for that many other sorcerers wouldn't.

For a moment I considered looking at him. Really looking, without the veil pulled across my eyes that let me see the same things everyone else saw. I'd learned to do that as a kid, a security measure against the chaos all around me. After a while it became habit, something that took effort to break.

Instead, I blinked and settled for the vision I already had. It hurt to stare at Bruce Mim too long already; I can only imagine it would be much worse without the shackles in place.

I looked from him to Carleton, trying to piece things together. "What are you?"

Carleton grinned and started pouring himself a drink. Bruce Mim just smiled his eerie fucking smile, shuffling cards in a slow shuffle.

"For the moment, on your side," Mim said.

"Beyond that, Mister Murphy, you don't really need to know. You've got your list. I'll loan you Mister Carleton, if you truly think you need help, but I'm sticking with my original plan as much as possible. I sit here, in this bar, and I drink until the end of the world seems like it's finally arrived."

He took a breath. Grinned at me. "If you need more help, I suggest you go check with your other allies. See if any of them have got it in their hearts to render assistance with your crusade."

I narrowed my eyes, but Mim's smile never faltered.

RECRUITING

I HEADED OVER to the Casino later that evening, once I was sure things were settled at the bar. Dale was working security on the floor, noticed me as soon as I walked down the stairs from the monorail station. He raised an eyebrow, pointed me towards the bar in the foyer. Excused himself from the other slabs of meat working as security to come and have a few words.

"Mister Murphy," he said. "We don't often see you in these parts. I thought you'd fallen into the habit of summoning Miss Holjack into your turf." He glanced at the bartender, held up two glasses. Didn't bother asking me what I was drinking; once upon a time I'd been a regular at the Casino. The demons knew my drinking habits as well as I did.

"I need to ask a favour," I said. "It seemed polite to come to Wesna, rather than asking her to come to me."

"Near as I can tell, she just did you a favour," Dale said.

"She does a lot of favours," I said. "That's kinda her job now, right?"

"She does deals, not favours." Our drinks arrived; two fingers of scotch over ice for me, a bottle of Coopers and a beer glass for Dale. He pushed the scotch glass towards me, drank straight from the bottle. He did a good job of that, setting himself up as a simple guy. Just another empty-headed pretty boy on the Gold Coast, more interested in surf and sand than anything else he came across. "She likes you. Some part of her, some part that's still human, it likes you. That makes you dangerous. Lots of the boys that used to follow Sabbath, they don't know if she's got what it takes to lead. She was great as the muscle. A perfect second in command. Now she's stepped up and it's favours instead of deals, you know?"

Dale's smile didn't budge, but his eyes glittered, cold and hard, behind his pleasant smile. "Not that I'm telling you what to do or anything, but if you were her *friend*, that'd be a thing worth keeping in mind."

"Alright," I said.

He tilted his head, raised the beer glass. His smile seemed almost friendly. "Now, tell me why I should let you go up and speak to the boss, then. Before I lose interest in this entire conversation and have you dumped in the gutter."

"I need to speak to Wesna."

"Lots of people want that. Very few get the opportunity."

"You got specific orders to keep me out?"

"No," Sale said, "but we haven't got orders to let you in. Wesna isn't Sabbath. She isn't obsessed with your destruction, to the point where she ignores business. She doesn't sweat the oncoming war, beyond making preparations that are necessary to safeguard what is ours."

"If a flock of valkyries come through from the Gloom, your preparations don't mean shit."

Dale's grin showed off his neat, white teeth. "That's why we have heroes like you, Keith. You keep us all safe."

"No, you stupid fucker," I said. "That's why you had heroes like Roark. Without him, it's just me and Langford. You're going to see plenty of things from the Gloom getting through our defences." I tilted my scotch glass back, drained the liquid contents. The ice clinked together when I returned it to the bar. "That's what I need to talk to Wes about, one way or another. You can let me go up and do it now, or I can go back to the bar and make a call, but one way or another, we need to discuss defences."

Dale opened his mouth, but I cut him off. "We're not preparing for war anymore. The war is fucking here. Go up to the thirteenth floor and tell her that, yeah? Then ask when she's willing to meet with me."

Dale didn't respond. He just stood there, staring down at me, trying to wait me out. It wasn't a battle he could win. Demon's are creatures of impulse; they get their restraint and their focus from their human hosts, when they first possess someone. Dale's host had been a surfer, disciplined enough to catch a wave and exactly no further. I spent days observing targets prior to making a move. I didn't have the discipline of a fully trained sorcerer, but I knew enough to hold a demon's gaze and slowly stare it down. That meant Dale was destined to lose. It took less than a minute before his dark eyes started dancing round, searching for something else to focus on.

He went upstairs and told Wesna I was there. I sat at the bar and ordered a second scotch, waiting for my summons.

Sitting in the Casino Bar got to me pretty quickly. The last time I'd been there, I was working for Sabbath, living up to a promise I'd made him in return for his help and protection. Back then, the end of the world seemed like a distant thing, averted when we wiped out the cultists trying to resurrect Michael Wotan. We were going to war with the local bikers, killing them off one-by-one. They weren't nice guys, but they were human. Untainted by magic, for the most part. We'd gone to war 'cause it was necessary, and 'cause Sabbath wanted my hands stained with mortal blood.

Wesna and I were friends back then, instead of fucking allies. She covered my back more than once, kept me out of the worst bloodshed whenever she could. Part of her remembered who we'd been before the demon arrived: old friends; old allies; the kind you tended to trust. All that'd changed when she took over Sabbath's organisation. She gave me the bar as a business decision, reasoned it was better maintained by someone independent. She'd kept her distance after that, kept discussions at an arm's length. I got the feeling we weren't really friends anymore, once Sabbath was taken down. Instead, I'd become a resource, someone to be deployed to benefit Wes and her lot. My circle of friends shrunk down to Roark and Holly Langford. With Roark dead and Holly MIA, that left me flying solo.

Two demons wearing security jackets appeared at the edge of the bar. They waited for me to finish my drink, led me to the elevator and up to the thirteenth floor. The elevator was cold and quiet, and we had it to ourselves. I stood between the demons and I kept my hands exposed. No room for misunderstandings when you're no longer part of the team. We hit our floor with a soft chime, and they led me down the hallway.

It was nine o'clock outside. The heavy clouds that'd started the day bunched up over the horizon had moved in and cloaked the city, spitting half-hearted bursts of rain onto the evening traffic. From the thirteenth floor of the Casino you could see the beach and the highway, the narrow stream of traffic heading north and south. There were only two directions on the coast. It was smeared against the coastline, clinging there like a limpet. You could walk across the city in an afternoon, with effort. It'd take you far longer to go from the southern border north.

Part of me wanted to throw it all in. Walk away from my escorts, my bar, and my problems. Climb into a car and start moving again, heading to a new city and researching a different target. I wasn't built to stay in one place, least of all here.

When she took over the organisation, Wesna moved into a smaller suite than the lavish penthouse Sabbath used. She called it an act of discretion, hiding their operations away from the opulence of the Coast. The truth, I think, was a hell of a lot simpler: you couldn't fit as many people into the small, one-bedroom suite on the thirteenth floor. Fewer guards, fewer visitors, fewer people watching her twenty-four seven. When you're trying to find your feet as the leader of a demonic cartel, that counted as good strategy in the short-term.

She was planted in one of the leather couches when the demons showed me in. Didn't bother looking up from the paperwork in her lap as they deposited me in the empty chair and excused themselves from the room. Wesna didn't bother with the veil in her quarters; the ashen, withered skin was fully exposed and her face looked like the rot had set in and claimed the soft tissue. No nose, no lips to speak of, a pair of dark pits where the eyes should have been. Withered, claw-like fingers held the paper steady, and the bright motes of humanity that once floated in her aura were dimmer and fewer than the last time I'd really looked.

Wesna set aside her papers. Studied me for a moment. "You look like a man who needs a holiday."

"Anywhere but here." I smiled. It was an old joke between us, the legacy of two kids who grew up among tourists. "Dale tell you what I wanted?"

"He gave me an overview."

"And?"

"If you need a spare to sorcerer, I can provide you with a sorcerer."

I eased back into my chair, turned towards the glowing lights of Broadbeach through the window. The storm was still out there, still making up its mind. Little spits of rain dotted the tinted glass. "To be honest, no, you really can't," I said. "If you had access to a sorcerer competent enough to do the job, then I'd be here dealing with Sabbath instead of you. Say what you will about Danny Roark, he was damn good at his job. Bruce Mim may be willing to do our research, but he's not going to put himself into the fight. That means we need muscle. Your people do muscle, Wes."

"My people," she said. Her teeth moved slightly, like she was grinning. "You're looking to fight a war. You're looking for soldiers. My people don't have that kind of discipline."

"Could have fooled me."

"No," she said. "We couldn't. What you think of as discipline was built by fear, and the thing they feared most was Sabbath. They feared me and Randall appearing to punish them. They feared being expelled and out there alone, trying to hold their own against the other entities that want the Coast for territory. Now there's no Sabbath, there's no Randall out there breaking thumbs if they don't obey. If I use a guy like Dale as a bludgeon, it only encourages him to do exactly what I've done—eliminate the top dog and assume the job."

"Still a dangerous world out there, for a demon on their own."

"It was," Wesna said. "Now entities are fleeing the

Coast, if they've got any sense. They can sense we're ground zero for something big, and they don't want to be here when it lands. There are stray demons out in the mountains, where the witches used to hold sway. They're holding their own, near as I can tell, simply because the witches aren't there to fight. There's fewer fey out there, fewer members of the Nipponese shadow or the supernatural Tongs out of China. All the people Sabbath used to fight, trying to keep his territory, they've realised this place is tainted now."

She left the couch behind, went over and unearthed two beers from the depths of the mini-bar. She opened one, underhanded the second in my direction. I caught it badly, bouncing it from fingertip to fingertip before it settled. Wesna shook her head. "It's going to foam."

"Yup."

"And you used to have such steady hands."

I grinned, a little half-heartedly. "Not sure what you're remembering. I never caught shit in high-school."

"Right," Wesna said. "That was me." She tilted the beer bottle, let the contents hit the back of her throat. She crossed over to the window, nursed the second half of the bottle as she stared into the distance. "You're lucky it's fucking cold out there, you know? A half-dozen times since we eliminated Sabbath, I've found myself wondering if this is some kind of long-play on your part, on Roark's. You set me up to eliminate Sabbath, take out half the enforcement arm so the organisation is crippled, then string me along as an ally until my organisation gets weaker. It'd be a perfect set-up for eliminating me and the rest of the demons, getting rid of our influence on the Coast for a while."

I drank my beer. "I don't plan that long term."

"And I can believe that of you. I don't know what Roark was like."

"He's good, but he liked taking risks too much. Treated magic like his own private extreme sport," I said. "Besides, he's dead. There's not much planning in that."

"Says the man trying to stop a ghost from ending the world." Wesna turned away from the window, studied me as she finished her beer. "He wouldn't be the first sorcerer to die in order to get stuff done. He wouldn't even be the first with a plan to come back to life. The only proof I've got that he's truly dead is your word, and Langford's."

I put my beer on the coffee table. Stood, so I could meet her gaze. "You got reason to doubt us, Wes?"

"Like I said, you're lucky it's cold out there." She drained the last of her beer, held the empty bottle in a tight grip. "You need help, I'm going to help you, Keith. Much as I'd like to ignore you, there's too much at stake to do that. Just be aware the size of the favour I'm doing you, and be aware that I'm going to ask it to be repaid."

She offered me her hand. I reached out and shook it. "You and every other motherfucker. I'm keeping a goddamn list."

INCURSION 22

THURSDAY NIGHT I was out in the back of Robina, down in one the construction sites between the train station and the three-hundred and fifty speciality stores packed into the Robina Town Centre. The excavated pit would be office buildings before too long, part of the mass rebuilding seeping through the suburb. For the moment, it gave us a few hundred metres between the next incursion point and the nearest block of units. Langford was already tracing her ward in the red dirt, preparing for the appearance of whatever came through. Wesna had brought out a half-dozen demons to provide a perimeter and back us up, and she sat on the stacked pallet of red bricks while her boys spread out into the darkness. Tim Carleton shadowed me, his bulky presence hovering by my right shoulder, piggish eyes focused on the book I was trying to read.

He'd come well-armed for an observer. An old-school .45 revolver tucked in the waist of his camouflage pants, a small wood-axe hooked onto his belt next to the sheath for a combat knife. There were dark, familiar stains on the edge of the axe blade, the kind of thing that came from grisly work and improper cleaning of the tools. I doubted he'd ever cut wood with the thing, let alone honed the blade.

"You put together a pretty good army," Carleton said, his oddly high-pitched tone at odds with his expression. "Almost feel kinda stupid for bringing the precautions, you know?"

I shook my head. "Never feel stupid for coming armed," I said. "This goes wrong, you'll be glad you have something to fight with as you die."

"Whad'ya mean, die? I can hold my own."

I looked up from my book. "You ever seen a valkyrie?"

He shook his head.

"First one I ever saw murdered sixteen or so Rebels before she hit us," I said. "Then, it took out two demons and one my friends after we trapped it in a warded room. Two demons who knew their shit, kid—

Sabbath and his favourite enforcer. We had guns, we had magic, we had wards and we had a magic fuckin' sword, and it was still a goddamn battle to put the bitch down."

"Don't blaspheme," Wesna said, her voice floating out of the darkness.

"The first thing that happened when I looked at the winged bitch," I said, "the thing that made it so damn hard to put her down, even though it needed to be done? I wanted her to kill me. Wanted it, like I've wanted nothing else, from the moment I first laid eyes on her. She's the gather of warrior souls, so it's like a fucking bee to a flower."

"Yeah, well, I like livin'," Carleton said. "I ain't planning on being no bee."

I shrugged and opened my book. "Like that's going to give you any choice in the matter, once the incursion begins."

Carleton grunted and walked the site, staring into the darkness. He pulled the axe free as he headed into the darker areas towards the back fence. Stood there for a while, tapping the flat of the blade against his thigh as he studied the night. Wesna came up and sat beside me, watching the kid move around.

"He's going to be in the way," she said.

"The deal with Mim says he's got to be here."

Wesna made a disgruntled noise in the back of her throat. "Should have negotiated a better deal, then."

"You know I'm trying to read here, right?"

She picked up the book, studied the cover. "Myths of the Vikings." She shook her head. "You should have gone to primary sources, read your way through all the eddas and shit."

"The eddas only tell me what people believed back then," I said.

"What people believed back then make this Ragnarok shit possible."

"Yeah," I said, "but what we believe today robs it of its full power. Otherwise, there's no way in hell we could have killed the Fenris Wolf when it pushed through. Roark or no Roark, your average harbinger of the apocalypse usually isn't quite so disposable."

Wesna shook her head. "You can take the fun out of anything, can't you?"

"Roark was the optimist. My job was picking holes in our plans." I went back to my book, re-read the beginning of a story about Odin hanging from the World Tree, staying there for nine days in order to earn the secret of runes from the universe. Myths and legends. The beginning of everything. Roark used to joke our job was easier, back when everyone knew what had to be done. All we had now was guess-work and the long-term effects of reshaping a story.

That, and modern technology, which had its own advantages. I kept the sword handy, laid out on the grass beside me, and I kept a loaded Mossberg next to the blade. It wouldn't kill whatever came through. I didn't really need it to. The shotgun was there to slow the enemy down, give them something to think about while I came in with the sword and did what needed to be done.

Wesna looked down at my arsenal, made a disproving noise. "You really should learn to use that thing," Wesna said, nodding at the sword. "I know you regard it as inferior to your beloved guns, but you and Roark pulled the damn thing out of the Gloom for a reason."

"I spend two hours a day going through the basics with Langford," I said. "With luck, I'll be good enough by the time we really need me to be."

"You and luck," Wesna said. "How's that working out for you?"

"We're still in the game," I said. "Sure as hell more than I expected this far into the process."

The experience of waiting with two trained sorcerers was damn well easier than shepherding a small crew of demons, sorcerers, and legbreakers through the uncertainty. We all sat there, waiting, the cold seeping in through our winter jackets. When the bitching started, there was nothing good-natured about it. Demons don't have a good nature to speak of, and

Carleton was more than happy to join in, working on their level. Only Langford stayed silent, standing inside her warding circle, working her way through a pack of cigarettes.

Wesna crouched beside me, shoulder to shoulder. "We've been out here over an hour. How much longer?"

I put down my copy of Myths and Legends. "This isn't an exact process. We get a window, we wait."

"And maybe that worked when there were only three of you, but patience ain't exactly the strong-point of your current hit-squad." She nodded at the far side of the lot, where Carleton was kicking rocks at the chain-link fence. "He's already your weak point. Letting him get distracted is only going to hurt you in the long run."

"You got a better plan?"

"Sure. I—"

I held up a hand to cut her off, pointed at the shadows in the centre of the construction site. For a moment they shimmered, touched by the oily darkness of the Gloom, its presence like a cold and ghostly hand running down your back and taking hold of your private parts. You felt the wrongness of it, the fear, deep in your stomach.

The demons went quiet, heads raised like bloodhounds who just caught the scent of prey.

"Too shallow," I said, going back to my book. "The next one, maybe. The one after it."

The demons didn't trust me. No reason they should, I guess, but they stayed alert until the Gloom dissipated, dissolving into the night as though it'd never been. Their hands didn't leave the guns until the Gloom was gone, and it took a few seconds for the bitching to resume.

Wesna shook her head. "That's going to cost you, you know?"

"I'm aware."

"I'm just saying there are options," she said. "It goes against your principles and all, but you've got people here who make their living calling things out of the Gloom. Langford could probably do it, one or two of my guys have definitely had the practice. You know this bitch is coming, why wait for it to happen on her terms? Call her and you get to choose the location, set the place where they manifest and trap them there."

"We're not calling them over," I said.

"Theoretically, it'd work." Langford turned, eyeing us both from the safety of her warding circle. "We could do it."

"I'm not arguing the logistics. Just 'cause it's possible, doesn't mean we should do it." I put down the book, grabbed hold of the sword. It was habit now, the moment a stake-out began. Never be more than a half-foot from the blade. "For one thing, I don't want Langford wasting energy she doesn't need to waste. Erecting a ward that will hold the damn thing is hard enough; trusting you can hold it in one place while pulling through an unfamiliar entity is running the kind of risks that aren't particularly worthwhile."

"That's Roark talking," Wesna said. "You played it his way. It didn't work out so good."

I swung on instinct, a right-handed jab at Wesna's jaw. It never connected. She was faster than me, stronger than me, ready for a fight. Even on my best day, putting all my weight behind the punch, it wasn't going to connect. Wesna leaned back, out of range. Grabbed my wrist and twisted it up behind my body, pushing my face into the cold earth.

"That's was stupid," she said.

"Acknowledged."

"And it proves my point." Wesna let me go. Rose and backed off a few feet. "You've got it into your head that you're a patient man, Murphy. That's who you needed to be when you worked with Roark, 'cause that played to his strengths." She held out her hands, indicating the crowd watching us, attention drawn by our brief exchange. "You're not working with Roark anymore, but you're still playing to his strengths instead of ours. We aren't sorcerers. We aren't bad-asses on the scale of whatever's coming through. But we are comfortable with the Gloom and we are strong enough to keep the bitch distracted. What we suck at is patience."

She offered me a hand. Hauled me upright.

"Let me play this my way," she said. "Trust me for once, will ya?"

Trust. Rarest fucking commodity in the world, once you start dealing with the things I deal with on a daily basis. Langford voted to give the demon's plan a try. I agreed so long as they kept Langford out of the summoning; she was purely defence, holding the thing in place once it manifested on our plane.

Wesna got to work straight away. Stepped out into the open, called her demons together. "Alright," she said, "We're going to do this our way; it's time to go looking for a fight, instead of hoping one finds us before we all get bored. Keating, you're doing the summoning. Reach into the Gloom, call whatever's lurking there over. It'll be big and nasty, so keep moving. Don't let it get its claws on ya. Hawke? O'Malley? Singe? You're responsible for getting the thing into the sorcerer's warding circle. Hammer it with everything you've got, but we've got to pin it down. Everyone else put together a perimeter; first thing we need to do when the incursion happens is keep that bitch from flying. Strong wings."

She took a deep breath, glanced over the demon's heads. "All of you know Keith Murphy. He's the trigger man on this one, 'cept the valkyries don't go down to conventional bullets. Ammunition is there to slow the old girl down a little, apply a little pressure. The thing that will put her down for good is the magic fucking sword strapped to Murphy's back, and I recommend against trying to liberate the weapon and using it yourself. He stole that bad-boy from deep in the Gloom, so it generally goes on the list of things we'd rather not fuck around with."

Red eyes turned towards me, studying the blade. I stared back. Showed no fear. There's no advantage in showing fear to demons.

They spread out, forming a ring around the building site, eyes burning in the darkness. Keating started chanting in a language I couldn't identify; something old and archaic, like most tongues that get used in magic. It started with a slow, steady rhythm that grew stronger as it went on, words building into short, staccato pauses as the darkness started to shimmer. My reading light flickered and went out, the gas lantern unable to keep up with the rush of magic. Shadows thickened into Gloom and bulged as something fought to be free.

I held the shotgun at the ready, finger resting against the trigger.

The valkyrie appeared faster than expected, bursting free of the darkness like a greyhound freed from a starting box. Tall and withered and immensely strong, taloned hands reaching for the demon named Keating and tightening around his throat. The long, feathered wings spread wide as the valkyrie squeezed and twisted, pulling Keating's skull free with a scream of victory.

Wesna barked an order and the rest of the demons went to work, three of us opening fire as the rest swarmed the valkyrie. I pulled the shotgun trigger, felt it buck in hands, but bullets weren't doing shit to slow down the valkyrie. She wheeled, dark eyes studying the clearing, picking her next victim as bullets bit into her flesh. The first demon to reach her—Hawke, I think—was met with a fist to the centre of his face. It connected with sufficient force to stop him in his tracks, his head jerking backwards as his feet tried to maintain the momentum of his charge. O'Malley was swept aside by the powerful wings, knocked off her feet as she approached.

Carleton crashed into the valkyrie, heavy arms wrapping around the feathered wings. The two of them tipped sideways, scrabbling across the grass, Carleton digging his boots in as he tried to push his victim into the warding circle. Wesna barked an order and the demons converged, the first two grabbing hold of the valkyrie's shoulders and preventing her from thrashing around. More bodies came in, some falling away as the valkyrie lashed out. One demon fell back, face bloodied by talons. Another had its arm broke, the audible snap a sickening noise accompanied by a strangled gasp.

I covered the distance between us, reversing my grip on the sword. Stabbed down through the mess of bodies, putting the blade through the valkyries shoulder. It keened like a wounded animal; a high-pitched, agonized sound that cut through to the bone. Blood stained the grass, black and altogether inhuman. I heaved the sword free, stabbed a second time.

The valkyrie struggled, wrestling against the mass of demons trying to hold her down. Blood loss weakened her, made it easier to push her into Langford's circle. I heard Langford's steady voice as she began the chant, locking the valkyrie down.

I readied the sword, held it in a two-handed grip. Looked out over the carnage she'd wrought, in her brief time on our plane.

"This is why we don't call them over any earlier than we need to," I said.

I swung for the valkyrie's head. Put everything I had into the blow, severing the neck.

VICTORY CELEBRATIONS

ROARK DIDN'T CELEBRATE victories, not really. What we did was necessary, but it wasn't worth celebrating. The only reward we ever claimed was the satisfaction of a job well done and the knowledge that, once again, the two of us had beaten the odds.

There was nothing of that in the demon's approach to the job. We'd barely finished clearing the incursion site and disguising our presence when Wesna announced the victory party in one of the casino bars. It was a morale booster for the nine of her demons who'd survived the crash, a way of keeping them onside and engaged.

I tried to beg off. "Some of us are still mortal enough to need sleep more than hard liquor," I said.

Wesna fixed me with a stare. "And exactly whose war were we out there fighting tonight?" she said. "You owe fucking Carleton a drink, if nothing else."

I was dragged along in the back of the SUV until we hit the club on top of the casino floor, a wide open place with sloped glass roofing that allowed you to look out over the glittering lights of Broadbeach as you drank.

The club was pure Gold Coast tackiness. Expensive drinks that came in fishbowls; repetitive dance music straight out of the top forty charts from a decade or so earlier; a mortal crowd, more or less, even on a Wednesday night, men and women in their early thirties who liked to pretend they were a little younger. The occasional stray lamb closer to eighteen than anything else who'd wandered in, not entirely sure how this place was different to the other clubs on the strip.

The demons drank hard and started dancing, giving in to the basic impulse. I found a dark corner and nursed a glass of scotch. Langford sat beside, her eyes never leaving the cluster group of allies.

"So, this is who we've become." She raised a glass of vodka in salute. "Succeed at any cost. Ally with whoever will get the job done. Shitty dance music to celebrate if we get something right?"

"You were the one who agreed with their plan to summon the bitch."

"Because I'm the one who lives here, after all this is done," Langford said. "You're the one that leaves town, Danny. I have to coexist with your old friend and her gang of thieves. That means you're the man who gets to be the bad guy when they're saying something stupid.

"Oh," I said. "I didn't realise."

Langford closed her eyes. "Not your fault," she said. "Roark didn't exactly train you to think about consequences, did he?"

"If we thought about the consequences, we'd never do the job."

She laughed and shook her head. "And now you're stuck with a crew who does even worse with impulse control than you do," she said. "If this is going to work, Murphy, you need to keep a leash on them. Today turned out okay, more or less, but there's all kinds of luck involved in something like this turning out as something to be celebrated."

I stared at the demons spread out on the dance floor, bouncing and thrashing, trying to get rid of the excess energy they hadn't been able to use in the fight. "Keeping a leash on them may be more than I'm capable of."

An hour ticked by and the club got muggier, the steady application of additional drunk bodies in motion generating a sweaty fugue that started to fog the glass panes. Langford disappeared, ostensibly to get another drink, but I caught sight of her dreadlocks bouncing through the crowd on the dance floor before too long. The music was getting older. Cheesy hits from the eighties and nineties. It was enough to entice most of the crowd. The beat grew louder, insistent. The kids working the bar in the centre of the room barely got a chance to pause.

Wesna appeared out of the darkness. Her black shirt clung to her, damp with perspiration. Her short, spiked hair lost its controlled appearance, the various products she used to hold things in place unable to hold up against an hour of wild movement. She slid into the vacant chair, stole the rest of my scotch. Grinned at me, a genuine smile. Like I was seeing the Wesna I'd known in school, instead of the woman who led the local demons.

"You look like you fucking hate this," she said.

"It's not really my thing."

"Of course it isn't," she said, leaning in to shout over the music. "Having fun never really did rate high on your list of priorities."

"We defeated one incursion," I said. "One, of the many that are going to roll through, as Ragnarok gets closer. It already cost us two of your demons. Having fun feels a little redundant."

Wesna shook her head. "So instead you're going to sulk your way through the apocalypse?"

"I'm not sulking."

"Murphy, you're one of the most miserable mother-fuckers I've ever seen," Wesna said. "You were when you left sixteen years ago. You were when you came back. Right now, there are demons doing a better job of celebrating the fact that they're still alive than you are." She closed her eyes and turned her face toward the ceiling. "Demons, Murphy. Seriously."

"Wes?"

She opened her eyes, fixed me with her stare. "Yeah?"

"You okay?"

Her grin went lopsided. "Just trying to picture what success looks like," she said. "If we pull this shit off. If we stop Ragnarok. I'm trying to figure out what that looks like for you."

I thought about that for a few minutes, watching the ebb and flow of the crowd.

"Well," I said, "I think it looks like another job done, and I'll try and figure out what the next job is going to be."

"Yeah, that's what I figured." Wesna shook her head as she laughed. "You're a truly sad bastard, Keith. I hope you fucking know that."

She leant in and kissed me on the cheek. Put my empty scotch glass on the table as she headed back to the dance floor. I stood there for a few moments, still feeling the press of her lips upon my cheek. The DJ segued from an old Ace of Bass track into something from Michael Jackson's *Thriller*.

I figured I'd celebrated enough for one evening. Headed for the exit without telling anybody.

I caught the elevator down and headed for the car park. Drove my rented sedan southwards, heading towards the apartment I was renting down in Palm Beach that month. It was early enough that the traffic had thinned out. The Gold Coast is a twenty-four seven kind of town, people always on the move regardless of the hour, but there was always a short pause a little before sunrise. A moment when all the drunks were busy getting home, and all the joggers and surfers who did the sunrise shift weren't yet on the roads. I let the car carry me forward, stereo blaring a CD of old punk songs I'd picked up at service station for ten bucks while getting fuel.

In my line of work, being followed is a pretty common occupational hazard. I knew the clues to watch out for, but exhaustion kept me from noticing the black SUV in my blindspot until we hit the stretch of Burliegh Heads where the highway did a little dogleg turn right on the goddamn beach front. They'd been on my tail since the casino, doggedly sticking to a distance of five car lengths. Amateur hour shit, but it's how I spotted them. If they'd done their homework even a little better, my tired brain would have missed them and focused on the problems associated with having demons on my side.

They were trying to play it subtle. Hanging back, out of the way. It made them just as obvious as if they'd sat on my rear bumper; real drivers vary their speed a little. They get closer and they fall back, more focused on their journey and their own shit than what you're doing. These guys were a tail. They wanted me, specifically, and that wasn't going to be good news. I cranked up the heat in the rental and slowed it to a cruise. Took a right off the highway and headed into the smaller suburbs. We were driving into the sunrise now. The red glow lit up my dusty windshield, forced me to slow it down even further. The SUV behind me kept pace. That was okay. I wanted them right there. The stretch of road we were following ran all out the way out to the hills in Mudgereebah. It was a long stretch of road without too much traffic.

The lack of traffic hadn't stopped 'em putting in a shit-load of streetlights.

I got lucky on the third stop. There weren't enough cars between us to keep the SUV from getting close. They changed lanes. Came to a halt behind the hatchbacks that occupied the right-hand lane. That was close enough to get a look at the driver. I tilted my rear-view and did a quick study. Three guys. Leather jackets and hair the same black as a raven's wing. The kid in the passenger seat had tattoos covering his arms and cheeks. I figured them for cultists; two thugs and a sorcerer. The thugs weren't a problem. Odds are, the sorcerer wasn't going to be one either. Every cult has a handful of dabblers, people who've crossed the line and brushed up against the Gloom without developing the mastery of a guy like Roark and Wotan. Experienced sorcerers like to guard their knowledge. It's how they keep the aspirational types dangling. How they push them over the line and convince them that things like human sacrifice are worthwhile if the exchange is a little more power.

The only cult I'd pissed off in the last year had belonged to Michael Wotan, and we'd eliminated everyone in his group with anything approaching real power. These guys were new blood, or the final hangers-on from Wotan's group. Either way, they were low men on the totem pole.

The lights turned green. I eased my foot down, sped up a little as we started getting into the hills. Took the right turn that lead me up the slopes of Springbrook and its national parks. The sun rose behind me. The SUV kept following.

I shook my head. Amateur hour idiots.

There's an art to indulging a tail without tipping them off. Part of it involves keeping your driving natural. Part of it involves resisting the urge to look over your shoulder. No doubt the boys in the SUV were already fretting they'd been blown. There were too few cars on the road to disguise it. Too few places I could be going out here, outside of trying to lose them. That was okay. I wanted them to think that. So long as they thought I was trying to escape, they wouldn't consider the possibility that things could get worse.

We hit the lower slopes of the mountains. Started going round the curves, past the signs that warned us to be aware of falling rocks and using too much speed as we took a sharp bend. The Eastern edge of the mountain slopes were mostly National Parks. We gained a little altitude. Got close to the rest-stops they built into the trip. I took a corner fast, sped up the next stretch like a bat out of hell. Pulled into the rest-stop and slid the car to a halt. I left my front door open, right next to the toilet block. High-tailed it across the road, scrambled a little further up-slope. It was steep going, using roots and tree-trunks for leverage, but there was plenty of scrub to cover my climb. I went a couple of meters up. Took refuge behind an old paper-bark, watching as the SUV pulled up behind my car. Two guys climbed out, left the third in the car. They produced a couple of guns, old .38 revolvers. One of the leather jackets advanced on the car, kept his bulk crouched low in case I was hiding inside. The other stood beside the car, jawing with the sorcerer holed up inside.

The first guy disappeared into the men's rooms. Took long enough that he either needed to go or he'd done a pretty thorough search. His buddy told him to finish the job, pointing to the other side. The first guy argued against going into the ladies. Went back and forth about it a half-dozen times. Eventually he gave in. Went in and out in half the time he'd spent on the mens side of things. It's funny the things that make people squeamish. Wotan's cult had killed a hundred women in their search for power. They'd done unspeakable things to women, before they finally let them die.

And a bloke in the ladies room remained unthinkable.

The argument started right after the first guy emerged from the ladies side. The guy by the car said he should have checked harder. The guy who'd gone in claimed he'd done a thorough job. They went back and forth again, killing time with the argument. Eventually, the guy by the car went himself, disappearing into the lavatories with the big revolver in hand. His comrade took position beside the car, attention focused on the toilet block.

I let go of the tree, eased my way down the slope. Hit the ditch that ran along the mountain side, crouched low until I was sure they hadn't noticed me. The guy outside the car had his back to me, still bitching about being made to go into the ladies room. The sorcerer in the front seat wasn't paying too much attention. He was studying the lookout, probably wondering if I was crazy enough to try and escape down the slope. I stayed low, crossed the road with the SIG held loose and ready. Crouched beside the driver's seat of the cultist's SUV.

When I stood, I fired two bullets through the window, plugging the guy in the passenger seat. The next two caught the complainer right as he turned around, his slack-jawed face caught in surprise as he tried to figure out where I'd come from.

I stayed low and scurried behind my car. Hunkered down behind the engine block, waiting for the third guy to emerge.

He played it cautious. Stuck his head out from behind the brick wall. Fired a few rounds to keep me honest. I stayed low and out of site. Said nothing. Did nothing. Waited for him to get curious and poke his head out again, trying to spot me. Waited a little longer until he picked his way free of cover, starting the short dash to the safety of the SUV. I rose and pulled the trigger. The third man saw me a little too late. His eyes went wide and he tried to get the .38 up, but there wasn't time. Two in the centre stopped him. Two in the head made sure. He slid to a halt, limp against the earth.

I stayed poised a moment, gun at the ready. My ears were ringing. The guns made a hell of a racket, enough to attract the wrong attention. When I was sure all three were dead, I went to work. Frisked the corpses for wallets, phones, and occult marks. Liberated what was worth keeping and threw the rest in the back of their SUV. I went through the firefight in my mind, counted off the shots. Went through the small lot until I'd recovered all the shells, slid them into my jacket pocket to take care of a little later. Wallets identified them as out-of-towners. The muscle were Adelaide boys; leftovers from Wotan's mob. The sorcerer was from Perth, probably part of the cult's diaspora. Just strong enough to start leading his own chapter. Just weak enough to be worth overlooking when shit went down. Two sets of keys between them. One of the SUV, with the number for a car rental down the airport. One a set of keys attached to a resort key ring; Magic Mountain, down on Nobby's beach. Pricey bit of real estate, despite the dodgy name.

They had a single cell phone between them. I went back to my Holden and threw it into the passenger seat. Closed the door and locked it. Went back to the SUV and sat in the driver's seat. Put it in gear and drove a little further up the road. Kept going until I found a tight corner. The kind most people would miss. The sun was over the horizon now. A glorious, eager pink and yellow sunrise. I stopped the SUV and climbed out. Hauled one of the corpses into the driver's seat. Put the whole thing in gear and let the slope do the rest. The big car rolled forward. Tipped over the side of the road and tumbled. I could hear metal crunching as it went down, bouncing through the undergrowth covering the slope.

I turned around and started walking back to the lookout. Climbed into the car and checked the cultists burn phone. There were two numbers in the recent calls section. I went through them both in order.

The first number rang out. No answer, despite my patience.

The second number picked up after the first few rings. The voice had a familiar whine to it.

"What's up?" Carleton said. "You get him?"

I killed the call and dropped the phone back on the passenger seat. Put the car into gear and got the hell away from there.

CONSEQUENCES

I PARKED IN the underground lot below the Oasis centre, went up to the Hell Bar on the second floor and took refuge in the office for the rest of the day. I spent part of my time dozing off in my chair, picking up a few hours here and there. I spent the rest of the time pacing back and forth, running through the possible reasons Mim's boy would be talking to the Raven cult. Around one o'clock I picked up the phone and made a call. Around five o'clock the bar staff appeared, getting ready for the late night opening. I went out in public, made it seem like everything was normal. Waited for Langford to shuffle in a little after dinner time, her hands disappearing into the pockets of her over-sized jacket. I waved her over, pointed towards the back room. She just nodded, walked ahead of me. I closed the door behind us, locked the staff out.

"How long did you stay with the demons last night?" I asked her.

Langford gave me a queer look, settling into the visitor's chair. "Not long, once you bailed. Wesna offered me a drink. I tried to be polite."

"You notice if Carleton was still there?"

She shrugged. "It really matter?"

I told her about the tail. About the hit up in the mountains and Carleton's voice on the end of the call. It didn't take long before she was thinking of the implications, thinking through the connection between Carleton and Mim, thinking through the trust we were forced to put into Bruce Mim's predictions for the sake of moving forward. She nodded slowly. "Can't say I blame Carleton for trying to have you killed," she said. "The thought's occurred to me a few times over the last couple of months. If I knew a few cultists who owed me a favour..."

"If you knew cultists who owed you a favour, I'd already be dead," I said. "You recognise competence when you're dealing with people. I'm not sure Carleton can even spell the word."

"He held his own last night," Langford said.

"There's a line between competence and stupidity," I said. "I'm trying to keep us on the right side of things, instead of doing something stupid 'cause it seems like the perfect time."

I stood and went to the safe in the back wall, pricked my thumb with a silver needle and used the smear of blood to unlock the initial wards. "I'm going to talk to Mim again," I said. "That means I need back-up. Someone who can watch my back if he starts throwing around magic, and someone who can cart my corpse out if things go wrong. I know I ain't got any right to ask this, but my short-list is pretty damn short these days."

"Figured, by this point, you'd have learned to stop asking," Langford said. "Save the world first. Pay back debts after you make sure the world's still here."

It was dark by the time we reached the Dell. I parked in the spot farthest from the pub, a good half-block's walk from the front door. Retrieved my SIG from the glove compartment and the sword from the backseat. Langford pulled up behind me in her pristine HR Holden. She stepped out, ground a cigarette into the concrete. The sky above us was the colour of ink. The crowd inside the Dell was thinning out a little given the hour, the honest drinkers and tradies heading home around dinner time. The folks who remained were the professional drinkers and those aspiring to professional status, young blokes with sufficient anger to make drinking away the evening an attractive prospect.

Langford pulled up in the space behind me, climbed out and stared at the Dell with a grim expression. The wards around the place were already starting to register our presence, offering up some faint resistance; a sense of pressure, like trying to walk against the tide, that wasn't quite strong enough to keep us from getting closer. I calmed my breathing, tried to put the idea of violence out of my head. Stumbled a few steps as the wards pushed back, but there wasn't enough bad intent to keep me out or cause me pain.

Langford, a few steps behind me, didn't even miss a step. Sorcerers play by different rules when it comes to warding against them and keeping a place safe. The wards would cut off access to certain kinds of energy if she started something, preventing her from doing anything that could be counted as a direct threat.

Fortunately, Langford didn't need to make threats that day. She just needed to jam the wards if anything went sideways, give me enough time to clear the SIG or draw the sword and do what needed to be done. She followed me into the common room.

She kept her back to the rest of the room, focused on the door. Her expression said she hated playing bodyguard almost as much as she hated scouting out a hit. I let her get settled, crossed the room to Mim. The old man was playing cards with a handful of blokes, obviously in the swing of things. He was shuffling, cards dancing a complicated twist as they moved from one hand to the other. I edged my way over, hands disappearing into the pockets of my jacket.

My shadow fell across the table. Mim didn't look up from his cards. "Your timing stinks, Mister Murphy," Bruce said. "This next hand was going to be spectacular."

The other players at the table exchanged a look and decided there was business at the bar. They had the looks of men who'd already lost the bulk of the money and needed to drown their sorrows. I took their place, sat opposite Mim. Tapped the wood with my knuckle. "Come on, then," I said. "Let's see what you've got."

Bruce Mim dealt fast, a small pile of cards forming in front of me. I picked them up, sorted them. Aces and Eights. A dead man's hand. I looked over and Mim sat there, trying to hide the smirk. "No secrets from a seer, Mister Murphy," he said. "I know what happened this morning."

"Yeah?"

"Yes." He discarded two cards. "You repelled an incursion. You were followed from the celebration."

"Did a whole lot more than that." I dumped the whole hand, motioned for him to deal again. "You want to tell me where you learned all that?"

"I'm a seer," Mim said. "Knowing things, charting

possible reactions and responses. This is my bread and butter, Mister Murphy. This is who I am. I know you dealt with an incursion because I sent you out there to do so. The tail I learned about because I have contacts everywhere. Friends who saw you leave the casino. Friends on the police force who reported a series of dead men found in their car, way up in the mountains. Men killed in a short gunfight and promptly disposed of, tipped over the edge of a hairpin turn and left to fall down the mountainside. It isn't hard to put two and two together. Not when you start out knowing what I know."

He dealt me a fresh hand, replaced the discards in his own pile. I picked up my cards, studied them carefully. The final eight showed up, an eight of hearts. The two of clubs, the seven of spades. Three queens in different suites, seated side by side. Across the table, Mim frowned at his own hand, arranged the cards with a certain look.

"Carleton isn't here tonight," I said.

Mim's glassy eyes looked up from the cards.

"Kind of surprising," I said. "From the way he acted, the first time I came, I could have sworn he was a bodyguard or something."

"Mister Carleton is an employee, not an indentured servant," Mim said.

"So tonight's his night off, then?"

"You amuse me, Mister Murphy," Mim said. "This is an unexpected line of questioning. I come across them so rarely, you understand. So very, very rarely, these days."

"Glad to be entertaining," I said.

Mim lowered his cards to the table, affable smile on his face. "Even so," he said, "perhaps we can simply skip to the question you truly want to ask, eh? I'm sure it's something truly troubling, given you've come out here with your sword and your gun and your sorcereress."

I nodded. Played my hand. The queens, the seven, the two of spades. "I took a phone off the guys who followed me this morning. A burn phone, pay as you go, only two numbers ever dialled in the damn thing's memory. One number rang out, when I tried to call it back. The other number was answered by your boy, Carleton. He didn't ask who was calling, just asked how the hit was going. He wanted to know if I was dead yet."

"And that establishes guilt, in the world of Keith Murphy," Mim said.

"It establishes guilt in lots of worlds, I said.

Mim laughed, softly. Left his cards face-down on the table. "Yet, that little monologue still didn't involve a question," he said. "Ask, Mister Murphy. We're getting no-where until you do."

"Fine," I said. "Here's my question: did you know your boy Carleton was working with the Raven cult?"

"Of course," Mim said. He flipped over his first card. A red king, holding a sceptre, staring out past the borders of the card. "But that isn't the question you truly want to ask me."

"Did he go and talk to them because you asked him to?"

Mim flipped more cards, revealed the jacks of Heart and Diamonds. "Did Roark ever tell you what the Gloom truly is?"

"Danny talked a lot of shit," I said. "Picking the stuff that was real was always part of the challenge."

"Humour me." Mim flipped the fourth card in his hand. The King of Diamonds. "Tell me what you know, eh? Let's see how well you truly play this game."

I gathered my cards together, put them in a neat pile. "Roark always called it a symbiotic reality; a black mirror of the real world that fed off the collective unconscious of humanity. It used to have other names, but they fell out of common usage as people gave up on magic."

"And the great fucking pity of the world is that you have no idea what that means." Mim shuffled the cards out of habit, not really paying attention. "There used to be borders in the Gloom, you know? Faerie was a place unto itself back then, like Valhalla and the infinite hells and the damned celestial bureaucracy the Chinese dreamed up. Little pocket universes reflecting the beliefs of a particular tribe or culture. The place where magic comes from, back when magic was something humanity still believed in. And when there were small tribes, there were heroes who stood at the forefront, men and women touched by the Otherworld and destined to shape its future. Then the world got bigger. Borders came to mean less and less. Stories went from one culture to the next, bleeding into one-another, appropriated for the storyteller's own ends."

He paused and coughed into his fist, grinned as he slid the final card in his hand across the table.

"It doesn't take much to sustain something. A handful of stories that capture the imagination. The fey still exist because of Tinkerbell lunch-boxes. Ghosts still exist because children will always gather around campfires, trying to scare one another. Monsters settle in as the bad guys in movies. The end of the world is still possible because you, as a species, still fear it. You gave it different names once you stopped believing in gods: global warming; nuclear war; global economic meltdown. You made them bigger and badder than any apocalypse your ancestors may have come up with. In trying to eliminate the things you feared, you simply raised the stakes and made it easier to wipe you all out. Lots of creatures in the Gloom were happy to play by those stakes, to let themselves be reshaped by the new stories you kept telling each other and the new dreams you forged."

He tapped his pack of cards, made a flourish with his hands. The cards disappeared, all except the one he'd placed before me.

"And some of those entities, which had fed on humanity and centuries of faith, chose not to play. They refused to become less than they once were and disappeared into the deep places where most entities of the Gloom do not go. Gods slumbering in the heart of darkness, sustained by the memory of what they used to be. Not everything in the Gloom complies with the rules you expect, Mister Murphy, but they all comply with rules laid down at some place, at some time. It's why a demon will always keep a promise, even as they're acknowledged as the masters of lies. It's why fragments of a sorcerer's essence are always caught up in the Gloom after death, as payback for the power they leached from it in life. It's why werewolves are hurt by silver and vampires recoil from items of faith, why holy water burns so many of the Other even if there are damned few holy men left to truly bless the waters."

Mim rapped his knuckle on the table and the card seated in front of me bounced and flipped face up. I'd expected a jack or another king, something to claim Mim victory. Instead, it looked like one of the tarot, a figure hanging upside down from a tree, a rope around his ankle.

"I knew Carleton was talking to your cult," Mim said. "I asked him to do it. There are rules for everything touched by the Gloom, including you and I. I don't see a single future—I see possibilities. Pathways to a desirable future that are, by no means, certain. In many of those futures, the cult and their attacks upon you are a necessary part of the outcome you desire. And so I make contact. I manipulate and nudge. I play games, as you no doubt call it, because that's the way things were done. That's my role in what's happening here. It's time for you to accept yours."

"Yeah?" I said. "And what's that? I'm the sacrificial lamb you get to send people after?"

Mim shook his head, his smile a little weary. "Your role is to be the hero," he said. "The man who makes choices and expects the world to follow. It's what your friend Roark was grooming you for, right from the very beginning."

STAKE-OUT

LANGFORD HAD A safe-house in the heart of Surfers Paradise. This small, three-bedroom place at the top of a tourist high-rise, high enough above the nightclubs that you didn't notice the din. She pointed me towards the spare room, disappeared into a bedroom with additional wards placed on the door. I slept for eight hours. Longer than I'd managed since the night Roark died. It felt weird, when I woke up. I'd been running on fumes and instinct so long that feeling awake felt abnormal.

Langford was up and making coffee by the time I emerged. Her dreadlocks were pulled back away from her face, held together by a length of cloth she'd tied into a bow. Her long coat hung over a partially buttoned shirt and a black t-shirt with a pentagram painted on the chest with gold paint. She pushed a cup across the counter, sipped the one she'd made for herself.

"You look like hell," she said.

I shrugged and sipped my coffee. "Healthy living disagrees with me."

"What part of the last twenty-four hours classifies as healthy?"

"Good coffee and enough sleep counts for a lot. Plus, no one's tried to kill me for at least twelve hours."

"There's a reason I always hated working with Roark." Langford finished her coffee and placed the cup in the sink. "Good to see you're endeavouring to keep up the tradition."

There were breakfast stools lined up against the kitchen bench. I pulled one out with my heel, settled into it. "Too much time around bad influences," I said. "You pick things up after a while."

She nodded and started moving around the kitchen, putting together the ingredients for breakfast. Hash browns. Spinach. Toast and beans. She lit a cigarette as she fired up the gas stove and started moving a dab of butter back and forth.

"Langford," I said.

"Yeah?"

"Thank you," I said. "For backing me, after what

happened to Roark. Sticking with this even though it looks... you know."

"Yeah," Langford said. "Feel free to say it." She sucked on a cigarette, exhaled quietly. "I don't kid myself, Murphy. No reason to, you know? But the way I figure, if we're going to go down, I'd rather go down fighting."

She went back to cooking, stubbed out the cigarette in an ash-tray on the counter. I sat quietly, ate when she slid a plate of food in front of me. Drank a second cup of coffee along with the meal.

I lasted about two hours before I told Langford I was heading out. Wotan's cult was out there, infesting the city again. I'd feel better if I knew where, and what they were up to.

I started with Magic Mountain, down on Nobby's beach. It'd been a theme park in the seventies, gone to seed by the time I was a kid. They shut it down in eighty-seven, left it derelict for a couple of years. There were rumours the old castle on the top of the hill was home to the local Satanists, that they'd booby-trapped the place to keep people out. All that was gone now. Wiped out in a fit of urban renewal sometime in the nineties. All that remained was the name: Magic Mountain Resort. A couple of hundred apartment blocks running up the slope, high fences keeping the outside world out and all the mountain's magic in. The cultists who'd tried to ambush me were carrying keys from this apartment complex.

It wasn't much of a mountain. The beach side were cliffs, the long slope on the far side connecting with the highway. The resort shared the slope with a small patch of scrubby parklands, a local high-school, and a church. I drove the long way round, parked in front of the school. They'd built a sign on their patch of the slope, this cruel mockery of the giant letters spelling Hollywood that loomed over LA. These spelled out Hi Miami High, like people could forget the name of the school. That was my way in. Across the open oval. Over the back fence. Use the letters as cover as I went up the slope, make a dash for the tree-line. Up on Magic Mountain.

There's magic in names. Magic in history, too. It made me wonder why the local Other hadn't tapped the site already, why they'd left it there, all open and waiting, for the Raven Cult to move in.

The first order of business was blocking out their territory, figuring which units they'd annexed for the cult. They wouldn't have the numbers to occupy the whole place, not based on what I'd seen of them. Michael Wotan, down in Adelaide, had kept his circle small. The offshoot he'd sent up here, a precaution against his eventual death, had been wiped out by the local demons just after I'd arrived. These guys were the remnant of the Adelaide arm, maybe a few additions from other cities where Wotan's disciples worked. They'd start recruiting locally, bringing in the weak and the desperate, using them for muscle, but that kind of growth took time and they hadn't been here long enough.

I opened the boot and hauled out the backpack with my kit, everything I needed for a full day of observation: snacks; water; a telescopic sight I could use to see things up close. A change of socks so I wouldn't sit there with damp feet after stomping through the scrub. I skirted the school oval, went up the side of the hill, moving fast and quiet to minimize the chance of casual observes watching from the street. Slowed down once I hit the trees, started picking my way up the slope.

The kids from the high-school definitely hid out in the scrub. I could tell that from the detritus scattered among the trees. Used condoms and empty coke cans, the occasional bong made out of a juice bottle and wedged into a tree branch where they thought no-one would notice. I ignored them all, kept moving towards the far side of the slope, searching for a patch where the branches provided sufficient cover but still gave a decent angle on the rows of apartments.

I understood this part of the job. The patience of it. The observation. Sitting and detailing the targets' movements, looking for the weaknesses we could exploit during the hit. It gave me a sense of control, the ability to relax and enjoy my job. I raised the binoculars, scanned the apartments. The keys I'd taken from the dead cultists were for apartments high up on the slope, close to the cliff edge that looked out on the Pacific. I started there. Identified the lookouts working the balcony. A couple of hours work, observing their behaviour. Separating the tourists enjoying their beach views from the cultists watching the streets for trouble. They all looked the same at first, rugged up against the cold. The differences were body language, the things the people focused on. Tourists looked out. Cultists looked down. They carried themselves a little differently, constantly alert. Their observation of the outside world was a little too intense; the way they moved, when they paced their balcony, was riddled with visible tension.

I changed my vantage point every couple of hours, sticking to the tree cover. It was an awkward way to run surveillance; lower than the targets, trying to get an angle on them. Destined to run into the hill before I could see if they had people on the northern side of the block. I used the lookouts to peg four separate apartments with cultists in residence. They were renting in a block, two on the ground floor, two above. They kept the curtains on each apartment drawn, making it impossible to see more than the boys on lookout.

That was okay. I could be patient now. I settled in and watched them for the rest of the day.

EXTRACTION

THEY CHANGED GUARDS on the balcony every couple of hours. I started tracking faces, putting together a rough idea of numbers. Identified at least twelve people before sunset made the job more difficult. Twelve wasn't a number that pleased me. I knew the cult had people to spare, that was obvious when they'd ambushed me, underneath the Oasis. But twelve faces on five balconies in the space of a day meant they had good numbers. Bodies to spare, sending people after me. Bodies to spare, constructing rituals and hindering our efforts.

It wasn't until the sun was set that things got really interesting. Additional men joined the lookouts working the balcony, started working together to prepare a climbing harness and belaying rope. Two men provided the anchor, while a third went over the edge. Rappelled down the cliff side of Magic Mountain, pausing every couple of seconds to do something to the rock. I dug out my sight, tried to get a close-up. Made out the sharp stylus one carried in the hand, an ancient thing built from copper and bone. When they paused, the climber scratched something into the rock.

My angle wasn't good enough to get a close look at the marking. I'd need to go beachside, get lucky enough to focus on the exact spot they marked things. I frowned a little, thought it over. Ran through my options for doing it safely. Nothing good comes from cultists scratching runes into the landscape. It changed the tenor of my surveillance, meant I needed to look at things a slightly different way.

I fished my phone out of my jacket, thumbed in Wesna's direct line. It rang a few times before she answered, her voice thick with irritation as she barked, "What, Keith?" down the line.

"I'm going to need a favour," I said.

"Like that's a damn surprise."

"It's a small one, compared to riding shotgun on incursions."

"Okay."

"We've got a small pack of Raven Cultists setting

up shop down in Nobby's," I said. "I've counted twelve standing guard, another handful coming out to do some ritual on the side of Magic Mountain."

Wesna's tone changed with that. Less irritated. More curious. "What kind of ritual?"

"Hard to say from my current vantage point. I'm going to need to hit the beach, take a real close look without the veil in place."

"And that means you're going to need a way out, 'cause puking on a cultists isn't going to slow him down any."

"You read my goddamn mind," I said.

"Keith."

"Yeah?"

"Don't blaspheme."

I grinned into the phone. "Sorry," I said. "Can you get me some help?"

There was a long pause on her end of the phone. "Keep an eye out," she said. "I'll send Dale down with some back-up. They'll meet you on the beach side within an hour."

Used to be, as a kid, I could see past the disguises used by the things that go bump in the night. I could see auras and the dark stain of magic on the ground when I encountered a ward on a house. I learned real fast what all those splashes of colour meant. Learned about the existence of demons, and fey, and the other species that make their home in the Gloom. I learned about Ghosts the hard way, on a road-trip to see my grandfather in a caravan he called home. I peered into very dark places and realised other worlds existed beyond our knowledge.

That's heavy shit to lay on a kid. It just about drove me mad. I spent years learning to ignore the gift, focusing on seeing the world as other people see it. Paying attention to the Veil, rather than the things that hide behind it.

But a gift like that doesn't disappear. It just punishes you for using it, after ignoring it for so long. I checked my watch, figured the demons were close. Closed my eyes and steadied my breathing, focused on the rhythm of it. In. Out. In. Out. Focused on the steady rhythm of the waves at my back. With a grunt, I let the Veil slip and stared up at Magic Mountain.

At first I couldn't see anything I could put into words. It was like staring at the night sky and seeing the mass of stars, without knowing how to identify constellations from the chaos. It took time to connect the dots, to see the shimmering strands of magic they'd edged into the cliff face and recognise it as a dark, tangled system akin to tree roots. My breath caught as I focused, saw the roots connect to a dark trunk that rose up towards the cult's apartments. Saw the trunk that rose further still, a dream of an impossible tree given birth by the shadows of the Gloom, the trunk rising higher and higher until the branches spread and reached for the sky, stretching until they disappeared into the upper atmosphere.

It took effort to focus, to see the tree in its entirety. It slipped away from me several times, my eyes refusing to latch onto its contours. They were attempting to manifest the fucking Yggdrasil, anchoring the Gloom to local landmarks in order to create a permanent incursion point. The ambition of it terrified me even as I felt myself wanting to start climbing, to see how high those shadowy branches truly went before they faltered.

Blood seeped from my nose. My head ached from the pressure of staring at the Gloom. I focused on my breathing. Tried to keep it steady. In. Out. In. Out. Saliva filled my mouth as my stomach began to roil. I spat and paid no attention to the queasiness, the growing desire to throw up everything I'd eaten since breakfast. It wouldn't work for long, but I was taking all the moments I could get with the tree. I stared at it until my vision started to swim and I felt myself falling backwards, my stomach registering its final objection before throwing up was no longer optional. I hit the ground hard, jarred my elbow and shoulder against the earth.

I blacked out a couple of seconds later, and the Yggdrasil haunted my dreams.

I woke up in a Jupiter's Casino hotel room, recognisable from its decor done in shades of olive green and sandy beige. I'd been dumped in a double-bed still wearing my clothes from the stake-out, left there to sleep off the worst of the vision. The digital clock on the bedside table said it was ten oh five, and the sunlight streaming in through the window meant I'd crashed there overnight.

I rolled out of bed, searched for my gear. Found most of it neatly stacked on the room's small writing desk. Clean clothes were folded and stacked on the desk as well, jeans and t-shirts from the gear I'd worn when working as one of Sabbath's flunkies, doing my best to meet the unwritten dress-code he seemed to demand from all flunkies. I'd hated the black-and-black look, particularly when coupled with Gold Coast business causal, which meant the part of my wardrobe I'd left behind after Sabbath's death didn't get thrown out by housekeeping.

I went through my weapons. Checked the SIG, then the combat knife, then the back-up piece. Made sure each of them were ready to go, if I found myself in need of them. When I was done, I hit the showers, climbed back into my dirt-streaked blue jeans rather than wearing the black. I emerged from the bathroom, still towelling off my stubbled hair, and noticed Wesna seated at the desk.

"The boys I sent to meet with you got lucky," she said. "They found you, passed out and dead to the world. Got to you before the Raven cult did, which is saying something given how many people they seem to have watching over their operations."

I nodded and scrubbed the towel against my right ear. "Obliged," I said.

"I've never seen you black out before, not from using the sight," Wesna said.

I nodded and went to work on the other ear. "I never really looked at something quite like what I saw there," I said. "The cult isn't just back. It's getting ambitious."

"They set off Ragnarok. That's ambitious enough

for me."

"That wasn't the cult, that was Wotan," I said. "In all the time I've known them, their sole ambitious activity was trying to bring Wotan back from the dead, and even that didn't work 'cause of what me and Roark did. The guys we're dealing with these days were probably the lower ranks when Wotan died; rank-and-file cultists who didn't have the magical skill to be worth bringing here. Now they've got people out there, dangling on a cliff face in the dark, so they can manifest their own fucking World Tree with its roots in Magic Mountain."

Wesna's eyes narrowed. "When you say World Tree, you mean—"

"The Yggdrasil," I said. "The thing that connects the nine worlds together, assuming all the places the Norse believed in were actually real."

She whistled and stood up, pacing the length of the room. "That's a big piece of mythic real-estate to try and reconstruct," she said. "How in hell are they sustaining it?"

"There were lots of urban myths about the mountain," I said. "Odds are there's a couple of soft spots in there, where they can tap directly into the Gloom. I don't think they've got it right yet—what I saw was big, but it was more like watching the ghost of a tree. Something that could have been real, but hasn't had a chance to truly exist yet."

"It's not going to get a chance to manifest, either." Wesna brushed the hair out of her eyes, offered me a feral grin that wouldn't seem out-of-place on your average lion. "We're going to shut them down."

"That'll be risky," I said, "and I can't ask you for that kind of favour."

"Screw favours." Wesna glared out the window, as if she could see the tree just beyond the glass. "They're staking a claim on my turf. They've put out hits on people that I haven't authorized. They're tapping the local Gloom to build shit that shouldn't exist. That kind of shit gets on my nerves. It's bad for fucking business, letting someone disrespect you like that, so I'm doing this one gratis."

She turned and slid her hands into her pockets, frowning as she focused her attention on me. "I've got a couple of boys packed into the cars downstairs. Big, menacing lads with some ugly fucking demons inside 'em, all ready to go somewhere and engage in a little mayhem. All we really need is a fucker with a magic sword and some sorceress with a hard-on for getting rid of these pillocks, and I think we can raise a little hell. What do you say, Keith? You and Langford want to go help me wipe the fucking Raven-cult off the face of the earth?"

I nodded and reached for my phone. "Let me call Langford, see if she's up for it."

EFFICIENT, WITH MINIMAL BLOODSHED

THREE SUVS FULL of demons parked at the base of Magic Mountain. Big men, professionally stoic, their attention focused on Wesna as she laid down the law. "We're doing this one quiet," she said. "No guns. No screams. No disembowelling. These fuckers are messing with our territory. We go in there and wipe them out. We do it quiet because we want to make a statement. We do it quiet because people need to know that this is our fucking city."

There was movement at the gate. Dale, standing by the wall, scouting ahead for cult guards.

"We've got five apartments full of cultists," Wesna said. "You three take out the ones the left. I'll be sending the other car to sweep the far side. Murphy, you're with me and the team going up the guts. With luck, you won't be necessary, but I'm hedging my bets. They summoned anything from the Gloom that could make a noise, I want you there with your sword, understand me?"

I nodded. I understood. It's half the reason they'd brought me along, instead of filling the spare seat in the SUV with another possessed thug.

Wesna's boys disappeared into the night air. Some of them went up, going up the side of the apartment blocks until they found a position on the rooftops. Others just disappeared into the shadows, better at hiding than any mortal was going to manage. Dale fell in beside Wesna. I took a position on her other shoulder, followed her long strides up the hill.

We found the first guard a hundred metres in. He was standing out the front of a small townhouse building, in the shadow of the peach-coloured garage that bordered the left side of the small garden out the front. He fumbled with a cigarette as we approached, trying to fake a reason for being out in the cold air, but his posture was all wrong. Wesna nodded and Dale leapt for it, grabbed either side of the lookout's head and torqued it sharply to the right. The soft crack of a snapping spine seemed louder than it should in the cold night air, and for a moment I slowed and held my breath, waiting for someone to notice.

They didn't. If there were lookouts along the road leading up the mountain, then Wesna's demons were doing good work, eliminating them as they discovered their presence. Wesna kept marching, a look of grim satisfaction on her face. Her eyes focused on the small knot of buildings towards the peak, the places where the cult activities were centred.

The cult had erected wards around the place, done a pretty good job on them. I felt the pressure on the side of my skull a good hundred meters out. Had me sweating as we got closer to the front door. Dale and Wesna faltered, doubling over, faces contorted in silent pain. Wards were always more effective against creatures from the Gloom, particularly those with bad intentions towards the one who created them.

I closed my eyes, focused on the ward. Imagined it as a physical thing, a wave that was crashing over us all and trying to sweep us away. It helped, having a visual. I knew that from experience. I grit my teeth and did as Roark had trained me to, murmuring the counter-ward beneath my breath. Breathed a sigh of relief when the pressure eased and I could think clearly again.

Wesna rose to her feet, teeth bared in a silent snarl. "You're better at that than you used to be."

"I've had far more practice," I said. "Ran into plenty of wards on the job. Roark made sure I could get past the shoddy ones without bothering him for an assist."

She helped Dale up, slapped him until he focused. His eyes blazed with anger as he regained his focus, fingers splayed wide as his nails elongated, becoming sharp talons.

"Quietly," Wesna said.

Dale nodded and took point, loping along on stealthy feet. Wesna and I came after him, crouched low and cautious. Covered the final hundred metres and gathered by the front door to the central apartment. It was one of the penthouse blocks. Large, expensive, and built to hang over the side of the mountain. The lights were on and we could hear people inside, muffled voices and the shuffle of feet against carpet. Dale pressed his shoulder against the front door, prepared to batter it down. Wesna clenched her fists, her expression grave. I drew the sword, just in case. Held it ready with both hands.

"Go," Wesna whispered, and Dale's shoulder hit the door. It splintered under the impact, broke in half the second time he threw his weight against it. The two demons hit the room first, their movement a blur I could barely see. They bounced the cultists into walls, tore open throats as they moved through the space. I came in behind them. Followed the carnage as they moved, clearing the penthouse room by room. We'd caught the cultists by surprise.

They'd counted on the wards to keep them safe, and the wards weren't going to do it.

The demons had the place wiped out inside of ten minutes. The final headcount was two-dozen cultists, spread out between four apartments. The penthouses had been damn-near cleaned out, furniture cleared to the edges of the room so they had sufficient space for rituals and weapon storage. There were more beds than bodies, so we figured some of the cult were out. Wesna assigned three of her people to stand guard here, in case they came back. She left me to toss the three apartments, trusted me to find things her demons wouldn't. The average person possessed by a demon is strong and incredibly fast, in possession of sight and olfactory senses that would make your average hunting dog envious. What they lack is the kind of patience that allows for a thorough search, which means human eyes still had an advantage when it came to doing things methodically.

It took time to notice the blood patterns connecting the three apartments. Partially because there was so much blood already, spilt during the demons attack, and partially 'cause the cult had tried to hide them, daubing the eaves with a few pinpricks of blood or concealing it low, at the level of the floorboards. I went through the apartments, tracking their locations. Tried to build a mental picture of the pattern in my mind. I couldn't do it, not with any accuracy. My sense of scale wasn't up to the task. The blood dots were like tiny constellations, marked out on the wall. Some of the blood was old enough that it'd turned black against the peach-coloured paint.

"Wes," I said. "We're going to need Langford."

Wesna pulled a sour face. "You're sure?"

I crouched and studied a trio of dots, placed low enough they almost touched the floor. "I'm really sure. They're doing something with this shit, but it's well and truly beyond me."

Wesna nodded. Produced a cell phone and started dialling. I kept moving, room to room. Found more constellations of blood scattered through the penthouse, always partially hidden by its location. I went into the bedrooms, started searching through them. Looked in the drawers. Looked under the beds. Poked around behind the furniture the cult had moved out of the way.

I found something in the final bedroom, underneath the bed. A small wooden box, hinged at the back, top and sides carved with warding runes. Velvet interior, like it was designed to hold jewellery, although the wards placed on the outside meant it had never been used for that. The lid hung open as I fished it out from under the bed, bounced a little as I turned the box over in my hands.

The wards were Roark's work. Roark's, and mine. The contents of the box had been mine for the better part of a year, right up until I'd handed the whole thing over in order to make an ally.

I closed the box and latched it. Put it on the bed. Stared at for a long, long time, right up until Wesna appeared at the bedroom door and told me Langford was there.

THE STARS ARE RIGHT

IT TOOK TWO hours for Langford to study the bloody markings, and she came straight to me once she figured out what they were. I straightened, took my elbows off the balcony rail. Wesna just took a step closer, bringing the circle in tight. Two steps and it spoke volumes: no need for her demons to hear Langford's findings. She'd let them know in her own time, when the information could be most useful to Wesna.

Langford looked at the two of us, waiting for an okay.

"Well?" I said.

"I think they're constellations," she said. "I mean, I can identify a good two-thirds. They're older than we're used to, spread out a little more, but they're definitely some kind of star chart spread out across the three apartments. Almost like they were trying to create their own orrery, assuming we could figure out what served as the central point."

She headed inside, waved two fingers to indicate we should follow her. Paused by the apartment kitchen and pointed a cluster of bloody dots painted into the ceiling. "My knowledge of astronomy isn't anything close to Roark's, but that's definitely Ursa Minor. They've got Ursa Major over by the floorboards, and there's three minor constellations that make up the Argo on this wall. I can use those as an anchor to figure out what the rest of them mean, but there's a point—"

She stood and wiped her hands, pointed to the bedroom at the rear of the penthouse. "Well," she said, "there's a point where things just start getting batshit crazy.

Langford lead the way, Wesna and I following. Heading into the master bedroom, the place where my old wooden box still sat under the bed, latched and closed and utterly abandoned, empty of its contents. Langford pointed to the wall, noted a cluster of dots so faint they were barely there. "These I've got no idea," she said. "There's about fifteen of them in this apartment, more in the ones above and below. None of them correspond to any constellation I know, but that doesn't mean much, really. We could call in an honest to god Astronomer, but—"

"That isn't necessary." Wesna pushed her way to the front, put her face very close to the wall. "I know this constellation. The demons call it Níðhöggr, after the dragon that chewed on the roots of the world tree." She turned to Langford. "The others you can't identify?"

Langford nodded, moved over to the northern wall. Pointed out another handful of dots. Wesna chewed her lip a moment. "The Beast of the Sea, named after the Christian Armageddon. That one's the Thunderbolt of Ba'al, son of Hadad, from the Canaanite faith."

"Not constellations I'm familiar with," Langford said.

"You wouldn't be," Wesna said. "They don't exist in this world. These were the stars you could see in the Gloom, back in the days when it still had a sky. My kind—the demons—haven't seen them in centuries."

"Someone knows them," I said. "That's probably not a good sign."

Wesna nodded. "They're not building an orrery," she said. "They're building themselves a map. They're waiting for some alliance of stars, some confluence of events that will allow them to pull something extraordinary." She had the beginnings of a smile. "They're up to something odd."

Langford snorted. "A cult trying to do something odd? That's a goddamn first."

"It's not funny," I said.

"It's a little funny. Cults, by default—" I crouched down and picked up the wooden box, forced it into Langford's hands. She stared at it a moment, pressed her fingers against the lid. Whispered a soft phrase before she opened it.

Wesna frowned at the box in Langford's hands. "Is that?"

"Yep."

"Did you?"

"Nope."

"Bruce Mim?"

"Most likely," I said, "but that's not the most pressing problem. We've got the box, but we don't have the contents. Which means one of the dead is keeping it on him, or the bullet containing Wotan's ghost is doing a tour with the boys who aren't here with the rest of the cult." I turned back to the dot-covered walls. "You got any idea when this sequence they're mapping is going to line up?"

Langford shook her head. "Not during daylight," she said. "I'll need to come back in the night, track it against some star maps. And even then, I'm no good with the stars I don't recognise. I didn't even know the Gloom had stars, let alone constellations worth following."

"Then we're not done with Mim," I said, "regardless of where Wotan's bullet has gone to. If neither of you remembers stars, we need someone older." I turned to Wesna. "I need one of your SUVs."

She grinned, showing off sharp teeth. "Want some backup to go along with it."

I shook my head. "This was my deal. It's my fuck-up to deal with if it's all gone wrong. I'm going to go have a quiet chat with Bruce Mim, the kind where he stops talking in riddles and gives me exactly what I want."

BETRAYED

I GOT OUT of Langford's old HR and walked into the Dell's front bar. It was early enough in the afternoon that there wasn't much of a crowd. Two barmaids, a couple of tradies who'd knocked off work a little early, and the hunched-over form of Timothy Carleton pretending he didn't see me come in. I walked over and sat down at his table, watched him try to find somewhere to put his eyes that didn't involve looking my way.

"Well, hey there, Timothy. Your boss around today?" I said it in a reasonable tone, trying to sound like the kind of person who wouldn't spontaneously break out into violence. I didn't succeed. I could see that in his face, the way Timothy went pale at the merest mention of his boss.

"Mister Mim is working out of office today," Carleton said. His piggish eyes danced to my face, danced away almost as fast. "If you'd care to leave me your message—"

"Carleton, please, don't do that," I said. "If you do that and I go back there, only to discover you're lying to protect your boss, then it's going to sour my good opinion of you."

He blinked a few times, processing that. His big hands left the table top, balled up into fists. He was a big guy, and fast enough for his bulk. That probably carried him through most fights, particularly the kind of guys who showed up the Dell for a drink. I wasn't like that, though. He swung at me and I saw it coming, grabbed his arm and twisted. He ended up face down on the table, arm stretched and hyper-extended as I applied pressure on his elbow.

"I swear to hell, Carleton, I've got no problem breaking your goddamn arm." I looked around the bar, took in the stunned expressions of the other patrons. I looked at the women behind the bar. "'Could one of you duck round to the back room and take Mister Mim a drink? Tell him that Mister Murphy's here to see him, and it's best for all concerned if it happens out here, where everyone can see us."

The first barmaid just stood there, her mouth formed into a tight O of astonishment. The second woman was older, a little more worn down by the surprises the Dell patrons threw at her. She nodded and pulled a pint from the on-tap, disappeared through a door marked Staff Entrance Only. She reappeared a few moments later, offered me a tight, controlled nod.

I let go of Carleton's arm, let him settle back into the chair. He rubbed at his elbow, glaring at me, no doubt convinced that I'd gotten lucky. I sat down opposite him. Waited quietly.

The door to the back room opened and Bruce Mim made his way out. He limped a little on his bad leg, gestured to the barmaid to pour him a beer. "I'd like to apologize, ladies and gentlemen," he said. "Mister Murphy is here on business with me, and he's gotten a little overexcited."

He limped over to the table, raised a pale white eyebrow at me. "You were overexcited, weren't you, Keith?"

I glared at him, both hands on the table. Mim nodded and tapped Carleton on the shoulder, signalled to the big man that he should find another place to be. "So, Mister Murphy, you're obviously upset."

"Upset and heavily armed," I said. "You're lucky I didn't walk in here waving a goddamn shotgun around."

"Luck had nothing to do with that." A barmaid stopped by the table, delivered Mim a pint. She turned to me, eyes full of fear, stammered her way through a question asking if I wanted something.

Mim waved her off, smiled at me. "Honestly, if I'd seen any future where you walked in here with gun or sword, threatening my people, there is no chance I'd agree to the conversations that preceded it. I don't raise armies like your friend, Miss Holjack, but these are my people, Mister Murphy. Threaten them, hurt them, do anything that makes their lives more dangerous than they've chosen it to be, and I promise you that Ragnarok will not be the thing that kills you."

He said calmly, the same bland smile fixed on his

face. Took a long pull of his beer when he was done. "So, Mister Murphy, you're obviously upset. What seems to be troubling you today?"

"We had a deal," I said.

"We did, although I wasn't aware our arrangement had moved into the past tense."

"It has," I said. "Be certain of that. I gave you Michael Wotan's soul. The part of him that could use magic—the part that made that mother-fucker a threat to me and to the world. I gave that to you, to bring you onboard. Now I'm asking you what happened to the bullet with Wotan's soul inside it?"

Mim exhaled heavily. "This is tedious, Mister Murphy. You wouldn't be here in such a lather if you didn't already know."

"Humour me," I said. "Confirmation is important in my line of work. Assumptions will get you killed, sooner or later."

He looked up at the ceiling lights as though he'd never noticed them before. "I delivered it to the chaps you and yours call the Raven Cult," he said. "What they chose to do with it is really just conjecture, but I assume they tried to revive their fallen leader or re-unite this part of his segregated soul with the spirit half that lurks around the Gloom from time to time."

He folded both hands before him on the table, waited quietly to see my reaction. I thought about leaping across the table, wrapping my fingers around his throat and jamming the SIG into the hollows of his jaw. I stared at him until that feeling died down, replaced by a need to understand.

"I was part of a raid on the cult compound today. They were dangerously close to getting Wotan back."

Mim nodded. "I assumed as much."

"You assumed?"

Irritation passed over his face. "Let's get something straight, boy: You talk a good game about wanting to stop Ragnarok, but only if it's done on your own terms. You're a crusader, Mister Murphy. For all your rhetoric about being a soldier, you want to be the shining hero and resolve things your way. If that weren't true, you could have stalled the apocalypse by doing exactly what I did, only you would have done it twelve months ago. You would have let your friend, Wesna, stuff a demon inside your mentor, simply because you needed his knowledge and weren't able to move forward without it. I warned you, from the beginning, that I was a pragmatic man. I have no need to play hero, so long as I survive."

Mim finished his beer, wiped the foam off his face with a serviette. "Pragmatism, Mister Murphy, is the lesson we creatures of the Gloom have learned from humanity. Pity you're so incapable of embracing it yourself."

"Roark didn't believe in pragmatism," I said.

"And now he's dead." Mim signalled the bar for another beer, eased his frame way back in his chair. "You, on the other hand, are still alive and fighting. And because the damn Raven Cult has Michael Wotan's soul, you actually have a fighting chance."

He smiled at me, like he had me all figured out. Maybe he did. I unclenched my fists, sagged into the chair. "You're a son of a bitch, you know that?"

"I'm that and a whole bunch more," Mim said. "I've lived with myself for centuries, Mister Murphy. That doesn't leave one with many illusions about who they truly are."

"They're building a tree," I said.

"Of course they are," Mim said. "They're ending the world. There's all sorts of scholarly theories about where people hide from Ragnarok, but the majority of them seem to suggest that hollows of the Yggdrasil are the best place to wait it out. They obviously need to build one, if they want to survive the coming apocalypse."

I scrambled for him, ready to swing a right hand at his face, but Carleton moved faster. He intercepted me, clubbed me to the floor with a swing of his right arm. I went down hard, started rolling as soon as I realised I was on the ground. It didn't matter. Carleton followed me, grabbed me. Hauled me up and twisted my arm behind my back.

"By the Gods, Mister Murphy, are you truly this stupid?" Mim said. "You've spent too much time around demons and their ilk, letting their poor impulse control manifest in your own behaviour. This is a time when you should be thinking, making smart decisions instead of placing your trust in instinct and half-cocked plans. I realise this doesn't play to your strengths, but I doubt it's beyond your capabilities altogether. Think."

Carleton deposited me back into my seat, loomed behind me in case I felt the urge to do something stupid. My arm hurt where I'd landed badly. I slumped in the seat, glared at Mim. He grinned at me, although the grin was close to a sneer. He was right. I was being stupid. There was satisfaction, in stupidity, compared to staying in the game.

"What did you really tell Roark," I said, "back when he first came to meet with you? Somehow, I doubt you really told him you wouldn't help."

Mim's grin didn't falter. "I told him he wasn't going to succeed in stopping Wotan. I told him, if he tried, that Ragnarok would roll through right on schedule, and everyone he knew and loved would die in pain and fire." The grin faded. Mim regarded me with a tired, hollow-eyed stare. "Then I told him the night that the Fenris Wolf would breach the Gloom and enter our reality, and I told him he had to die if there was any chance of you doing what he could not."

"Alright," I said. "Now tell me about the bullet. Where is it?"

Mim raised his shoulders.

I raised an eye brow. "Seriously?"

"Seriously. I don't know," he said. "It is one of those variables that is no longer trackable, which suggests it's no longer accessible on our plane of existence. That would be unfortunate, but it's not our main concern."

"No?" I said.

"Not at all," he said. "It was turned over to the cult. That part is done. In thirteen days, the stars are right. The seed the cult's been planting will bloom and the Gloom will ensure the Tree of Life is more than a mythic metaphor. This will be your one, last chance to stop the apocalypse. You can waste that being mad at me, or you can gather up your army, rag-tag though it is, and take the fight into the Gloom in order to stop Wotan's cult." He paused and tilted his head to one side, a ghost of smile on his face. "Or you can make the same decisions Roark made, and do the thing that will tip the odds in favour of mankind surviving Ragnarok. You can go to the Gloom and you can let yourself die, and you will give humanity the fighting chance you seem so desperate to give it."

We watched each other for a long time. Two poker players searching for a tell.

"Mister Carleton," Mim said, "I think this would be a good time to escort Mister Murphy from the premises."

ON THE JOB

THREE DAYS LATER I was back on an incursion site, pulling into the Currumbin Alley parking lot and parking next to the unmanned guard tower. It was cold and wet. The incoming clouds obscured the stars, the horizon lit up by the occasional flash of lighting. The rain hadn't hit yet, but you could taste it in the air. It was coming and it would be a cold, aggressive downpour. High winds came off the beach, carrying the salt spray and grains of sand that attempted to lacerate the legs of our jeans. Distant thunder cracked and boomed, following the lightning by a couple of seconds. Langford stood by the HR, hands shoved into her pockets. She glared at the storm, then glared at me.

"Yeah," she said, her expression sour. "This is going to be all kinds of fun."

I walked round to the rear of the car, caught the keys she tossed me. Unloaded the sword and strapped on the sheath, pulled out the Mossberg latched to the top of the trunk. The big shotgun was a comforting weigh, more than the sword poking into my back. I'd loaded it with handmade shells—a combination of iron and silver shot, soaked in a mixture of holy water and mistletoe. Those four substances were the bane of a dozen entities from the Gloom. I was counting on at least one being able to effect a valkyrie. With Roark gone, we needed the extra firepower. I rested the Mossberg against one shoulder, pulled Langford's kit free with my other hand. She grabbed it and started scanning the ground, trying to find the best point to paint in her warding circle.

Langford rolled her eyes at the shotgun. "If the cops come past, they're going to arrest you."

"We're not going to see cops. Not tonight," I said. There were a half-dozen demons spread along the beach, each of them armed to the teeth with blades just in case something went wrong. Wesna's boys, keeping watch, protecting the investment she'd made on my life. No way she was bringing cops into this, not with her people nearby.

I dug my book of Norse Myths out of the car, nursed it in my lap as I sat down at the picnic table. Kept the unsheathed sword beside me, kept the loaded shotgun beside that. My position gave me a pretty good vantage point on the beach and the mouth of the river, the long stretch of sand and the lights of Surfers Paradise glowing in the distance. Behind us, Currumbin Hill was a mass of darkness, all the houses and estates kept away from the ocean-facing slope. Langford paced back and forth along the parking lot, picked her spot about twelve feet from the HR. She crouched, just inside the yellow glow of the streetlight, pulled a small pot of paint from her kit as she started to daub a warding circle into the rough bitumen. Once she'd finished a rough outline, she stood and frowned at her handiwork. "So, this is Mim's intelligence, yeah?"

I could hear the accusation in her tone. Chose not to engage. "He hasn't led us wrong so far," I said, nose still buried in the details of Norse myth. "Everything he's given us is right on the money."

"Everything he's given us, sure." Langford crouched again, fingers dipping into her jar of paint. Her long dreadlocks skittered against the bitumen as she turned a slow circuit, filling in the gaps in her circle. "Seems to me there's plenty your friend Mim is keeping damn quiet about."

"He's a sorcerer," I said. "Near as I can tell, you all keep secrets for the sake of it."

Langford's cheek dimpled when she smiled. "Mine aren't likely to get you killed."

"We going to place money on that?"

"Maybe," Langford said, "if the world lasts long enough to demonstrate the truth of it." She finished her second attempt at the circle, stared at it intently. Bitumen was a bitch to work with, I knew that from experience. The uneven surface made it easy for the ward to be broken, and she looked a little uncertain as she tested the circle's strength.

"He keeps quiet," I said. "He does things without telling us. He's willing to be practical and do the things we aren't. At this point, if I'm honest, I don't really care what he does, so long as he's got good reasons. And his reasons all seem reasonable enough, when he lays them out."

"The man's a goddamn sorcerer, Keith. One of the oldest on the goddamn planet. It ever occur to you that making things sound reasonable is one of those skills he's picked up over the years? That maybe he's willing to embellish his talent with a little Gloom-based voodoo?"

"Yeah," I said. "I've thought of that."

"And?"

"The same was true of Roark. I chose to trust him."

Langford smirked as she finished the circle. "'Cause there wasn't anything dysfunctional about that goddamn relationship."

She fished around inside her kit, produced a pack of cigarettes. She backed away from the circle a couple of paces, not willing to risk damaging it while she lit her smoke. "It's going to be a cold, ugly bitch of a night," she said.

It was two o'clock when I got the phone-call, twenty minutes past the time Bruce Mim had given me. I was still on the park bench, rereading the same page for the forth goddamn time. Langford hovered by her circle, studying the darkness, waiting for something to come. The rain was closer now, close enough to taste it in the wind. My phone was on vibrate, twitching in my pocket. I pulled it out, thumbed it to life. Held it against my ear.

"Pack it in," Bruce Mim said. "It's not going to happen tonight."

I didn't reply immediately. Just sat there, phone against my ear, watching Langford by her circle, waiting for something to happen. I took a deep breath and let it out, made sure I wasn't being stupid. "Can I get you to repeat that? I want to be sure I heard you right."

"There's no incursion," Mim said quietly. "The chain of possibilities that would have led to a valkyrie crossing over in that location have been diverted by recent events, resulting in new possibilities."

"In other words, you got this wrong."

"In other words," Mim agreed. "Believe me, I'm as surprised as you are."

"Surprised wouldn't be the word I'd use." Thunder cracked out over the ocean, heralding the start of the rain. The downpour hissed against the bitumen, rattled against the corrugated covering erected over the picnic tables. I pressed my finger against one ear, trying to focus on the phone. "We've got a dozen of Wesna's demons, standing out in the rain," I said. "If I go tell them it was all for nothing, they're going to try and eat my spleen."

"Blame me," Mim said. "They're more than welcome to try and take mine, and Carleton needs the practice dealing with demonic threats."

"I've seen Carleton' attempts to deal with mortal trouble. He'll need a lot of practice."

Mim said something I couldn't quite hear, against the rattle of the rain on the roof.

"Can you repeat that?" I said. "We just had a storm hit."

"I said, this is good news, for all it doesn't seem like it," Mim said, raising his thin voice til he was nearly shouting into the phone. "When we hit the point where my abilities are uncertain, Mister Murphy, there is the possibility of doing something that truly changes the direction of things."

"Yeah," I said, "and it also means there could be incursions you're totally unaware of."

Mim paused, considering the implications. "That," he said, "is a slightly disturbing thought."

I hung up. Waved Langford in, under the cover. She ran for it, dripping cold rainwater onto the concrete, her dreadlocks hanging limp and damp around her face. She looked me over, then shook her head. "Before you say what you're about to say, I'm very wet and very cold and extremely easy to piss off."

I grinned at her, trying to think of a joke that would make it all okay. Langford stood there, shivering in her leather jacket, skinny hands balled into fists. Her eyes met mine and there were no jokes that would fix what I saw there. She was scared and she was pissed. She had been ever since Roark's ward broke and the wolf sank its teeth into his shoulder. Langford had walked away from all this. She'd left Roark's war behind and settled on the Gold Coast, laying low and bothering no one.

"You know," I said, "if we actually pull this saving-the-world thing off, I'm going to spend the next twenty years paying back the favours I owe you."

The fear didn't go anywhere, but it did cause Langford to crack a smile. "Don't worry," she said. "I've been running a tab ever since you blew up the first safehouse I found you."

I grinned at her. She grinned back. For a moment, we felt like a team again, for the first time since Roark's death.

Then my phone rang again, vibrating in my pocket. A message from Dale, further down the beach. It said: *incoming.*

I looked up and spotted the SUV cruising along the beach front, high-beams cutting through the storm as they drove twenty K's over the limit. They took the left into the Alley parking lot, tyres skidding on the bitumen.

I reached for the Mossberg. Langford grabbed the sword, turned and sprinted for the HR. I walked out into the rain, got close enough to open fire and but a blast into their windshield before the SUV's doors started opening. Cultists spilled out, weapons in hand. Five guys with small, automatic handguns. A driver who sat there, bleeding, behind the wheel of the vehicle. I heard the HR's engine growl, watched Langford floor it and head for the second exit. Two of the cultists opened fire, bullets connecting with the rear of the Holden.

I pumped the action on the shotgun. Even in the rain, with the sharp crack of their guns to distract them, the distinctive click of the pump-action got their attention. Five gun barrels pointed in my direction.

"Put down the shotgun, Murphy," one yelled. "We don't want you dead yet, but we'll work with your soul if we have to."

Tyres squealed as Langford took the corner, gunning the big engine inside the HR. I stared at the assembled guns, at the frightened faces of the cultists behind them. I couldn't help smiling at their threats.

"Put down the shotgun." The voice was insistent this time, demanding I comply. I removed my hand from the trigger, held the shotgun in one hand.

"I'm putting it down," I said, lowering the weapon. "But you already fucked up, boys. The sword is in the car that just left. It's getting the fuck out of here, and Langford can cover her tracks."

A nervous titter ran through the cultists. "We aren't here for the sword, Murphy. Get your hands behind your head."

I raised my hands, locked my fingers on the back of my head. Kept grinning at the cult boys through the pouring rain.

"I'll give you one chance to get into your car and fuck off," I said. "One chance, 'cause I'm feeling generous tonight."

"Fuck you, Murphy." This time it wasn't the guy who'd been giving me orders. That meant the group was getting cocky, ready to relax a little. A bad habit to get into, when you've got a target cornered. Worse, when you don't know what kind of back-up's coming.

I didn't really see Dale charging in. Motivate a demon, convince them it's worthwhile, and they'll move a whole lot faster than the human eye can track. That's one of the reasons people accept having the fuckers possess them. It makes them faster, it makes them stronger, it makes them nigh immune to pain. Dale crashed into the side of the cultists like a wrecking ball with claws. The SUV rocked with the force of the impact, two cultists pinned against the steel chassis of the vehicle. A second demon came in from the opposite side, leapt at the closest guy with the gun, a feral grin in place. There were another three demons on the beach. All of them wanted in on the action, a chance for a little mayhem in light of the failed mission.

I crouched and picked up the Mossberg again. None of the cultists tried to stop me. I walked back to the cover, picked up my copy of Myths and Legends. Waited for the carnage in the SUV to end so I could hitch a ride home with Dale and his boys.

It was nearly dawn when Dale and his cohort dropped me outside the Hell Bar. I hid the Mossberg beneath a long jacket, carried up two flights of stairs until I hit the rear door to the club. The wards pressed against me, trying to keep out the weapon, but they gave way as I slid the key into lock, letting myself in and heading for the back office.

I put the Mossberg in the gun case and locked it down. Sank into the desk chair and rubbed at the grainy exhaustion settling around my eyes. I pulled Roark's book out of my pocket. It'd gotten damp, despite my best efforts. There were pages stuck together, delicate enough that they tore when I tried to separate them. It didn't matter. I knew the contents well enough. Myths and Legends were a form of self-preservation in my line of work, where obscure knowledge about the things that go bump in the night could often come in handy when things went south. I'd spent twelve years with Roark memorizing eschaton scenarios, charting all the ways the world could end, whether mythical or man-made.

I started dreaming about Roark's book of myths and legends, on the history of Odin as a guide for the dead. One of a hundred mythic psychopomps that evolved into something more complex over time. Raven the one-eyed god, who'd traded his right eye for a draught from the well of wisdom. The god who'd hung himself from the world tree for nine days and nine nights to procure the gift of writing for the world.

Odin, who'd stood against the monsters and the giants, until Ragnarok came to claim him. I dreamt of the myths in Roark's book, saw the tortures the old man went through in the name of knowledge.

But I wasn't a god. I wasn't hanging on the world tree, hoping for knowledge. I was passed out in my office chair and someone was shaking me, their firm grip on my shoulder and their voice repeating my name. I opened my eyes, found myself looking up at Wesna's sharp features and the fringe of black hair that framed her face. "I think that's the first time I've ever seen you sleep," she said. "You actually looked...defenceless. Like anyone could show up and put a bullet into you."

I pushed my chair upright and ran my fingers over my face. "Guess that's the flaw of thinking this place is mostly secure," I said. "I keep forgetting it's got a few holes that let undesirables in."

Wesna grinned and settled into the spare chair in my office. "You were twitching in your sleep."

"I was having a weird dream."

"A dream, or a *dream*," Wesna said.

I shrugged. "I'm no sorcerer. I'm not sure there's a difference."

"There's always a difference," Wesna said. "Sorcerer's just know how to pay attention to the important things."

"You're the one who asked about the twitching."

Wesna raised both hand in defeat, folded them over her right knee. "So you had a dream," she said, "which was merely a dream. Noting particularly special about it."

"It's nothing," I said.

"Yeah, right." Wesna stood, thrust her hands into her leather jacket. "That sorcerer you hang with—Langford, not the one I found you—she called me tonight and asked me for a favour. Seems the events of this evening rattled her, and she wants you to meet her at a safehouse she assures me you know how to find."

"I'm fine," I said.

"Like hell you are. There's a cult out there, looking for you. We don't know if we can trust the man you're trusting. You're abandoning the people who've had your back for weeks, Keith, and you're doing it for what?"

"I don't know," I said. "Hope, maybe?"

"Hope." Wesna shook her head. "You really are an asshole, you know that? I respect your desire to go down fighting, but eventually you reach a point where it's time to admit defeat."

"I don't admit defeat," I said. "Roark drilled that into me. Do enough research and there's always a way to win. If you're not sure how to put something down, hit the books and study—"

I looked down at my book.

"You okay?" Wesna said.

"Yeah. Just, you know, tired," I said. "Should probably get back to Langford's and abuse her hospitality. It's more comfortable than sleeping here, and almost as secure."

I let Wesna leave the club before I made the phone call. Gathered up my SIG and my book before I treated to Langford's safe-house. She'd already gone to bed by the time I arrived, although she'd left me a handful of pizza slices ready to be microwaved. I sat at her kitchen table, running my finger along Roark's book. Reading and re-reading the myths until I had the damn things memorized. When I was done, I made a phone call and caught a lift down to the ground floor. Walked down to the cab rank on the highway and caught a cab up to the Dell.

It was closed, at that hour, but I hammered on the door. Kept at it until the lights upstairs went on and Bruce Mim made his way down to ground level. He grinned when he saw me, wryly amused by my presence.

"Mister Murphy," he said. "I apologise for earlier this evening. I gather you were attacked?"

"It doesn't matter," I said. "I need your help."

He straightened his blue suit, touched a finger to the sprig of mistletoe at his pocket. "I fear we're now beyond my help, if my predictions can no longer be trusted."

"I don't need your predictions. I need your knowledge," I said. "I think I know how to get the information we need to stop this thing."

Mim raised an eyebrow and let me in. Listened, over a glass of beer, as I explained what I had in mind.

"I don't know if you'd call this a plan," he said.

"It's more blind hope and desperation, even if the theory seems sound."

"Roark always said the strongest magic was rooted in symbolism. Nothing in the Gloom holds power unless it's got an earthly analogue that people recognise or believe in. This particular symbol may be out of vogue, but there's plenty of analogues in Christian faith that keep the possibility alive."

Mim smiled. He liked that. "You're a smarter man than you look."

"Yeah, if you say so." I finished my beer and wiped my lips with the back of my hand. "So what do you say we go hang me from a tree and see what I learn from the experience?"

Mim grinned at me and rose from his seat. Froze, instantly, as he turned towards the door. I dropped my hand to the holstered SIG before turned around, but it wouldn't do me any good. Carleton stood at the Dell's open doorway, his ancient .45 in hand. The big hand-cannon was pointed in my direction, dwarfed by Carleton' massive hands.

Mim shook his head. "Timothy," he said, "put down the gun."

Carleton shifted his glare to the old man. "Fuck you," he said. "Fuck you both, for that matter. Six years I worked for you, old man, listening to you ramble about possibilities and time-lines. Six fucking years, and when someone shows up talking shit about the end of the world, you just shrug and pretend it's no big deal. Play both sides against the middle."

Mim's dry laughter sounded hollow against the emptiness of the bar. "You think that's what I've been doing, Timothy?"

"Shut up," Carleton said. "It doesn't matter what you've been doing. I've seen the things that are coming through from the Gloom. I've read what's on the paper, all the predictions of things that are coming. I've heard the lies you told along the way, helped give the cult back the very thing they needed in order to get the end of the world moving again. And now, well, I'm officially done. I'm joining the side that actually knows what it's doing."

The sorrow in Mim's expression could have made a stone cry. "You disappoint me, Timothy. I had such hopes for you."

I didn't see him produce the gun. Didn't even see him pull the trigger. I just heard the loud retort, echoing against the empty bar, and watched Carleton list sideways, his .45 hanging loose in his grip.

"Well, then," Mim said, stepping over the body. "Shall we do this, Mister Murphy?"

I followed him out of the pub.

We took the long walk up Magic Mountain, heading for the cult's apartments. It was a clear night, the stars a series of bright points in a cold and empty sky. Mim limped along beside me, rope looped over his right shoulder. He used a walking stick to steady himself, took his time going up the slope.

"Do you know the story of Mimir, in the eddas?" Mim said. He glanced at me, grinned when I shook my head. "Legends say he was one of the Vanir, predecessors to the Norse gods. It was Mimir's Well where Odin sacrificed his eye, in the name of knowledge, and when the other Vanir cut off Mimir's head, Odin used magic to preserve the skull and asked it to speak prophecies and otherwise advise him."

The old man paused a moment, blew his cheeks out before sucking down huge breaths. "When I started reading portents, when I first realised the directions my life would take me, it seemed a reasonable name to take on as my own, just as Michael Wotan borrowed his name from Odin's precursor, a psychopomp from Germanic myths that put him closer to the dead."

"Both got a taste for the pompous, then?"

"Spoken by a man who doesn't yet understand power," Mim said. "You remind me a great deal of your friend Roark."

"I know," I said. "I take it as a compliment."

That earned me a soft wheeze of laughter and we finished the climb in silence. One of Wesna's demons emerged from the darkness, blocked our path as we went to walk the last twenty feet towards the apartment.

"No one in or out," he said. "Wesna's orders, you know?"

"I should have access," I said. "I negotiated with Wesna when we first took this place."

"Call came through revoking that permission," the demon said. "No one goes on or off the site."

Mim swore beneath his breath, whispered a second word I didn't recognise. He reached out with his walking stick, rapped the demon across the skull. The demon blinked once, then closed its eyes and fell backwards into the concrete embrace of the penthouse suite's front walk.

Mim offered me a toothy smile. "Irritating little beasts," he said. "They really could do with being quieter, now and then."

He edged past the sleeping demon and stepped into the house, let out a low whistle as he felt the energy thrumming though the place. I felt it too, once I crossed the threshold. The build-up of something untapped and primal, still mild and eager to be unleashed, but building and looking for viable escape routes. My skin tingled just standing inside the door, and I could see flares of Gloom from every surface.

"They were definitely building a gate," Mim said. "Once those stars align, this entire building is getting pulled into the Gloom." He let loose a peel of wheezing laughter. "Desperate bastards, Mister Murphy. Never underestimate a truly desperate pack of bastards."

The darkness gathered in the corners of the room seemed to shiver. I drew the sword and stood beside Mim, let its soft glow provide us with light. Shadows bled together on the walls around us, congealed into pools of Gloom that shivered and writhed. A tentacle wormed free, searching blindingly. Another emerged from the wall behind us, curled around my right arm. I jerked backwards, swinging the sword on reflex. It passed through the Gloom without effect.

Another tentacle reached out, wrapped itself around my ankle. A third grabbed me wrist. My arm. My throat. They held me tight as the room shook and the cold, frosty touch of the Gloom closed around me. I twisted, trying to avoid getting pulled in all directions.

Kept my teeth clenched as I fought off a screen, wary of one of those tentacles forcing its way down my throat.

"Relax, Mister Murphy," Mim said, but his voice sounded like it came from some place a very long way away. "We want to be transported, remember?"

I kept the sword clasped in a death grip, unwilling to break my hold.

But I let the Gloom take me and carry me someplace else.

It's not a tree, not really. I can make out details against the darkness—the wide canopy of its branches, the dark trunk that extends in all directions, the tangled roots that claw at the earth and spear it like an invading army—but these things are just facsimiles of the trees we know on earth, larger than you can image in the emptiness of the Gloom. It isn't a tree, not really; it's the nightmare of a tree, the kind of tree mother trees use to frighten their saplings when they've been disobedient and need the threat of a monster.

Bruce Mim sat on one of the tangled roots, steadied himself with the walking stick as he studied the rise of the trunk. He pointed at a low-hanging branch that still seemed incredibly high, unfurled the length of rope and stretched it between pale fingers. "That's the one," he said. "That's the place you hang yourself."

I looked up until my neck hurt. "And then what happens?"

"You hang for nine days," Mim said quietly. "Then, I guess, you die."

"Odin survived it."

"You ain't Odin, kid. This ain't really the Yggdrasil. It's just a version of the tree, an idealised image sucked from the collective unconscious. This shit is far more dangerous than any myth could be. Yeah, Odin hung from the tree for nine days, all in the name of receiving wisdom. Earned this thing a new name." He hawked and spat in the darkness. "You ever heard the gallows called Odin's Horse before?"

"Never," I said.

Irritation flickered across Mim's face. "No reason

you should have, I suppose," he said. "Given the scarcity of hangings in your stretch. Makes me wonder what Roark taught you 'bout magic, though."

"That's easy enough," I said. "I never really bothered letting Danny teach me anything." I craned my head back, peering into the shadows. "How high do we need to get for this to work, do you think?"

Mim found the end of the rope, knotted out a noose with practiced ease. "Not far," he said. "We're just making sure your feet can't touch the earth, such as it is."

I nodded and crouched, fascinated by the tree. My life was spent coming into contact with myths, facing down against the things that no-one truly regarded as real. I knew about vampires and werewolves, had encountered the possessed that could have given rise to mysteries about ogres and trolls. I'd gunned down fey and slipped into the Gloom because it was useful.

This was the first time I'd come close to one of the primal metaphors, standing so close to it I could see the enormity of it. Even if people didn't believe in the Yggdrasil directly, its myth had taken hold and transformed it enough to established a site of power. I hesitated, unwilling to touch it. Bruce Mim grinned. "You afraid, little trigger man?"

"Mate, I'm fucking terrified."

"Good," he said. "You should be. The magic that runs through this thing, it's old and it's primal. Those roots reach down to the places where the elder gods sleep and I wouldn't be surprised if a couple of them had ol' Yggdrasil growing into their brains. If we weren't doing this right, making contact would snuff your pitiful existence."

He handed me the noose, waited quietly as I pulled the loop of rope over my head.

"I could lie," Mim said, "and tell you this wouldn't hurt, but the truth is—"

"Bruce," I said, "I signed up for this,

"It's good that you think so," the old man said. He threw the rope, looped it over a branch high above us. "You ready to climb?"

I wasn't, but I couldn't think of a reason to stay on the ground.

I stepped to the side of tree, using Mim's rope to brace myself against the rough hardwood. I took each movements slow and steady, focused on getting where I needed to be. Going faster wouldn't have helped much. Mistakes would be made, slippages could occur. It didn't seem like a long way to fall, but it was best not to trust your eyes in the Gloom.

I touched one hand to the noose, glanced at Mim for confirmation. He grinned at me, nodding once. "All you've got to do is step off," he said. "We'll take care of all of it."

I felt the weight of the noose on my shoulders, the coarse scratch of the rope brushing against my neckline. Mim smiled his encouragement, knotting the rope to the branch. He was halfway out on the limb. I was still standing close to the trunk, appreciating the width beneath my feet. When Mim was done, he gestured for me. Urged me out onto the black limb with him. I let go of the black trunk and inched my way across, keeping my precarious balance.

Gravity exists in the real world. It's scientific fact, inescapable and immutable. Gravity exists in the Gloom because the sub-conscious of almost every living mortal insists it should be that way. It's no longer fact, but it is commonly understood. I thought about that as I tilted my weight forward, hit that point where balance disappeared and gravity did the rest. For a few short, endless seconds I fell through Gloom.

Then the noose pulled tight, tight against my neck. I felt something break and figured it for my neck.

NINE DAYS

THE NOOSE DID exactly what a noose is supposed to do: pulled tight as my weight hit the end of the rope; just enough torque to snap my neck, the tight fit of the rope cutting off the carotid arteries. Cut those off and the brain starts to swell inside your skull, plugging up the top of your spinal column. Once that happens the Vagal nerve is pinched, setting off the associated reflex. No more heartbeat. No more breathing. It's a slower way to go, if the snapped spine doesn't kill, but it'll get you in the end, whether it takes a couple of minutes or the slow agony of a half-hour.

I felt the cold pain in my neck, the slowing rhythm of my heartbeat as it came to a halt.

I hung from Yggdrasil. I didn't die.

And somewhere high above me, far further than I'd fallen, I could hear the raspy wheeze of Bruce Mim's victorious giggle.

When I say *I didn't die,* this may be a lie. For a time there, hanging from the tree, I was pretty sure I was dead.

Time doesn't pass in the Gloom. Not in the way we're used to. I heard Mim's giggle for a long time. Hours maybe. Days. None of the usual signifiers were there to mark the passage of time. No sun moving overhead. No moon. No shifting shadows or passing seconds. Every moment folded in on itself, connected to every other moment.

It was dark. My spine wasn't working right. I couldn't see the stars. I didn't breath anymore.

It was cold, but the Gloom was always cold. The only thing that suggested I might not be dead was my ability to wonder whether or not I'd passed on. I tried to move my fingers and failed. Tried to move my toes. Tried to close my eyes, then wondered if they already were. It made no difference to the darkness, which meant I was staring into a deep, unmoving part of the Gloom or my eyes were already closed and I could not open them.

I may have been asleep when the first visitor

arrived. I don't remember him coming closer. I don't remember where the light came from, so I could make out his familiar face.

"Do you know what happens, when Ragnarok starts?" Sabbath said. "All that time you spent reading the book Roark gave you, did you ever actually pay attention to the sequence of events?"

I tried to respond, but the noose was tight around my throat. I couldn't breathe, and the lack of air robbed me of any sign of speech. Sabbath watched me through his small, round glasses. A small, fit-looking man in his fifties, tanned and dressed in white. His close-cropped hair a distinguished grey, a pleasant smile on his face.

"All this time you spent worrying about incursions and valkyries," he said. "Fenrir you stopped, even though it cost that damned bastard Roark his life, but the Norse were wrong about his role in things. They thought it was the wolf that came out and devoured the sun. The wolf that took away that moon and the stars. They thought it would be a wolf that shook the mountains and split the earth. They didn't understand things the way you and I do, Keith. The wolf is just a metaphor. It's the Gloom that does the damage. All those shallow spaces where the borders between my home and yours are thin, those are the places that break. They break here on earth, and up there—" he gestured "—well, you know where."

He took off his glasses. Polished them with a square of white cloth.

"I'm almost disappointed we won't see the next stage," he said. "The demon in me relishes the chance to see a serpent unleashed, and you have to admire the imagination that proposed the great ship Naglfar, bearing a squad of giants to the fray on a ship of dead men's nails. The sky breaks and suddenly there are giants, giants everywhere. Giants made of fire and giants made of frost and the guard-dog of the dead that mauls the great god Tyr."

He shook his head and slid the glasses back onto his face. "So much closer to the truth than the myths people still believe in, yes? They were closer to things, in those days. Understood the implications better. All those monsters coming out of the dark, from whence they'd been relegated, it feels so very like the borders between two dimensions crumbling and all the nightmares of humanity coming home to roost."

I opened my mouth. It seemed glacial; an act of enormous effort, accomplished over the span of centuries. I sucked a slow, hesitant breath through a space as wide a sewing needle.

I croaked a single word: "dead."

It left me feeling like a deflated balloon, limp and spent, unsure if I'd ever inflate again. Sabbath's corresponding laughter was the dry rustle of leaves in the wind.

"Of course I'm dead, Keith. You fucking made sure of that." He shook his head, affronted by my ability to state the obvious. "It's almost a mercy, at this point. It'll be no better for demons, after the borders break. We're too young... too weak... to stand up against the creatures from the deepest parts of the Gloom."

I croaked another word: "Stop."

I'm not sure where I found the breath for that. I don't remember drawing it.

"You amuse me, Keith," Sabbath said. "You should have helped me with the valkyrie. I could have stolen its power, done what I could to protect us all. You had my word that I'd do that. That's what it meant to be part of my crew."

It went dark. I think I closed my eyes, that I made the darkness crash around me, but I can't be sure. But it went dark. Dark and cold. And I let myself sink into it.

It was easier than staying there, listening to Sabbath talk.

I surfaced, later, when I heard a familiar voice.

"Ah, kid," it said. "What are you doing here?"

It wasn't phrased like a question. Roark's voice jerked me to wakefulness. I felt a pang of loss as I stared at his ghost, a wispy thing made of Gloom and memory that lacked the substance of the man I'd followed. He stood on a tree branch, cigarette on his lips. He grinned at me and ashed the cigarette, looked at the length of rope leading into the darkness.

"So this is the best plan you have," Roark said. "Hanging yourself in the middle of the Gloom." He breathed against the cigarette. Exhaled to the side. "Shouldn't have left you alone. First time I do it, you think selling your soul is a viable thing. Now you agree to this."

It sucked at the air, tried to speak. It was easier, this time. "Didn't know... what else to do."

"So you thought dying was the best option?"

"Seemed... sensible."

Roark sucked on his cigarette. Thought about that.

"There's not many ways this can turn out, kid," he said. "Most likely, it means you're dead already. Your necks broke. Your brains been starved of oxygen. That's the most likely option, but there's no way of telling for sure. And if it does work, well, then you've got the next problem. You're walking the same path Wotan did. You're binding yourself to the same damn powers. That way lies madness kid, even if you aren't dead. I didn't prepare you for this."

"S'okay," I said. "Wouldn't have let you... prepare me."

Roark smiled. "I could have insisted."

"Didn't want... to be a sorcerer," I said.

"Yeah," Roark said. "I should have respected that, maybe, a little more than I did." He considered his cigarette a moment, shook his head. "Truth is, kid, you couldn't do this job without knowing about magic. There's no way in hell you could have survived it without knowing how to defend yourself. I kept telling you it wasn't necessary, but you picked up a hell of a lot. I should have been straight with you. Prepared you for what's coming."

"S'okay," I croaked again.

His laughter was old and bitter, devoid of any real humour. "When you're hanging from a tree, by the neck, in an effort to stop the apocalypse, okay is probably one of those words you stop using. I fear it may be without useful context, these days."

I'm not sure how long I'd been hanging there when I dreamed of killing of Michael Wotan. It's possible I wasn't even dreaming.

I dreamt of the warm, dry Adelaide heat. I dreamt of the Italian restaurant, longer than any restaurant I'd ever seen, the glass cabinet of desserts to my left and the wall full of photographs to my right. Michael Wotan seated at a dark, wooden table in his business suit. The empty socket where his right eye used to be, tattoos barely concealed by his silk shirt. I could feel the thrum of Roark's magic in my veins; the chant taking place in a nearby hotel room, stripping away Wotan's defences, making it possible to do what I did.

I dreamt of the SIG in my hand, heavy and comforting. The impossibly loud retort of two gunshots in close proximity, the two flowers of blood that appeared on Wotan's chest. Two more shots, in the head, to ensure he was dead. The quick chant that trapped his soul in a bullet before it could escape into the gloom.

I dreamt of a single, blue eye staring at me as he died.

My lips twisted at the memory. I smiled into the darkness.

"You truly are a cocky fucker, aren't you, killer?" Wotan said.

My eyes snapped open. He loomed over me, tall and one-eyed and dressed in an expensive suit, substantial as he'd been as a living sorcerer. Panic surged through me, told me to run, but my body remained limp and swaying at the end of the noose.

Michael Wotan smiled a crooked smile. "The middle of Brunelli's, in the middle of a fucking latte," he said. "Who fucking dies like that? Who fucking thinks a hit in the middle of the goddamn open is a good idea?"

He pushed me with one hand, watched me swing. "I came here once, a very long time ago," he said. "I walked the Gallows Path as you did, I cut a deal that gave me power over all manner of life and death. And it all it cost me was the promise that the end of the world would come. That one day, when I finally passed on, my spirit and my soul would find their way here to wake them and start the process of Ragnarok."

He held up a 9 millimetre bullet, dull and utterly plain. "Ingenious little thing, you and Roark devised. It's the only reason you survived as long as you did. Part of my spirit made it to the Gloom, came down here to wake the slumbering gods and prod them into motion, but there isn't much power in half a ghost. It needed the weight of a soul to truly matter, to allow me to speak with the authority I needed to rouse those who have slept for thousands of years."

He lowered the bullet. Glared at me. "And now you're here."

"Yes."

"You've ridden the Gallows Road, with your bright and shining sword and your desire to be a hero."

I still swayed back and forth, although the momentum was ebbing.

"Yes," I said.

"What good has it done you, coming all the way here? When Odin rode the Gallows Road, he learned the secrets of the runes. He learned to heal wounds and bind enemies. He learned to destroy an enemies weapons and free himself from bondage. He could put out fires and banish malevolent magic. He could wake the dead, protect allies from harm, charm himself a lover, and more than that besides. What have you learned, killer, hanging from the tree?"

I didn't know.

I wasn't there yet.

But when he asked, for the first time, I started to feel pain. It started as a burning sensation in my neck, a feeling of weight and warmth and the certainty something was wrong.

It got worse.

It got so much worse.

Michael Wotan stood there, watching me. Laughing as I finally passed out.

When I slept, it felt like falling. Falling into a darkness deeper and wilder than the Gloom could ever hope to be. A dreamless place, empty, untouched by the presence of other minds. For the first time in my life, I realised I was alone. No one asking something of me. No one expecting me to behave.

I fell a long, long way.

When I woke, the Gloom was thick and the ground beneath uneven. I was splayed against a stone crag, jagged rocks digging into my flesh, the cold wind whistling over the lip of a precipice dangerously close to my left. I crawled back from the brink, stone cutting at my palms. The pain in my neck was gone. My heart was beating, soft and steady. My lungs inflated, and I exhaled with measured calm. The air filled with strange, alien whispering that ebbed and flowed like waves against the stone.

I wore the clothes I wore the night I killed Michael Wotan. A leather jacket. Blue jeans. A black-shirt. Black boots. I could feel the weight of the SIG at my hip, the heavier pull of the sword slung over my right shoulder. When I rose, I was standing on the edge of a cliff, the familiar ashen of the Gloom spread out around me. I took a few steps towards the edge, peered down into the depths below. Amid the shadows, there were leviathans moving. Great, slumbering beasts that twitched and turned in their sleep, edging their way towards wakefulness. My brain reeled, trying to focus on them, unwilling to comprehend their size.

“Sleeping gods,” a familiar voice said, “or close enough to it. The terminology won’t truly matter, once they wake.”

I turned and saw Michael Wotan, seated on a rock nearby. Not the pale spirit formed from the stuff of the Gloom, as he’d been since I’d first killed him. This Wotan had access to his soul. It had weight and size and power.

“You can feel them now,” he said. “They’re in your head. You can feel them the same way I can.”

I nodded. The things below us weren’t really gods, not in any way that mattered. Maybe they’d deserved that title, once, but they'd devolved so far from contact with our world. They were formless, reflections unsure of what lay on the far side of the mirror, waiting for something to appear and give them form. That's what Wotan had promised them, in exchange for his magic. Forms they could use to stride the earth. A way to break the sky and slip back into a world that forgot them.

"We don't have to wake them," I said.

Wotan shrugged. He produced a SIG, made a show of sliding a bullet into the chamber. "I'm afraid I made a deal," he said.

"You did," I said. "I didn't. We followed the same path here. All you need to do is let me calm them, sooth them until they return to their slumber."

Wotan stood there, one-eyed, gun in hand, smirking as he considered my offer. "So you buy the world another couple of centuries?" he said. "Why bother going through the rigmarole, killer? Neither you nor I will be around to see it. Let the old gods have their time, and we may yet eke out a new level of existence."

I reached for the sword. Wotan raised his gun.

"None of that," he said. "I intend to start the end of the world, and I already owe you a death. It would be a pleasure to put a bullet in you, killer. It—"

I drew the sword, swung at him. Wotan fired the SIG, it's retort oddly soft in the cold darkness of the Gloom. I felt the sword bite into flesh, slicing open a chunk of his left arm. Wotan's blood soaked his pristine jacket. My own blood spilled from a gash beside my right eye, opened when the bullet ricocheted off my skull. I fell back, more stunned that he'd got a gun working in the Gloom than the bloody gash.

I went to stand and Wotan kicked me in the face, the side of his boot smashing open my lip. I spat blood. Shook my head. Tried to regain the ability to focus. Another kick rocked me, spun me over until I lay face-first in the rocky ground. My blood dripped onto the black stone. My lungs heaved with the effort of breathing, of keeping me moving and conscious and alive.

Wotan stood over me, swaying from side to side.

He wasn't steady on his feet, not with the blood he'd lost already. It didn't matter. Not at that range. He raised the SIG and tied to focus, squinting as he lined it up with my skull. I swatted at his gun arm. A desperate, foolish push against the hand. His gunshot filled the silence of the Gloom. The bullet caught me in the shoulder. Lots of pain. Lots of blood. I was okay with both of those things. I staggered to my feet, hit him with everything I had in me. He staggered, fell back into the rocks. I staggered too, heading for the sword. Forced my tired arms to lift it and hold it. Advanced on Wotan's ghost with the blade held at the ready.

He raised the pistol. Pointed it at me. He stared at the action, snapped back to expose the open chamber. Blinked at it like he expected another bullet to be sitting there.

I grunted, stumbling the short distance towards him. Heaved the sword into motion as I moved. Wotan turned to look at the incoming steel, didn't quite manage to duck it. The blade impacted with the side of his skull, crumpled bone beneath the weight of the swing. Wotan teetered. Fell backwards onto the black rock. I could feel his soul trembling, eager to be released.

I knelt and whispered over the sword, pressed my hand against the runes Langford carved into its surface. The pale, indistinct shape of Wotan's soul reappeared, wavered as it attempted to dart over the side of the cliff. Slowly, I advanced on it, whispering the spell beneath my breath. A slow advance, leading with the sword, consigning the soul to a second prison.

The dead do not scream. I know that from experience. They do not cry or rant or express their rage. If you do the spell correctly, it's like a change in the humidity. One minute you're aware of the soul hanging in the air, a distinct and unfriendly presence still coping with its death.

Then it's found solace in whatever resting place it can, and if you're lucky, it's the ghost-cage you've elevated to keep it inside.

I staggered over to the edge of the cliff, dragging the sword behind me. Held onto it as I stared at the formless giants below, the things that had been great and terrible and would be, eventually, when they reclaimed their place in the world. And slowly, carefully, I started to sing to them. I don't remember words, just the undulating rhythm that wove in and out of their whispering voices, the way it soothed and healed and eased the tormented agony of formlessness.

There are some things we're just not meant to remember. Some knowledge, once deployed, is best left where it came from.

PAIN

I WOKE TO the steady beep of a heart monitor. Breathed in and out through a tube. White walls and blue curtains swam in front of my vision, refusing to come into focus. I blinked a few times. Struggled against the stiff, unyielding weight that covered my chest and neck.

"He's awake," someone said, and Langford's face appeared in my field of vision. She smiled a tight, relieved kind of smile and disappeared from view, replaced by Wesna's frowning features. I gurgled something, tried to lift my right hand.

"You want the tube out?" Wesna said.

I tried to nod. Couldn't. Mumbled something against the alien plastic occupying my throat. Wesna grinned and took a little pleasure at removing me from the breathing tube. Hovered on the fringes of my vision as Langford reappeared on the far side of the bed.

"Hospital?" I said, and my voice was weak and raw.

"You disappeared from the safehouse twelve days ago," Langford said. "Sneaked off without saying shit, disappeared from sight altogether for the best part of nine days. Then a couple of Wesna's demons found you at the base of Magic Mountain. You'd cracked a couple of vertebrae, which is why they've got you're paralysed. Doctors say your injures are consistent with a fall from the cliff, except for the bruising around your throat, the eye-damage, and the spinal cord damage."

"We told them some shit about you being an amateur rock climber," Wesna said. "You know, in case someone asks why you were there, and why you fell."

"Thank," I said. My throat was too dry, too raw to manage the S.

"They've fused part of your spine," Langford said. "They've put you on more painkillers than I knew existed."

"Yeah?" I tried to smile. "Good."

"Some doctor is going to come along soon and tell you how fucking lucky you are," Langford said. "Man doesn't know the half of it."

"On the plus side, it's a fucking warm day outside, too," Wesna said. "In case someone mentions it. Three days you've been asleep in here, and it got seasonably warm out."

She smiled and pushed the few strands of hair out of her face. "I don't know what you and the old man did in the Gloom," she said. "I suspect I'm happier never knowing. But whatever you did, Keith, I think it worked."

I nodded and went back to sleep. Real sleep, this time. The kind that's full of dreams.

The doctors released me from the hospital a week after I woke up. I was banged up, taking a shit-ton of medication, and generally unable to do anything more strenuous than shuffling the length of a bedroom, but I was glad to be away from the beeping machines and out in the world again. The warm days seemed odd, after a year spent in the cold, but the skies were clear and blue and Langford drove me home in her pristine HR Holden and took the long way around, past the beaches, so I could see the empty horizon.

We drove out to Currumbin Valley. Pulled up out the front of the farm house she'd lived in right up until we'd destroyed her wards as part of the plan to kill Sabbath. She hadn't had time to rebuild her defences due to the hustle of saving the world, but she'd moved back while I was in hospital, rebuilt the place into the fortress it had been. She opened the passenger side door and helped me out. We stared up at the winding driveway for a few moments. Studied the house halfway up the slope, partially hidden behind the ancient gum trees.

"You know what's surprising?" I said.

Langford tilted her head towards me.

"Somehow, this place didn't end up getting blown up," I said. "I always figured we'd burn the place literally, you know? After what happened to the bar, and the safehouse down by the beach."

"Please don't joke about that," Langford said. "My

friend will be back in a few weeks. I figured I wouldn't need to explain that fire, but now that we actually pulled things off..."

She shook her head. Crouched low and rubbed her hand against the dirt. "Holy shit, Murphy. You actually pulled this off. You stopped a goddamn apocalypse."

"Not stopped," I said. "Just delayed a little."

"You bought us a couple hundred years," Langford said. "Most people would take the win."

I grinned. "Most people didn't see what's coming in a couple hundred years," I said. "Trust me, I'm taking the win, but someone needs to give the poor bastards who face this apocalypse next time an honest-to-god fighting chance."

I retreated to the car, gave Langford a couple of moments to strengthen the wards at the front gate. When she was done, she climbed into the driver's seat and edged us up the steep slope of the driveway, helped me unpack the small supply of painkillers into the spare room on the east side of the house. I'd heal faster, outside of the hospital. Langford's magic could speed things up, and I'd retained bits and pieces from my trip down the Gallows Road. More than a song to soothe old gods had found its way into my skull on the tree; not all of it had found its way out yet.

Eventually, Langford drove us up the driveway. Her house remained as I remembered it: a neat, warm kind of place with mismatched furniture and cluttered shelves. The kind of place someone lived in and stayed in for a long time, wearing their presence into the dwelling like grooves worn into wood. Langford set me up in the spare room, let me get a few hours of sleep. I dreamed of the tree, of Roark, of the expression on Wotan's face as the sword slid through him.

I could smell dinner cooking when I woke, along with a warm cup of tea on the bedside table.

I shuffled into the kitchen. Found Langford cooking, slicing onion and garlic on a marble chopping board, a wok steaming over the stove behind her.

"I've talked to that kid who runs your bar," she

said, the rapid click of knife against stone punctuating her statement. She scraped the diced garlic into her palm, turned to dump it into the wok. "I told him he's in charge for the next few months, while you heal. You can make the decision to keep the place or not once you're well enough to run again, but not fucking before."

I nodded. "Thank you."

"Don't thank me yet." She put the knife down, fished a notebook out of her pocket. Threw it into my lap. "That's the list," she said. "Everything you owe me, all the favours you owe me, after you ran out of Roark's credit back when all this started. Take your time looking through it. Let me know if you dispute anything."

I picked up the book. Flicked through the pages. "Comprehensive."

"I told you I was keeping track," Langford said. She smiled and went back to chopping. "Thought it best to get it out of the way now, so it can inform your thinking 'bout what happens next."

"I thought I focused on healing," I said.

Langford snorted. "Yeah, but after that. Roark's dead. Going back to what you used to do ain't much of an option. Wesna's already asking me if I think you'll hang around, already putting plans into motion about how that will look." She scooped up the onion, dropped it into the wok. "Sooner or later, you'll need to put some thought into what happens next. I wanted to make it real clear how much you owed me, before you did that."

"A-huh." I opened the notebook again. Worked my way through the first few pages. "Hell of a lot of debt to clear up."

"My point," Langford said.

I closed the notebook and slid it into my pocket. "You ain't planning on starting a war with anyone? Having me kill some laundry list of enemies?"

"I thought about it, but there's better uses for a man of your talents," Langford said.

"Could have fooled me. I always thought my talents mostly involved killing people."

"Yeah," Langford said. "I thought that about myself once. Then I stopped working with Roark, figured out what else I could do with what he taught me." She turned to the wok, prodded the contents with a wooden spoon. "Trust me, Murphy. It's not that bad."

She found me in the Hard Rock. It was a Thursday night, a little after ten. They were getting a good crowd, all things considered. Lots of girls with inscrutable, backpacker accents clustered around the bar. Plenty more heading up the stairs, attracted by the heavy guitars of the band playing the Thursday night gig. Lots of blondes, natural and peroxide. The Gold Coast could always provide you with another blonde, regardless of gender. I'd forgotten how omnipresent they were, in the years I'd spent away. Now I barely noticed, except for the nights when I sat and watched a crowd.

I'd been there maybe fifteen minutes before Wesna arrived. She cut through the crowd easily, made a beeline for my table wedged between one of Keith Moon's Polyester shirts and Mark Occhilupo's surfboards. "So Langford let you out," she said. "Didn't think she'd do that until you were fully healed."

"You'd think right," I said, "but there are some advantages to being a sorcerer. Certain magics that can speed up recovery once you're outside the watchful eyes of medical professionals. Which I'm not, quite, not yet, but I got tired of being on painkillers. I'm willing to risk a few conversations about my recuperative qualities, in exchange for the ability to get about on my own devices."

Wesna nodded and settled into the empty seat at my table. She stared at me through the fringe of dark hair that hung over her eyes. "You could have made an appointment, you know? You didn't have to just surface and let word filter back to the Casino."

"The last time I tried to make an appointment, one of your demons pointed out I was a sign of weakness in your organisation. That was when you had good reason to talk to me; now that the danger's dealt with—" I paused and shrugged. "Shit, Wes, I don't want to cause you trouble, no more than I already have, you know?"

She grinned at me. “I run a cartel of demons, Murphy. You think I come and investigate every sorcerer who intrudes on my territory personally?”

“When you put it like that,” I said.

“Yeah,” she said. “Idiot.”

We stared at one-another, then I glanced over her shoulder. Made out a couple of her demons scattered about the crowd. Three or four, possibly, a bodyguard to the boss. One of them—Dale—smiled at me and touched two fingers to his forehead in salute.

“So,” Wesna said, “you made a decision about leaving, yet?”

I eased back in my chair, retreating from the question. “Langford’s got me thinking about it.”

A waitress came by our table, asked if we’d like to order. I went for a coffee. Wesna did the same. The waitress rolled her eyes, like we were freaks for ordering caffeine instead of the usual array of Hard Rock cocktails and bottle booze.

“So,” Wesna said. She stared at me.

“Do you remember, when we were kids, how much we used to hate it here? Hanging out at school, feeling like freaks, telling each other how quickly we’d bail when we finally got the opportunity? It didn’t matter what got us out of here, so long as we got out.”

Wesna nodded. “I remember.”

“It kind of irritated me,” I said, “when I finally got out and did all that shit with Roark. I was out in the world, away from the Coast, ready to go and figure out exactly where I belonged. And all it really got me was sixteen years of shitty hotels and a new town every couple of months. That’s what it meant to do what we did. I always believed in it, which made it worthwhile. I could take comfort in the mission, you know?”

Wesna looked at me, brushed the dark hair out of her eyes.

“It’s going to piss me off if I have to find another idiot willing to run the Hell Bar,” she said. “I was kinda counting on having you to keep the peace, once the local Other start returning to the Coast.”

“If I stay, you and I are going to end up on each

other's shit list," I said. "You're a demon, Wes. That's inevitable. I can't turn off the part of me that exists to keep people safe."

She frowned at that, but she nodded. "I'd already started putting together contingency plans," she said. "You know, just in case. Most of them were... non-lethal."

"Mine wouldn't be," I said.

She nodded. "So that's it. You pull up stumps and go on the run again, fucking off for another decade or so?"

"No," I said. "Not unless you want to reinstate Sabbath's ban on having me in the city. I've still got debts to Langford. Still got debts to you, for that matter. I figure I'd try having a base of operations for a while. Operate out of the Hell Bar, make sure people know where to find me if they've got problems. Keep the peace when it needs keepin' around these parts, be elsewhere, from time to time, when the job demands it. Split my time, you know? Commute to the places I'm needed. Catch up with friends, when I'm not."

Wesna settled back in her chair, fixed me with a stare. "And you think that's enough to keep us from trying to kill each other?"

"I think it's worth a try," I said.

"Right," Wesna said. "But when it all breaks down, I'm going to make you eat those words." She was smiling as she said it, though. As much as Wesna ever smiled. She raised her coffee cup. "Til then, here's to sensible decisions."

"Yeah," I said, joining the toast. "Gotta start making those, sooner or later."

GLOAMING

Stories from the Gold Coast

LOCAL HEROES

THINGS YOU CAN'T PAY BACK

Summer on the Gold Coast is like a little slice of Hades. Scorching days and humid nights, the temperature pushing forty on the Celsius scale, a sweltering heat that makes you regret being alive. Air so thick with moisture you could chew it up and spit. Tourists everywhere, including the fucking *Hell Bar* I inherited after shit went down. Reminded me why I left, first time I got an offer. Made me think real hard about leaving again, first chance I could, even if the Coast was safer than being out there solo.

I was thinking all those kinds of thoughts the night Holly Langford showed up on my door. I stepped out of a cab at four AM, crossed the sun-blasted grass that masqueraded as a yard. Didn't notice her parked on my front step, dreadlocks pooled around her skinny arse, killing time with a Winnie Blue while I crossed the sun-blasted lawn.

I stopped short, stared at her. Wondered how the fuck I'd missed her. It wasn't like Langford blended, not in the white-bread coastal suburbs pressed up against the shoreline. She was six-three and bird-thin, piercings through her nose, lip and brow. Tattoos covered her leathery skin. Some of them I recognised. A lot of them, I didn't.

"You're late," she said.

"Didn't know we had a meeting."

"Doesn't mean you ain't late." She exhaled a final cloud of smoke, hauled herself upright with the cast-iron railing.

"Could have waited inside," I said. "You still got a key, right?"

"Didn't want to fuck up your wards. Figured you might want to fix 'em up so they'll actually keep stuff out." She stepped aside. "Just open the fucking door, eh?"

I did, stifling a yawn. Twelve hours at the bar meant I wasn't real fit for visitors, but that didn't mean much when Langford showed. You don't say no to people you owe, especially not when you're so deep in that you'll never quite pay things off.

My place wasn't much to look at. One bedroom, one bathroom, a small kitchenette. Habits of a lifetime meant I didn't keep much there. A handful of clothes, some second hand books, enough weapons to hold off a demon or two if the situation demanded it. A go-bag, tucked beneath the bed, in case I needed to bail on the place and didn't have time to pack.

I pointed Langford towards the leather arm-chair, headed to the kitchen bench to set the kitchenette. Langford settled in, rolled a cigarette on the coffee table.

"You look okay," she said. "Considering."

I grunted. "Coffee or tea?"

"Tea," she said. "Black. Two sugar."

She watched me spooning things out, waiting for me to give her some sign the eye-patch was causing problems. I put the spoon down. "Depth perception was a bitch, the first few weeks," I said. "But I figured shit out, yeah?"

She nodded. Perched on the edge of the chair like a falcon, ready to swoop in. I made the fucking tea, handed her a mug. She took it, sipped it. Nodded her satisfaction.

"So," she said, "you're settling in?"

"I'm doing okay."

She tapped a finger against her occipital bone. "The eye isn't—"

"I'm doing okay." I put an ashtray in front of Langford, went to claim my mug. Then we stared at each other, waiting. I was going to lose that, one way or another. You don't win staring matches with a witch.

"So," I said, "what's up?"

Langford ashed her cigarette. "I've got a job for you."

"Right," I said, quietly. "What kind of work?"

"The usual kind," she said. "Your kind of thing."

My kind of thing. Not running a bar. My kind of thing meant something needed killing.

Something, and not someone.

I took a deep breath and nodded. "Alright."

"No questions?"

"Not how this works. You need something done, I do it."

"It's not—" she hesitated. "Shit, Murphy, I'm not fucking Roark. No need to jump, just 'cause I said so."

"Should have thought of that before calling in a favour," I said. "Old habits, and all."

She scowled at me. Truth is, I would have done it even without the debt. Running the Hell Bar wasn't a bad gig, but it wasn't my thing. I'd spent the better part of a decade hunting things that go bump in the night—demons and warlocks and rogue entities from the Gloom. All that came crashing down, when me and Danny Roark fucked up, but it was one of those jobs, you know? Serving drinks and handling payroll didn't exactly cut it, after all those years doing hits.

"The job," I said. "Tell me."

Langford screwed up her face, stared at her mug of tea. "I got a friend," she said. "Gareth Cottee. He works up at the university, helps out with stuff occasionally. Good guy, once you get past his habit of talking shit. He's been watching one of the local talents, up around Brisbane way. Says it's starting to hit the point where we should look at curbing its influence. Never bothered with that sort of thing much, before you got here, but since you're around and looking for things to do..."

"You need a trigger man."

She nodded.

"All I need to hear," I said. "Tell me about the target."

Langford pushed a flyer across the coffee table. It promised a thing called Rampage Pro was heading back to the Nundah Community Hall, headlined by Rocky Malice versus Eddie Coltrane. Glossy photographs of the two men sat underneath the logo. Malice wore black trunks and painted his face like that kid from *The Crow.* Coltrane was a chubby kid, the fold of his gut hanging over his jeans, greasy hair hanging over his Cheshire-Cat grin.

The other names on the card were equally improbable, but at least they spared me the photographs. One of them was circled in red pen: Ketch.

"You're kidding, right?"

"I'm not."

"Pro-wrestling?"

"I don't pick where the target works."

My eyes dropped to the flyer. "So long as your friend ain't the fucker in the face-paint."

"That's not Cottee's scene," she said. "He's more an observer."

"Fan?"

"Researcher. Part of his thing at the uni." She waved her hand towards the door, like the campus was just outside. "Cultural studies and modern mythology, all that kind of crap."

"He know any magic?"

Langford shook her head. "Interested amateur. Knows enough to get into trouble, but—"

She stopped, took a short breath. "Look, he knows stuff. Enough that I take him seriously. Isn't the first time he's mentioned this particular problem, but he's getting a little urgent about it. Wants me to come out and see the show, take a look at what's going on."

"So we're going?"

She grinned. "You're kidding, right? It's a goddamn wrestling show."

A whole bunch of things clicked into place for me. "Ah," I said. "So I'm going."

She nodded. "Let me know if it's something that needs to be dealt with."

I picked up the flyer again. Saturday night.

"I'll get someone to cover my shift."

GOOD THINGS

Gareth Cottee was built like a wheelie bin: squat, thickset, wrapped in a dark green Ninja Turtles tee and camouflage-pattern Chucks that had seen better days. Flannel shirt tied around his waist, the knot completely missing beneath the overhang of his gut. Lank hair and an untamed beard that left the existence of his neck a matter for speculation, jeans with a hole torn into the right knee. He parked his SUV out front, bounded up the path to my flat like an over-excited puppy. Grinned at me, when I answered the door. "So, you're Keith Murphy," he said. "I've heard brilliant things about you, sir."

Not words I'm used to hearing from folks I've just met. "Brilliant?"

"Holly speaks very highly of you, says we owe you pretty big for stopping some kind of apocalypse." He nodded, enthusiastically. "I make a point of paying attention, when she says things like that. It's a rarity, since she stopped taking an active interest in—"

Shit. I cut him off. "Mister Cottee, I—"

"Gareth, please."

"Gareth, this isn't—"

"Oh. Yes, of course not. Say no more." He tapped a blunt finger against his nose. The green eyes squinting at me from underneath those heavy brows gave the impression of an unfocused, if brilliant, intelligence trapped inside of a woolly mammoth. "Discretion. Discretion. One of the reasons Holly rarely liked to use me in the field. Never really stopped me, of course, but—"

"Gareth?"

He raised his eyebrows.

"We're running late," I said. "Maybe we should get moving?"

"Oh," he said. "Right. Of course, of course."

It's a long drive to Brisbane, from my neck of the woods. Longer with a man like Cottee at the wheel, working his mouth a mile a minute as he wove through the highway traffic. He shared things at a pace that left me feeling dizzy: thirty-four years old, lecturing in cultural studies; interested in folklore and semiotics and other shit I barely understood, which is how he fell in with Langford in the early days of his degree. Held forth on the cultural importance of the Bee Gees during the final twenty-minutes as we took the tunnel to the north side.

I stopped listening, chimed in with a nod or a-huh every few minutes. I'd worked with men who liked to talk before, back when me and Danny Roark still travelled as a team. You learn the art of faking interest and getting ready for a job.

I'd like to say it taught me I shouldn't dismiss guys who liked talking to burn off nervous energy, but truth is, Gareth Cottee gave me the shits. By the time we hit Nundah, I was daydreaming about leaving him in a ditch.

We pulled up out front of the Nundah Community Hall. Dinky little building nestled up against a cricket pinch, a handful of pine trees marking out the edge of the car-park pushed to capacity. No signage to signal the wrestling show, but the crowd was in full-swing, queued up against the side of the building and waiting for doors to open. Maybe two hundred people, all walks of life: fathers with their kids, out for a night's entertainment; small clusters of goth-faced kids in black jackets and fishnets; sullen men in their thirties who looked like they'd raided Cottee's wardrobe. Island kids, dressed in baggy jean and tight tees, tattoos on full display as they talked shit from their place in the queue. A couple of obvious gym-bunnies, muscles pumped up like balloons. Lots of them talking like they knew kids in the show, one way or another.

Cottee and I fell in at the rear. He twitched with nervous energy, eager to be inside. He said: "You've never done this before, right?"

I raised an eyebrow. "This?"

"Wrestling shows," he said.

"Not here to see a show."

"Yeah," Cottee said. "Your enthusiasm shows."

I shrugged. "Always struck me as ten kinds of stupid."

Cottee nodded. "Yeah, I get that. Heard it a whole lot, when I first started writing papers about it. Like most things, it gets more interesting when you pay close attention."

"I'll take your word on that," I said, hoping to stall the conversation.

Turns out, I wasn't that lucky. The doors swung open and we shuffled forward, tickets in hand, but it wasn't enough to shut him up. "I got interested during my undergraduate, reading Roland Barthes. He wrote an essay about the semiotics of a wrestling match, the way each man embodies notions of heroism and villainy," he said. "All this? It's one of the last true passion plays left in Western culture. The hero who suffers does so for no other reason than embodying the act of suffering. The villain who cheats does so for no other reason than embodying the act of villainy. The man who is defeated... well, you get the picture."

We shuffled inside, got our first look at the slightly sagging ring. It didn't exactly inspire confidence, but the hall buzzed with conversations as the crowd searched for seats. "So," I said. "You're a fan?"

"Yes, but not *just* a fan. I got hooked, as I said, studying the modern incarnation of the sport. After that, there was..." He trailed off, smile wilting. Pointed to some seats up the back row, close to the exit. "I'll be honest with you, Mister Murphy. I'm surprised it took this long for an entity of the Gloom to discover this sport. The wrestling ring is a microcosm for studying the Other—every man who steps into that ring draws power from being part of the story, becoming a symbol of something greater than himself. It doesn't play with subtlety and metaphor, it simply puts it out there, as part of the spectacle, and asks people to believe. Given the nature of magic, as I understand it..."

The heat in the small community hall was oppressive and thick with humidity. The buzz of the crowd rattled against my skull, too many people crammed into a small space. "Okay," I said. "I can see how that'd be bad."

The grin returned. "Worse than bad," Cottee said. "I can think of no better place for an entity to hide out, soaking in his power without anyone picking up on it. Who pays attention to wrestling, after all?"

"It's still just play-acting."

"Not play-acting, iconography." Cottee gestured toward the ring. "The whole foundation of magic is simple semiotics, just like everything else. One thing stands in for another, the symbols connected to esoteric meanings, the signified and the referent drawing power from the signifier. You learn to decode them and poof—" he snapped his fingers in front of my face "—magic. A stage is not a wrestling ring, a movie villain is not the same thing as a wrestling heel. The space shapes the performance, re-codes the symbols in slightly different ways."

There was an eager fervour to the big man's voice. "You know they're not really fighting, right?"

Cottee sighed, rolled his eyes. "If they were fighting for real, Mister Murphy, trust me, none of this would be a problem."

FIRST FALL TO A FINISH

The show was slated for a seven-thirty start, but it was closer to eight before they actually dimmed the lights. The first two fighters came out, both young, both skinny. Eighteen, nineteen years old, still with the scrawny look kids get before they start to bulk out. Painful to watch, when they started fighting. Bad holds, sloppy punches, a quick gouge to the eye by the smaller of the two in order to get the pinfall. A handful of people booed the victor, the rest of us just sat there. Cottee lapsed into quiet commentary, explaining the pattern of the match: the shine where the hero controls the match; the heat when the heel cheated and took the upper hand. The comeback that's cut-off before the hero finally ends things, then a chain of big moves leading towards the end. There was a pattern to it, a rhythm.

It didn't make it entertaining.

The second match featured another skinny kid, all sinew and bone, squared off against an evil looking fucker with a beer gut and a perpetual scowl. These guys did a better job of making sure things connected, Beer Gut slapping the hell out of the kid and raising welts on his chest. More cheers, when this one ended, after the skinny kid landed a lucky kick and picked up the three-count.

We made it to the fourth match before I excused myself, went over to the concession stand where a crew of older women were serving hot dogs and cans of Pepsi. I paid for one of each, lingered over by the back wall while I ate. Respite from Cottee's rambling in addition to settling the itchy feeling in the center of my back.

I ate mechanically, discovered my hot-dog was still cold in the middle. The match was still going when I was done, ticking into its twelfth minute. I went outside, dialled Holly's number. "This guys a freakin' lunatic," I said.

"Doesn't mean he's wrong."

"He doesn't stop talking," I said. "He's been lecturing non-stop since I arrived."

"Gareth's a little weird, but he's rarely wrong. If he says there's something to look for, get back inside and look."

She hung up on me, left me to stare at the phone. I went back inside right as they announced a short intermission. Cottee found me against the back wall, settled in beside me.

"The next match," he said. "Keating versus Hangman Ketch."

"What?"

"That's the one to pay attention too," he said. "If you want to go, after that, then you're done."

He went back to his seat. I followed him, settled in. Debts, man. What can you do? You pay 'em back anyway you can.

They announced the fifth match fight after the lights dimmed.

And then the demon turned up.

I'd known plenty of demons, killed my fair share of 'em. This one walked like a predator, weight on the balls of his feet. An ebony forelock hung over a gaunt face rendered in stark, monochromatic make-up. Bone-white skin, kohl-rimmed eyes, lips marked with black ink that bled into the pale white around his mouth. A noose hung 'round his neck, the knot dangling between his pectorals, and he rippled with lean muscle.

Dark, shimmering eyes studied the crowd,

ignoring their jeers. I found myself wishing I could sink into the wall, slide away from that stare without being noticed. The demon climbed into the ring and roared, showed off teeth filed into sharp points. The fans hated him, right on cue, and Ketch's low-laughter mocked them all as he lounged against the ropes, one hand lifting the end of the noose and stuck out his tongue in a vulgar mockery of a hanging.

His opponent was older, a tall blonde with the physique of a front-row forward, all jaw-line and shoulders and focus. In a fair fight the blonde looked like the kind of guy who'd dismantle the leaner, sleeker opponent, and you'd be just as likely to be wrong. The demon moved fast, all grace and quick bursts of power. They locked up, arms gripping one-another's elbows, and started forcing each other around the ring.

"Jesus," I said.

"Yeah," Cottee said, "he's something, isn't he?"

Something wasn't the word I'd use. Outright bloody terrifying came a lot closer. Every demon I've ever met was some kind of dangerous, but they only crossed over from the Gloom when they found a human host. Relied heavily on corruption and wheedling to get their way, right up to the point they finally subsumed the host's memories and eliminated the human feeling.

I'm not sure the fucker inside the ring had ever felt human emotion.

They went through the motions, wrestler and demon: shine, heat, come-back, cut-off. Cottee explained every step along the way, made sure I understood why it was happening. First a little something to show the good guy could win, then a whole lot of time where the bad guy dominates, cheating like hell to stay on top until the comeback was due to begin. The good guy rallied, all fury and good fortune, only to get stomped the moment it started getting good.

My breath caught every time Ketch slammed his opponent into the canvas.

"Wait," Cottee said, "it'll pass, soon enough."

For a moment the demon hovered, lips curved into a cruel line. It soaked up the derision of the crowd, feeding on it, ready to plunge the wrestler head-first into the mat. The air of menace that surrounded the creature grew thicker, stronger. I could taste it, thick and bloody, in the back of my throat.

"Shit," I said. Cottee nodded.

The demon spiked the rangy blonde into the canvas, crashing him head-first into the mat. The blond kid sprawled across the mat, still as death while the demon made the cover. I held my breath, fingers drifting towards the gun holstered beneath my jacket. Cottee laid a warning hand against my wrist. "Wait," he said. "Just give them a moment."

The referee counted off the victory, hand falling to the mat three times. Hangman Ketch looped his noose over his opponent, pulled it tight. Stood and smirked at the crowd, before stalking out of the ring. Got so close to us that I could see the beads of sweat on his bare chest. He lingered a moment, giving the kids in front of us the finger. Looked up and flashed Cottee a mocking wink.

Two ambulance officers came to remove the other wrestler. They got him to his feet, lugged him backstage. I let them get through the next act before I got out of my chair and left, took deep breaths of air the moment I got outside.

STEPS

Hangman Ketch was a character, played out in the wrestling ring. I got the address of the Rampage Wrestling School from Cottee, staked it out for two days before I finally saw the demon a second time. Dressed down, this time, showing up for training. Sweat pants and a singlet, a pair of beat-up docs on his feet as he climbed out of the car. I sat tight in a rented hatchback, waited for him to emerge.

Followed him for the next couple of hours, tracked him to his home. A little rental duplex out the back of West End, down by the river that flooded back at the start of the decade. Enough to track the kid through Facebook, get the name that probably appeared on his license. 'Course, from what I'd seen, Toby Vennis was just another character, a kid who'd been real way back when, but the demon inside him ate all that away, left behind nothing but a shell and some attitude.

I dialled Langford's number from the car. "Well, your friend Cottee definitely found something."

The news was met with silence on her end. Then: "You're kidding."

"I'm really not. We got a kid, looks maybe nineteen years old, any semblance of his mortal half long gone from the looks of him. Whatever shit Cottee's rambling 'bout when it comes to symbols and wrestling, turns out he may not be entirely full of crap."

"Damn," Langford said. "The demon, it's—"

"Not done a damn thing, so far as I can see, 'cept wrestling and train and hang around his house. That's never a good sign, you know?"

"Keep on it," Langford said. "Let me know if it needs to be taken care of."

She hung up the phone. I sat in the car. Drank bottled water, I'd picked up with the rental, and settled in for the long haul while I studied the duplex block.

There's a process, when it comes to eliminating a demon. A lot of it requires a shit-ton of patience and the willingness to lie low and avoid detection. That's how you figure out what defences they've got in place, from magical wards to booby traps that'll blow your damn hand off if you pick the wrong lock. I'd encountered both on the job before, back when I first worked my way up the food chain. The longer a demon's been around, the more it's settled into its host, the more dangerous they tend to be.

After you've got the defences down, you start in on the pattern. Figure out the safest places to hit them when you want to avoid detection. Figure out where you go when the job is done, since most dead demons just look like dead bodies, and the cops ain't exactly buying the defence that you killed 'em for the good of humanity. It's half the reason we let some demons keep walking around, if they limit themselves to the kind of bad shit that doesn't cross a line.

The demon inside the kid upstairs hadn't crossed

any line that I knew about yet, but I knew he wasn't paying his rent by wrestling. That was usually the first sign steps needed to be taken.

A demon taking shortcuts was always going to be trouble.

I tag teamed the surveillance with Langford, focused on the physical while she handled the other stuff. Met up with her fourteen days later, in the McDonalds down in Palm Beach, not far from my house. Langford ordered a couple of shitty cheeseburgers, along with a coke. I ordered a coffee, sat down to wait. Let her eat for a stretch before we started.

"Cottee says there's another wrestling show coming, next week," Langford said. There were hollow pockets beneath her eyes, dark and sleepless. She didn't look over, but idle fingers twisted her eyebrow ring while she contemplated the problem. "Based on what I've seen, we want him eliminated before that happens."

I nodded. Drank my coffee. "He still hasn't done anything worth killing him over."

She hesitated, cheeseburger in hand. "Yeah."

"But we're doing it anyway?"

She bit into the burger. Spoke with her mouth full. "Cottee asked."

"I asked for your help in saving the goddamn world and I'm going to be paying that favour back most of my damn life," I said.

"You're point?"

"We're killing a dangerous demon, no questions asked," I said. "Seems funny, is all. He doesn't seem like the kind of guy who inspires that kind of loyalty."

"And yet, here we are. Preparing to do the job." Langford unwrapped her third burger, bit into it. Chewed and swallowed. "Cottee's rarely wrong about things. When he says something needs killing..."

"Never said we weren't going to do the job. Just thought it was odd, is all."

"Keith, head in the game," she said. "If any other demon figured out this trick, started using it as way of helping others strip away their human half a little faster…"

"Yeah," I said. "I get it."

"So you're in?"

"You really need to ask?"

She pushed a notebook across the table, along with a pencil. "Then let's start getting a plan together. I want this done before the next show and it all gets a little harder."

FORTIFIED

It was hot, the night we set aside to kill Ketch. Langford in the back of the van, setting up for the ritual that would break down his wards. Me in the front, watching his duplex, leaving sweaty marks on the fake-leather upholstery. The air thick with incense and oppressive humidity, the moon a pale sliver and the streetlights on his street flickering as we waited. Technology and magic have never been a strong combination. Magic flows out of the Gloom, tainted by the shadows there. No lights on in Ketch's home, although I doubted he really needed them.

It wasn't much of a place. I figure the kid who'd been Ketch rented it, before he got possessed; semi-furnished, cheap, and perched on a steep slope, the drive little more than a breakneck drop between the roadside and the door. Stubby palms filled the cramped yard and burnt-orange brick walls secured things to the hillside, a desperate attempt to keep soil erosion from sweeping the duplex away. Big windows gave me multiple points of entry, even if they were likely to be loud. I unearthed a SIG, a knife, and a set of lock picks, kept watch while Langford finalized her work.

"We're good." Langford settled in the centre of her circle, crossed her legs and closed her eyes. I slipped free of the van, whispered a short spell to discourage attention as I covered the two blocks between us and Ketch's home. I edged closer to the duplex, counted down from five hundred. The air hummed as I sidled towards the front door, half-slid down the grass, goose bumps on my arm as Langford's magic did it's thing. I crouched low and worked my picks into the locks, prodded the tumblers until they clicked. Slipped in before anyone noticed - you can trust magic to cover your tracks, a little, but there's no point taking risks that aren't necessary on a hit. I pulled the door shut behind me, quiet as a breath.

It was dark, inside. Longs shadows cast by the thin seam of moonlight peeking in through the heavy drapes. I took a moment, blinked rapidly until my eyes adapted. Kept still and hoped the lingering effects of my spell would keep my scent obscured. I knew the layout of the duplex, courtesy of city plans: two bedrooms to the left, after leaving to the lounge room; small kitchen and dining space at the end of the wall on my right, with a doorway to the garage halfway there. Just enough room to swing a cat round, if you didn't mind giving the cat a concussion. The chewy stink of rotting meat came from the garage. The frisson of unravelling magic filled the air with an ozone scent. The soft splash of tap-water, up and round the corner. Ketch lived alone, near as we could tell. I held my breath, edged closer.

He stood at the sink, filling a glass. Boxers only, in the muggy night air, the muscled lines of his frame silhouetted against the open window. Head low, attention foggy thanks to Langford's magic. I took aim at the broad back and the SIG kicked three times. Two shots to the chest, one to the head. Standard operating procedure, whether you're killing men or monster. Ketch fell forward, sprawled across his kitchen bench. Didn't move for the space of ten seconds, which was long enough to get me curious.

I took a step forward, kept him covered.

Big mistake.

He swung blind, glass in hand, smashed it against my blind side. Sent me stumbling backwards with blood streaming down my cheek, a jagged stump of glass still clenched in his fist. I'd nailed him good with the first two in the chest, but the headshot had been wide. Glancing shot to the side of the skull, not enough to scramble his grey-matter like you want in a demon-shoot.

Should have known better, after months at the target range. Stupid missing eye was going to get me killed.

Ketch charged, dark flecks of blood dribbling from his chest. Professionals don't panic, but I came close: I backed off, tried to get the space to plug him with the SIG. Groped for the knife sheathed at the small of my back with my other hand. Ketch kept coming, all claws and snarls and pain. My retreat hit the wall, forced me to skid sideways. Ketch put his fist through the space where my head had been.

"Cottee's friend," Ketch hissed. "Recognise your scent."

I don't do up-close, not if I can avoid it. I put a bullet in his leg, tried to slow him down. Didn't work. He came after me, nails elongating into talons that raked my shooting hand. Latched on and wrenched sideways, hammering my fist against the wall. Pain lunged up my arm and numb fingers dropped the SIG. I got lucky, wrenched the knife free. Held it, awkwardly, in my left hand as I jabbed and gave ground.

Ketch leapt at me, hit me with the blunt force of his shoulder. Knocked me to the floor while he kept his feet. The first kick caught me in the ribs. The second, in the soft parts of my flank, just short of the place where the ribs would protect me.

The third kick hammered me in the skull, bounced my head off the floor real quick. The pain in my wrist didn't bother me, after that.

Nothing really bothered me at all.

HEAT

Ketch threw water into my face and I came too, spluttering, desperately fighting to return to the pain-free darkness. Awake wasn't good. My wrist hurt. My face hurt. Cold water dripped from my nose.

I wasn't dead, which surprised me, but there wasn't much else that seemed like good news. I was seated on an office chair, beside an archaic laptop. Wrists taped to the chair, feet hanging free. Ketch perched on the edge of his couch, lights turned on. Up close, his features were bone-white and ugly, the fluorescent globes giving him a wan, faintly ill appearance. Lips pulled back from sharp teeth, yellow and stained with stringy lines of drool. "Your pulse just shifted," he said. "Don't bother trying to pretend you're not awake."

I blinked a few times, lolled my head backwards. Ketch leaned back, showed off the puckered scar-tissue where my first two bullets had caught him. My jaw set, and I regretted it, felt pain down the side of my face. "You should be dead."

"And yet, I'm not." Ketch scratched at a scar, flashed me a grin. "Odds are your little wizard fucked up, or you're not as good as I'd heard. You've got a reputation, killer, after all that shit went down. The local boogiemen are all a-twitter about your presence. No one really trusts you, working at your bar. They show up to keep an eye on you, wait for you to fuck up."

I wanted to nod, but I didn't. That way lay pain. I retreated into stillness, matched the demon's gaze. It was one of Roark's rules: keep your cool, work the situation. Talk it through until you get an opening. "Seems like your kind need more to talk about, if all you've got is me."

He punched me in the mouth, got his weight behind it best he could from his perch on the couch. Still hit me hard enough that the office chair did a bunny-hop, rolled backwards a few inches before the drag of my feet slowed it down. I could taste blood, my whole face burning.

"Don't mistake the fact you're still alive for a good thing," Ketch said.

"Noted."

"I'm not a patient man," he said.

"Not much of a man at all," I said. "Far as I can see."

Ketch nodded. He liked that. "When a man heads to the Gloom, stops himself an apocalypse," he said, "my kind pay attention. When he cuts a deal that keeps him alive, my kind pays attention. We let each other know there's a big damn hero on the block, that it's time to step wary if you're going to do wrong." He came forward, clawed hands clamping down on my forearms. Pressed his face real close to mine. "I don't like being wary, hero. It makes me irritable."

I flinched, despite myself. Screwed my good eye shut, waiting for the next punch. Instead I got treated to his warm breath against my cheek, the faintest hint of brimstone every time he exhaled.

Then he was gone, the weight of him no longer looming over me. Ketch was standing again, hoisted upright far too fast for anything human, like he's used some magic trick that disconnected his bulk from the rules of sinew, gravity, and human muscle movement. Sharp talons tore at the tape around my wrist. "Get up," he said. "I've got no further interest in hurting you, right now."

I hesitated and the order came again, lowered to a feral growl. "Get. Up."

I stood, unsteadily, expecting a trick. Pressed my wrist close to my chest as the pain settled into a dull throb. I could still see dark shadows at the edge of my vision and my body felt weird, like I'd been made of out flesh and helium before getting weight down with bring sparks of pain. Concussion, maybe. No condition to make a fight of it.

It didn't stop me from scanning the floor, searching for the SIG. It was there, half-hidden beneath the coffee table, like we'd kicked it there during our scuffle. A temptation. Demons liked doing that. Inviting you to do something stupid and making it seem like a good option.

Didn't stop me from faking a stumble, blocking his view with my body as I slumped against the coffee table and reached for the weapon. I got it left-handed, swung it round towards Ketch as I rose.

Ketch shrugged one shoulder, fire burning in his eyes. The long, muscled frame pulled itself back to full height and the demon glanced at the window, idly scratching at his chest as he sighed. "Shit," he said. "I mean, seriously, hero, you really want to do that? I'm letting you go, you stupid fucker."

I glanced at the door. Another temptation.

Ketch shook his head. "Get out," he said. "I mean it."

My first instinct was to run, flee with all the speed I could manage, but that was the kind of instinct that got you killed. I braced myself, adjusted my grip on the gun.

"Your friend is long gone," Ketch said. "There's no one worrying at my defences, no one to give you an advantage if we get into a fight. No way to win here, hero, except trusting me and leaving."

"I tried to kill you."

"You failed. I'm not holding a grudge."

I blinked, not sure how to process that.

"Get out." Ketch smiled and I could see the cruel points of his teeth. "Tell Langford she's getting sloppy as hell, and she should do better the next time you try this. Won't do her any good, but it'll make things amusing. Give me a worthwhile fight, you know?"

I tried to hold the SIG steady and failed. Lowered my arm and limped toward the door, waiting for an attack that never came.

SECOND CHANCES

Used to be, when I was a kid, it was easy to find a pay phone. Not so easy anymore, in the age of cheap cells, which hurts like hell when you're limping away from a job gone wrong and your back-up's already absconded with your ride.

These days, when you fuck up, you grit your teeth and lug your aching carcass three kilometres to the nearest Seven-Eleven with a pay phone, then you stand around out-front until your partner comes to collect you.

Langford didn't say much, when she showed up. I stayed quiet the entire way to the safe-house, distracting myself from the pain by running through each step of the job, trying to figure out exactly where it went wrong. Got as far as the front door before I passed out, didn't come-to until we were back on the Coast and Langford's skinny arms were trying to help me into a safe house on the twenty-third floor of a holiday resort, down on the beachfront.

Langford made coffee, grabbed a first-aid kit from the bathroom. Directed me to the spare bedroom where she started to patch me up. Stitches and antiseptic, to hold my face together. Bandages and a splint, when we got to my arm. I sat there in silence, glaring at her the entire time.

"That was a fucking fiasco," I said.

Langford focused on wrapping my wrist, pulling the bandage tight. "Fucker had wards we didn't pick up during the surveillance. Didn't help that he was awake, when we got there."

"Awake I can deal with. Awake is the natural state of most demons, and it's never been a problem. Going in with half-arsed intel, that's a recipe for shit going wrong."

She paused a moment, glanced up at me.

"He knew you," I said. "Said you were getting sloppy."

She hit the end of the bandage. Tied it off and stepped back. "That work?"

I flexed my fingers. The pain wasn't gone, but it'd receded a little. "It'll do. Sprained?"

She nodded, dreadlocks shifting.

"And Ketch?"

She sighed. "You got all kinds of lucky."

"Lucky is escaping. That isn't what happened here."

"Demons don't let people live after a botched hit."

"No," I said. "They don't." I closed my eyes and listened to the waves, the irregular hiss of them rolling in and thumping against the shore. "Tell me about Cottee."

Holly snapped the lid of the first aid kit shut. "He's a friend."

"And his beef with the demon?"

She settled back, stared at her hands. "A mistake," she said. "One of mine, and one of Gareth's.

He was being, well, groomed, I guess, back when we first met. A bright kid who understood the basics of the Gloom, started dabbling with magic. Never going to be a full-fletched sorcerer, but he could pick up enough to do what you do, backed up by someone like Roark." Holly cradled the aluminium box in both hands, fingertips rubbing the red cross on the white surface. Moonlight caught the silver stud through her eyebrow as she glanced towards the window. "Thing is, I'm not Roark. I taught him a few things, figured he'd keep them to himself, but Cottee experimented. Tried a few minor rituals. Next thing you know..."

Things clicked into place. "Ah," I said. "So it's personal."

"Very."

"And you've tried taking care of it before now?"

She nodded. "Me and Gareth, and Gareth on his own. We were looking to save him, originally, but as we saw how his power expanded..."

"Yeah, well. Ketch was, what, a friend? A brother?"

"A lover," Langford said. "They were both of them young and stupid, too enamoured of comic books and theories to listen to any warnings I had. Cottee's holding a grudge for what he's lost. Ketch is playing a different game, but make no mistake, if there's anything human left in him..."

"Roark always said things go wrong when it gets personal."

"Which is funny, 'cause every job for him was as personal as it gets."

"Why didn't you tell me?"

"We hadn't tried in years."

"And you figured, what? He'd forget it ever happened?"

"I figured Cottee made peace with it. Turns out, I was wrong," she said. "Ketch wasn't doing much, near as we can tell. He didn't sign-on with any of the local crews, didn't bother trying to recruit other demons. No reason to go after him, outside of Cottee's hard-on. I figured you'd go in there, see there was nothing worth worrying about. And then..."

"Then, there was something worth worrying about."

"Yeah."

"Weeks of surveillance," I said. "Weeks of fucking surveillance and intel, and this didn't come up."

"I'm sorry." Langford retreated to the doorway of the bedroom, paused there with one hand resting against the frame. "Listen, we made the attempt. You don't owe me any more than that, and you sure as hell don't owe Gareth. I'm sorry we didn't warn you of that. It's been years and... well. Look. Go back to the bar, heal up. Let me figure out some other way of taking care of all this."

Tempting. Very fucking tempting.

"You owe him, I owe you. It's a vicious fucking circle." I made a tight fist with his right hand, getting used to the pain. "Get Cottee down from Brisbane, tomorrow morning. One thing hasn't changed: we can't let the fucker keep running around."

LOCAL HEROES

We met Cottee in the KFC out on highway, just round the corner from Currumbin Beach. He pulled up in an ancient Honda hatch-back, half-rust and half green paint. Climbed out and mopped his forehead, sweaty in the muggy heat. I sat with Langford, watched him shuffle through the car park. The heat gave him a sweaty sheen and damp stains on his shirt. I waved him over and he edged closer, hands fluttering as he tried to figure out what to do with them. "Mister Murphy," he said. "It's good to see you."

"Sit." My voice was little more than a growl. Cottee nodded once, eyes on my splint.

"Listen," he said. "I—"

"Ketch is still alive," I said.

His face fell. "Oh."

"Chose not to kill me," I said. "Said some interesting things."

"Oh," Cottee repeated. He sat. "I should apologize,

I suppose."

"Fuck your apology."

"Listen—"

"No." I reached for my paper cup of Pepsi. "Tell me what you were hoping for, sending me in there. Tell me what you wanted."

Cottee ground the ball of his thumb into the other hand. "Revenge, maybe. I'm not sure. Holly mentioned what you'd done, prior to ending up here. I figured... maybe, this time..." Cottee's mouth opened and closed, saying nothing.

I glared at him, fists bunched. Langford put a hand on my arm. "It's okay," she said. "Just tell him, Gareth."

Cottee looked away. "It wasn't love," he said. "Maybe it was, once upon a time, and that was a long time ago and I'm not trying to get him back. Call it obligation, I guess. I owed it to him to fix my mistake. Holly thought—"

"I know what she thought." I sipped on my straw. Watched Cottee and his eyes flicked from me to Langford, then back again.

"I'm sorry," he said. "I don't really know what to say here."

I put my cup down. "You're the closest we have to an expert. You knew the guy he used to be, and you know wrestling. I want you to figure something out for me."

He nodded.

"Why did he let me go?" I said. "We botched it. Two shots to the chest and he didn't go down, but he didn't rip me apart like most demons would in that situation. It let me leave with my gun, dared me and Langford to make another attempt. That isn't normal."

He frowned. Nodded. "For demons, no."

"For wrestling?"

He shrugged. "It's what bad guys do," he said. "There's a tradition in wrestling, when you're trying to get a bad guy over. You send him out there, night after night, to make an open challenge. Let him bring in local kids for a last-five-minutes-and-you'll-win-a-prize kind of thing. 'Cept no one really lasts five minutes. They get out there and they get killed. Metaphorically killed, I mean. Submission holds and pain and..."

He trailed off, frowning. "Beating on the local boy makes the crowd hate 'em, and heels that get hated are the lifeblood of the sport. It gets people to pay money, week after week, just to see when they finally get beat. So you do this bit, show after show, 'til people really want to see the guy beat, and that's when you bring in your new gold boy, the hometown hero whose sticking with the company. He doesn't get to win, not at first, but he lasts the five minutes and then he gets beat down for his presumption. He's the one who feuds with the heel. He's the one who finally gets to beat the unbeatable arsehole and become a hero."

The big man paused and took a breath. "You've been beat," he said, "and you're still kicking. Ketch is drawing strength from that, just like he does when he's inside the ring. He's saving you up. Letting you live for the rematch, so it means more when he kills you. "

"'Cept your bad guys get beat, eventually, and I didn't last five minutes."

Cottee's fingers drummed the table. "This is all just a theory."

"It's something." Langford grinned. "I've got an idea."

"I don't owe you enough to die," I said.

"Sure you do." Her grin widened a little. "Shouldn't come to that, though. We go back to first principles: locations matter. Symbols matter. If he's drawing power from the rituals of wrestling, maybe we can do something with that. Get you an audience and a ring..."

I nodded. "Location matters."

"It does." Cottee's his hands grew still. "But I don't like your chances. You can't wade in there with guns to fight him, not if we're playing it this way. You'd have to go in there and... well, you know." He threw a couple of punches at the air. They looked like crap.

"New plan, then," I said. "No way I'm taking on a demon bare-handed." I held up my splint. "Especially not with this."

"Then we'll cheat," Langford said. "Take the sword and use it."

"The sword would be cheating," Cottee said. "Good guys don't cheat."

"Ever?"

"Not never, but they don't start the process."

"We can work with that," I said.

REMATCH

The sword: three feet of dull, serviceable metal we'd stolen from one of the deepest parts of the Gloom in order to save the world. The kind of weapon that had a dozen names, when you traced its mythology, a dark reflection of every magic blade swung in the name of doing good. Me, I never took to it. Swords were a bad idea, no matter which way you sliced it. They needed you to get up close to whatever you wanted to kill, into the range where it could do bad things and try to kill you back.

I preferred to shoot things. It played to my strengths. But debts need to be paid back in this line of work, and that meant digging the sword out of the lock-box in my office.

I sat in the driver's seat of Gareth Cottee's hatchback, watching the gym where Ketch and his fellow wrestlers assembled to train each Thursday. It didn't look like much, just a stainless-steel shed in the middle of an industrial estate, a small car-park out the front for the wrestlers who drove over. We'd been watching a few hours now, waiting for the others to leave. Finally, Cottee checked his watch, nodded to himself. "It's time."

He was pale, beneath the sweat. I couldn't really blame him. Sweat prickled the back of my neck as I exited the car, hauled the sheathed sword out of the back seat and slung it over my shoulder. It was getting dark, shadows growing longer as the sun set. A poster out the front of the wrestler's shed advertised their next show, three days away. I glanced over at Cottee.

"Ready?"

He didn't really nod, just inclined his head a little. He led the way as we headed into the shed, not bothering with anything like stealth. The faint sourness of too much sweat clung to the walls and canvas. Ketch was up the back of the room, lifting weights. He looked up, grinning, as we entered, his arms still moving in a smooth rhythm, muscles bunching beneath his grubby singlet. "Gareth," he said, "and the hero. You two."

I climbed up the side of the ring and clambered through the ropes. Handed the sword to Cottee and turned towards the demon. "No guns, this time," I said.

Ketch's lip curled. "Gareth's been talking, I see."

"Light it up," Gareth said, his voice squeaking.

Ketch laughed. "Gareth, love, did you really just attempt an order?"

"Light it up." Gareth's voice was steadier this time, and he circled around the ring. "You want an opponent, you want an audience, I'm giving you both."

A bare bulb flared to life over the ring, illuminating the red and blue cables running from post to post. The demon dropped its barbell and stepped forward, sneer growing deeper. "Is that true, hero? You really want a rematch?"

"You saying no?"

"Stupid," Ketch said. "You're injured. You left your sorceress at home. You left your guns behind. This is my house, my ring."

"I'll risk it," I said.

"You will."

I didn't see him move, not really. Just a flicker of movement in the corner of my eye, a blur as he charged the ring. Then something hard and unyielding smashed against my jaw, sent me reeling back into the ropes. The impact rolled through me like the flash-wave of a bomb, a precursor to the pain that followed in its wake. I groped for the ropes, used them to stay upright. Another fist caught me in the stomach, doubling me over. Strong hands lifted me, slammed me into the mat. Ketch grated my cheek against the canvas, opening up my stitches.

I swung a wild elbow, caught him in the face.

Ketch backed off, just a little, gave me space to get to my feet. There wasn't anything slick about my approach, nothing stylized of rake. I bunched my fists and swung, hammered Ketch hard as I could. He gave ground, grinning the entire way. I followed, half-stumbling, trying to get my weight behind a punch. Tagged him below the right eye and his skin broke, blood seeping free.

Ketch grabbed my injured arm and twisted it behind me, the pain sending me to my knees. He dragged my dead weight to the side of the ring and jammed it against the ring apron. "You're lazy, hero, and you're not built for this."

Splinters from the wooden splint dug into my arm. I cried out, grabbing the ropes with my free hand. Tried to kick my way free with both legs.

Ketch slapped me across the face. "Get up," he said.

I stood, moved my weight onto the balls of my feet, just like Danny Roark taught me. Swung a few times without connection before Ketch put a boot into my stomach. I went down hard, his weight on top of me, both hands locked around my throat. Hot breath pressed against my ear. "I like your persistence, hero. It's worth more, killing you here. Far better than snapping your neck in my kitchen."

I gasped, my face burning. Desperate to break free. Ketch cinched his choke a little tighter, squeezing the life out of me.

"Toby."

The demon faltered a moment, gave me a moment to catch my breath.

"Toby, stop," Cottee said. He was up on the apron, against the ropes, pleading with the demon. "This isn't you, man. This isn't—"

Ketch planted a right hand in Cottee's face, knocked him off the canvas. A hard shot that'd hurt like hell in the morning, if it hadn't done something permanent.

I crawled to the corner, collected the sword. Pulled it from the sheath.

Ketch laughed, spreading his arms wide. "Not what this fight is about, hero-boy."

I didn't bother talking anymore, just charged in and buried the point of the sword deep into his chest. Ketch snarled, stumbling backwards. Sagged against the ropes. Ketch's blood stained the canvas, along with my own. He swung at me, hard and wild, knocked me to the floor. I landed hard on my right shoulder, felt something pop that shouldn't.

I forced myself upright, stabbed again. The fire in Ketch's eyes went out and he sank to his knees, trying to hold his guts in.

Gareth Cottee's rapid breathing echoed in the darkness, the big man scrambling through the bottom rope. "Toby," he whimpered. "Shit, Toby."

Ketch closed his eyes, breathed in and out. I tried to pull the sword free, stab him again, but a single bloody hand closed around my wrist. "Not Toby," Ketch said. "Not yet."

Cottee closed his eyes, tears spilling down his cheeks.

"Watch," I said. "This needs an audience."

Cottee nodded, sniffling, backed away from the ring. Cried as I jerked my hands free of Ketch's grip, leaving bloody smears where his fingers had been.

I stabbed a third time, twisting the blade. Blood made my grip slippery. Cottee winced, but he held steady, his puffy eyes focused on the mess I was making in the demon's stomach.

"Enough." Cottee's voice was muted. I barely heard it.

"Enough," Cottee repeated, louder this time. When I glanced across the ring, there were tears dribbling into Cottee's beard. "It's done, Mister Murphy. It's done."

WINNER, AND NEW CHAMPION

I put through a call to Langford, told her the job was done. "One less you owe me," she said, and I agreed, that was true. I told her she sounded tired and hung up the phone.

Gareth Cottee was out front, slumped up against his car, his eyes and nose red as he sniffled and fought the tears. No-one around that time of night, in the heart of the estate. Not unless a security patrol rolled past, and we'd timed those out earlier to give us a chance to get the job done. I limped out, my arm pressed close to my chest. Wished I had it in me to drive for the poor bastard, but that wasn't going to happen. I needed to re-splint my arm, take a metric ton of painkillers, and sleep for the better half of a week. Unfortunately the bar wasn't going to give me that long. That's the curse of staying in once place, after a job is done.

"You okay?"

Cottee looked up, blinked at me. "Yeah," he said. "No. I'm not really sure."

"Yeah, I totally get that." I limped round to the driver's side, forced aching fingers to open the door. "You think you're right to drive?"

He nodded.

"Well then," I said. "Before anyone arrives."

He huddled in the driver's seat, put the car into gear. Struggled with the gearstick as he tried to move into third, although he got it there and started winding his way out towards the highway. My right arm burned the entire way, aching every time I shifted in my seat. My shoulder protested as loud as the wrist, now. That wasn't a good sign. "Every instinct I have tells me to get out of town," I said. "First rule of hitting things from the Gloom, get out before the death-curses start."

Cottee's voice was weak. "Demon's don't have death curses."

"No, but they leave corpses. They attract cops."

"Oh," Cottee said. "Yeah, I guess they do."

We drove four blocks without saying a thing. Cottee started searching the radio, kept finding the empty crackle of static instead of settling on a station. He sniffled and wiped his nose with a sleeve.

"First time I ever ran," I said, "I left a girl behind. Didn't think much of it, at the time. Figured it was necessary. Told myself that the entire time I was away, right up until circumstances sent me home again." I shifted. Winced. Looked out the window. "Didn't end all that well, when we reconnected."

"I heard she tried to kill you."

"Lot of old friends tried that. Wasn't unique to her."

That earned me a weak smile amid that heavy beard. "Not the same as killing her, though."

"No, I guess it ain't."

He nodded, followed the road out onto the highway. Followed the highway south, back to the Gold Coast. Neither of us said another thing the entire way home.

TITHES

AN EASY NICKEL

Last stop, Gould's Antiques, up on Wickham Terrace. The three of them skulk in, trying to disappear amid the furniture and the ball gowns and rows of glass display cases. The same routine every visit: Angie slinking to the rear of the store, breathing in the scent of the ancient leather jackets; Byron down by the glass-fronted cabinet, crouched so low his coat brushes the concrete floor, peering at the flintlocks and gasmasks and colonial knives; Nate just kind of wandering around, not really looking at anything except his watch, fretting about the possibility of missing their last train home.

Nate's only there because they are a team, the three of them. Refugees from the land of misfit toys, as Byron's so fond of calling them, sharing a shitty fibro shack in a city that has no use for them. They spend their days, three against the world, the punk-girl, the goth-boy, and whatever Byron calls himself, a witch or a warlock or just strange weird.

They come to Gould's because Byron wants to, telling stories about the occult paraphernalia auctioned to secret bidders, but Nate's never seen any magic here, never seen much of anything but antiques and junk, and he's not even sure there's a difference between the two. He hates Gould's because Brisbane's supposed to be a break, one damn day in a city where their pale and black-clad existence doesn't stand-out amid the sea of tanned surfers and overweight tourists, and Gould's is the one place they go on these trips where the stern gaze of the owner makes Nathan Heaney feel like just a child playing Halloween dress-up.

The owner is an old man, squat and heavily jowled, with thinning white hair brushed back from his scalp. Despite sitting there, day after day, surrounded by the grandeur of ancient ball gowns and uniforms, he seems content with his drab cardigan and the gilded bifocals that enhance his already formidable scowl. Nate finds himself meeting the stare, caught and almost trembling, weight shifting from foot to foot.

"So," the owner says. "Just browsing?"

"No, I, uh—" Nate looks away, searching for back-up, but the others are gone. "I'd like to buy something. I mean, I've got..." He thinks about his wallet, empty except for a ten dollar note. Fingers dart into his pockets, searching for change. "I've got money."

"Right." The old man picks up a newspaper, folds it in half. The side facing upwards contains the crossword, the white boxes half-filled with messy scrawl. Nate stands there, hands plunged into pockets, face burning. He forces himself to step towards the counter, heavy boots clumping against the concrete floor. There's jewellery in the display cabinets, rings and earrings and antique lighters. Old coins arranged on velvet displays, faces turned towards the heavens. He crouches, peering in, eyes drifting from face to face.

He stops when he spots the nickel. It's small, an interloper among the disused halfpennies, shillings, and sixpences. Nothing antique about it; just an American coin with a skull carved into the face. It's the details that catch Nate's eye, the silver metal buffed until each jut of bone and hollow socket is visible. The old man still sits on his stool, scribbling words onto his paper.

Nate can't say why he wants the coin, why he does what he does, but he leans forward, hands pressed to the glass, and feels the door slide sideways beneath his fingertips. He lets go, breath hissing as he inhales, fingers thrown back. Feels the world slide into freeze frame as he stands there, waiting for someone to notice the cabinet left unlocked and open, the old man showing too little attention, the skinny little goth-boy crouched down and waiting to see what happens next.

Nate exhales, fingers back against the glass, easing the door open millimetre by millimetre. Angie squeals, sharing some joke with Byron on the far side of the store, and the old man glances up, once, in irritation, before going back to his seven letter word. Nate's fingers tremble as he slides the glass pane back, creating a space just wide enough to fit three fingers.

For a moment he hesitates. In their trio, their little team, it's never been him that's done the stealing.

Angie walks off with candy bars. Byron is more ambitious. Nate is always the nervous one, too distracted, too fretful of the consequences.

And yet he sees the nickel sitting there, the grinning skull sitting side-by-side with the faces of dead queens and kings, and Nate calmly slips a hand inside the cabinet and claims it. It's cold and small against his palm as he nudges the glass closed, eases his way back. He tries to remember Byron's lessons: stay calm; don't rush things; wait for a distraction.

Then Angie squeals again, and there's a crash as a rack of dresses give way, and Nate slips out of Gould's while the old man shuffles off to investigate. He waits outside, pulse hammering in his ears, until the exhilaration of the theft wears off.

Hours later, on the train home, the steady click-clack of the wheels lulling them into sleepiness, back to the Gold Coast where there's no place for things like flintlocks and ball gowns and antiques. Brisbane aspires to be a city to house things that are laden with the burden of history, but the Gold Coast is beaches and tanning salons and tourists by the hundreds. It measures its history by minutes instead of years. Nate gets out the coin and stares, puzzled by his desire to steal the damn thing. The skull seems less distinct in the murky light of the train carriage, the nickel oddly unpleasant to hold now it's been warmed. He holds it and the shadows in the carriage grow longer and deeper, a little darker than they have seemed.

The others don't seem to notice, not right away. Byron is staring at the window, watching his own reflection. Angie's asleep, the shaved half of her head resting on Byron's skinny shoulder, the half left to grow long hanging like a purple veil over her face. Nate knows better than to trust Angie when her eyes are closed. Sometimes it means Angie's sleeping, sometimes it does not. He can't tell which until he eases the coin back into his pocket and Angie's eyes flick open, wide and eager, grinning as if she's caught him doing something illicit.

"What's that?" she says.

"Something I picked up." Nate hesitates, coin in hand, then opens his fingers to show her. "I think it's a nickel."

Byron shrugs Angie free of his shoulder and leans forward. "Where in hell do you pick up a nickel in the middle of Brisbane?"

Nate closes his fist around the coin. "Gould's."

Angie's eyebrows rise. Bryon snorts. "No way," Byron says. "No way did you rip that place off."

"Cabinet was open," Nate says. "You and Angie caught his attention for a minute."

Angie clicks her fingers, opens her palm to accept the coin. Byron whistles. "Jesus," he says, "you did."

"I figured they wouldn't really miss it."

"Jesus." Byron glances at the coin, shakes his head. "Cabinet full of antique shit, and you steal a five cent piece?

"Maybe it's magic," Nate says.

"They don't keep that stuff on display." Byron crosses his arms, tattooed wrist peeking free of his sleeves. "You should have grabbed something cooler. Something we could sell."

"Sell where?" Nate says. "Who buys this shit back home?" He sits there, watching Angie examine the nickel, unable to take his eyes off it. Byron looks out the window again, face set into a scowl.

"I don't think I like it, "Angie says. "It's cool and all, with the skull, but...."

"But?" Nate says.

"But it's weird." Angie rubs the coin between her fingers, frowning at the way it feels. Nate reaches out, plucks it from her fingers.

"So I'll keep it in my room," he says, "where neither of you need to see it again."

GREEDY SHADOWS

I hate this place, Nate thinks, and he takes another hit of the joint Bryon rolled for them, a little something to get them through the afternoon heat and the oppressive humidity of summer. The three of them gathered on the back steps of the house, clustered there with the joint and bottled water, watching the breeze catch the hills-hoist and the unwashed grass. Nate dressed up in his black shirt and jeans. Byron perched, stork-like, on the step above him. Angie pressed against his knees, taking a hit on the joint, the long hair on the left side of her scalp died pink in the three weeks since Brisbane.

Nothing ever happens here, not down on the Gold Coast, nothing but summer and rain and the heat that turns their fibro rental slick and humid as a sauna. The neighbour's cat climbs over the fence, a flash of grey fur disappearing into the long grass, its presence only heard because of the jaunty, tinkling bell on the collar. Nate stares at the grass, at the shadows, looking for the creature. All he sees is their overgrown yard and the weeds growing in the shadow fence line, a shadow the cat seems too cautious to go near. Not that Nate blames the feline, not since he started carrying the coin. There's something about dark places—hallways, ditches, the leeward side of buildings—something about their presence that leaves him uneasy.

"Jesus," Byron says, "I'll almost be glad when uni starts again. At least the classes have air-conditioning."

Angie nods, breathing against the joint, the same agreement they've made every time one of them makes that complaint. Nate grunts, bored with the exchange, digs through his pocket in search of the nickel, sorting through the shrapnel of unspent coins until his finger finds the one that feels warm and dank as a mangrove floor. He doesn't pull it out, just runs his fingers across the surface, tracing the skull. A bad habit that's formed in the last few weeks, ever since he made off with the coin to begin with.

"We should go to the movies," Angie says. "Go see something stupid and get out of the heat."

Again there's agreement, silent and universal, but they're all broke, too broke to go out, too broke for anything but smoking their last joint. *Jesus*, Nate thinks, and he slips the coin out of his pocket without really meaning it, just pulls it out and holds it in his left fist.

"Hey," Angie says, "what the hell's that?"

They follow her finger, eyes searching the fence-line for God-knows-what.

"What's what?" Byron says, standing to get a better look. His eyes are bloodshot and his shirt hangs open.

"Next to the second missing slat," Angie says, "down by the clump of dandelions," and this time Nate sees it, a twitch of movement in the overgrown weeds, a flicker of darkness. He tightens his grip on the nickel and the movement stops, the thing in the shadows halts, but now they can all sense its presence. Sense, but not see, like the shadows themselves are a living thing, hunkering in the overgrown grass. Something that watches, its presence tangible, and everyone's struck by this feeling that's cold and terrible and empty as a lost soul, and Angie, at least, starts shaking.

"Let's go inside," Nate says, and he knows Byron is nodding, Byron who's already standing but not willing to look away. And then the darkness, the emptiness they're looking at without really seeing, congeals and spreads through the overgrown weeds, creeping forward like a rising tide, until Nate finally panics and pockets the coin, letting it drop down amid the twenty and fifty cent pieces, and the panic that gripped them melts, all of them breathing and slow to move.

"Jesus," Angie says, "Nate, that was you. What the hell did you do?"

"Nothing." Nate reaches for the dropped joint, rescuing it from the rotting step.

"Bull," Angie says. "Get out your nickel again."

"I don't got it on me," Nate says.

"You've got it," Byron says, his voice still shaky. "You've always got it."

"So what?" Nate says.

"So it's doing something," Angie says. "It made that thing come. It made it go away."

"Like magic?" Nate says, trying to make a joke of it without knowing why.

"Yeah," Angie says, and her voice is very small. "Yeah, just like magic."

"Jesus, Angie, you're fucking stoned."

"She's not," Byron says. "No more than you and I are."

"It's just a damn coin."

Angie glares. "You saying you didn't see that?"

"No," Nate says. "I'm saying—"

"Fuck you," Angie says, and she runs her hand across the stubbled half of her scalp, fingertips teasing the side left long. "Fuck you, Nate, for trying to make me feel crazy about this. Fuck you very much."

She stands and retreats, preferring the sweat-box heat of their house than sharing the steps with him, and Nate watches her go with his mouth clamped shut, fighting the urge to shout that he's sorry, to give in just like he always does whenever Angie doesn't get her way. Byron waits, then shakes his head, then disappears to comfort her, leaving Nate out there alone with his joint and the brewing storm and the nickel he doesn't dare touch.

They spend four days avoiding one another, facing a silent detente. Nate finds himself touching the nickel without noticing, feeling the same cold terror. He tries to leave the coin alone and discovers that he can't, that he'll absently pick it up and fondle it until he feels something watching from the shadows and lets go. He smokes endless cigarettes to cover his nerves, prowls the house like a caged beast.

"This isn't fair," Nate argues, cornering Byron in the kitchen. "She can't expect me to take her seriously, right?"

Byron doesn't turn away from the counter, attention focused on spooning instant into a chipped and dirty coffee mug. "She's scared, Nate. Something weird happened, has been since you got the nickel."

"That doesn't mean it's magic."

"We both saw something."

"We all saw something," Nate says. "I don't think the nickel's the cause. It's, I don't know, an illusion or something. A natural phenomena. A coincidence."

"That's three things." Byron's voice is steady and even. He picks up the kettle and pours, stirs gently. He drinks while staring out the kitchen window, watching the fence and the long grass. "So how do you really explain what happened?"

"I don't," Nate says. "Not in this house. Shit, the amount of—"

"Nate."

It cuts him off mid-rant. His name said softly, with gentle calm. Byron slowly turning to look at him, dark eyes open and wary. "Nate," he says, "what's up? Why's it so important that this have nothing to do with the coin?"

"'Cause it doesn't," Nate says. "It's just some bloody metal."

"Maybe," Byron says, "but it's more than that to Ang. It's more than that to me, and I think you know that as well. It's doing something weird, Nate, and it worries us both. What we saw, it wasn't normal."

"We didn't actually see anything," Nate says.

"I know people," Byron says. "People who'll take it off our hands."

Nate clenches his fists and stares Byron down, forces the taller man to look away.

"All that shit you used to tell us about Gould's selling magic shit, that was just talk, By'. None of us took you seriously, you know that, right?"

"I know people," Byron says, but Nate isn't listening. He charges out of the kitchen, disappearing into his room where he knows he can hide.

Later, hours later, Nate walks up to Angie's door. He says her name, not shouting it, but forcefully, says he just wants to talk, and eventually she opens up, standing there in the doorway of her cluttered, clothes-filled room, looking at him with wounded eyes.

"Well?" she says, hands on hips, her jaw set and ready in case he decides to be arsehole.

"I'm sorry," Nate says. "I'm really sorry. I didn't mean to imply you were, you know..."

"You saw it, Nate. You felt whatever was out there."

"I saw something," Nate says, and he leans against the mould-covered wall, wishes it wasn't so damn hot in the house. "But I don't think it's the coin, Ang. I have it out all the time, Ang, and..."

"And what?" Angie reaches for the door, one hand on the brass knob.

"And nothing," Nate lies, trying not to think about the sensation of eyes upon him, the nightmares he has every night. "Nothing happens with the shadows. It's just a coin, yeah? A little freaky lookin', kinda cool, but just a coin."

For a moment he thinks she buys it, because she doesn't slam the door. Lies have always been Nate's talent, the thing he brings to the house. Angie leads, Byron does, Nate creates the half-truths that allow them to stay friends.

"Show me," Angie says. "Get the coin out and show me nothing happens."

For a moment Nate hesitates, 'cause he can feel the coin in his pocket, warm and getting warmer like it anticipates coming out. His instincts tell him not to do it, that the lie is surely over once she sees that the shadows are omnipresent, that Nate has seen them time and again since he acquired the coin and given them too little notice.

But he reaches into his pocket and produces the nickel, opens his fingers to display it to the world. The shadows in Angie's room start to congeal, faster and thicker than they were in the daylight, far quicker than the dim fluorescent bulb can truly slow down.

"Fuck, Nate," Angie says, "put it away, okay?"

Nate tries to close his fingers, tries to conceal the coin once more and return it to hiding. But his fingers won't cooperate, and the shadows start reaching forward, stretching like the wings of some great bird trying to envelop Angie. She tries to run, but Nate's in the way, blocking the easy path out. The shadows grab her, envelop her, bulging and swelling as she struggles. He can hear Angie screaming, but the scream is very distant, like she's in another house instead of an arm's length away.

Through it all Nate can't close his fingers, can't lock the coin away in a tight fist until the screaming is even fainter, so faint it's almost lost and gone within the swirling darkness.

Then Byron arrives, following Nate's own screams, and Byron's strong fingers work against Nate's hand, forcing him to drop the nickel against the hardwood floor.

"What happened?" Byron shouts. "Nate, where's Angie?"

Nate points to the centre of Angie's room, where the shadows are thinning and retreating to their usual place, where Angie lies amid the puddle of her dirty clothes, cold and pale and barely breathing, like something almost dead and waiting for its funeral shroud.

Angie lies in the hospital bed, all wires and tubes and pale skin. The room beeps, beeps, beeps, constantly beeping and hissing, reminding you that the machines are doing part of the work that keeps Angie breathing. Nate hates this place. Sand-coloured walls; sand-coloured curtains; another fucking permeation on the endless beige the Gold Coast embraces.

"Hey," Nate says. "Hey."

He's holding the nickel, has it coiled tight in his fist, thumb tracing the ridges cut into the side. He wants to give it to her, to tuck it into her hand for luck, to do whatever magic it can to help her out, but the coin is moist and unpleasant to hold, and he knows in his gut it'll just make things worse. He reaches out with his other hand, places it over Angie's still fingers. She's smaller here, in the hospital, but Nate is ready for that. Hospital's reduce people, shrink them away to nothing.

"Hey," he says, "just, don't die, okay? Hold on a bit. Hold on. Byron's got a plan."

He leans forward and kisses her forehead, just in case it helps, but it doesn't and Angie keeps on sleeping, keeps on breathing and beeping and hissing away. He can feel something watching her sleep, the same empty feeling he had in the yard. Nate keeps the nickel clenched in his fist as he exits, finds Byron in the hall with a cigarette in hand, unlit but nervously fiddling with it, giving the nurses cautious looks.

Byron looks up, stares at Nate with glistening eyes, fighting back tears. "We're getting rid of your fucking coin," he says, high forehead covered in a sheen of sweat.

Nate bites his bottom lip and tightens his grip. "It's just a coin," he says, and damned if he knows why, just another untruth he can't help himself speaking.

"That's bullshit, and you know it," Byron says. "I'm making the fucking call."

He disappears down the hallway, cigarette still in hand, making his way to the bank of payphones only pensioners and dero's ever end up using. Nate stands there, watching him go, unwilling to open his hand. He's afraid that letting go will free the thing that watches him, let it retreat back into the room and savage the sleeping Angie. He's afraid that maybe what Byron's saying is true, and that everything that's happened is all his fault.

TITHING

Byron lines up a meeting for three in the morning, drags Nate down to the lot out front of the local shopping centre. Australia Fair is close to water, like everything on the Coast, nestled next to the highway that runs down the beach-front, and beyond that the estuary where river meets ocean. It's the dodgy end of the Coast, home to junkies and students and the mentally ill, the parks on the far side of the highway a camping ground for the homeless.

Nate stands there, waiting, nickel in his pocket, wondering if someone is really going to show, if Byron is really serious when he says *he knows people*, and why they have to meet in the middle of the fucking night. "You sure about this?" he asks, not for the first time, and Byron's frown is all the answer Nate needs, angry and nervous at the same time.

"I've been thinking," Byron says, "about you and the coin. About how you ended up with it, up at Gould's. I think he let you steal it. I think he wanted it gone."

"Maybe," Nate says, 'cause he doesn't want to agree, 'cause he still wants to pretend that there's nothing wrong. "You never said who we're meeting out here, or why they'd want to take the coin."

Byron searches his jacket for a cigarette, casting furtive glances down the street. It's dark there, in the shadow of the shopping centre, and the soft tick of the streetlights seem loud and alien in silence. "This guys a friend of a friend," Byron says. "Not someone I know, but he's probably, you know..."

"Dangerous?"

"Maybe," Byron says. "Definitely not above board. Definitely not white magic."

"Definitely?" A voice asks, and they realise too late that it wasn't the other. The figure that walks down the car park ramp is one of the biggest men Nate's ever seen. Six-five, broad-shouldered, head shaved down to grey stubble. His dark suit blends seamlessly into the gloom of the night and there's a short, stubby weapon in his right hand. Not a gun, not quite, but its shape is close enough. "So," the big man says, "which one of you has the coin?"

"That depends," Byron says. "You Sabbath?"

The big man snorts. "Sabbath doesn't make house calls, mate. He sends me."

Byron hesitates, chewing over the information. Nate's eyes twitch back and forth between the stranger's weapon and the cheerful grin. He makes the circuit three times before Byron digs deep, finds the courage to say, "You got a name?"

"Randal," the big man says.

"I'm Byron. He's—"

The big man, Randal, fires and two darts thump into Byron's chest. He falls to the ground, twitching, the steady click of electric current breaking the silence.

Nate backs away. "What the hell?"

"Taser," Randal says. "You've got the coin, you make the decisions. I didn't want this munter getting in your head."

"The coin—"

"The nickel," Randal says. "Little thing, skull, ugly as sin. You do have it, right? I'd hate to reload and go through this again."

"I've got it," Nate says, hand dropping to his pocket, and as he does it Randal darts forward, strong fingers wrapping around Nate's wrist, pulling it up and away and around, locking it up behind Nate's back where it hurts.

"None of that, mate," Randal says. "No touching it, not out here. Trust me, it's better for all concerned. You got that?"

Nate nods.

"I want it said aloud, mate."

"I've got it," Nate says, "no touching the coin."

Randal lets him go, and Nate stumbles forward, ends up on his knees on the concrete sidewalk. "I don't get it," Nate says. "It's just some weird-ass nickel."

"Lots of weird things in this world. This one's a long way from home." Randal produces a cigarette and lights it, flame blossoming without any lighter that Nate can see. "Can't say we're fond of it, me and Mister Sabbath. Too bloody disruptive, you know?"

Byron stirs, coughing, whimpering like an injured animal. Randal takes a short step, builds momentum for a kick that catches Byron in the teeth. Nate flinches, looks away, tightens his grip on the coin.

"That's—" Randal turns and the words die in Nate's throat, stick there until he coughs them free and forces himself to speak. "That's not exactly going to convince me to... you know... deal."

Randal smiles, transferring his cigarette to his left hand. "Look at the stones on you," he says. "Good for you, kid. Good for you." He buries a punch in Nate's stomach, folding Nate over in one smooth movement. "Now stop being a fucking idiot, yeah? I'm not here to deal with you. That coin, it's all kinds of bad news. One curse if it's stolen, another if it's given away. More effort than I'm willing to put in, mate, all things considered."

Nate coughs, splutters, forces himself to breathe. "Then... what..."

"What do I want?" Randal lifts the cigarette to his lips, breathes with casual ease. "I want you to give it back to the original owners. You want rid of it, they want it back. Seems easy enough, yeah?"

No, Nate thinks, *not easy at all,* but what comes out of his mouth is a small, reluctant, "Yeah, I guess."

"Good call," Randal says, and he heads across the highway, long and easy strides that carry him away from Nate and the sucking, unpleasant sound of Byron trying to breathe through his wrecked lips and teeth. Nate hesitates, just a moment, hand hovering over his pocket, but Randal calls out and he finds himself moving, jogging across the empty highway in an effort to catch up. He follows the big man down to the riverside park, along the pebble paths no-one but the homeless use regularly.

"Whatever you do," Randal says, voice floating back through the darkness, "don't throw a ciggy into the water. Damn shit'll go up in flames if you give it half a chance."

Nate's already wheezing with the effort of keeping pace, staying close enough to see the vague shape of Randal's silhouette in the shadowy night. He can barely think of smoking, think of anything but the coin and the big man leading him into the darkness, the prickly points of fear digging their tines into his intestinal tract. He's so focused on it all that it catches him by surprise when Randal stops, settling down on his heels, and lights a small candle.

"We're here," he says, and nods towards the path, the thickly-packed pebbles leaving the shoreline and winding towards the underpass that runs beneath the highway, a convenience no-one bothers to use. There were stories about the tunnel, local tales about rape and murder and worse, stories that may be bullshit for all Nate really knows. But standing there, next to Randal, with the flickering candle lighting up the concrete mouth and the urine scent in the air, he can't help but acknowledge that there's something wrong. Some aspect of the tunnel mouth and the darkness that seems too thick to be real, obscuring the far end just two hundred meters away where Nate knows, instinctively, he should be seeing the light of a streetlight.

Randal kneels down, sets the candle on a patch of grass, using his body to shield it from the wind. Nate stands by, arms slack at his side, legs hollowed out with a fear he can no longer explain. He takes two uncertain steps, stands at Randal's elbow. The big man smells of cigarette smoke and cologne and, very faintly, of a mixture of sugar and sulphur.

"This here," Randal says, "it's very do-not-try-this-at-home, yeah? One of those things that's going to happen, and you're going wake up tomorrow and your sheila will be on the mend, and you're going to pretend like none of this happened. You understand what I'm saying, mate?"

Nate offers him a mute nod. "Out loud," Randal says.

"Yes."

"So here's what you're going to do." Randal points. "Get up there, close to the tunnel as you can, and leave the coin on the fuckin' ground. Once that's done, you're done. You get out of here before anything else can happen, right?"

Another mute nod, this one met with a stare, and it takes Nate a few seconds to realise he should be moving instead of saying yes. He takes a few uncertain steps up towards the tunnel mouth, leading the way with the fist holding the nickel tight. He blinks uncertainly, trying to get his vision to adjust, to penetrate the darkness of the tunnel. There are meant to be lights in the tunnel, a few inches of moonlight at least, but there is something impenetrable about the wall of black he's facing and no matter how his pupil's adjust there's no peering through it.

"In and out, kid," Randal says. "Don't fuck around."

Nate nods, nods and takes a few more steps forward, but that's as far as he gets before he does see something, a kind of thickening in the darkness. Frost-touched air flows out of the tunnel like an exhalation and the sudden bite of it makes Nate open in hand, the nickel dropping and bouncing on the pebble path, rolling towards the tunnel mouth. For a moment, Nate watches it go, mutely trying to process what just happened, then he kneels and reaches forward, dimply aware of Randal shouting *something, something* he can't make out.

And as he reaches, fingers stretching, the darkness in the tunnel congeals into something, some long and twisting tendril that slides across the ground and curves around the coin, and Nate is still kneeling there, still leaning forward, frozen with a fear he can't quite explain. He can't make himself move when a second tendril congeals and slides across the path towards him, advancing with the same sinuous slither Nate associates with snakes.

"Hey," Randal says, and he's suddenly there, grabbing Nate by the shoulder and hoisting him back along the path. "None of that, mate," Randal says, "Mister Sabbath made you a deal, got you back your coin. Leave the poor bastard alone, yeah? He's only the messenger."

For a moment Nate thinks he sees the tendril hesitate, poised in front of the big man who shows no interest in giving ground, no interest in anything but staring down whatever it is that exists in the shadows of the tunnel.

And Nate, he sees the nickel going, sees it being dragged into the shadow, and the part of him that doesn't want to let it go makes one last desperate dive and reaches for it, crossing the tunnel's threshold and plunging into the shadow beyond.

For a moment, the moment before he starts screaming, Nate marvels that what he feels creeping up his wrist isn't cold, not for all the ways it bites and numbs and chills him down to the marrow. No, not cold at all, but it's the only word he has for it, this feeling that's more like an absence, and that's all he can really think before the pain becomes too much and he starts to really scream.

Later, when he comes to, Randal is standing over him, cigarette in hand. Nate blinks and stares at the shaved scalp, the little point of orange light that is the burning cherry. Randal leans down, forces one of Nate's eyelids open, waves the cigarette back and forth. "You'll do," he says. "Better get up."

Nate doesn't want to obey, but he does it anyway, levers himself into a seating position. They're back in the car-park, in the shadow of the shopping centre, Nate's hand strapped to his chest with strips of white fabric. Byron's leaning against the fence, shirt missing, hands pressed to his nose. There's blood splattered down his pale and skinny chest, and he doesn't look in Nate's direction.

"Just so you know," Randal says, "you truly are a stupid fucker."

He offers Nate a hand, hauls him to his feet with casual ease. "Really should have let the coin go, mate. It would have cost you a little less."

Nate stands there, nodding, taking it all in. "I can't feel my fingers," he says. "My fingers. My hand. Nothing."

Randal exhales, drops his cigarette on the concrete. "Like I said, mate, stupid. Get your friend, go to a hospital, let the doctor's take a look at it. Get used to spending the rest of your life doing things with the other hand."

Nate opens his mouth to say something, then shuts it when he sees the look in Randal's eyes. There is something burning there, something Nate can't quite place, but it scares him. Scares him almost as much as the darkness in the tunnel, the unseen thing that came with the coin.

"So, all this?" Randal says. "Never happened, yeah? Mister Sabbath isn't going to hear from you, or that dipshit, ever fucking again. Whatever happened down there, it was just a bad dream. Agreed?"

Nate says nothing, and Randal steps forward. Steps and looms, a big man with the ability to inflict harm, and part of Nate wonders that he can still be afraid of that, still get that quickening of the pulse when he sees Randal's fingers bunch into a fist.

"Agreed," Nate says. "Just a bad dream."

Randal nods, once. "Good call," he says. "Now fuck off, mate. Call in on your girl. See if she's doing better now the bad voodoo's gone back home where it belongs."

Nate looks at him, stares at the eyes with the glimmer of red light in their pupils. "And she'll be okay, right? Angie, she'll be okay."

"Sure, kid, she'll be fine," Randal says, and he pulls out the pack of cigarettes, taps a new one free and plants it in his mouth. His holds Nate's stare the entire way, as if daring him to call the bluff. "We're done?"

Nate nods, once, and says, "We're done."

He turns and walks, leaving Randal and Byron both, walking into the night that smells of saltwater and petrol fumes and the faint scent of brimstone, and as he makes his way along the block, heading for the mall and the streets beyond, the path that'll lead him to the hospital. Nate's careful to move from streetlight to streetlight, spending as little time as possible walking through the dark.

He hears Randal laugh, a soft and gentle sound that's almost filled with respect, and soon, very soon, Byron realises he's left there, alone with the big man whose done nothing but hurt him, and Nate hears his friend calling out his name out, again and again, as Byron runs down the path.

ABOUT THE AUTHOR

PETER M. BALL is a writer from Brisbane, Australia. By day he manages the Australian Writer's Marketplace and runs the bi-annual AWM GenreCon. By night he writes, and his short fiction has previously been published in magazines such as *Apex*, *Shimmer*, and *Strange Horizons*, as well as the *Dreaming Again, Interfictions II, and Eclipse 4* anthologies. His faerie-noir novella, *Horn*, was published in 2009 by Twelfth Planet Press, and was followed by *Bleed* in 2010. He can be found online at www.petermball.com and on twitter @petermball.

If you enjoyed this book by Peter M. Ball, you may enjoy one of these other Urban Fantasy books published by Apocalypse Ink Productions

The Karen Wilson Chronicles

Jennifer Brozek

The Karen Wilson Chronicles

Follow Karen Wilson, a 911 operator, who discovers her city is not what it appears to be. Pulled in by a mysterious phone call, Karen discovers the hidden, supernatural world of Kendrick, becomes the Master of the City's representative, and gets adopted by a baby gargoyle. Join her and her allies as they fight to protect the city, themselves, and its denizen from dangers within that threaten to consume them whole.

This omnibus is composed of all four of the Karen Wilson Chronicles books as well as bonus content including the never before published short story, "The Fool's Path."Find this on http://www.apocalypse-ink.com

DYLAN BIRTOLO

The Sheynan Trilogy

This dark urban fantasy adventure by Dylan Birtolo is an omnibus of three novels: The Shadow Chaser, The Bringer of War, and The Torn Soul, and features three new short stories.

The Shadow Chaser: Darien Yost is a young man haunted by blackouts and vividly realistic dreams. When mysterious strangers start to appear, claiming that he has a power which makes him unique, he finds himself entangled in their world; a world of shape shifters. Soon, he is thrust into the middle of a centuries long war, and must master his ability before either side claims him... as an asset or a casualty.

The Bringer of War: Months have passed, and the Arm of Gaia and the Shadows still struggle to control Darien's destiny, attempting to use him to tip the balance of their war. But Darien has embraced his power. He and his allies have gone on the offensive, hunting down those who are trying to enslave him. Meanwhile, another renegade shifter has appeared, trying to pull Darien away from his friends for reasons of her own.

The Torn Soul: Time is running out for Darien. As new players and new dangers enter the scene, Darien must confront his past, and convince the Arm of Gaia and the Shadows to work together against a new enemy—before his mind is lost to the Sheynan's curse.

Apocalypse Ink Productions is an independent press focused on dark speculative fiction and horror in its fiction line and online based writing education in its non-fiction line.

Please visit our website at http://www.apocalypse-ink.com to learn more about us, and to find information on other books—both digital and print—that we have available.

CPSIA information can be obtained
at www.ICGtesting.com
Printed in the USA
FFOW01n1107220516
24172FF